ADIRONDACK
DETECTIVE
RETURNS

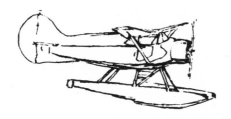

John H. Briant

Chalet Publishing
P.O. Box 1154
Old Forge, New York

ADIRONDACK DETECTIVE RETURNS

Library of Congress Catalog Control Number 99-96188

ISBN 0-9648327-3-9

VOLUME II

Graphics and book design
by
John Mahaffy

Printed in the United States of America

Chalet Publishing
P.O. Box 1154
Old Forge, New York 13420-1154

Dedication

*To all the Adirondack people who reside within the
Blue Line. And to all the people, who love and visit
this special place on Earth, known as
the Adirondack Park,*

and

*To my wife, Margaret,
who inspired me and kept the oil lamp lit.*

ACKNOWLEDGMENT

I wish to extend thanks to
John D. Mahaffy
for his creativeness and
"steering the canoe."

FOREWORD

The author has traveled to many places in this great country and has met many people from all parts of the world and from all walks of life, but his journey inside the Blue Line seems to be his favorite of all. The author's desire as a young man was to reside in the Adirondack Mountains and for him it became a reality. He considers it a privilege to live where the deer, the moose and the black bear roam freely. And, where our fellow Americans give of their time to assist their neighbor. To hear the call of the loons on the lake in the middle of the night, or to view the swift fox, are a part of Nature's gifts and hopefully the present generation and generations to come will be able to enjoy this place of pristine beauty, known as the Adirondack Park in Northern New York State.

It is through the daily trials and tribulations of JASON BLACK, Private Investigator, that you may glean a series of events that occur in some of our hamlets and towns where the interaction takes place. Some of the places that you read about may remind you of places you have visited on your journeys through the mountains.

Other books by the author

ONE COP'S STORY: A LIFE REMEMBERED
ADIRONDACK DETECTIVE

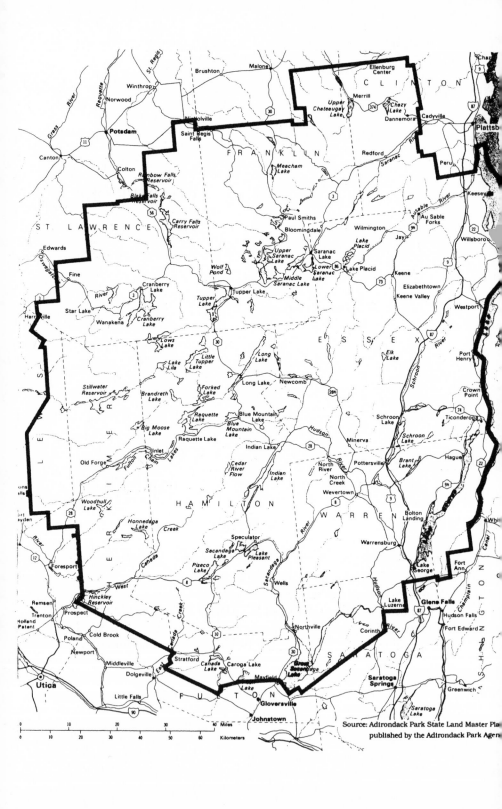

Source: Adirondack Park State Land Master Pla
published by the Adirondack Park Agen

CHAPTER ONE

It felt like a year, but it was only a month that I had been away from my home in the Adirondack Mountains. My name is Jason Black. I'm forty-nine years old, been married twice and divorced twice. I'm a private investigator. When I retired from the State Police I settled in the Adirondack Park of northern New York State. You don't make a lot of money doing what I do, but I love the mountains with the pristine beauty that they offer. The solace that I experience is relaxing, and I thirst for the out-of-way places to hike and explore. The five years that I've been retired from the State have been rewarding, not in a pecuniary sense, but from the privilege of experiencing the view of society from another perspective. I'm fortunate to have a K-9 companion. His name is Ruben, a German shepherd also retired from the troopers.

At the moment the plane is twenty thousand feet above the earth winging it's way towards my home. I was fortunate to catch a red-eye flight from Phoenix to Pittsburgh. I'll have a two-hour stopover and then catch a flight to Syracuse.

I've been assisting my former US Marine buddy, Jack Flynn, a private investigator with a sensitive case in the State of Arizona. I didn't want to leave Old Forge, but Jack called, pleading for an extra hand on a custody dispute case involving a ten-year-old child and the divorced parents. The case ended before a family court, with the father and mother going into reconciliation in the best interest of the child.

1

The father had taken the child to a remote area in Arizona, and hid out in an old prospector's cabin. The mother had informed Jack that her husband had spent considerable time in that region and had mentioned to her an old cabin located between two mountains near Jerome, a town known for copper mining years ago. Jack and I spent two weeks in the area before we overheard two older men talking about a man and a child living in an old cabin about four miles west of Jerome. We rented a Jeep and conducted a search for the cabin and the inhabitants. We located the man and the ten-year-old boy who had been reported missing by the mother. They had very little food and water to sustain them much longer. After Jack finished talking with the father about the possibility of criminal action that could be taken against him, the father decided to follow us back into Phoenix. The matter went into the hands of the Arizona Family Court System. Jack was pleased that we had located the father and child and thanked me for assisting him. With my work completed with Jack I am now returning home.

My stopover was less than two hours. The flight from Pittsburgh to Syracuse took about an hour. I had called a friend, Wilt Chambers, on my cellular-phone, and he was waiting for me on my arrival. Wilt's from Boonville, New York, and works in the Adirondacks.

I know I'll have plenty of work waiting for me when I get home. I work on bad check cases, white collar crime cases that usually end up being turned over to a police agency, missing person cases, and background investigations for Adirondack attorneys.

I haven't mentioned the main reason why I'm eager and happy for my return to the mountains. She is thirty-seven years old, stands five-foot three inches and has blond hair. Her name is Patty Olson. She has a wonderful personality. I love her so much. Wilt had taken care of Ruben, my German shepherd, while I was away and had put him in the dog run before coming to Syracuse to pick me up. On the way home Wilt filled me in on the happenings of the Old Forge area. I was glad to be back inside the Blue Line, the place I loved and cherished.

It was April and winter was waning as the signs of spring filtered through the mountain air. Tracks from the hundreds of snowmobilers that permeated the region were beginning to disappear as the snow melted and the runoff filled the rushing streams which in turn would fill the Fulton Chain of Lakes.

Ruben was lying on the dog run pad when we arrived. Only his eyes moved from right to left and left to right as a spunky striped chippie teased him through the wire fence. Ruben's ears were straight up as though they had been soaked in starch. High above in the sky a V-shaped-flock of Canadian geese were honking as they moved in rhythm homeward-bound.

"Ruben! Come here, boy!" I said. I put my suitcase down and Wilt put my small suitcase on the porch, then came over to the dog run. The chippie took off toward the woods. Ruben jumped up on me and licked my face. When Ruben settled down Wilt leaned over and rubbed Ruben's back. I was glad to see my K-9.

"Well, Jason, I've got to be going. I'm glad you're home and will see you later," Wilt said with a big smile on his face.

"I want to give you some money toward your fuel for the Dodge," I said as I reached for my wallet.

"No, you're not. Someday you can return the favor." We shook hands. He smiled as he turned and walked toward his vehicle.

"I'll see you later, Wilt, and thanks again for the ride home," I said.

"See ya, Jason."

I carried my suitcases into my log home and put them into the bedroom. I would empty them later. I went into the office and called John's Diner. Patty answered the telephone.

"Hi, honey. I'm home sweetheart!" I was so happy to hear her voice.

"Darling! I'm so glad you're home. I've missed you so very much! I'm very busy, honey. Can we talk later on?" she asked hurriedly.

"I'll talk with you later, sweetheart." I could tell she was busy.

I decided to take a walk with Ruben. The strong bond between this highly decorated K-9 and me was strong and everlasting.

"Let's take a walk, Ruben."

The big dog pushed against my forest green trousers. The trail was covered with melting slush as we made our way into the pines.

A white-tailed doe stood at the edge of the forest watching us.

This region of Old Forge was a small part of the six-million-acre Adirondack Park with many scenic places; however, I had opted to purchase a piece of property just north of this popular hamlet to call home. My close friend, Jack Flynn, who had served in the US Marine Corps with me, now a retired homicide detective from the Phoenix PD and now a private investigator in that southwestern city, had on several occasions, begged me to join his busy detective agency; however, I will not leave the great Adirondacks.

While I was in Phoenix assisting him, Jack had again badgered me to stay on in Arizona and work for Flynn Investigations. His offerings of a high salary tempted me, but I turned him down. Yet when we parted at the Sky Harbor Airport he told me about a case he was working on that could require a helping hand in New York State. I assured him that I'd be glad to assist him, but only if the matter involved the Adirondacks. "Semper fi," he said as I left.

"Semper fi, Jack," I replied.

The only reason that I wouldn't take Jack up on his offer to move to Arizona was due to the hot weather. I wouldn't be able to tolerate the temperatures of 120 degrees. The Adirondack region was much cooler to live in. And, I don't believe that Patty would be able to take the heat of that desert region.

It was getting dark when Ruben and I finished our walk. I was wondering if Patty had had a busy day at John's Diner. Ironically, since our engagement it seemed that our times together weren't as frequent. I knew one thing, though: our love for each other was as strong as ever. Although we had been engaged almost seven months no date had been set for the wedding, although our friend, Wilt, kept pressing us to unite in marriage. We both told him that we would eventually tie the knot, but we wanted to wait for a while to be certain that our forthcoming marriage would be an everlasting one.

The winter had been a cold one. My month in Phoenix had offered warmer temperatures. Despite my time away though, I had used about all my firewood. Concerning my private investigation work, my trips to Lake Placid and the Long Lake areas were made only on a need-to basis. The bad checks were still being passed at numerous business places, but not as frequently as the summer season when the region was flooded with masses of tourists.

During the winter I had attended a couple of promotion celebrations in the Troop S area. Frank Temple, former BCI Captain was now a Major and Lieutenant Roy Garrison was now the BCI Captain. A new BCI Lieutenant, Jack Doyle, filled the number two slot in command of the BCI. I had known Jack Doyle for many years. He was a dedicated member of the division. And, when Jack was around, there was usually something going on in the world of law enforcement.

I missed the division and the day-to-day operations of the BCI. I hadn't had to retire, but I'd known it was the appropriate time to put in my retirement papers. That had been almost five years ago. The lifeline was working on those bad checks and recovering funds for numerous businesses inside the Blue Line of the Adirondack Park. But checks weren't the only activity in the private-eye world.

It was almost 10:15 p.m. when Patty called. I picked the phone up on the second ring.

"Hello, honey. I just got home. I've missed you, Jason." She sounded exhausted.

"Hi Patty, did you have a busy day? I'm so glad to be home. I've missed you, too, darling." Hearing her voice made my heart skip a beat.

"It was hectic. But Lila has given me the day off tomorrow. Would you like to spend the day with me?" she asked excitedly. "I don't want to interfere if you have previous plans."

"Nothing I would rather do than spend the day with you, sweetness. Do you want to drive over here or do you want me to pick you up?" I queried.

"I'll drive over. Will you prepare one of your great breakfasts?"

I noticed the lift in her voice. "Sure will. Anything special?"

"Surprise me. Goodnight, hon. I'm going to turn in now. I'll look forward to the morning now."

I heard the click. I knew she was dead tired after ten hours of working at John's Diner. Patty was so well known that people would visit the diner frequently. She always had a big smile when she greeted her customers. I know I was one of them when we met.

I let Ruben out for another quick run into the woods. The timer on my security lights clicked on and I saw the swish of two white-tailed deer as they scurried away from the lighted yard. It wasn't long before Ruben bounded onto the porch. He slurped some water from his water dish and went to his sleeping pad. He turned three times and lay down, placing his nose between his paws. I checked the doors and went into my office to check my telephone calls. They were numerous. I jotted down all the numbers before going into the bathroom to brush my teeth. The almost empty tube of toothpaste indicated the need for a shopping spree. I undressed, slipped on my pajamas, pulled the covers back, and lay down. I read for awhile, set the alarm, and eventually fell off to sleep, looking forward to the morning and the numerous bad check cases, my bread and butter.

CHAPTER TWO

As Jason Black slept in the great Adirondacks near Old Forge, Jack Flynn was sitting in a booth at the Cactus Café on 51st Avenue. The lighting in the place was dim, and shadows of the dozen customers moved in ghostly gyrations on the dingy white walls. Jack was dressed in old clothes and his head was bent forward. He wore a baseball cap with the name Phoenix Suns in large letters above the cap's visor. Jack, formerly a homicide detective with the Phoenix Police Department, was not known in this part of the city. He was working on a routine divorce case, hired by a local lawyer to gather evidence. The target of the investigation was Bernie Draper, who was sitting at the bar with a freckle-faced redheaded woman known as Hilda Furman. She was in her mid-forties, about five-foot-seven-inches in height. She was wearing a short tight gray skirt and a low-cut maroon blouse. Her bosom was partially exposed and Draper's right hand was resting on her left kneecap. Draper and the redhead were apparently an item. They were talking loudly. The couple had downed three manhattans apiece, and Draper ordered two more.

Jack didn't like this type of case, but his firm didn't turn anyone away, especially if they had plenty of funding. Local attorneys held Jack Flynn, private eye, in high esteem, because they knew they would get the best bang for their dollar. The lawyer who had hired Jack warned him that Draper might also be involved in a large-scale drug operation that operated from Phoenix to Cornwall, in Ontario, Canada. Draper owned and operated "Over-The-Road-Freightways," which consists of ten semi-trailer trucks and a number of smaller delivery trucks used for local deliveries.

The tiny lens of Jack's camera, which he operated from his jacket pocket, was busy capturing the scene of the two lovers as they pawed each other. Jack smiled as he rose from the rickety chair. He pulled his baseball cap low over his eyes and shuffled toward the door. Draper's wife, Cynthia, would do well in divorce court. These were the final photos and observations that would complete this particular case, but Bernie Draper was involved in much darker things than a divorce action. Jack had other files in his cabinets and one of them contained confidential information as to Draper's alleged drug dealings. He planned to acquire all the information he could and pass it on to Captain Jay Silverstein, his former associate with the Phoenix PD.

CHAPTER THREE

I had just put Ruben in his runway when Patty's red Jeep pulled into the driveway. I glanced at my watch: 9:30 a.m. She turned the ignition off and got out of the Jeep. Ruben let out a bark and she ran over to his runway to pet him.

I rushed over to Patty. Her long blond hair flowed off her shoulders. She fell into my arms as I embraced her. We held each other closely.

"Honey, I've missed you so much. That month in Phoenix seemed like an eternity. I never want to be away from you again, especially for long periods of time." We kissed. "Are you ready for breakfast?" I asked.

"Yes, and I'm starving," she responded giving me another kiss.

Ruben whined as we went into the log home.

"I'll whip up some sour-milk pancakes, bacon, and a couple of sunny-side eggs. How does that sound?" I asked, reaching over to hold her hand.

"Sounds delicious, Sherlock," she said.

"You have been busy at the diner. When Wilt and I drove by yesterday, the parking lot was packed."

"Yes, we have been. Honey, that was nice of Wilt to pick you up in Syracuse. Everybody at work has been asking for you. The bowling teams had their annual breakfast. You know how that is, busy, busy. But I don't mind. They're a great gang." Patty sounded excited as she spoke.

"Oh, yeah, I know. We've got some great folks here in the

9

mountains," I answered as I continued my preparations.

I poured six small pancakes onto the hot grill. I then went to the refrigerator and took out three fresh eggs. I placed four slices of bacon in my medium size iron skillet. The orange juice had already been placed on the table by Patty. It wasn't long before we were sitting across from each other. I said grace and we began eating breakfast. We said very little as we enjoyed our meal. Patty got up and refilled our coffee cups.

"Shall we take a ride today, Patty?" I asked, as I looked at her lovingly.

"I'd love to," she replied, sipping her hot coffee. "Isn't it a shame about the three or four snowmobilers who went through the ice last month while you were away. A couple of them almost drowned. The rescue squad and Chief Todd Wilson saved them. They weren't local people," she remarked, shaking her head. "Look at all the rescuers who place their lives in jeopardy."

"Patty, you know I do feel sorry for those folks, but that's a dangerous sport and before anyone takes a heavy sled out onto the ice they should be aware of the possibility of thin ice. They wear heavy clothing and it doesn't take much to sink to the bottom of the lake. I maintain that anyone snowmobiling should go through a safety course and be a responsible sled operator. Someday, Patty, the Chief or one of the rescue people could be in jeopardy."

"You're so right, Jason. And not only snowmobiles, wave runners and all water craft should be included." She went on.

"That's true, Patty. People in all sport activity should be careful and think of where their carelessness could lead. But that's enough depressing talk for the morning. Let's get back to us," he said, reaching over to hold her hand.

We both cleared the table and did the dishes. I worked on the grill. It wasn't long before the kitchen was spotless.

"Jason, can we take Ruben with us today? I'm sure he's missed you," she asked, coyly.

"Sure, honey, we can. I have to call the Mountain Bank concerning some bad checks. While I do that, why don't you take Ruben for a short walk and then put him in the back of the Bronco." I realized this would be a treat for the big K-9.

The call to the bank lasted only a few minutes. Two of my clients had been reimbursed and the bank had advised them that their accounts were corrected. I had a good relationship with this savings institution and wanted to keep it this way.

I joined Patty and Ruben. Patty had placed some water and dog food behind the front seat of the Bronco. Ruben was sitting in the back of the vehicle. Patty was in the passenger front seat. I ran back to check the door. Soon we were motoring north on Route 28. We passed through Eagle Bay and Inlet. Traces of snow could be seen along the highway and into the woods. Just weeks before, snow had blanketed the whole region from a late spring storm. North of Inlet we went by the large sand pile, which had been reduced considerably during the winter months.

The winter had been difficult for some of the senior citizens who were confined to their residences. The younger people enjoyed the season on their snowmobiles, following the trail system and, for the most part, having a good time. The local police had been busy investigating some thefts and investigating accidents, mostly fender benders. Before going to Phoenix I had managed to keep busy investigating for the local attorneys and pursuing some collection work.

Route 28 had survived the winter onslaught with minimal wear and tear. Spring had arrived and here we were, Patty and I and Ruben, out for a day's journey in our favorite place on Mother Earth. The Adirondack Park, six million acres of state and privately owned land where the rich and famous played in the 1920's and where today, the hearty Adirondackers work hard and strive to eke out an existence.

We were just north of Raquette Lake when we spotted a cow moose crossing Route 28, placing one lanky leg ahead of the other.

"Jason, look! Look at the moose!" Patty cried out excitedly.

"I see her, honey!" I was relieved that we hadn't collided with her.

Before I could stop the Bronco and activate my 35 mm camera, the cow had lumbered over a knoll. I told Patty that next time we saw a moose we'd stop sooner and have the camera ready for action. She just smiled and shrugged her shoulders.

We drove on. Of course, Ruben had to let out a bark, just to inform us he was still with us.

CHAPTER FOUR

The temperatures were warming in Phoenix, Arizona. Jack Flynn was en route to his 99th Avenue office to meet with Cynthia Draper. The sun blinded Jack for a few seconds as he pulled into his parking lot narrowly missing the left front fender of the night janitor leaving for home. The janitor, Wayne Johnson, laid on his horn as the two vehicles passed. Jack pulled into his space next to Ruby Wolkowski's white Mazda 626. Ruby was Jack's secretary. Before exiting his car he looked in the mirror and straightened his tie.

Cynthia Draper, age forty-five, wearing a gray suit and high heels, was sitting in the waiting room. Her auburn hair flowed onto her shoulders. She had been married to Bernie Draper for ten years and had filed for a divorce based on Bernie's continual adulterous adventures with one Hilda Furman. Cynthia Draper had been Cynthia Roth before her marriage and was from a well respected Arizona family with investments in cattle and oil and many out-of-state holdings. She had met Bernie Draper at an auction and fallen in love. Adultery wasn't the only reason Cynthia was divorcing Draper. She had learned that her enterprising husband was deeply involved in the transporting of cocaine, marijuana, and guns. She wanted no more of Bernie Draper and his illegal activity. The Drapers did not have children.

"Good morning, Cynthia," Jack said as he briskly approached. "I hope I haven't kept you waiting."

"Hello, Jack. Sorry to bother you again, but I have some information for you that may prove useful," she said rather anxiously.

"Please step into my office." Jack held the door open for her.

The office of Jack Flynn was spacious. There was a large bookcase with glass doors containing law books and manuals, along with framed pictures placed on top of the highly polished walnut wood. The walls were covered with plaques and commendations earned during his time in the US Marine Corps and his years with the Phoenix Police Department. A large picture was situated in the middle of smaller photos in gold-trimmed frames. The larger photo was that of two young US Marines: Jason Black and Jack Flynn. The picture had been taken at Camp Pendleton years ago.

Cynthia sat down in one of Jack's brown leather chairs and crossed her legs.

"I understand from my secretary that you have some more information concerning your husband's activities." Jack was probative.

"Bernie is involved in the transportation of drugs and guns. He secretes cocaine and guns in the middle of his loads in two of his refrigerator units that transport oranges into Cornwall, Ontario." She was eager to share this information with Jack Flynn, who listened to her every word. She was visibly upset.

"How do you know this?" Jack questioned, furrowing his brow.

"I've searched through his office desk at home. I know that the drivers use highways other than the New York State Thruway or I-87 north of Albany. I read this in one of his journals that he keeps locked up. He inadvertently left his keys home one day. He uses a highway north of Utica." She referred to some notes she had removed from her purse. "I believe it is Route 12 to Route 28 to Route 30, which goes into a place called Tupper Lake. They take Route 3 to Route 56, where Bernie's refurbishing an old barn into a terminal and a gift shop. They then proceed into Potsdam, crossing over the bridge near Massena into Cornwall. I believe he is smuggling contraband into Canada." She spoke softly, looking intently at Jack Flynn. "I hope this additional information will aid your investigation."

"Interesting! Interesting!" Jack listened intently as he took notes. "This added data will be useful in my case."

"I believe he is being paid a large sum of money to do this from someone. I have also learned that he is sending large money transfers to a bank in Switzerland and a bank in Quebec City. And that's not all, Jack. He is renting an apartment near here, in Glendale, for his red-headed mistress," she said with vengeance.

"Cynthia, have you made any personal observations of this activity?"

"No, not actually, but by accident I overheard a couple of his drivers talking, while they were drinking coffee in the coffee room of his company. I believe, Jack, that the New York authorities might be able to catch them." She caught her breath and continued.

"The bookkeeper is a friend of mine and she can let me know when they make the Cornwall run. They make that trip about twice a month. I trust Sally Parsons. I'm the one that got her the job with Bernie's company. I didn't go to the local police and I was told that you have contacts all over the country, so that's why I'm sharing this information with you."

"I appreciate you confiding in me. This sounds as though it could be a major drug case. I assure you that I will check this information out. By the way, according to your attorney, your divorce proceedings should go smoothly. I'm sorry that you got yourself involved with Draper. It appears that he has a dark side."

"Jack, Bernie has all kinds of political friends here in Arizona. I've heard that he's financing several illegal massage parlors along with his other activities. I had to be blind when I married him, but he drenched me with his charm. I finally wised up, Jack. As I said before, maybe the New York authorities can come up with a solution to his illegal activities," she added, bitterly.

Jack was taken by surprise when Cynthia got up from the leather chair, and came toward him, and gently kissed him on the cheek. He didn't pull back.

"Jack, I appreciate your efforts in my case." She smiled and turned toward the door, nodded at Ruby, and left the office. She was gone before he could say goodbye.

"Jack, she seems like a sophisticated lady," Ruby said approvingly.

"Yes, she is, and beautiful, too." He mused to himself momentarily. "Place a call to Jason Black in the Adirondacks. "I think he is about to return a big favor to me."

Ruby quickly placed a call to Old Forge. She had not spoken to Jason since he left. The phone rang several times and the answering machine came on. "You have reached the office of Jason Black. Leave your message after the beep and I will return your call as soon as possible." Ruby spoke clearly into the receiver.

"Jason, this is Ruby at Flynn's Investigations. Please call Jack as soon as possible. It's important."

CHAPTER FIVE

We took our time driving north, stopping occasionally to snap pictures. Patty wanted to stop at Hoss's Country Corner to browse. When we entered the store, we were greeted by one of the clerks. Patty proceeded to shop while I occupied myself at their well-stocked book section. Before we left the store, Patty had purchased me a brown leather belt with a brass buckle, which I loved. I chided her for giving me such an expensive gift. I gave her a big hug.

We bid farewell to Laurie and Ginny, as they emerged from the storage room and left the store. We climbed into the Bronco. Ruben was in the back seat and barked as we put on our seatbelts. I turned right onto Route 30 and we headed north. We didn't stop at Gertie's Diner because we were still stuffed from our big breakfast.

Early spring was always slow for business in the Adirondacks. Normally it was a time to breathe a little before the busy summer season started. Across the street from Gertie's, Tracy Winter, a local seaplane owner and operator, had the cowling off his Cessna float plane. Wearing a pair of coveralls, he was intently checking connections. He didn't notice us as we went by, but he waved at us when I tooted the horn. At age fifty, he had many hours as an Adirondack bush pilot.

When we passed the site of the old Skip-Jack Campgrounds I commented, "Honey, years ago I used to spend some time camping here in Long Lake at the Skip-Jack. The owner was a retired over-the-road trucker. He was a great fellow, always trying to please his customers. A friendly chap. I felt so bad when he passed away." My thoughts always returned to the many chats we had shared in the past at the campground.

"I would have loved to have met him, Jason. He must have been a special person."

"Believe me, he was." I changed the subject. "I'm so glad that we have a day to wander through the region. Being with you, sweetheart, makes it extra special." Jason smiled at Patty. She returned his smile lovingly.

It was 1:30 p.m. when we pulled into Tupper Lake. We had just passed the village sign when I spotted Bob Wallace's brown Ford pickup truck heading south on Route 30 toward Long Lake. We blinked our lights at each other as we passed. Bob waved, as he had recognized me. My vintage Bronco was well known to him.

"Patty, you know Bob Wallace from Long Lake. He's a hard worker, a good husband and provider for his family. Both he and Gertie work hard in that diner."

"Yes, they do. Last year I remember when they stopped at John's Diner. John and Lila talked with them for quite some time. I guess they were comparing notes about the restaurant business. You see, Jason, many of their customers are also our customers."

"That's true, sweetheart," Jason acknowledged.

We were just north of Tupper Lake on Route 30 when a state police car came up behind us with red lights flashing and siren blaring. I was startled, for I wasn't speeding. The troop car sped by. I looked over at Patty.

"I wonder where he's going in such a hurry!" I mused.

"He's really moving fast. Must be some problem ahead."

The speeding troop car brought back so many memories of another day and time. "So many times I chased speeders at breakneck speeds. I remember the perspiration on my fingers and hands as I firmly gripped the steering wheel. A law enforcement officer doesn't know why the person is speeding. Could it be a person late for an appointment, a husband or wife who had a quarrel, a car thief, a bank robber? That question can't be answered until the stop is made. Then other questions come to mind. What will I find behind the wheel? A mentally deranged person? A person with a weapon? A smiling eighty-year-old lady who was a former race car driver? Those possibilities all become individual mysteries and have to be played out."

We soon learned why the trooper was hurrying. At the location where Route 30 turns north toward Paul Smith's and Route 3 continues on to Saranac Lake, two vehicles had met head on. Both drivers were crushed from the violent impact. The trooper was busy calling on his radio. We pulled off the highway onto the shoulder.

Patty stayed in the Bronco and I exited the vehicle. I put out a couple of flares, I always carry some for emergencies. After I placed the flares I ran over to the troop car. The tall trooper was Ralph Jensen. I introduced myself.

"Oh! I've heard of you, Jason," he said, extending his hand.

"Can I be of any help?" I volunteered.

"I've got assistance coming. Thanks just the same." The trooper was polite.

I could tell that Jensen was a seasoned officer. He checked both of the drivers for a sign of a pulse. It appeared they had both expired. There was a broken whiskey bottle lying on the pavement. I bid farewell to him. I walked slowly back to the Bronco.

"Can I replace those two flares, sir?" I heard Jensen ask.

I turned around and said, "Not necessary, Trooper. Glad I could help."

As I climbed into the Bronco, I could see the tears streaming down Patty's cheeks.

"Oh, honey, don't cry. They probably died instantly. I'm certain they didn't suffer." I took my handkerchief and dried her cheeks. I kissed her gently on her forehead.

"Don't cry, honey." I said, consolingly.

I pulled onto Route 30 heading north toward Paul Smith's College. Two troop cars, followed by an ambulance, were bearing down on the scene. Trooper Jensen's assistance had arrived.

We were quiet as I steered the Bronco northward. Ruben had lain down in the back and I could see his head moving as he licked his paws. He yawned a couple of times. Patty had closed her eyes and was leaning against the passenger side door. I was going to turn on the radio, but did not want to disturb her. Traffic was light. Two New York Department of Transportation trucks were parked near the entrance of Paul Smith's College when I passed by. One of the trucks still had the snowplow attached.

Patty awoke as I turned toward Santa Clara.

"Hi, sleepy head. You feeling okay?"

"Jason, that was a terrible accident! The families of those victims will be destroyed." She was still visibly upset.

"Yes, they will feel the pain. No one likes to lose a family member." I knew that the accident that we came upon was deeply affecting Patty. She had seen death the way I had.

"Honey, I brought you up here today for a purpose. When you were in the Saranac Lake Hospital last year recovering from your injuries from the accident with the two fleeing killers, I was up here. In fact, right over by the old Collier Hotel here in Santa Clara."

"Is that the hotel, all boarded up?" she asked, pointing to the abandoned building.

"Yes, that's the one, right over there." I stopped the Bronco.

We exited the vehicle and took Ruben out of the back with his leash. I turned him loose for a few minutes and the big dog ran into a wooded area nearby. In a few minutes Ruben came running toward us. I fastened the six-foot leash to his collar. We walked over by the old stately hotel and walked around it a few times.

"Patty, this is where I was parked when the escaped killer, Jewell Norris, came out of the woods, right over there." I pointed to the location and Patty looked over. I knew that she would never forget her abduction from Old Forge the year before when she had stopped to help a vehicle that appeared broken down. In my own mind, I knew that Patty Olson would never stop to help another motorist unless she knew them personally.

"You were lucky, Jason. That Norris was a violent person. He could have shot you." Patty shuddered.

"I was lucky, Patty, darn lucky. We were both fortunate." Ruben was becoming restless as a chippie raced by. I held the leash tightly.

Patty and I decided to stop by the Red Fox Restaurant for dinner. It was approaching 5:30 p.m., and if we drove directly to Old Forge it would be difficult to prepare a meal at my log home. We arrived at the Red Fox at 6:30 p.m. and received a warm greeting from the owner. He took us to a corner table and placed two menus before us. The restaurant was crowded, and therefore we didn't have time to catch up on the Saranac Lake happenings.

Walter Scott was in his early sixties and had lost his wife. Since her death he had put a great deal of effort into the operation of the Red Fox. Among his many talents he was an accomplished pianist.

"What are you having, Patty?" I asked as I scanned the menu.

"I'm going to have the grilled salmon and a baked potato," she replied.

"Sounds good to me."

The waitress appeared and we placed our order. We learned her name was Iris.

She looked about thirty years old, and wore a pleasant smile. The ice waters she brought to our table were complemented by lemon wedges. The water was refreshing. Both of us were thirsty. Patty and I discussed the day and wondered how the families of the two deceased drivers were doing. The impact of the two vehicles hitting head on must have been horrible. Probably the operators didn't know what hit them.

"Are you really hungry, Patty?" I queried. "We haven't eaten since breakfast."

Yes, sweetheart. I am," she said, smiling at me.

It wasn't long before Iris returned to our table carrying a large tray. She set the tray on a stand and served Patty first. The salmon was steaming and both plates were garnished with parsley and lemon. She poured us two cups of decaf and added water to our glasses.

"I love salmon, Patty. This is cooked just right, nice and flaky and tender."

"It is excellent. And, it's good for you, too," she added.

Patty was always looking out for my healthy diet.

We finished dinner and decided not to have dessert. Iris brought the check and I paid her, leaving a suitable gratuity. On the way out of the restaurant, the owner thanked us and indicated that we should get together in the future. I introduced Patty to Walt.

"Patty, that was a close call you had last year when those two killers abducted you. All the folks around here were praying for you when you were in the coma."

He spoke with concern.

"Thank you, Walter. Believe me, I appreciated those prayers. It was something that I don't want to go through again. I'm pleased to meet you. You have a lovely restaurant. And we really enjoyed our dinner."

"Thanks, Patty." Then he added solemnly, "It isn't the same without my Mabel."

"I'm sorry to hear of your loss, Walter. Jason informed me of your wife's passing."

We both bid farewell to Walt and headed to the Bronco. It had been a full day. Ruben had drunk most of his water and had only one dog biscuit left. He was glad to see us. His tail swished back and forth as I let him out of the Bronco for a quick run and relief. He soon returned and jumped into the back of the Bronco. We headed to Old Forge. I wished that Patty could have heard Walt play the piano, but I realized he probably didn't have the heart to play at this time with the recent loss of his wife.

The trip back to my log home was in the dark. We could see the eyes of deer along Route 30 and Route 28. Fortunately, no deer decided to take that trip across the highway in front of us. The Bronco purred along as we headed south. This was definitely a special place on earth, the great Adirondack Park with its mountains and pristine lakes and winding highways. And, of course, the people residing within. Ruben was asleep in the rear of the Bronco and Patty's head was lying against my shoulder deep in sleep when I pulled into my driveway.

"Wake up honey, we're home," I said tenderly. Ruben started barking.

"Dear, I—I must have fallen asleep. I'm sorry," she said groggily.

"Both of you dozed off. Would you like to have a cup of decaf before you head for home?"

"I'd love some, but I have to open the diner in the morning at 6:00 a.m. I'd better go."

"Okay, sweetheart. Give me your keys and I'll start your Jeep for you." She reached into her pocketbook and handed me her key case.

I let Ruben out of the back of the Bronco, and the big dog bounded toward the woods.

The Jeep started on the first turn of the key. It purred like a kitten. I got out of the Jeep and embraced Patty. She held me close to her bosom and her lips met mine. We were both waiting for our wedding day before we would go much further.

But, we wanted each other. There was no doubt about that. I helped her into her vehicle.

"Do not stop to help anyone on the way home unless you know them. Remember what happened the last time you went to the aid of an alleged fellow motorist. Call me before you go to bed."

"Don't worry, Jason, I won't! I promise!"

I certainly didn't want to see Patty abducted again. She was lucky to be alive! I loved her so much. I watched her turn around, head toward Route 28, and make the right-hand turn onto the highway.

"Come on, Ruben, let's go inside." It had been a wonderful day and I was certain that the K-9 had enjoyed his ride. I unlocked the door and we entered. Ruben made a beeline to his favorite spot for the evening and I went to the bathroom. I had just finished placing the towel on the rack when the phone rang.

Right away I noticed that I had a call, the red light was flashing. I answered the phone.

"Hello, Jason Black here."

"Hi, Sherlock. How's my favorite private investigator? I'm home safe and sound, sweetheart. Wish we were going to cuddle up together."

"Anything going on in town when you went through?"

"I did see Dale Rush dropping some mail into the outside post office box, and Wilt Chambers' big Dodge pickup was parked in front of John's Diner. He must have been having his nightly coffee."

"Get some sleep. You've got a full day tomorrow. Sleep tight!" I wished that I could be with her.

"Goodnight, Jason."

I hung up and quickly pressed the button on the phone. There were several calls from various businesses. The last call was Jack Flynn's secretary.

"Jason, this is Ruby at Flynn's Investigations. Please call Jack as soon as possible. It's important."

I went into the bathroom, brushed my teeth, and prepared for bed. Ruben was already lying on his small air mattress. I checked the doors. The security lights were on, and when I looked outside two does were slowly passing through the yard.

Just before I climbed into bed I reached for a newly purchased police novel, *Nightbird*, authored by Ed Dee, a retired NYPD Lieutenant. I had finished reading his book, *Bronx Angel*, which I had enjoyed. I was eager to start reading his new book. My eyelids became heavy after about an hour. I placed the book on my nightstand, turned the light off, and in a few minutes drifted off to sleep. I was soon dreaming of chasing a perp who had snatched an elderly lady's pocketbook and was running through the Fulton Fish Market area in New York City. When I tackled the perp I woke up holding my pillow. My heart was pounding. I glanced at the Big Ben alarm clock. The numerals indicated that 6:15 a.m. had arrived. Ruben was wagging his tail, sitting in the entrance to my bedroom.

I threw the covers back, got out of bed, and headed for the shower. The soap bubbles slithered down my chest. The hot shower penetrated my aching back and I could feel the relief. I asked myself a question. "What does Jack Flynn want?" I'd wait until 9:30 a.m. before calling him, remembering that Phoenix was on mountain time.

Ruben bolted out the door as soon as I opened it. He made a beeline for the woods. Two chippies scattered as the retired K-9 approached. This time Ruben didn't chase them. He had one thing in mind. He returned shortly, and I put him into his dog run with filled food and water dishes. His ears were straight up. I would have to take him to the Eagle Bay Kennel for grooming soon. I owed it to Ruben for his loyalty.

Breakfast consisted of two slices of fried bacon under two over-easy brown eggs with hash brown potatoes. A little ketchup added to the crispy potatoes satisfied my taste buds. I was hungry this morning. I blamed it on the dream I had had of the foot chase through the Fulton Fish Market of the Big Apple. After breakfast I rushed to do the dishes, as 9:30 a.m. was soon to arrive.

CHAPTER SIX

Jack Flynn and I had served in the United States Marines together and had been in the South Pacific. Upon discharge, Jack went with the Phoenix, Arizona, Police Department and I opted to join the New York State Troopers. The only thing that kept me from the Phoenix PD were the hot, dry summers when the temperatures rose to 125 degrees. Jack went into the homicide division and I ended up in the BCI (Bureau of Criminal Investigation). Both Jack and I retired about the same time, and we were now in our own individual private investigation businesses: Jack in Arizona and me in the Adirondack Mountains. Again, it was the high temperatures that kept me from working with Jack. He had made his choice and I had made mine. But our respect for each other was very much alive, and we had promised to help one another whenever the occasion presented itself. Jack's selection of cases was more abundant than mine, but I was able to sustain myself working on bad check cases throughout the region and other casual cases that came my way. We both maintained good working relations with our former departments.

It was exactly 9:40 a.m. when I dialed the 602 area code for Arizona. After three rings I heard, "Good morning. Flynn Investigations. May I help you?" Ruby Wolkowski said.

"Good morning, beautiful. Jason Black here."

"Jason, it is so good to hear your voice! How was your flight to New York?"

"Good. I had a two-hour layover in Pittsburgh," I replied.

"Thank you for calling back. Just a minute, I'll get Jack. He's in the file library. We are so busy we had to create a special room for our files. We could use you out here, Jason."

"We won't even go to that subject, Ruby."

"Take care, Jason. Jack will be right with you," she spoke assuredly.

Jack, Ruby, and Lieutenant Jay Silverstein of the Phoenix PD Homicide Division were business partners and had bought an old rundown shopping plaza on 99th Avenue in Phoenix. They had fixed it up and now rented out various stores to tenants. All money taken in from the rent was considered the retirement fund for the three of them in their old age. Papers had been drawn up and it was all legal. Jack set up his lucrative private investigation agency in one part of the plaza, a suite consisting of three offices, a new file library and a waiting room. Jack and Ruby had selected the furnishings for the business.

"Jason, Ruby just told me that you had a good flight."

"Hello, Jack. Yes, it was a good one. I'm returning your call. What's up?"

"Today, I mailed you a report and a letter explaining some information that I have received as the result of a divorce case I'm working on. The package I mailed is self-explanatory. Although it is a divorce case, it hinges on something much broader involving the husband of the divorcing couple. In fact, Jason, it involves a large scale drug operation which includes the transportation of cocaine, guns, and other contraband from Phoenix to Cornwall, Ontario."

"Where do I fit in this?" I asked with curiosity.

"I want to hire you to be on the watch for a trucking firm believed to be involved in the case. I'm working closely with the Phoenix PD Narcotics Unit, but this is a highly sensitive operation. I thought possibly you might do some probing in your region, and here's why! The wife who is in the divorce case has personal knowledge that her husband is behind the operation and is also a suspect in three homicides in Arizona. As you are aware, I won't mention any names over the phone. They're in the paperwork I sent you. The wife of the suspect doesn't know any of the details of the murders, except some rumors around her husband's office. She knows about the drug traffic. Jason, she is a respectable woman who got tied up with the wrong guy."

"Is she the only source for your information?" I was thoroughly curious now.

"No, I have a snitch that has worked for the company for a few years. All I can tell you is that he is a former Marine and a concerned citizen. I left the snitch's name out of the documentation I sent to you. See what you can do on your end. You never know, Jason—you might become a hero. Ha, ha!"

"Come on Jack. Be serious." I knew that he liked to kid.

"I am. Okay, that's the scoop. All the information is in the report I sent you. You should receive it soon. By the way, Jason, how's your love life? You still seeing Patty? I bet she missed you while you were out here for a month."

"She did. No date has been set for the wedding yet."

"Congratulations! Jason, I wish you both the best. Let me know when and I'll fly east."

"We'd love to have you."

I hung the telephone up and went into the living room. I noticed that dust was accumulating on my furniture. I decided to spend the rest of the morning cleaning my log home. I knew that when Patty and I tied the knot, she'd probably help take care of the housework. But I wasn't quite ready to give up my bachelorhood, yet!

I was anxious to receive Jack's package. Three days after our phone conversation, I found the priority mail packet in my box. The brown manila envelope was heavy. I could hardly pull it out of my post office box, as it was in the middle of a dozen letters and magazines. I went over to the table and quickly thumbed through the mail. The letters contained more protested checks. I didn't mind because they were my lifeline and I depended on them. And the businesses throughout the park depended on me to aid them in the retrieval of their funds. Generally, the check passers made them good, but once in a while, it had to be turned over to the police for criminal action remedies.

I was just getting ready to enter the Bronco when I heard two loud blasts on an air-horn. It was my friend, Charlie Perkins, gripping the steering wheel on his Peterbilt log truck. The spray behind the trailer splattered against some parked cars. I knew that he was headed to Vermont with a load of hardwood. Charlie's family consisted of his wife and six children, and he couldn't miss a day of work. Charlie, another logger, Wilt Chambers, and I were close buddies and often had coffee and breakfast at John's Diner in Old Forge. John and Lila were the owners and operators of the busy diner and went out of their way to give their customers generous portions at a fair price. Of course, Lila's pies were the best in this part of the Adirondacks, because she made them fresh each morning.

The Bronco caught up with Charlie as he kicked down into a lower gear climbing the hill just north of Old Forge. I followed and turned into my driveway.

Charlie flashed his taillights. He wouldn't return to the Boonville area until late the next night.

Ruben was in his runway and didn't bark as I got out of the Bronco. I went over to see if he needed some water or dog food. He was okay. I petted the big dog and went inside to my office. I placed the mail on my incoming basket and immediately sat down in my swivel chair. I took my pearl handled letter opener and opened the recycled envelope, part of Jack's business stationery. I slowly read the letter, which I knew had been typed by Ruby.

The content mentioned the "Over-The-Road Freightways," owned and operated by one Bernard Draper, aka Bernie Draper, of Wickenburg, AZ, Post Office Box 10868. The letter briefly mentioned details of the divorce action of Draper vs. Draper.

On reading further I was somewhat startled as the names of Old Forge, Tupper Lake, Potsdam, Massena and Cornwall, Ontario appeared. There were specific routes of travel: Route 28, Route 30, Route 3, Route 56, and several secondary highways. "What the—" I said to myself. My friend, Jack Flynn, Private Investigator, was apparently looking at part of a large-scale drug operation that might be using these highways and an old barn in the Adirondack Region. He went on to elaborate that the reason for using these roads was the fact that the transporting vehicles, Over-The-Road-Freightways, would be less likely to be stopped by roving police patrols.

The report indicated that two trips each month would begin sometime during the middle of May. The semi-trailer trucks were white with Over-The-Road-Freightways painted in black letters on the doors of the Brockway Tractors. Both the trailers and tractors would bear Arizona registration plates. I noticed that Jack noted the highways to be traveled just in New York State. In addition, he advised that when the rigs left for New York, he would call me. Jack stressed that this information was confidential and my only function was to alert the authorities and make them aware of the fact that an Arizona trucking company might be transporting drugs or other contraband into Northern New York State. Further information indicated that near the intersection of Route 56 and Route 3, east of Cranberry Lake, an old barn converted to a warehouse might be a stopping off point for the trucks, where they would unload the drugs or other contraband for storage purposes or until other associates involved in the scheme would make a pick-up to further distribute the illicit drugs, believed to be cocaine and marijuana.

Jack didn't mention the name of his informant who had access to the main headquarters of Over-The-Road-Freightways. He indicated only that he was a reliable source of information. I knew that Jack had numerous snitches in Arizona. I remembered that he had told me about the time he was in a wild gun battle with two murder suspects in South Phoenix. Jack was alone checking out a lead when he stumbled onto two dangerous killers wanted in the State of Washington. Jack was pinned down. Bullets were flying over his head and striking the metal of a dumpster. This went on for twenty minutes. Jack had not seen Willie Thurston holding a paper bag to his lips downing a combination of beer and cheap wine. Willie had seen Homicide Detective Flynn dive behind the dumpster and had watched two large hair bags firing AK-47's at Jack. Willie, intoxicated as he was, slipped away and called the police. In a matter of minutes an elite S.W.A.T. team appeared without sirens and returned fire. On the ground near the alleyway were the two killers silent and dead. From that day on, Jack had developed dozens of informants. He went out and found Willie Thurston. He drove him to the YMCA, where Willie shaved and showered. In the meantime Jack went out to a store and purchased Willie some new clothes. Later that evening Jack bought Willie the biggest Porterhouse steak he could order. Jack had always told me that on that day, years ago, Willie Thurston had saved him from being gunned down. And, since that day, Willie, a highly decorated former U.S. Marine, had been one of Jack's informants.

I finished reading Jack's epistle and placed it back in the envelope. It would appear that the alleged drug operation was sizable and that local authorities would eventually become involved in the matter. I opened the bottom drawer of my desk, placed the envelope in the drawer, and closed it, turning the key to lock it. Jack's letter had stressed confidentiality in handling this sensitive information.

I had just completed running the vacuum cleaner when Ruben started barking. I looked out and could see that Dale Rush had just pulled into my yard. I went outside to greet him.

"Quiet down, Ruben," I stated firmly.

"Hello, Jason, haven't seen you around lately. Some winter we've had."

"Hi, Dale, you can say that again! We certainly had many, many snowmobilers this season."

"I agree with you. The more sleds, the more accidents. They should run everyone through a safety course at the beginning of winter or have them show a certificate or evidence that they participated in a safety course before applying for their winter trail permits."

"That's a good idea, Dale. I love to see the snowmobilers have fun, but safely. There are too many accidents."

"Did you do much ice fishing over the winter? Some of the fellows have caught a few perch, but they're smaller than usual."

"Been out a few times, but they didn't bite. I must have been using the wrong bait." I knew that Dale was an avid fisherman. "What's up, Dale?"

"I'm taking the Stinson up tomorrow. Would you like to come

along? The ice has disappeared and I've got room to take off."

"Sure, I'd love to." I could tell that Dale, a former US Marine Corps Ace, was itching to go aloft. He was wearing a brown leather flight jacket.

"Okay, I'll pick you up around 10:00 a.m. Dress warm! See ya."

"Yep."

Dale, before he got into his Chevrolet pickup, rushed over to Ruben's runway and threw him a dog biscuit. I knew that Dale wanted to keep on good terms with the big K-9. I waved at Dale as he left. I turned around and saw a large buck run into the woods on the end of my property. He was moving fast.

I went into my office and spent most of the day doing paperwork, writing letters, cleaning out old files and making telephone calls. One of the calls was to my good friend, Lieutenant Jack Doyle of the Bureau of Criminal Investigation, at Troop S Headquarters. I congratulated him on his promotion. We promised to meet for coffee in a week at Gertie's Diner in Long Lake. I told Jack that I had something of importance to discuss with him. I trusted Lieutenant Doyle. Troop S could be proud to have him. I knew that Captain Roy Garrison and Jack would make a good team. The BCI unit in Troop S were seasoned investigators and were diligent in carrying out their assignments. Even though Mother Nature was good to the great Adirondack Mountains, she couldn't keep out the criminal element. Historically, the case files of Troop S have contained many interesting cases. I, Jason Black, a retired BCI man, was only a part of the equation, but the memory bank does hold a few of those cases that came my way.

As I sat at my desk looking over my old cases as a private investigator, I couldn't help but remember that one I was involved in on a cold winter night in the wee hours of early morning. It was near the border of Canada. I had the reserve from 11:00 p.m. till 7:00 a.m. that particular duty day. An alert US Border Patrol Officer checked out a car east of Malone. Two individuals were arrested for possession of 10 kilos of cocaine. It was a father and son team, in a rental car headed to Pennsylvania, with the intention to sell the drug to dope dealers. I can remember that the father would talk only with the feds and sought immunity for the exchange of information that would take down a large drug cartel, whereby no state charges would be entertained against the two. I had heard a rumor months later that the two people involved went free and the information they offered the feds never materialized. I could never refute the rumor, much to my concern. Two known lawbreakers could have duped the criminal justice system. The recovered drugs had a street value of thousands of dollars at the time. Just one of many cases that get lost in the shuffle at no fault of the police. I shuddered a little as I reviewed the case I was about to enter. Would this one develop into another of the same? "Not if I have anything to do with it," I whispered to myself.

I placed a call to Chief of Police, Todd Wilson, and requested that he stop by my office. Chief Wilson and I had become good friends, and he was an honest hard-working officer. I continued to clean off my desk and sealed thirty envelopes addressed to people who wrote checks without examining the balance in their accounts.

My wristwatch read 2:15 p.m. I knew Patty would be pulling into her driveway. I waited till 2:30 p.m., then called her.

Patty answered on the first ring. "Hello, sweetheart," I said.

"What've you been up to, Jason?" she asked.

"Honey, I've been right in my office cleaning out files and doing some much needed housework. How'd you like to come over for dinner tonight?" I wanted to see her. "I've got a small roast of beef we could have."

"I'd like that. Would you want me to come over and help you cook?"

She was waiting for my answer.

"Sure, see you about 5:30 p.m. Stop for some rolls at the store, would you?"

"I will, Jason. Anything else?"

"Just yourself, funny one." I knew she was excited about coming over.

I finished in my office and took Ruben for a brisk walk into the woods. We returned and I placed the big dog in his runway. His dishes were watered and filled with dog food. I went inside and peeled some Idaho potatoes. I had just finished peeling the spuds when Chief of Police Todd Wilson came to the door.

"Come on in, Todd," I said.

Todd opened the screen door and entered.

"Good to see you, Jason. Some winter we had, just like the old fashioned ones. I wish the visiting snowmobilers would display more caution in the operation of their sleds."

"You know how it is, Chief. However, I do feel that they are exercising better safety practices. Let's face it, Todd, you and I have had several sleds over the years and we experienced some of those falls and narrow misses."

"I guess you're right. We tend to forget," he added thoughtfully.

"How about a cup of coffee and a piece of banana bread?" I offered.

Todd nodded in acceptance.

I reached over, turned the burner on, and slid the old teakettle onto the hot flame. It wasn't long before Todd and I had hot steaming coffee along with generous slices of homemade banana bread. As we sat at the kitchen table sipping our coffee, I couldn't help but think about the various cases we had worked on. Old Forge was generally a quiet mountain town in the south central Adirondacks where most people behaved themselves and interacted in community events. A good town with good people. During the summer tourist season and winter snowmobiling events, the townspeople would go all out to host their guests in a friendly manner. Todd kept his thumb on the pulse of the community and everything usually went smoothly.

"Todd, Patty's coming for supper tonight. I was just getting the potatoes peeled a little ahead of time." I was glad that he stopped by, as I wanted to discuss the Draper matter with him. "While you're here, I want to share some confidential information with you."

"Sure, go ahead," he said with a quizzical look.

I confided in Todd. I shared with him the contents of Jack Flynn's letter and the possibility of drug traffic through our region. We discussed the matter for several minutes. Todd's immediate jurisdiction took in the Town of Webb, a large area. I informed him that as developments took place he would be kept abreast of the facts. In addition, I told him that I was going to be in touch with Troop S Headquarters. I stressed that this information was strictly confidential. He understood.

We finished our coffee. I thanked Todd for stopping. He was a tall man and had to duck when he passed through the doorway. When he got outside he turned and said, "I can see that Ruben is frisky as ever." My dog was standing up with his paws on the fence of his runway.

"Yeah, he's still a young K-9 at heart. I think he misses riding on patrol with his partner. I know when I have him on a leash he still pulls hard. You wouldn't want that big jaw clamping onto your arm or leg."

"You can say that again. See you later, Jason."

Chief Todd Wilson climbed into his patrol car and he was gone. Ruben let out a couple of barks and ran over to his water dish.

I went back into the house and placed the small roast in the oven. I set the temperature at 325 degrees. I made a salad with fresh lettuce, cucumbers, sliced radishes, and tomatoes, and I browned some croutons. The table was set with a blue candle at each end. The napkins were folded and placed by my best china.

I took a fast shower and shaved. The hot water was relaxing. The razor removed my whiskers; however, I nicked my right ear-lobe. The styptic pencil I ran over the small laceration stung me. I slipped on my bathrobe, hurried into the bedroom, opened the dresser, and took out fresh underwear and socks. The closet seemed to be getting smaller or else it held too many clothes. Changes in our closet space appeared to be inevitable after our forthcoming marriage. I selected a light shirt and a pair of blue jeans, then dressed, combed my hair and, last, splashed some aftershave lotion on my face. The cut on my right ear lobe stung again.

It was 5:35 p.m. when Patty's red Jeep Wagon pulled into the yard. Ruben was going crazy in his runway. I looked out and his tail was going around like a windmill. Patty got out of the Jeep and ran over to the big K-9. She stroked his neck and patted his head.

I didn't rush out to greet her, but when Patty came into the house I grabbed her gently and put both of my arms around her. Our lips met. She held me firmly and our feelings for each other held us close together for several minutes.

"Jason, I love you, darling." She was breathless.

"I love you, too, sweetheart." I looked down into her beautiful blue eyes. Their color matched her light blue blouse and the southwestern jewelry on her hand and wrist. She was wearing a dark blue pleated skirt. I hung up her leather jacket. Her eyes followed me to the closet. She smiled warmly at me.

"Can I help you with anything, dearest?" she asked, as she set the rolls on a plate, placing them on the table.

"I think we're all set, Patty." We were both hungry, and the aroma of the roast beef permeated the room.

The blade of the carving knife was dull. I sharpened it and ran it under hot water, drying it off with a clean towel. I opened a bottle of Burgundy wine and poured our glasses half-full. I lit the candles and, as they flickered, shadowy figures danced on the wall. I sliced into the roast and then we started eating.

"Jason, the beef is delicious." She chewed slowly. Her eyes sparkled in the candlelight.

"It came out well. I kept the temperature at 325 degrees. Yes, it is tender, honey."

We sat quietly at the table sipping our wine. I could see Ruben out in his runway. He was watching a chipmunk darting in and out of the woodpile. I looked into Patty's eyes.

"I love you, Patty. I think that we should think about tying the knot when you're ready. How do you feel about it?"

"When you're ready, Jason. I love you, too." She smiled and looked directly into my eyes.

"We love the autumn. Should we plan it then?" I waited for her response.

"That would be great with me, honey!" she answered excitedly.

"I have some work that I'm doing for Jack Flynn, and I'd rather wait until after it's completed," I went on to explain.

She nodded her head, showing her understanding. "How is Jack, honey?"

"He's busy in Phoenix. In fact, he's so busy he is hiring some operatives to handle the case overloads. I'm so glad that I didn't go to work for my buddy. I've told you how hot it gets in Arizona."

"Yes, you've mentioned it several times." She smiled knowingly. "I'm glad you didn't move to the west."

I poured us some coffee. After our coffee, we did the dishes together. I didn't serve dessert after dinner. Both of us were trying to keep our weight down.

"Patty, Dale is stopping by in the morning and picking me up. We're going flying."

"You lucky guy. I have to be at the diner by 6:00 a.m."

Patty and I looked at some of my old photo albums and at 9:30 p.m. she left for her home. It had been a wonderful evening. Before she left, I held her closely and kissed her goodnight. It was a good thing she left when she did, as our passions were mounting and autumn was still some months away.

I called Patty at 10:00 p.m. and said goodnight to her. She was already in bed and sounded sleepy on the phone.

"Goodnight, darling," she said softly.

"Goodnight, babe. Have a good day tomorrow."

I walked outside and let Ruben make a run into the woods. The night air had a chill in it, so I didn't stay out. I went into the office after he returned. I typed reports and wrote three or four letters. It was after midnight when I got ready for bed. My toothpaste tube was almost empty. I climbed into the covers after I set the alarm clock, then fell off to sleep.

CHAPTER SEVEN

The Big Ben alarm sounded at 6:15 a.m. Ruben was sitting by the side door. I rubbed my eyes and let him out. He soon returned. I looked out and he was sitting on the porch, so I let him into his runway.

The hot water felt good on my back. Soapsuds bubbled and found their way into my right eye. After the hot shower I turned on the ice cold water and spent a few seconds under the showerhead. I was thoroughly refreshed.

When Dale pulled into the yard I had just perked a pot of fresh coffee. I thought I'd give him a treat with scrambled eggs and thick, lean bacon. The toast had just popped up in my new toaster.

"Good morning, Dale." I let him in. Before we leave, I have breakfast ready."

"Jason, you son-of-a-gun, how'd you know I'd be hungry?"

"It's my sixth sense, I guess," I answered with a grin.

We both sat down. I could tell by the way Dale dove into the eggs and bacon he was hungry. So was I. Dale talked about his Stinson Reliant and indicated that over the winter he had taken the engine apart and put it back together again. Dale had been a U.S Marine pilot—an Ace—and came out of the war with a chest full of medals.

"Good breakfast, Jason. Next time I see you at John's Diner, I'll pick up the tab."

"Not necessary, Dale."

The sun was bright this spring morning. Dale's GMC SUV was brand new, and as we headed to Kirby's Marina on Fourth Lake, he explained some of the new features he had ordered for his vehicle.

"How come you decided on a red color?" I asked.

"Red's my favorite color. I also believe other motorists can spot it easier on the highway. Jason, you know how some of these drivers cross the double lines and pass on curves. I've almost been hit head on numerous times between Old Forge and Otter Lake." Dale had a point there.

"Yeah, you can say that again. Some of them drive like maniacs, especially folks coming to this region on Friday nights." I agreed with Dale.

Traces of snow could be seen in the woods, but spring had sprung and a few woods flowers could be spotted along the shoulders just inside the tree line. We turned into Kirby's Marina. The one-lane dirt road was curvy. Dale pulled down to the lake's edge and parked.

"I'll be right back, Jason. I have to see old man Kirby for a minute."

Dale and I exited the vehicle and I walked along the shore, while he ran up to the office. Kirby had been in the area for quite some time and had a lucrative business. His yard crew was getting boats out of the storage areas. I waved at one of his helpers as the guy was placing rollers under a Chris Craft wooden boat, which appeared to be well maintained. I could never feel comfortable dealing with Kirby after a part on my Glaspar was removed and sold. I had ended up selling my boat when I couldn't replace the part. Old man Kirby never could look me in the eye after that.

There seemed to be a slight breeze. Visibility was good and you could see clearly across the lake. I turned around and headed back toward the plane. Dale was already there giving the plane a cursory examination. He checked over everything. I climbed aboard and Dale handed me a flight jacket. We both knew that it would be cold up there in the wild blue yonder.

"Jason, I've brought some hot coffee along, if you'd like some, and sandwiches for our lunch later. Hope you like liverwurst?"

"I like it." It wasn't my favorite, but I wouldn't hurt Dale's feelings.

The 245-horsepower Lycoming didn't sputter on starting. He warmed up the engine at dockside. Soon we were slowly heading to the center of Fourth Lake. It was a beautiful day for flying.

"Jason, is there any special place you'd like to see?" Dale asked thoughtfully.

I wanted to share the confidential information I had received from Jack Flynn, but I couldn't. It was too sensitive. I pondered over Dale's question before I answered.

"Dale, would it be possible to fly over toward the Star Lake area?"

"Sure, why not? This is just a pleasure jaunt," he replied.

Dale headed north down the lake and the powerful engine pulled us up and over Inlet. The church steeple glistened in the morning sunlight. Dale banked the sturdy red and white Stinson to the northwest. Below us was some of the finest forest land in the country. Dale climbed to 3800 feet. Visibility was excellent. Off to the right of us we had spotted a flock of Canadian geese headed north. Their wings strained against the strong breeze. Dale was soon flying over NY State Route 3 between Tupper Lake and Cranberry Lake. Raquette River was now below us, Conifer was slightly to the south, and Childwold was next. I asked Dale to circle around the intersection of Route 56. I didn't tell him why. We circled twice before I spotted the large old barn situated in a cluster of pine trees.

"What's your interest in that barn down there, Jason?" He had noticed my observation.

"Nothing special. I would like to snap a couple of pictures, though, if you can get a little closer." I already had my 35mm camera in hand.

Dale came in from the north and banked to the left. I clicked the camera twice and told Dale I had the pictures I wanted. Dale pulled the Stinson up and headed toward Cranberry and Newton Falls. He continued on to Star Lake. My memories of Star Lake were many. I remembered the songfests I had attended at the Allen residence and all the hunting trips into the back country. Lefty had been Sheriff of St. Lawrence County. His mother was an expert in making patchwork quilts. And, of course, I couldn't forget the wonderful home-cooked meals. Three local gentlemen would furnish the guitar music and the rest of us would sing. It was a nice get-together of Adirondackers. One night we went to Tupper Lake and visited the Wakesha Inn, where one of the lumberjacks would clog and everyone in the place would watch the performance. By the time the evening was over, everyone was trying to clog.

Dale climbed to 3500 feet and headed toward Newton Falls.

"Jason, I'd like to fly over the Newton Falls Paper Mill. My grandfather used to be a foreman there in the 1930's. I wish you could have met him. He was a hard worker and took me in when my dad's health failed. Gramma and him were always there for me. They are both buried in the Star Lake cemetery."

"They must have been special folks." I couldn't help but notice that Dale's eyes were watering. Talking about his grandparents must have struck a chord.

The liverwurst sandwiches tasted surprisingly good. And in my eagerness, I clumsily spilled some coffee on the flight jacket Dale let me wear. The thermos kept the coffee nice and hot. Dale had finished his sandwich and decided to take a closer look at Cranberry Lake. He banked the Stinson and headed down, flying low over the lake. Some of the cottage owners could be seen removing their window coverings, and in fact two of them waved. Dale circled them and dipped his wings to the left and then to the right.

I couldn't share with Dale the reason for taking the photos of the large wooden barn. Jack's letter had indicated that Bernie Draper, through a real estate agency, had purchased the barn and five acres of land. Almost certainly Draper was going to use the barn for a storage facility. Jack Flynn had been somewhat vague in his letter; however, I was able to glean enough information to determine probable criminal activity. I was under the assumption that Jack was receiving information from Mrs. Draper, his client, and from his contacts at the Phoenix Police Department. I had already decided to contact Lieutenant Jack Doyle of the Bureau of Criminal Investigation, a division of the New York State Police. Jack was a trooper who was thoroughly dedicated to locking up the bad guys, but he was fair in his appraisal of any given set of circumstances—

and he had proven over and over that he was a cop's cop.

Dale climbed to 2500 feet and circled the water again. All the ice was out of Cranberry Lake. I had fished the lake several years ago in my small aluminum boat on a windy day when the water was choppy. The area used to be busy when the Jones and Laughlin Ironworks was in operation. The foundry employed almost a thousand people. The paper mill in Newton Falls had about five-hundred good paying jobs. Now a much different job climate existed in the region.

I was looking out the right side window when Dale spoke.

"Let's fly around the barn again."

"Good, maybe I can take another photo." I readied my camera.

Dale came in from the south and banked left. I clicked the camera twice.

"Got it, Dale. Thanks."

"Good. Let's get out of here."

Dale decided that we'd set down at Long Lake instead of going to Lake Placid. The time was approaching 1:00 p.m. The wind had come up and we were enjoying a tail wind into Long Lake. There were a few cars and log trucks crawling along Route 30. The 245 horsepower Lycoming engine was purring like a kitten. I knew my friend would rather fly than do anything else. I wanted to share with him the case I was going to be working on, but Jack had requested that the matter be strictly confidential. This case could mushroom into something more than the running of drugs from Arizona to New York. I knew that one of my next steps would be to contact Captain Roy Garrison and Lieutenant Jack Doyle at Troop S Headquarters located at Raybrook. It was fortunate that Dale had wanted to fly today. I had saved gas money. I did offer Dale the use of my credit card in the event he wanted to fuel up at Long Lake.

"No, Jason, I asked you to take a flight with me. I'll take a rain check."

"Just thought I'd ask." I knew that Dale was a proud person and very independent.

Dale brought the Stinson down near the Adirondack Hotel and taxied to the public dock. He cut the engine about a hundred feet from shore. I climbed out and stood on the float as the plane drifted to the dock. I secured a line to the ring and left a little slack. Dale made arrangements to have the Stinson fueled.

When we walked across the street to Gertie's Diner, we were surprised to see a note tacked to the door. The message read: "Closed, had to go to Rochester for the day." Dale and I looked at each other in wonderment. I commented to Dale that this was unusual. He agreed. We went across the street and Dale paid for his fuel.

A wind had come up and the lake water pounded against the shoreline. We climbed aboard the plane as Dale untied the line. Dale checked the instruments and started the engine. The Lycoming engine purred.

"Make sure you put the seat belt on, Jason. It's going to be a bit rough," he cautioned.

"Will do," I replied as I secured my belt.

The white floats cut through the water of Long Lake. I could feel waves striking against the pontoons. Dale gave the Lycoming plenty of power as we lifted off against a stong wind. It seemed like we were temporarily suspended in air, but the 245 horses took us toward the heavens. We both understood that a storm was coming in. The flight to Old Forge was slightly rocky. We were at 3400 feet over Raquette Lake when Dale started his descent. I looked out as we passed over Drew's Restaurant. The red roof that Mike, the owner, had painted last year stuck out like a beacon. The sun was still shining in the Inlet area, although the clouds were beginning to come in. Dale banked to the right and came in about 600 feet over Drew's. The parking lot had a few cars and pickup trucks.

Dale didn't waste any time. He landed the sturdy seaplane in front of Kirby's Marina. One of the workers ran over to Dale's rental space waiting for us. I didn't recognize the young fellow. Dale told me that his name was Josh Lincoln, from the Port Byron region. Dale cut the engine about thirty feet from the dock area. We glided in, and the young man tied us up.

"Dale, I imagine the folks at Drew's are in awe about a low flying seaplane," I jested.

"Oh yeah! We'll probably hear about that the next time one of us stops by Drew's," Dale said with a devilish smile on his face.

"Thanks for the ride. It was a good flight."

"I worked on the engine over the winter and it performed well. Jason, the plane is old, but I think I keep it in good shape."

"Yes, you do, Dale." I could almost see the pride illuminating from his face.

Dale gave Josh a two-dollar tip for tying up the plane. He gave the Stinson a cursory look and locked it up. We didn't see Kirby around, so we proceeded to Dale's GMC SUV. Dale let it warm up for a few minutes and then we left the Marina. I told Dale to drop me off by my entrance. The storm was beginning to hit the area and a few drops appeared on the windshield.

"Looks like we're going to get some rain," I remarked.

"Yeah! I guess we're in for a good soaking. Typical spring weather."

Dale pulled up in front of my driveway, and I got out after thanking him again.

"Take care, Jason. Until next time."

"Best to you, Dale."

I watched Dale disappear down Route 28, then walked toward my log home. As I approached, Ruben greeted me with a series of loud barks. He had missed his master. I walked over to his run and opened the gate. The large German shepherd retired K-9 came over to me and rubbed his big head against my knee. I reached down and petted him. I had missed him and he had missed me, too. I checked his water and food dishes and filled each of them. Ruben ran into the forest and returned, heading for the porch, indicating he wanted to come inside. It was getting cool, and a wood-stove fire would warm up the log home. Ruben followed me inside, and in about fifteen minutes the kindling wood was beginning to set the larger pieces of maple to flame. After I got the wood-stove going, I washed up. Ruben had settled down on his air-cushion with his nose lying between his two front paws. His eyes rolled to the left and then to the right, constantly watching his master. Our bond was strong. He loved to chase the chippies as they darted into the high grass and brush piles that lined the edge of the forest. He knew, as I, spring was finally here.

The red light on my answering machine was blinking. I pressed the button and listened to the calls. The first was from owner of the Breakshire Lodge in Lake Placid.

"Jason, this is Tom Huston. Please call me when you have an opportunity."

The remaining calls were from various business establishments. All those calls contained the same theme, bad check cases. I noted the calls in my telephone log.

I'd contact my clients in the morning. I looked at my watch and noted that it was 4:30 p.m.

I called Tom Huston, sensing he would still be in his office.

"Good afternoon, Mr. Huston. Jason Black returning your call."

"Jason, how are you? Thank you for calling. Have you been involved in any more kidnapping cases?" He was making reference to Patty's abduction by the two Ohio prison escapees.

"No, I haven't. Thank goodness for that," I replied.

"How is Patty, Jason? And are there any wedding plans in the future?" he asked, adding "Or perhaps it's none of my business."

"She is doing well and is still working five days a week at John's Diner in Old Forge. The wedding is in the planning stage. You know I consider you almost family," I said sincerely.

"I want you both to know that I wish you every happiness, and if there is anything I can do on this end, do not hesitate to let me know. Promise me that, Jason." Tom Huston was sincere. And he appreciated the assistance I had given him on some internal matters at the Breakshire Lodge. "I'm calling about some bad checks that my cashier took in from a New York City guest. They are protested. I'll send them down to you with all the information we have on the guest. By the way, when are you coming up to see us?"

"You remember Dale Rush. We were flying earlier today in the Tupper Lake and Star Lake region. We had considered coming over, but Dale didn't know if the ice was all out of the lake."

"He could have landed all right. Well, maybe next time. I'd love to go up with Dale myself." I was aware of Tom's love of flying.

"That could be arranged, Tom. I'll let you know the next time we're going to be in the area." Dale would be honored to have Tom as a passenger.

"That would be nice, Jason." Even over the phone I could sense his smile of appreciation.

We promised to meet soon and concluded our conversation. I was glad to know a man who was such an asset to his community.

I went into my office and straightened up my desk, then took a moment and called Patty. She advised me that she was just getting ready to help her landlord, Harriet Stone, with a project. It seems that Harriet was caning an antique chair and needed some assistance. I told Patty that I would call her the next day. Although I would miss her, I realized she enjoyed her outside activities.

Ruben stirred from his comfortable air-cushion and went to stand by the door. He wanted to go outside. I opened the door and he bounded off for the forest. It wasn't long before he returned. I could see him from the opened door. I went out to meet him. He ran into his run and drank some water from his dish. He finished and came to me and rubbed his big head against my right knee. His ears stood straight up when a large doe crossed our property, but he didn't bark. I rubbed his back and we went inside. It was just after 8:00 p.m. when I heated some chicken soup and made a grilled cheese sandwich. After I finished my late meal, I cleaned up the kitchen and continued to put my office back into good order. *Brady's Book on Checks* was opened on my desk. I closed it and inserted it into the bookcase. All small business people should have a copy of Brady's book, especially if they receive checks for their products or goods.

CHAPTER EIGHT

My log home always afforded me peace. I pondered in my mind what it would be like having Patty as my wife and wondered how the solitude in my world here, in the great Adirondacks, would be changed. I enjoyed this existence, away from the turmoil of an urban setting. The hikes that Ruben and I had taken were filled with enjoyment. The animal inhabitants of this wonderful place were always in our presence, but, unlike people, they rarely disturbed the peaceful environment. I knew in my mind that changes would take place inside the Blue Line. There were always forces at work, whether it be the elite looking for more vast amounts of property to elevate their status of importance or the proposing of legislation that would place a heavier burden on the poor and middle classes. I wasn't against progress, but I didn't like to see hardworking, struggling people left out of the loop. Historically, my family had come to this country in 1709. They had carved their existence out of the land and the forest with hard work, axes, two-man saws, horses, and mules. To exist in that difficult way of life, one had to possess creativity and intestinal fortitude. As their descendant, that's why I chose inside the Blue Line to live and exist.

It was time to retire for the evening. I let Ruben out for his last run into the woods. Soon he returned and pawed at the door. I opened it and he entered and headed for his sleeping area. I went into the bathroom, brushed my teeth, and prepared for bed. I still wore heavier pajamas, as the air in the mountains was on the cool side.

I went over and petted Ruben, checked the doors, and had a glass of cold water. I climbed into bed and started to read. My eyelids became heavy after a few minutes, and I fell off to sleep.

The handle on the two-man saw came apart when I felt a tugging on the bedspread. I awoke to find Ruben at the foot of the bed with the end of the spread in his mouth. My dream of cutting wood was interrupted.

"Ruben, drop it," I commanded.

I rolled out of bed and let Ruben out for his early morning run into the woods.

While he was outside, I turned the gas on under the teakettle, removed a cup from the cupboard, and acquired a green teabag from the pantry. I looked out the window and saw Ruben racing to the door. I let him in. He went over to his cushion and lay down. I decided to shave and take a quick shower. I hadn't been to John's for breakfast in a week, and I missed Patty. I glanced at the clock. I had overslept. No wonder Ruben was tugging on the covers. It was 8:30 a.m. Patty had been working at John's for two hours already.

The shower felt good as the soap bubbles popped against the force of the water. I had replaced the water pump, and the new one added a stronger flow. Jack Falsey had told me when he changed it that my old pump was malfunctioning. I always appreciated Jack's input because he knew his business. My soap supply was getting low, and all the Ivory was gone. I had just one cake of Lifebuoy soap left, and I was using it. I rinsed with ice cold water, which felt refreshing. I reached for my robe behind the bathroom door. I dried my hair with my dryer. Ruben sensed that I would be leaving the house soon for John's Diner to have breakfast and, of course, to see Patty. I got dressed and finished combing my hair.

I took Ruben out to his run and checked his water and food dishes. He looked at me and I petted him. I went back inside and checked my desk for mail that was ready to go to the post office. There were three letters, stamped and sealed, to three Adirondack Mountain businesses concerning bad check cases. I checked the answering machine and noted there were no new calls. I locked the door, headed to the Bronco, climbed in, and started the engine. It coughed from the night air dampness. I let it warm up for a few minutes. I turned around, tooted at Ruben, and headed out of the driveway. The sun's rays were making long shadows in the tall pines. The air was cool. Just as I was about to turn toward Old Forge, I observed Charlie Perkins' log truck approaching. The stacks on the Peterbilt had long trails of white smoke pouring out. He spotted me and laid on the airhorns. I grabbed my CB.

"Where are you headed, Charlie?" I asked.

"Heading to Vermont, Jason. See you when I get back." Charlie sounded tired.

"Have a good trip and watch out for the moose," I retorted.

"Sure will, Jason, old buddy."

"See you later." The CB audio was weakening. I couldn't hear Charlie anymore.

I continued south on Route 28 to John's Diner. The early crowd had left, and only four pickups were in the parking lot. One of them was Wilt Chambers big white Dodge. Charlie and Wilt had become good friends of mine. Charlie had helped me out on several of my cases in the past and had towed me out of more than one snow bank over the winter. Wilt was always there to help anybody who needed a helping hand. He and Charlie were independent loggers. Charlie was always looking out for two-man saws to add to my collection. He would pay for them and I would reimburse him. Wilt and I would visit the New York State Woodsmen's Field Days held at the Boonville Fairgrounds every year. It was a great display of skill by the participants, and the booths were interesting to visit.

I pulled in next to the white Dodge pickup. I assumed Wilt was inside. As I approached the door, I could hear his booming voice and laughter. I entered. Wilt had his back toward me and didn't see me enter. Lila was busy at the grill flipping some flapjacks, and I could see Patty at the far end of the dining room carrying a tray of food to three men. Wilt was talking with John, the owner of the diner. John saw me, but didn't alert Wilt that I was approaching from behind. He was telling John about the new log skidder that he had purchased and was explaining some new features on the machine. John was listening intently. I hadn't seen Wilt since he picked me up at the Syracuse airport. I placed my finger against his back.

"Wha…. What's going on here?" He appeared startled.

"Wilt, where have you been? I haven't seen you around," I asked with concern.

"Jason, how are you? " He was genuinely pleased to see me.

The giant of a man got up, turned toward me with a big smile, and extended his hand. I clasped his hand in friendship. I shouldn't have done that. He put the squeeze on and I thought he'd break my bones, but he released the pressure. He was wearing a forest green work jacket and brown trousers. I could tell that he must have dropped thirty pounds.

"You're looking good, Wilt. I can see you've been taking off some weight," I said approvingly.

"I feel great! I've lost about forty pounds and had to purchase some new duds."

"Would you like to join me for a diet breakfast?" I asked.

"Sure would," he replied, rubbing his hands together.

Patty saw me and waved, and I waved back. Wilt and I took a table in the corner of the dining room. Patty approached us with a big smile. She had already poured our coffee and two large glasses of ice water. Wilt ordered a poached egg and toast, and I settled for a short stack of wheat cakes with crisp bacon. In a few minutes, Patty brought our piping hot food. Wilt rolled his eyes when he saw the three golden wheat cakes and the bacon strips. Patty re-filled our coffee cups.

"Jason, this diet I'm on is starving me," Wilt groaned.

"I imagine you're having a difficult time getting used to the smaller portions. Keep it up, Wilt. You're looking good," I replied.

"It is a difficult task to limit the food intake." He reached for his coffee cup.

"I hear you've invested in a new skidder. I bet that set you back a few dollars."

"Yep, it did, but the old one was beginning to cost a fortune to maintain and I've been contracted to cut a hundred acres near Star Lake," he explained.

"Well, Wilt, I wish you good luck with your project," I added. "And, Wilt, I appreciated you picking me up at the airport and taking care of Ruben, while I was in Arizona."

"I was glad to do it, Jason. Ruben missed you. He paced back and forth all the time you were gone. I never saw anything like it. He's a great dog."

"I know he is, Wilt," I said, nodding in agreement.

We sat around the table and chatted for a while. Patty was busy waiting on a busload of senior citizens who apparently were headed to Blue Mountain. Some of them must have been hard of hearing, as they were talking loudly. Wilt reached for his wallet, and I placed my hand against his arm.

"I'll take care of this, Wilt." Wilt always paid; now it was my turn.

"Thanks, Jason," he replied, appreciating the gesture. I beckoned to Patty and Lila as we left John's Diner. John was busy in the kitchen and we didn't have a chance to say goodbye. Wilt told me that he had four or five two-man saws for my collection and that he would drop them off in a few days. I bid my good friend goodbye. He climbed into the big Dodge and backed up to make the swing toward Route 28. I headed to the post office to check my box and to mail my letters. Wilt headed south toward Thendara.

I went into the post office after parking the Bronco. Chief of Police Todd Wilson held the door open for me. I spoke as I passed him.

"Chief, I'll be in to see you soon. Everything quiet in town?"

"Looking forward to it, Jason. Not much going on, except some criminal mischief cases. Nothing serious."

The Chief had his thumb on the pulse of the community. He and his staff did a good job with the public safety issues. I checked my mailbox, which contained numerous letters and magazines, then closed the box and went over to the letter drop to put my letters to be mailed through the slot. I purchased some stamps and envelopes, chatted a few minutes with the post office staff, and left.

I drove over to Brussel's and asked Don some questions about the Bronco. While there I had an oil change and checked the tires.

"Jason, when are you going to trade this Bronco in for a newer set of wheels?"

He had a grin on his face acknowledging that he realized how much the Bronco meant to me.

"When the wheels fall off," I retorted.

"Only kidding, Jason. The Bronco still looks in good shape."

"Well, I've got a good mechanic. That's the reason, and I keep it washed and waxed. The prices today for these vehicles are out of reach for the people in the low pay scale range."

"True, true, Jason." His grin was gone.

I paid my bill and thanked Don for his good service.

I went home after stopping at the Big M Market for a newspaper. When I entered the yard, a raccoon was making a beeline for the woods, and Ruben was standing behind his fence. His ears were standing up straight, but he didn't bark. I got out of the Bronco and took Ruben for a walk. The buds were coming on fast with the rain that we had been having, and the wildflowers were beginning to spring to life. Ruben sniffed the pile of brush for a fast moving chippie that darted into it. We were in the woods for about half an hour. The retired K-9 still looked in good shape. When we returned to the log home, Ruben ran over to his gate of the runway. I swept the porch and walk and went inside.

I opened my mail and placed some of the insufficient fund checks in the case folders. I typed several letters to the people who had issued the checks. After I finished taking care of the office work, I took Brady's book from the shelf and reviewed "stale dated" checks. I then placed the bible of the check world back on the shelf.

I placed a call to my old friend, Lieutenant Jack Doyle. After going through about three different people at the Troop S Bureau of Criminal Investigation I finally heard; "Lieutenant Jack Doyle speaking. Can I be of service?"

"Hello, Lieutenant. Jason Black here." I was glad to hear his voice.

"Jason, how in the hell have you been? I haven't seen you since my promotion party. When can we get together?" He was always happy to hear from me.

"That's why I'm calling. How about lunch tomorrow?"

"Good idea. I'm busy, but we can grab a quick lunch. Any special place?" he asked.

"How about the Breakshire Lodge? I've got to come to that

area in the morning, and if you can meet me at the Breakshire around 12:30 p.m., that would be great."

"I'll be there, Jason. I'll look forward to seeing you then."

I wanted to talk with Jack about the possible drug case out of Arizona. I was certain that he wasn't aware of it. I knew that he would be the one to talk with. In the past I had worked closely with Roy Garrison, now promoted to Captain, and Frank Temple, now a Major. I felt that Jack would handle any case that might arise, in the finest tradition of the troopers.

Jack and I conversed about the old days and promised to meet for lunch the next day. I had just hung up when the phone rang.

"Hello," I said, picking up the receiver.

"Jason, it's about time you hung up that phone. I've been trying to call you for several minutes." It was Jack Flynn.

"Hello, buddy. How are you?"

"Better now, since I've got through to you," he shot back.

"Jason, the property that has been purchased by the trucking company guy in the North Country is being converted into a warehouse. They are going to have an office there and space for storage. Have you been by the property lately?"

"I have flown over it and secured some photos. They are being developed as we speak." I could tell he was pleased.

"That's good. Will you send me some copies for my file here?" he asked excitedly.

"Sure will. Just as soon as I get them from the drugstore. Jack, I'm meeting my contact tomorrow for lunch. In fact, I was talking with him when you were trying to call me." The excitement was contagious.

"Do you think he is up to the job? It's going to take a great deal of surveillance and some wires." He went on speaking hurriedly. "This thing is a sizable operation, and all the T's and I's have to be crossed and dotted. The main principal is a bad guy."

"Believe me, Jack, he is one of the best." I knew what Jack meant. It was an important case. He didn't want anyone incompetent handling it.

"You know, I'm working closely with the Phoenix people. This guy would haul anything anywhere for a buck, Jason. He's making big dollars, and it doesn't appear legitimate." Jack was getting wound up.

I tried to reassure him. "You can count on me."

"Jason, we've been down the trail together. Thank God for our US Marine Corps training."

"Those were tough days, but good days, Jack. How's Ruby? Is she keeping you in line?" I guessed Ruby would have placed the call had she been there.

"Great! Sorry she's not here right now. She has gone to the post office and has to run some other errands."

"Give her my love, Jack."

"I will."

"How hot is it in Arizona?"

"Only 100 degrees, as we speak."

"Take care. You know I don't envy you those triple digit temperatures," I said jokingly.

We hung up.

I made some notes in my journal and notebook. Jack was right; it was going to be a tough case putting all the facts together, but I knew that Jack Doyle would be up to the task. For my part, I would even donate my time in order to keep our great Adirondacks crime free, which probably was impossible, but we'd try to keep it a level playing field.

Noon had arrived. I heated a can of cream of mushroom soup and grilled a cheese sandwich on rye bread. I also brewed a pot of green tea. When I looked outside, Ruben was walking back and forth in his dog run. I would have rather let him run free, but to avoid any difficulty the run was his daytime place to be. I returned to the stove and filled my soup bowl. I sat down and enjoyed my lunch.

CHAPTER NINE

Working as a private detective in the mountains is different than working in an urban setting. There was process serving and work from various attorneys' offices throughout the park. Occasionally some more complicated cases would come my way. It all blended in with a good lifestyle that I enjoyed. I had many friends, and living inside the Blue Line surrounded with this majestic beauty was inspiring. I couldn't ask for anything better. It was true you couldn't please everyone, but I always tried my best. On the other side of the coin, we do have a few miserable folks, but then you have to analyze what made them that way. I believe everyone tries to enjoy a good day every day.

I called John's Diner and talked with Patty. I told her that I had to leave early for Lake Placid and that we should plan on dinner the next night. She was pleased. I told her that I'd call her later that night before going to bed.

The information concerning Bernie Draper and his organization was contained in the report that Jack had sent me from Arizona. I reread it and made some notes relative to points that I would raise with Lieutenant Doyle at our meeting the next day. Draper had to be a greedy person. He ran a successful legal trucking concern. But he apparently had been taken in by somebody who needed to have a way of transporting contraband. Draper, according to the report, was intelligent, and for a small trucking outfit he did well in the transportation arena. The report went on to say that Draper's wife was from a family of prominence. Something had to have soured the relationship to send her down the path of a forthcoming divorce.

I was in the midst of typing several letters when Ruben began to bark. I got up from my desk and looked out the window. It was Wilt. He shut the big Dodge off and climbed out. He went over to Ruben and threw him a dog biscuit. Wilt had made friends with my dog a long time ago and always carried a supply of biscuits for Ruben. I took the letter I was working on out of the typewriter and placed it in the drawer. I went outside to greet Wilt.

My friend looked up and waved.

"Wilt, what a pleasant surprise."

"Jason, I had to come over to the Old Forge hardware stores for a number of things, so I threw those two-man saws on the truck. They are in good shape, and I want you to know, Jason, I sharpened them for you."

"Wilt, that was wonderful of you to do that. I could have had them sharpened here. How much are the saws?"

"I picked them up over the winter. There are five of them. Oh, give me ten dollars apiece and we'll call it square. That includes my time for sharpening them."

"Are you certain that's enough, Wilt?"

"That's plenty, Jason." He had a big smile on his face. "You must have a good collection of those arm builders."

"This will bring my collection up to thirty-five saws, not counting the band saws and ice saws I have."

"That's great! Jason, if you ever start collecting single-bladed and double-bladed axes, let me know. I've got several over at my place. My cutting crews replace them often. And, if you ever start collecting chain saws, I can help you out on that, too."

"No, I'm sticking with the saws for now. I'll let you know if I broaden my collection. Would you like to have a cup of coffee?"

"Sure, I will. I'm not keeping you from your work, am I?" he asked. "I wouldn't want to be any bother."

"Not at all. Let's go inside." I could see that Wilt was still losing weight.

We went into the kitchen and Wilt sat down at the table. He no longer needed two chairs or two stools to sit on. I turned the gas on and lit the burner. I fixed Wilt a cup of coffee without cream or sugar and prepared myself a cup of green tea. Both cups were steaming as I joined Wilt at the table. I wasn't prepared for his next comment.

"Jason, when are you and Patty going to tie the knot? You've been dating long enough. It's high time you get down to business. Ha! Ha!" he chided.

"Wilt, we haven't set a date yet, but we're both thinking about it."

"Jason, that young lady loves you. Well, it's none of my business, but when you do, I want to be best man."

"I understand that, Wilt. I can't promise the best man, but when and if we do, you, Charlie Perkins and Dale Rush are going to be in the wedding party. I promise."

"You mean, the three of us will be in the wedding?" He acted surprised.

"Well, Patty and I discussed that several months ago, and that's what we decided."

"Do Charlie and Dale know about this?" he asked quizzically.

"Yes, I told them about it. I'm asking you to keep it quiet, too."

"I won't say a word. I promise."

I told Wilt that it would be a while yet before the wedding knot was to be tied. I took my next week's grocery money and paid Wilt five ten dollar bills for the saws. Then I helped him carry them to my storage shed. I had several pegs that I hung them on. They looked good, and sharp, too.

Wilt and I walked over to the run. He gave Ruben another dog biscuit. Ruben licked the man's big hand. Wilt had made a good friend.

"Good dog, Ruben," the big logger said.

"Wilt, thank you for stopping over and thank you for bringing the saws. Maybe some day I'll have a display and invite some of the old-timers to look them over."

"Jason, that's a good idea. Some of those fellows are getting up in age, but I bet it would bring back some great memories of their days in the forest."

"Yes, it would, Wilt." I nodded my head in agreement.

We shook hands and said goodbye. I watched Wilt climb into his pride and joy and turn around. He tooted when he left the yard. Wilt was a good man.

I let Ruben out for his late afternoon run. He took off toward the woods. While the big dog was taking care of his chores, I grabbed a rake and used it on some of last fall's leaves. I put them in a plastic bag and placed them in the shed. It wasn't long before the retired K-9 bounded out of the woods directly toward me. He wanted to play. I took a few minutes to toss the ball at him. He loved to bounce it off his nose. What a dog!

I prepared myself a light supper consisting of scrambled eggs and toast and a pot of green tea. After washing the dishes and taking Ruben for a short run, I got ready for bed. Five o'clock in the morning would soon be here. I set the Big Ben alarm clock, read for a while and dozed off.

Dale was in a full power dive. I was yelling at him to pull up. I awoke with a start. Big Ben was winding down and Ruben was at the foot of the bed pulling on the spread. I let him out and turned the burner on under the teakettle. He soon returned.

"Ruben, you're going with me today, big fellow." He wagged his tail as if he understood.

I took a fast shower, shaved, and dressed. It was cool, so I elected to wear a new pair of Dockers with a matching shirt. I'd take my jacket, too. My plan was to have breakfast at Gertie's in Long Lake and then swing over to the Cranberry Lake area and look over Mr. Bernie Draper's recently purchased real estate located on Route 56 just north of Route 3. I knew I didn't have to meet Lieutenant Jack Doyle until noon.

Ruben's food and water were placed in the rear of the Bronco. I brought a small cooler along containing three ice packs, several cans of soda, and two bananas. Ruben jumped into the back of the Bronco and lay down. I seldom carried my 9mm semi-automatic pistol, but with the possibility of rabid animals, I thought it would be a good idea. There had been recent reports of rabies in the region. We left the log home at 6:45 a.m. As we left the driveway onto Route 28 heading north, a spike-horn buck ran in front of us. I slowed down just as a doe ran directly in front of the Bronco. Luckily, she also darted across in time.

I didn't call Patty, as I knew she'd be busy at John's Diner. Hopefully I'd see her that night. Ruben and I didn't run into any traffic except for a bread truck making a delivery in Inlet. When we passed through Raquette Lake, there were some fisherman taking a boat off a car. Ruben was sitting up now and his ears touched the roof of the Bronco. Guess he wanted to see what was going on. I had brought along some letters to mail, so dropped them off in the mailbox as we entered Long Lake. Back in Blue Mountain, some of the workers were driving into the Adirondack Museum. The summer season would soon begin.

Gertie's Diner was busy. I had to park next to the Adirondack Hotel and walk a short distance to the diner. Ruben was sitting in the rear of the Bronco watching me. I had lowered the window so he would have plenty of cool mountain air. I went into the diner, where and Bob and Gertie were busy at the grill. There were two servers on duty, one carrying a pot of regular coffee and a pot of decaf. The aroma of bacon was permeating the air as it sizzled on the hot grill. Flapjacks were golden brown. My taste buds, as always, were sensing a good hearty breakfast. I found a small table in the corner and sat down. Bob saw me and waved. Gertie turned around.

"Jason, good to see you. Somebody will be with you in a moment." Her face was flushed from the heat of the grill as she acknowledged me.

"Plenty of time. No hurry," I replied. Hunger pains were starting.

"Can I help you?" the smiling waitress asked as she approached my table.

"Yes, I'll have a small glass of orange juice, a cup of decaf, and a stack of flapjacks with an egg over medium and some bacon. And a glass of water, please."

The newspaper had not yet arrived at this early hour, but I didn't have to wait long for my order. The waitress returned carrying a tray. She placed the plates of hot food in front of me and left to clean a couple of tables. I didn't know any of the customers dining at Gertie's this morning. I figured that most of them were folks passing through Long Lake. If I had been there an hour earlier, I might have known some of the locals. I finished breakfast. The waitress dropped the check off. She told me that her name was Trudy and she had just started working at Gertie's. I left a gratuity. On the way out the door, I told Bob and Gertie that my breakfast was perfect.

"Wish we could chat, Jason, but the crowd is heavy this morning," Bob said.

"I'll catch you two later. Have a good day," I replied.

When I returned to the Bronco, I took Ruben out on his leash for a short walk. I looked out over Long Lake. The sun was climbing into the sky and the lake was calm. It was a beautiful scene here in the center of the Adirondack Park. I opened the door for Ruben and he jumped in. In my trooper career I had met so many fine folks in these mountains with their families enjoying the pristine beauty that God created. I could not help but think of those weekends camping at Skip-Jack Campsite just over the Long Lake bridge.

I backed the Bronco out onto Route 30, as there was no room to turn around by the Adirondack Hotel. Luckily there was no one coming down the highway. I headed toward Tupper Lake. Traffic was light. When I got to Route 3, I went toward Cranberry Lake and Route 56, which was located several miles east of Cranberry Lake.

I hadn't been to the area since Dale and I had flown over the newly acquired Draper property. I noticed that the barn had a large addition built, and a huge parking area. Floodlights had been erected. Several pickup trucks were parked near the barn. The workers could be observed cutting lumber and installing electrical service. A pole had been erected, and several meters could be seen mounted on the pole. It was apparent that the work was being rushed to meet some sort of a deadline. I was able to take some pictures with my telescopic lens. I didn't want to be observed, so I took them from an adjacent woodlot close to the site. I scanned the area with my binoculars. None of the pickups displayed company names. I did notice a black Ford ¾-ton pickup bearing an Arizona license plate. I could not make out the number, as the plate was partially covered. It was apparent to me that Draper had big plans for his newly acquired property here in the Adirondacks. I said to myself, "We'll see about that, Draper. If you're legitimate, fine, but if you're planning criminal activity, you're out of here."

I made my way back to the Bronco and Ruben. I headed for Cranberry and Star Lake. I'd look up Luther Johnson, a friend of mine. I knew that Luther was trustworthy, as he had helped me on several major cases over the years. Luther was a retired Marine, and he and his wife Libby lived just outside of Star Lake. They were private people, but Luther knew everything that went on within a fifty mile radius. He was a quiet fellow, but he remembered everything he heard or observed.

Luther's black Jeep was parked in front of his garage door. I pulled in behind it. The first thing I heard was the sound of a saw coming from the garage. I could see the six-foot-tall former Marine bent over his ban saw. He was in the process of cutting out some crows for lawn ornaments. He looked up, startled.

"Is that you, Jason?" he asked in surprise.

"Yep, that's me, Luther. How are you?" I asked, grinning broadly.

"Not too bad. Gee, it's good to see ya." Luther came toward me after turning the saw off. He extended his hand and I extended mine.

"You still have a good grip, Luther." He was applying firm pressure to my hand. I applied pressure, too: a mutual ex-Marine greeting.

"So do you, Jason."

"Luther, do you remember some of the old cases you assisted me on years ago?"

"Indeed I do. The good old days when there was still a lot of respect in our society," he added.

"We had some close calls, especially on that lumber theft investigation at Newton Falls."

"Yep, that was a good arrest you made there."

"Luther, I have been meaning to stop by before this; however, I've been busy doing my private investigation work."

"I heard that you apprehended a kidnapper last year. And I heard that you and that Old Forge waitress—I believe her name is Patty—are going together. Oh, yeah, I still hear the news from around the mountains."

"You hear well, my friend. Luther, I'd like you to assist me on another matter. I'd like you to keep an eye on a building by the intersection of Route 3 and Route 56." I spoke in a muted voice.

"Do you mean the one the fellow from Arizona purchased?"

"Yes, that's the one. I'm working on a matter that concerns that location, but it has to stay strictly confidential."

"Oh, I understand, Jason." I knew that I could depend on Luther.

"What have you heard about the guy from Arizona?" I asked.

"I heard that he is a big-shot trucker that hauls freight to Montreal, Quebec, and that he is going to convert the barn to a storage area. He's building a gift shop on one end of it for the purpose of selling southwestern jewelry and knickknacks. One of his workers is staying at the motel in Cranberry and has hired some local carpenters for the project."

"You hear well, Luther."

He smiled and hung his head. "Jason, tell me what you want and I'll do it. This foreman or boss, Scott Austin, is about fifty years old, six feet tall with a slim build. He probably weighs 165 to 170 pounds and is a white male. According to what I hear, he drinks straight whiskey and doesn't mingle or talk to any of the locals, except the carpenters he has hired. Supposedly he has worked for this trucking company owner for several years."

"I appreciate the information, Luther. Remember it has to be kept quiet. I can't pay you much, but I would appreciate any information that might come to your attention as it pertains to that project. I can't go into detail about the situation, but as I indicated to you it's imperative to be low key. Call me right away if anything develops."

"You've got my word, Jason."

"I know that, Luther. I can tell by your brush cut you're still a Marine."

"You know how it is. When I was a DI instructing those raw

recruits with their shaven heads, I felt out of place with black curly hair, so I got a brush cut and never have changed back to the longer style."

"Luther, it works for you, especially in this black fly country."

"You got it."

"How's Libby?" I asked.

"Good. She's with some of her lady friends today shopping at Potsdam. They have a new dress shop over there, and you know how the ladies love to shop."

"Indeed, I do." I shook his hand. "Luther, you take care of yourself and keep me posted."

"Don't worry, Jason. My eyes are open, my ears are listening, and my mouth is shut. Take it easy." Luther restarted his ban saw.

I walked out of Luther's garage, got into the Bronco, and headed toward Tupper Lake and my meeting with that raw-boned BCI Lieutenant Jack Doyle. I was pleased with the information that Luther had shared with me. I had told Luther for years that he would have made a damned good trooper, but Libby had wanted Luther home at night, and many times over the years I had had to agree with her ideology. He had seen enough in his Marine Corps career. He had been a master sergeant for years and had been a good leader.

CHAPTER TEN

The Breakshire Lodge, owned and operated by Tom Huston, was like a stately New England Inn. Tom was in his sixties, about six feet tall with white hair. He was from Long Island and old money. I pulled into the parking lot and looked around for Lieutenant Doyle's state car, but he had not arrived as yet. I got out of the Bronco and put the window down for Ruben. He had been lying down in the rear and had slept all the way from Star Lake. I let him out and put him on his leash. We went for a short walk and then he went back into the Bronco. He leaned over to his water dish, lapped some of the water, and lay back down.

"Good, Ruben. Good boy," I said as he rolled his eyes at me.

I entered the lodge as Mr. Huston was walking toward his office. He approached as he recognized me. We shook hands.

"Good to see you, Jason." He flashed a big smile.

"Hello, Tom. It's good to see you. I'm meeting BCI Lieutenant Jack Doyle for lunch today."

"That's great, Jason. Before you leave, I would like to talk with you about a matter, if I wouldn't be imposing on you."

"You're not imposing at all. As soon as my meeting is over, I'll stop by your office, sir."

"Cut that 'sir' stuff, Jason. It's just 'Tom'," he said emphatically.

"Right. See you in awhile, Tom." I stated his name with a grin.

I took a seat in the lobby. The large leather chairs were comfortable. I knew that my friend, Jack Doyle, should arrive momentarily. I hadn't seen Jack since his promotion party. What a celebration it was! Roy Garrison was elevated to Captain of the BCI in Troop S, and my old boss, Frank Temple, was now the Major of Troop S. That was a good team, including Jack, the new ramrod of the unit. Former team member, Melvin Nemyer, had retired to become a county Sheriff. Mel had been a great trooper and had retired as a senior investigator. I always remembered fondly the conversations we shared over our chili-dog lunches—one of my lasting memories from my many years in the Troopers.

As I sat in the lobby of the Breakshire Lodge waiting for Jack, I looked around this elaborate room. The lobby was large. Paintings were displayed on the walls, and two water fountains had been added to the lobby. One other artwork stood out, and that was the huge wooden carved black bear that Wilt Chambers had created for Tom Huston and his lodge. The eyes of the bear pierced from their sockets. The claws looked razor sharp, but were honed pieces of ivory. Wilt and I had gone in together and presented the bear to Mr. Huston as a tribute to the lodge, the visiting tourists, and the local community. Standing in the lobby, it was definitely representative of the Adirondack Region. Tourists and local people had clicked the shutters on their cameras more than once. The big black bear looked real, and to add to the ambience, Mr. Huston had prepared a tape of a black bear growling; when anyone pressed the button, the loud growl got everyone's attention. People came from miles around to press that button.

I had just picked up an Adirondack publication when the front door opened and Jack Doyle entered, wearing a navy blue three-piece suit, a white shirt, and a matching blue tie. He was just over six feet tall, and slender, and he walked with a military swagger. He spotted me as I placed the paper on the oak table.

"Jason, I'm sorry I'm late, but I had a meeting with Captain Roy Garrison, and you know how meticulous he is for details."

"He's a good man." I had worked for Roy and I knew how efficient he was.

"Yes, he is. My desk is piled high with reports. What have you got for me, Jason?" he asked quizzically.

"Let's enjoy a nice lunch, and I'll explain what I have while we eat."

"Okay, that's fine with me. I'm hungry."

"You look sharp in that blue suit. Do you miss wearing the gray?" I knew he did.

"Jason, you know I miss it. My dad and my late brother both wore the gray."

"I know they did, and they wore it well, Jack. I know you still miss them."

"Jason, how are you doing? I hear that you might tie the knot again. I wish you well. It must be tough living alone."

"Yes, my girl Patty and I are thinking about it. But I'm not really alone; you know I have Ruben, the retired K-9. He has been a friend, believe me. Still in good shape, too."

"Yes, I did hear that you had him," he acknowledged.

"He's out in the rear of the Bronco. I'll introduce you to him after lunch." I knew that Jack respected the K-9's in the Division of State Police.

We were led to a large table in the corner of the massive dining room. Customer traffic was light, and only a few senior citizens were finishing up their lunch with coffee. The hostess seated us and advised that a waitress would be with us shortly. We looked at the menu. One of the specials was a large spinach salad with boiled eggs and ham chunks. The waitress appeared and took our drink order. Both of us ordered iced tea with lemon. She returned shortly. Jack ordered a broiled chicken sandwich with honey mustard, and I selected the spinach salad.

"Are you on a diet?" Jack asked.

"Yes, I'm beginning one as of today. Two hundred and forty pounds is a little too much to be lugging around."

"You're probably right, but you have a large frame and seem to carry it well." I liked Jack's comment. He was the eternal diplomat.

"What information do you have for me, Jason?" Jack's voice let me know he was anxious to hear what I had to say.

While we waited for our lunch to be served, I told Jack the information I had received from Jack Flynn. I told him about Bernie Draper and his operation of transporting contraband to Cornwall. I didn't leave out any of the details. Jack pulled out a small notebook and took notes in shorthand, a skill he had learned in high school and honed well. I could tell by the expression on his face that he was anxious to acquire all the facts. We were interrupted when Isabella, our waitress, arrived. She was a graduate of Mount Holyoke and the niece of Tom Huston. She carefully set the tray on a folding tray holder. I noticed that Jack's sandwich looked great, with two slices of dill pickles on the side. My spinach, served in a large wooden bowl, was covered with slices of boiled egg and garnished with black olives and bits of radishes. A small basket of piping hot rolls accompanied the salad. Isabella refilled our glasses with iced tea.

I noted that Tom had made some changes in his tablecloths and napkins. They depicted the high-peak region of the Adirondacks and were eye-catching.

"How do you like your chicken sandwich, Jack?" I asked.

"Delicious, Jason. They must have a great chef."

"They have three chefs here and several cooks. Two of the chefs graduated from the Culinary Institute of America, and one of them graduated from Paul Smith's College. All three are outstanding in their field, and Tom pays them well."

"I'm impressed, Jason." Jack held his napkin to his chin.

"Yes, they serve excellent cuisine for a fair price. You don't mind paying a little more, if the food is good."

The waitress refilled our glasses with iced tea. I continued to explain the scheme that Draper was masterminding from Arizona. I told Jack that Flynn's letter indicated that Draper was setting up a gift shop and warehouse with the gift shop as a front, offering southwestern jewelry and western gear, including shirts, belts, cowboy boots, western hats. I shared with him my belief that Draper, hauling freight to Canada, would undoubtedly be carrying drugs and guns secreted in the loads of commercial freight. Included with the contraband, it was believed that he also had whiskey and untaxed cigarettes. I told him that the possibility of a large-scale smuggling ring could be in the making.

"Jason, I've taken down most of the information. I should have brought a recorder, but my shorthand caught just about all of what you told me. What about the feds?"

"That will be your call, but my Arizona contacts want this matter to be handled carefully by good surveillance and information gathering. I couldn't think of a better person than you, Jack, to handle this sensitive investigation. Keep in mind I'm not part of the division anymore, but I have already set up a damned good informant to keep an eye and ear open for any information. I have photos of the barn in my Bronco. But since they were taken, the barn has changed. As we speak, they are building the gift shop and expanding the warehouse. Another thing: that is a residential area, and someone had to give big bucks to change that particular location to a business area. Big bucks!!"

"You can say that again." He mulled it over for a moment. "I'll have to know who your informant is. We will have some undercover surveillance people in the area as well. Don't worry, they'll never be made. I can't tell you who they are at the moment, but rest assured, they will be around." His tone was reassuring.

"I understand. We should stay in touch often to keep everything running smoothly. Jack, Town of Webb Police Chief Todd Wilson is a close friend of mine, and a former BCI man as well. He is aware of what is coming down and will be watching for the vehicles involved. My buddy Flynn, in Arizona, is working closely with the narcotics people at the Phoenix PD and will feed us the information as it develops. Bernie Draper is also a suspect in the killing of three Mexican Nationals, who were working out of a day labor office and who were in the states illegally. Those crimes are being looked at closely by the Arizona authorities, immigration, and other federal agencies." I wanted to share all the information that I could.

"Interesting, Jason." Jack was taking shorthand rapidly, filling the pages of his notebook.

"I'm treating today, Jack. Next time you can have the privilege."

"Thank you, Jason. It really isn't necessary. Thank you."

I paid, and Jack and I went out to the Bronco. I took Ruben out of the rear and attached a leash to his collar. Jack smiled when he saw my dog.

"This was the K-9 that was involved in sniffing out drugs. Am I correct?"

"Yes, you are. His handler worked Ruben well, and as a team they were very successful."

"I feel that I know Ruben, as I've heard the dog handlers talk about him and the good results he produced." Jack patted his head. Ruben sniffed Jack's pant leg.

"Good boy, Ruben," I added.

"Well, Jason, I want to thank you for lunch, and sometime I'd like to meet Tom Huston, but I have to hurry back to headquarters. Don't worry; this information will be kept secure. We appreciate your contacting us about it, and you'll have our cooperation. You were a great investigator on the job, but you know how organizations are. At least, Jason, you can think for yourself, and you never kissed anyone's butt."

"We won't go there, Jack. Let's concentrate on Draper, and I'll help you all I can to take him and his kind down. We have too many people on drugs in our country, and it is Bernie Draper and people like him that helped spread it. Can you imagine the impact on our society? He and his kind are making millions of dollars. The statistics are there." I was adamant in my statement.

"That's for sure," Jack agreed. "Take care, good friend. I've got to rush,"

"Talk with you later. I'll keep you posted."

Jack Doyle would do his best to stop Draper's organization from getting a foothold in New York State, and in particular, the Adirondack Park. Now he smiled and turned and walked to his troop car, a shiny black Mercury with four antennae. I watched him wheel out of the parking lot. He waved goodbye.

I went back inside the lodge to see Tom Huston.

When I entered the lobby, Tom motioned me to come into his office. He must have anticipated our meeting, as a pot of green tea and cups were on a nearby table.

"Jason, how have you been?" he queried.

"Keeping busy with spring coming on. Plenty of bad check cases coming in by mail." I sat down in the deep leather chair. Tom sat down in the other leather chair after pouring us two cups of tea.

"Do you take cream or sugar, Jason?"

"No, just the tea." There were two small end tables by each chair. I sipped the green tea. It was hot and tasted good.

"How is Patty? I hear through the grapevine that you two will be getting married soon." He seemed pleased with the news.

"Where did you hear that?" I was inquisitive.

"From one of the salesmen," he answered coyly.

"We are talking about it, but it may be in the fall. No definite date has been set." I didn't mind Tom asking, but it wasn't any of the salesmen's business.

"It has been about a year since Patty was abducted by those two killers. You did an admirable job in apprehending that fellow in Santa Clara. People are still talking about it."

"I was fortunate that it turned out the way it did. I'm glad that no one got hurt. Patty still has nightmares about those two bastards." I could feel my blood pressure rise. He quickly changed the subject.

"Jason, I have been meaning to come to Old Forge and have dinner sometime at John's Diner. We hear about that place way up here in Lake Placid. They talk about Lila's pies constantly in our kitchen. My chef has dined there. I'd love to hire her as our pastry chef." I could tell that Tom was serious.

"Yes, she turns out some fine desserts. Personally, the thick apple with vanilla ice cream is my favorite. You should try that sometime, Tom," I advised him.

"I will. The restaurants in Old Forge all have good reputations for serving fine cuisine."

"Yes, we're lucky. We're blessed with many hardworking folks. You know how it is in your business; Tom, the service to the public is important."

Tom paused, and his tone changed. "Jason, remember you always told me to let you know if something out of the ordinary should come to my attention."

"Yes, I remember that. Why, Tom. What's up?" My curiosity was aroused.

"Well, I may have something that you might like to look into. I have a guest here that is trying to sell some oil paintings. He has

asked me if he could use the lobby for a display this coming week-
end. His name is Oscar Winton and he's from Detroit, Michigan. I
told him that he could use one corner of the lobby. I feel that something isn't just right about this guy. My night clerk caught him in
the act of taking some cigars without paying for them. When the
night clerk challenged him, Winton turned pale as a ghost and
claimed that he was going to pay for them, but the night clerk
caught up with him going down the hall at a fast pace. He did give
the night clerk a ten-dollar bill and apologized. I know it isn't
much to go on, but my inner feelings tell me that this gentleman is
up to something. Could you discretely check him out?" he asked.

"I'll be glad to. All I need is his name, his address, and his registration plate number."

"I have it right here for you. He is driving a Ford van with
Michigan plates."

I copied down the information and told Tom that I would make
an inquiry about Mr. Oscar Winton. There could be something to it,
or maybe the gentleman was legitimate. We'd find out. We finished our tea and shook hands.

"Jason, say hello to Patty for me. It will take her some time to
get over that ordeal, but she'll be okay. You wait and see."

"I know she will. She's got true grit." Patty was a strong
woman, both physically and mentally. She had to be, to have survived the abduction incident.

I bid farewell to my friend, and left the Lodge. I would be going right by Troop S Headquarters, so I thought I'd drop this new
information off with Lieutenant Jack Doyle. He would have one of
his investigators check out Oscar Winton from Michigan. When I
pulled into the parking area, I found it hard to believe that Lieutenant Doyle was just exiting his Mercury. He must have made a stop.

"Hey, Jason, twice in one day. Didn't think I'd be seeing you
so soon." He looked at me with a quizzical expression.

"Jack, I'll only take a minute of your time."

I gave Jack all the information I had on Mr. Winton and told
him about the forthcoming art sale. I knew that Lieutenant Doyle
would discretely handle the matter well. We chatted a few minutes
and then I departed for Old Forge. I stopped at a local gas station

and filled up. Ruben seemed to be getting restless, so I put him on his leash and took him for a short walk. I knew that the retired K-9 was happy, as he pushed against my pant leg with his big head. I rubbed his neck before I put him back into the Bronco. He slurped some water and had a few dog bits.

Traffic on the way back to Old Forge was medium. There were a few slowpokes ahead of me who had a top speed of 25 mph, but I managed to get around them. I was tired when I pulled into my yard. I put Ruben into his dog-run after I let him run free into the woods.

When I entered my log home I checked the answering machine, as the red light was flashing. One of the messages was from Patty.

"Pick me up around seven o'clock." I looked at my watch. It was now 5:15 p.m. I would have to take a shower and get ready to pick her up. I listened to the rest of the messages. Several were from business places relative to bad checks. The last one was from Chief of Police Todd Wilson. The Chief's message was to call him in the morning.

I shaved, showered, and took out some casual clothes from the closet. I felt like a new man. I would soon be with my love. I was just about to lock the door on the way out when the telephone rang. I went back inside and picked up the receiver. It was Lieutenant Doyle.

"Jason, you've really opened up a bag of worms for us. I'm calling you to thank you for that information regarding Oscar Winton. All I can tell you right now is that he is a con-artist and is in possession of stolen expensive artwork and a stolen Ford van from Michigan."

"Holy cow! Are you kidding?" I asked, astonished! "That was fast work."

"No, I'm not kidding. This guy is smooth. Your friend Tom Huston's hunch was on the money. Seems that Winton had gotten close to a wealthy lady who is an artist. He conned her out of the paintings and the van. She is Julia Estey, a well known artist from Detroit. She didn't waste any time. Her uncle is a Captain of the Detective Bureau, Detroit Police Department. Mr. Winton is in deep trouble. Thank you for steering us to him. We got a hit on the National Crime Info Center."

"You're welcome, Jack. And I'll let you know what I hear on the Draper matter."

"Good. I'll appreciate it. Oh! By the way, I've already set into motion a surveillance on the Route 56 site. You're right; they are doing a lot of building there. Our undercover people indicated that the power and phone companies are installing their service already. Keep in touch—and remember, we appreciate it."

Jack Doyle sounded excited about the events. He loved police work and he loved the state troopers.

"Take care, Jack." That was a good job.

I went back outside, locked the door, checked Ruben again and headed to Patty's. I was just going out of the driveway when a spike-horn buck darted into the edge of the woods adjacent to my property. I drove through Old Forge. The parking lot at John's Diner was full.

Patty was on the porch when I pulled into her driveway. Harriet Stone, her landlady, waved at me and entered her house. Patty looked stunning. She was wearing gray slacks with a pink blouse. Her long blond hair flowed down onto her shoulders. Her warm smile was captivating. I got out of the Bronco to walk around to the passenger side and meet her there. We embraced. Someone from the diner went by and blew the horn just as we kissed. I opened the passenger door and she climbed in.

I waved at Harriet as she stood watching us leave the driveway. Patty and I chatted all the way to the Edge Water. We hadn't been there in a long time and thought a table overlooking Old Forge Pond would be relaxing and enjoyable. I was able to find a parking space near the entrance. I turned to Patty. She looked radiant.

"Honey, how did your day go at John's?"

"We were busy all day. People seem to be coming up to Old Forge a little earlier each year." She smiled.

I opened the passenger side door for her, and she stepped out. We walked slowly to the door. As we entered, I looked into the bar area and several of the patrons waved. We both waved back. The hostess was standing by the entrance to the dining room holding two menus. She smiled and led us to a table overlooking Old Forge Pond. I seated Patty and sat down. Patty remarked, "Jason, this is a wonderful view looking out over the water." Old Forge Pond looked like a picture through the window of the Edge Water.

"Yes, sweetheart, it's very relaxing," I acknowledged.

Several wild ducks were bobbing in the choppy water. They seemed not to have a care in the world. A party barge was approaching the Edge Water's dock. There were several people aboard. Many of the customers travel by watercraft to the restaurant for dinner. We watched as the barge docked and was secured. Our waitress came to the table.

"Hello, Jason. Hi, Patty. Did you folks see the specials we had posted by the door?" The waitress was Julia, who had been with the restaurant for several years.

"Yes, we did," Patty responded.

"Would you care for a drink before dinner?" she asked as she placed the menus in front of each of us.

"We'll have two glasses of your iced tea with lemon wedges," I requested.

I gazed over at Patty and we looked at each other intently for a moment before we turned to view the menus.

"Jason, I think that I will have the New York Strip Steak with a baked potato."

"I think I'll order the same." I was hungry.

Julia brought our iced tea and we ordered our meals. Both of us opted for medium rare steaks, baked potatoes, chives and sour cream. We sipped our tea. It was cold and refreshing. Both of us got up and went to the salad bar. The cream of mushroom soup was nice and hot. Each of us had the soup and piled our salad plates with crisp lettuce, adding slivered carrots, onions, peas, and other assorted veggies. Blue cheese dressing topped both of our salads. I cut three slices of loaf bread for us. We returned to our tables to begin our feast.

The salad was delicious, and I could tell that Patty was enjoying it, too. I looked around the dining room and noticed that my friend, Dale Rush, was having dinner alone. He was on the far end of the dining room and apparently had not seen us. One of the other waitresses was filling his water glass.

"Patty, look over there. Dale is dining out tonight."

Patty glanced over. "He must have a lonesome life, living alone. He's so quiet when he comes into the diner. I've heard local people mention that since his military days his personality changed from a cavalier attitude to one of solitude. He just seems to be interested in his seaplane and the painting of his Victorian home."

"I know exactly what you mean, hon." Patty seemed concerned.

Julia approached, carrying a large tray and our dinners. She sat the tray on one of the folding serving tables and served Patty and then me. The steaks were still sizzling and the baked potatoes steamed. There was plenty of sour cream, butter, and chives. The carrots were covered lightly with orange glaze. We took our time eating our dinner. The atmosphere was romantic and, with the lit candle flickering, the evening took on a special aura. It was indeed a moment to remember. We conversed incessantly and talked about our upcoming autumn wedding.

"Jason, if things work out and we marry, I would like to keep the event small. You know how private I am."

"Yes, dear, I know how you are. In a way I am, too; but, honey, our lives have touched the lives of many wonderful people. I realize that we won't be able to invite everyone we know, but we'll have to think about it and discuss it more fully as the time gets closer."

Patty looked down, deep in thought. "I know you're right, Jason. We'll discuss it further, as you say." She appeared dejected.

"Don't be glum, precious. It'll work out, you'll see. By the way, you're off duty tomorrow. What do you say if we take the canoe out for a couple of hours? The exercise would be good for the both of us."

Patty brightened, and a big smile crossed her beautiful face. "Oh! Jason! That would be great! Can we?" She was excited. I could tell.

The dinner was perfect and we couldn't have asked for anything better. Julia brought our check and I put the meal on my credit card. I left currency for the gratuity. I was just helping Patty up when we heard a loud crash.

Everyone in the dining room got up from their tables and rushed to the windows and deck to see what had happened. We looked out and saw several men running toward the dock. At the same time I heard the siren go off on the firehouse. Before our eyes was a tragic scene. A wave runner had hit the dock head on, apparently at a high rate of speed. Two people, apparently the riders, were severely injured. One was in the water and the other was sprawled on the dock. The wave runner was splintered and partially submerged. You could hear the men down below checking the injured. They were not moving and they appeared to be unconscious. The area was filled with people as the ambulance arrived. I could see Chief of Police Todd Wilson with one of his officers pushing the crowd back so the emergency people could assist the injured. I saw Dale joining the emergency team. He had left his meal to respond. Dale was a member of the fire department and rescue team. I looked at Patty, and tears were flowing down her cheeks. We didn't go down to the dock, as about a hundred people were milling around. The EMT's could be seen making their evaluations. It was hard to believe that the operator of the wave runner hadn't seen the dock ahead of him. Fortunately, the wave runner didn't catch on fire.

Patty and I left the restaurant a little shaken up from the incident and concerned for the people involved. I told Patty that I would check with Chief Wilson to see how the people were. The injured looked to be in serious condition, and it was a shock to the community. On the job with the troopers, I had seen so many deaths and injuries that I was hardened to those ghastly scenes; however, deep in my heart the concern for the injured was ever present and paramount in my thoughts. So many accidents in all types of vehicles and watercraft could be avoided if the operators only would use common sense and caution.

"Jason, I hope those young people will be all right." She had tears sliding down her cheeks.

"Honey, the ambulance arrived in a short time and our EMT's know their business. Don't worry so much." I felt badly for the young people, too.

"Jason, I'm looking forward to our canoe trip tomorrow," she said, wanting to change the subject.

"So am I, honey. I don't know how long a trip we'll have. I haven't had it on the water since last fall."

"Well, at least we'll be together. I love you, Jason."

"I love you too, beautiful." She looked like an angel.

"I'll drive over to your place, Jason, and maybe we can have breakfast together."

"I was just going to mention that. I've got plenty of eggs and bacon and some Italian bread we can toast."

"Sounds good to me, sweetheart."

Patty decided that I should take her home instead of going to my place. We would be up early in the morning and would be spending the day together. I drove through town. I saw the red flashing lights in my rearview mirror and immediately pulled over to the curb. The Old Forge ambulance flashed by us heading to one of the hospitals in Utica.

"There they go, Patty. I hope those young people will be okay."

"So do I, Jason."

When we pulled into Patty's driveway, Harriet apparently had just finished sweeping her front porch. She was known to engage in this activity about four times each day. I tooted the horn, and she stopped sweeping and gave us a big wave. With the passing of her husband, Harriet had gone through the usual period of depression, but since Patty had come into her life as her tenant next door Harriet wasn't depressed anymore. She treated Patty as though she were her own daughter and watched over her as good mothers do. Patty leaned over and kissed me on the cheek.

"See you tomorrow, honey," she said.

"I'll look for you in the morning about 8:00 a. m., sweetheart. Give my regards to Harriet and tell her that I'm waiting for that baked apple pie she promised me."

"I will, Jason." She exited the Bronco and walked over toward Harriet's porch. I waved at Harriet and tooted the horn while backing onto Route 28. Patty and Harriet waved as I headed for home. Tomorrow would come quickly, and hopefully we'd have a good day on the lake. I stopped at the Big M and purchased a few groceries, including some additional bacon, bread, and milk, and some dog bits for Ruben. He loved those bits.

I went by John's Diner, and there were still some cars and pickup trucks in the parking lot. I knew that Gracie Mulligan was working, as her old red Toyota was parked where she always parked, under the maple tree at the end of the lot. Gracie had helped Patty with some good pointers about waitress work in the Adirondacks, and whatever the instructions were, they had worked for Patty. Both of the waitresses were popular with the local customers and had made many friends with the tourists.

I finally reached my driveway and pulled into the yard. Loyal Ruben was standing, legs stretched on the dog run wire fence and ears standing straight up. I parked, got out, and locked the Bronco. I hadn't been locking it, but with the busy season forthcoming, it was a wise thing to do. I had noticed that since Patty's abduction last year, the local town people seemed more alert as far as their safety was concerned. I knew that Chief of Police Todd Wilson, had focused on informing the public about safety and we need to report any unusual incidents to his attention. I knew, too, that during my past career in law enforcement I had always kept the welfare of the citizens up front. It just made good sense for a smoother-run operation between the department and the community. We all had to live in the community and work in the community. Today it is called community policing, which I had adopted years before it became a reality.

Ruben followed me out of his dog run and we took a walk into the woods. He was frisky and I had all I could do to keep up with him. If I hadn't known better, I would have thought that the local chippies around my log home sat in a waiting stance for Ruben. He was in the process of chasing two or three of the chippies as they darted from one brush pile to the next, making those squeaking sounds that they do. I truly didn't believe that Ruben would actually chomp down on one, if he were fortunate enough to catch one.

The deeper into the woods we went, the less the chippies seemed to engage in their activity, and I could understand why as we heard the crackling sound of something coming toward us. Ruben came to me, and we stood quietly waiting to view whatever it was. We soon found out. It was surprised as much as we were.

Standing before us up on its hind legs was the largest black bear I had ever seen. I took a hold of Ruben's leather collar. My dog remained still. The bear bellowed an ungodly growl!!! I didn't move. The bear must have been about forty feet from us. I could feel the nerve endings tingle on the back of my neck. I wasn't armed!! It seemed like an eternity that we glared at each other. He went from the standing stance to all four feet on the ground floor of the forest. He slowly came toward us, then turned to the left and slowly sauntered away from us in the general direction from which he had come. I looked around for any cubs, but saw none.

"Whew! Ruben, that was close," I whispered. "Real close."

I released Ruben's collar and we walked hurriedly to our home. I wondered where the bear had come from. I would have guessed that he weighed at least seven to eight hundred pounds. I couldn't believe that, with the landfills closed, a bear would be carrying that much weight. It was obvious that this big creature had been feasting some place. It was dark when Ruben and I entered the log home. He went to his air mattress and lay down. I went into my office and noticed the blinking on my answering machine. I sat down at the desk and pressed the call button. I knew the voice well. My old Marine Corps buddy, Private Investigator Jack Flynn of Flynn Investigations. The call was short: "Jason, call me in the morning! It's important."

I continued to play my incoming messages. The next was from Luther Johnson of Star Lake: "Jason, call me when you get a chance."

The remaining calls concerned some bad check cases from business people inside the Blue Line. My mind raced. One call from Jack, and one call from Luther. I would call them both in the morning. While in the office, I checked my bad checks file and wrote two letters to a couple of clients.

Trying to sleep was difficult for me, especially with the pending telephone calls in the morning. I got up about 1:30 a.m. to have a glass of water. My mouth was dry. Ruben lifted his big head momentarily and plunked it down between his two paws. Apparently I had disturbed him when I made my way to the kitchen. Before I got back into bed, I looked out into the front yard. The usual deer that frequented my yard were absent. I went into the bedroom, stubbed my toe against the dresser, and fell into bed in agonizing pain. The Big Ben alarm clock was set for 6:00 a.m. I reached over to the night table bed and clicked the light off. I fell asleep. The next noise I heard was a fire engine clanging its bell. The bell was getting louder and louder as I awoke to find the Big Ben running down.

CHAPTER ELEVEN

I got out of bed. Ruben was nervously pacing back and forth, looking toward the door. I let him go outside. I went into the bathroom and splashed some cold Adirondack water on my face. It was refreshing. The water pump clicked off. The soft towel felt good against my skin. When I looked outside, Ruben was waiting by the gate to the dog run. I went out and let him in.

The shaving cream was cool on my skin as the razor did its job. The shaving lotion felt refreshing. My mind was going a mile a minute. Patty was due to arrive in about an hour. I decided to make my phone calls early. I figured that Luther would be up and about, but Jack would still be sleeping, as the Arizona time zone is two hours earlier than our time here.

I dialed Luther's telephone number. It rang three times. He answered the phone.

"Good morning, Luther. Sorry to bother you so early."

Luther sounded sleepy. "No problem, Jason. I just wanted you to know that the activity on Route 56 is increasing. They have added onto the barn and they have attached a rustic gift shop to the north end of it. In addition, they have constructed two docking areas with large roller type doors. They have even landscaped the grounds surrounding the complex," he explained excitedly.

"That's interesting, Luther." I jotted down the information in my notebook.

"They have also erected a sign in large letters. It says 'Southwestern Jewelry.'"

"Boy! They've worked fast, haven't they?"

"Sure have, Jason. By the way, there are a couple of bearded painters in the area. They've got two or three ladders on a rack and a large paint sprayer mounted on an old pickup. They look suspicious, Jason."

"Hmm! Is that so?"

"Yeah, it sure does." I felt that Lieutenant Jack Doyle had already started surveillance of the new "Southwestern Jewelry" complex.

"Luther, I appreciate your call. Sometime we'll have lunch together. By the way, Luther, I'm especially interested in the fellow with the pickup that has Arizona plates on it."

"Jason, it's a late model GMC ¾-ton with Arizona Registration #19230. He goes by the name of Scott Austin. He is about 50 years old, and stands about six feet tall with a muscular build. He is supposed to be the foreman and is from Casa Grande, Arizona, and works for a Bernard Draper in Phoenix."

"Yeah, you gave me some of that information before. Where did you get all that information?" I queried.

"I'm a good listener, Jason, and I figured you'd like to know who that dude was. He struts around Cranberry Lake and Star Lake as though he owns the place. He's been buying drinks for the locals and seems to be making a lot of friends. Gee, I even saw him having a drink with those two bearded painters in one of the local gin mills. When he first arrived here he didn't speak to anyone, except the carpenters he hired. Now he's changed. He's friendly and has the loudest voice in the bars."

"Hmm! That's interesting, Luther. He's probably drumming up business for the jewelry store. I can always depend on you."

"I've got my eyes open and my hearing aid turned up."

"Be careful, Luther. Play it cool and keep me posted if you hear anything you consider important. I'd like to know who issued the building permit and who the people were that sold that parcel with the barn on it. Had to be some fast exchange of big bucks on that deal."

"This Austin flashes a lot of money around town, Jason."

I thanked Luther Johnson and hung up.

My next call was to my ex-Marine buddy, Jack Flynn. I knew he wouldn't appreciate me calling him at this hour, but I felt it necessary. I dialed his private number at his home. The phone rang six times.

"Hello, hello, what the hell can I do for you?" he grunted angrily.

"Jack, this is Jason in New York. Wake up. I've got to talk to you," I shot back.

"What are you calling me so early for? It's only 6:30 a.m. here." He sounded sleepy.

"Had to, Jack. It's important."

"I'm only joshing ya. What's up?" He sounded more alert.

"You called me last night. Remember?"

"Yes, I remember. I've been so damned busy with the heaviest case load I ever had. Concerning the Draper matter, one of his trucks is headed your way, tomorrow." He spoke rapidly.

I listened to Jack intently as he gave me details of the case. I in turn related some of the information that Luther had developed for me. I told him about the barn conversion and the jewelry shop and about Scott Austin. Jack confirmed that Austin was one of Draper's men, who was close to Draper and knew Draper's operation, inside and out.

"You want to be careful around that guy, Jason. He's bad news. He is suspected as a possible hit man for Draper, and he's a tough cookie. He is a weight lifter and a former student of martial arts. The Phoenix Police Department has a record sheet on him. He is a good carpenter, as was his father, but his association with Draper has influenced him toward another direction. Be careful. He always carries a gun." Jack sounded concerned over my welfare.

"I will be; you can count on that."

"How are your police contacts, still intact?" He waited for my response.

"Yes, the best. I have alerted a lieutenant in the BCI who has already adopted this case on this end. He is strictly business and is a dedicated officer."

"I'm glad. This Draper puts up a good front, but when you turn the coin over, you get a different picture. He's greedy, and if the authorities give him a little rope, they will close down a large-scale illegal operation."

"Jack, is this semi that is leaving tomorrow going to take those specified routes into New York State?" I asked.

"The information is excellent and it came from a charming lady, Draper's wife—or, I should say, soon to be former wife. Her divorce is on the court calendar as we speak. Remember, Jason, there is nothing like the wrath of a woman who has been treated badly."

"That's true, Jack."

"I'll let you know when that semi enters New York."

"Jack, we have a low train bridge just south of Old Forge. The semi will have to cross the track by our scenic railroad. Just make certain that you alert me when it enters New York. I'll take care of the rest. Okay?"

"That'll be fine." I could sense Jack smiling at the other end of the line. "I still wish that you'd come out and work with me in Phoenix."

"Not on your life, Jack. Too hot."

"You can't blame me for trying." I heard Jack chuckle.

"Best to you, buddy."

We said goodbye and Jack promised me that he would advise me when the truck entered New York. Ruben was uneasy and he was pacing back and forth, wanting to go outside. Patty had just arrived in her red Jeep. Apparently Ruben had heard her coming down Route 28. Now he started barking in excitement.

I immediately put Ruben into his dog run. I then rushed over to Patty as she got out of the Jeep. She came toward me and we embraced. My lips found hers and we stood holding each other closely.

"Good morning, dearest," I said, so very happy to see her.

"I hope that I didn't arrive too early. Charlie Perkins passed me on the right as I turned left into your drive. He gave me a toot on the air horns. Did you hear him?"

"No, dear, I didn't. Usually I do, but they must have been quiet toots. He holds the button down when he wants to get my attention. He loves those horns." I took her hand.

"Before we hit the lake, how about some breakfast? Do hotcakes sound good?"

"Great. I'm hungry, hon." She loved my hotcakes.

"Go over and say hello to your friend, Ruben, and I'll start cooking."

We kissed once more and I watched Patty walk toward the run. Ruben's ears perked up. I went inside and began to pursue one of my favorite hobbies, the culinary arts. I went to the sink and washed my hands and dried them. I decided that I would make hotcakes from scratch. Flour, eggs, shortening, pinch of salt, baking powder, sugar, and milk. I blended all the ingredients in a large bowl and prepared a medium batter. I went into the refrigerator, brought out my favorite bacon, and cut off four thin slices. Next I opened the orange juice. The coffee was just beginning to perk when the back door opened and Patty entered.

"Can I help you, Jason?" She sounded eager to assist me.

"You can finish setting the table, honey."

"Before I do, I had better wash my hands. I've been petting Ruben." She ran to the sink, then opened the cupboard door, reached in, and brought out two plates, and two large coffee cups. Next came napkins and silverware from the drawer. When she had finished setting the table, I began pouring the hotcake batter onto the hot grill.

"Patty, would you like an egg on your hotcakes?" I asked as I flipped them. I knew she loved that combination.

"Yes, honey, I would."

I took two eggs out of the refrigerator and cracked them into a small iron skillet. The aroma of the bacon was permeating the air. We were both famished.

"Okay, Patty, bring both of the plates over here." The hotcakes were golden brown.

Patty went to the table and picked up the plates, which had been warmed. She held the plates out in front of her, and on each plate I placed three hotcakes, two slices of the bacon, and one egg over easy. Patty returned the plates to the table. I followed with the freshly perked coffee. After saying grace, we began our breakfast feast.

"Hmmm! Good! They are delicious." Patty turned to me with a

big smile.

"They are tasty," I agreed. One thing we shared was our love of food.

We ate slowly and looked into each other's eyes. I knew that she was right for me. I loved her dearly.

"Honey, I'll refill your coffee cup." She pushed her chair back and rose to get the coffeepot. The brew was still steaming hot.

We finished breakfast and quickly cleared the table. Patty started doing the dishes. I replaced the tablecloth and swept the kitchen floor. When I had finished I dried the dishes and put them into the cupboard. I sensed Patty's eagerness for the canoe ride on the lake.

"It should be calm on the water this morning," I commented.

"Jason, we haven't been out on the lake since last year, when you proposed to me," she exclaimed rather wistfully.

"We wanted to, Patty, but with you working a full schedule at John's and my investigative work, we haven't been able to squeeze in any time. However, we'll give it a try. Today's clear and the sun is not behind any clouds, so far."

Patty was wearing jeans with a denim top. She looked rested and ready to paddle. We finished cleaning the kitchen. Patty tended to Ruben and filled his water dish. I went outside, loaded the canoe on top of the Bronco, and secured it. Then I went over to the run and checked Ruben with Patty. I wanted to take the big fellow along, but the canoe just wasn't big enough for the three of us. I asked Patty if she would mind waiting for me in the Bronco while I made a confidential call. She told me that she'd walk Ruben, while I was busy.

I went back inside the house to make a quick call to Chief of Police Todd Wilson. I informed him that one of Draper's semi-trailer trucks was headed our way and that I would stay in touch with him. I then dialed Troop S Headquarters and spoke with Lieutenant Jack Doyle. I gave him the description of the semi-trailer outfit. Jack indicated that he would arrange for a surveillance team, and as soon as Draper's rig entered New York State they would be engaged in watching the truck's movement as it proceeded east and north toward the Adirondack Mountains. I thanked him and hung the phone up. I then locked the house and joined Patty in the Bronco.

We drove north toward Inlet and took the South Shore Road to the boat launch site. When we pulled in, a fisherman had just launched his fishing boat and had tied it to the dock. I found a suitable parking spot. The large crowds hadn't invaded the area yet and there were plenty of spaces to park. We got out. Patty helped me lift the canoe off the Bronco, and we carried it down to the shoreline. I ran back to the vehicle and picked up the two paddles. There was a slight breeze and the sky was blue, with just a few fluffy clouds.

I helped Patty into the canoe and handed her paddle to her. I climbed in and pushed us away from the dock.

"Are you comfortable?" I asked her.

"Very comfortable, honey." She wore a big smile.

The slight breeze felt good as we moved south along the shoreline. We paddled in rhythm. Two inboard motorboats were in a race headed toward Inlet. I couldn't tell who they were, as they were quite some distance from us. When they came out of Third to Fourth Lake channel, they appeared to be doing at least 25 knots. The NO WAKE signs posted along the channel didn't mean too much to these speeding boats. We were hoping that a sheriff's boat patrol was in the area. There was none. Boaters always seem to know when the patrols are on duty, as they obey the law when officials are in sight. When the patrols are absent, it's another story. As we continued to paddle across Third Lake into Second Lake, we observed two loons diving and watched them bob up as they resurfaced. Patty expressed her amazement at the length of time they were able to remain submerged. We both enjoyed the show the loons were performing. Finally, they disappeared out of our view. We continued to paddle until we both became weary and tired. When we reached the boat launch site, Patty announced that her arms were getting heavy. I had to agree; mine were, too. Jim, from the boat launch site, was standing on the dock as we approached.

"Jason, can't you paddle that canoe just a little faster?" He asked with a big grin.

"Jimmy, if we lived on the lakes like you do, we'd be in a heck of a lot better shape. I've got to admit, I'm out of shape," I answered good-naturedly.

"You've just got to practice more, Jason. Patty is in better shape than you are."

"You know, Jim, maybe you're right, but I'll tell you, I've got enough energy to throw your butt into the lake," I said as I exited the canoe and made a move toward him.

"I was only kidding, Jason."

All three of us laughed.

Jim helped me carry the canoe to the Bronco and we lifted it on top. I secured it. I thanked him for his assistance and shook hands, giving a little added squeeze.

"Ouch, Jason, not so hard on the hand." I had applied some pressure.

"Oh! Sorry, Jimmy."

We laughed some more. He knew I was getting even with him for his comments.

Jim and I had been friends for years and he was a good sport. He was in charge of the launch site and took good care of the camping sites on Alger Island. The three of us chatted for a few minutes. I thanked Jim for his assistance, and Patty and I left for Drew's Restaurant outside of Inlet. We were just driving away from the site when we saw a marten run across the highway. We watched it go under a downed tree and disappear.

On the way to Inlet we went by Quiver Pond. Two fishermen were sitting on small beach chairs holding their fishing poles. I told Patty that they should have been there in the early morning hours when the fish are biting.

"Are you hungry, honey?" I asked her.

"Not really, darling." She snuggled closer. "There's something about the lake air that is refreshing. I'd love a cup of coffee."

When we pulled into Drew's, there was one space left in the parking lot, just room enough for the Bronco. We got out and I checked to see that the canoe was secure. It was. We walked across the parking lot and entered the restaurant. Al was at the bar waiting on some lunch customers. When he saw us he waved and we did likewise. Patty and I found an empty booth and sat down.

Mike Drew, the chef on duty, came out to the dining room to

say hello. Mike was a hard-working young man and always took good care of his customers. We talked for a couple of minutes and then he rushed back to his chef's duties. Patty and I looked at the menu, but both of us decided to just have coffee as we were still full from the lumberjack breakfast. The lake had been cool, and we just needed a good cup of coffee to warm us up. Paula, the waitress, brought us two large glasses of ice water along with the coffee.

While we sipped, we talked about Patty's family in Kentucky. Since her abduction, she had stayed in touch with her brothers by mail. She reported that all the brothers were doing well and were busy working and raising their families. Paula came by with the coffee pot and refilled our cups. When we had finished we went out to the bar and talked with Al and Mike for a few minutes. As we were leaving, two pickups wheeled into the parking lot. Each contained a canoe. I figured that these fellows had worked up an appetite. They nodded and smiled as they walked passed us in the parking lot.

"Do you know those fellas, Jason?"

"No, honey, I don't," I replied. "Why, do you?"

"Oh, I thought I recognized them from the diner. It's not important."

I opened the Bronco passenger door for Patty, and she climbed in. When I went to get in the driver's side, I noticed the names on the rear license plate brackets. The trucks were from the Syracuse area. One was from Brewerton and the other from Central Square. Probably friends enjoying our great Adirondacks. I got in behind the wheel. Patty leaned over and kissed me.

"Thank you for the coffee, Jason. That's less calories, my dear."

"The coffee hit the spot."

I backed the Bronco around and we headed back to Inlet, Eagle Bay, and home. There were a few tourists walking in Inlet as we passed. It wouldn't be long before the long lines of cars and trucks would be an everyday adventure for people going through the region. Complicating matters even more were the various construction zones along Route 28. It went with the territory. The winters were long and sometimes difficult. Construction in the winter months was impossible. The short spring and summer season had to accommodate any ongoing construction. However, to me, it was the greatest place on earth to live. Patty agreed.

We were finally at my driveway entrance. We pulled in and immediately we could see Ruben sitting in his dog run. His ears were pointing skyward and, as always, he was on alert. I pulled close to the run. Patty got out, ran over, opened the gate, and let Ruben out.

"Let's take Ruben for a walk, honey," she suggested. "The dog needs some exercise, too."

"Okay." I was tired, but agreed. "I know you're right."

Ruben ran ahead of us, sniffing the brush piles. At the second one a chippy darted out, ran around Ruben in two or three circles, and scampered back into the pile. Ruben gave up his search and ran into the woods. I held Patty's hand as we followed him. She looked tired, but beautiful. Inside the woods we stopped and embraced. She held me close and kissed me warmly. Her breath was rushed. We pulled away from each other. Our passion was put on hold. My heart was beating rapidly.

"Jason, I've got to be leaving. Tomorrow I have to open John's at 6:30 a.m."

I understand, Patty. We've had a full day. I'm tired myself."

I called Ruben. We walked back to the log home and put him into his dog run. Patty helped me lift the canoe off the top of the Bronco and place it behind the house.

"We had a wonderful time, darling," she said.

"Indeed we did. We'll do it again, soon. The lake got a little choppy today."

"Yes, it did."

"Patty, call me when you get home so I don't have to worry."

"I will, dear," she promised.

We embraced once more, and I opened the door to her Jeep. She climbed in, started the engine, backed up the Jeep, and turned toward Route 28. I watched her until she pulled out of sight. The Jeep needed a new muffler; escaping exhaust made a slight roar. I wouldn't want her to get a summons for an inadequate muffler. She had promised that it would be replaced with a new one.

I turned toward my log home and slowly walked to the side door. My mind was racing. We loved each other very much. I knew that all I had to do was ask her to set a date and we'd be joined in wedded bliss. Yet I felt that we should wait a little longer before getting married. I looked over at Ruben sitting quietly in his run with ears extended skyward. I felt the big K-9 would approve, and I was certain that Patty would spoil the big fella. I unlocked the door and walked inside. I went into my office, grabbed the newspaper and read while waiting for her call. A few minutes later, the phone rang.

"Hello," I answered.

"Sherlock, I'm home safe and sound. My landlady left a note on my door. She is going to visit her cousin in Saratoga Springs for a couple of days."

"Oh! How nice."

"I'm going to bed early, as 6:00 a.m. will be here before I know it. That will give me a half hour to get ready for work. Love ya!" I heard the click.

I hung up the receiver. How I wished we were together at this moment.

I punched play on the answering machine. The calls came in one after the other. There were messages from Lieutenant Jack Doyle, Wilt Chambers, Charlie Perkins, the Eagle Bay Kennel, Tom Huston in Lake Placid, and several banks from inside the Blue Line. I realized it was getting late and decided to return all the calls in the morning. There was no mention of any urgency.

I went outside and let Ruben out of the dog run. He ran into the woods and quickly returned. He followed me inside. It was cool outside, and I debated whether to turn the furnace on to take the chill away. With the price of fuel I decided that two heavy blankets would do the trick. Ruben lay down on his mattress. I went into the bathroom and brushed my teeth. I then went into the bedroom, opened the chest of drawers, and removed my flannel pajamas. They felt good. I took a book from my bedroom bookcase and climbed in between the covers, then reached over and turned the light to a brighter position. As soon as I started to read, I must have dozed off.

I felt a tugging at the foot of the bed. Ruben had woken me up. I glanced over at the Big Ben, my trusty alarm clock, and the time read 7:30 a.m. In my tired state I pushed the covers back and sat up. The night had passed so quickly. Ruben headed toward the door, and I shuffled across the room to let him out. In a few minutes I looked out the window and observed him sitting inside the dog run.

The shower felt good, though the soap smarted when it entered my left eye. I then nicked my chin with the razor while shaving, and the soap made it sting. I turned the shower to cold and rinsed off. The icy Adirondack water did the trick. I was wide awake and ready for the day. I dressed; made a breakfast consisting of two scrambled eggs, toast, and coffee; washed the dishes, and swept the floor.

CHAPTER TWELVE

My office desk was cluttered with paperwork. The outgoing mail basket contained letters to some bad check passers and a couple of attorneys. I consulted my calendar.

In my first return call, Jack Doyle at Troop S Headquarters informed me without going into detail that the semi-trailer outfit from Arizona had entered New York and was under surveillance. He offered no specifics. I shared with him the information about my contact in Star Lake. I reassured the Lieutenant that any information I received would immediately be passed on to him. He indicated that the converted barn and gift shop was also under surveillance and the crew working on the remodeling had about completed the work. He shared with me that the two painters with the beards hired to paint the buildings were his undercover men.

"You are clever, Lieutenant," I complimented him. I had already surmised this fact about the painters from Luther Johnson's conversation; however, I did not mention my suspicions to Jack Doyle.

"Jason, as you know, you have to implement your manpower in the best possible way." His Irish brogue came through.

"If there is anything I can do to assist you, let me know."

"You know I will, laddie. We appreciate the information. This is going to be a large-scale operation and it will take some time to build a good case. Don't worry, Jason; I'll keep you updated. Any substantial information I develop will be passed on to you. By the way, give Captain Roy Garrison my regards." I often thought about my former supervisors, Roy Garrison and Frank Temple, both good guys.

"I'll do that." Lieutenant Doyle sounded pleased.

I said goodbye to Jack Doyle and hung up the receiver. I got up from the desk and made myself a cup of coffee. I ran outside and filled Ruben's food and water dishes and closed the gate on the run. The big dog came over to me and rubbed his head against my pant leg. I went back inside to finish making calls.

The next was to Wilt.

"Chambers Logging and Wood Products. Can I help you?"

I recognized his voice. "Wilt, Jason here. What's up? I'm returning your call."

"Where have you been hiding?" he inquired.

"I've been busy working on a sensitive case."

"I'm calling to let you know that we're going to have a breakfast at John's Diner in the future. It's going to be a special occasion and we'd like you to attend. Chief Todd Wilson and Dale Rush are going to be invited, and a few more. Just wanted to let you know about it. I'll fill you in on the date and details later."

"What's the occasion?" I asked, puzzled.

"Nothing special, just thought it would be a good idea. By the way, Jason, you know I don't have to use two seats anymore."

"That's great, Wilt. I'm happy to hear you're doing so well."

"I knew I had to do something. Getting around was beginning to be an effort. But I'm happy with the results."

"You should be. It really is beginning to show! I have to call Charlie Perkins now. Any idea why he called me?" I asked.

"No, none at all. Well, take care. Oh! By the way, Jason, I picked up three more two-man saws for your collection. I bought them over in Glenfield from an elderly farmer."

"That's great! How much do I owe you?" He was always looking out for saws for my collection.

" Only $21.00. They were $7.00 apiece."

"Thanks for thinking of me. Take care."

"That's what friends are for, Jason. So long." He laughed.

I called Charlie Perkins next and left a message on his answering machine that I was returning his call. I would get back to him later.

The next calls I made were to the banks relative to bad check cases. My contacts there informed me that several of the checks had been paid. I turned to my files and made the appropriate notations in each.

I called Lynn at the Eagle Bay Dog Kennel. She sounded so sad on the telephone, and asked me if I would stop by the kennel. I told her I'd drop by later that day.

"Lynn, I thought I paid my bill last month."

"You have, Jason. This is something different. I would rather not discuss it on the telephone."

"I'll see you in about two hours." I glanced at my watch.

"Thank you." Her voice cracked. I wondered what was wrong. She hung up the telephone.

I dropped everything. Lynn sounded sad, and she always takes such good care of Ruben. I decided to leave for the Eagle Bay Kennels immediately. I locked the house, took Ruben out of his run, and opened the rear gate of the Bronco. He leaped in. I got in and started the Bronco. Ruben was glad to be with his master. He sat down, as obedient always. It took us fifteen minutes to get to Lynn's. I put the rear window down so Ruben would have plenty of fresh air. I ran up the steps and into the kennel office.

"Jason, hello! I didn't expect you so soon." I could tell that Lynn was relieved to see me. Tears started rolling down her cheeks.

"What's the matter, Lynn?" I felt concerned to see her so distraught.

"Jason, someone cut the fence to my dog run and stole Brian of Widmere, my Alaskan malamute. I had to go to the post office and the store. Brian was the only dog in the run at the time. I was gone for about a half-hour at the most," she said, trying to dry her eyes with a tissue she pulled from her pocket.

"Did you call the police?" I asked as I put my arm around her, consoling her.

"No, Jason, I haven't. The reason I didn't call is that I have an idea who may have taken the dog. If it is the person I think it is, I don't want to press any criminal action against her, for she has cancer. I thought you might possibly be able to check to see if she has Brian."

"Why do you think this person may have the dog?" I was probative.

"She stopped by the kennel last week and asked me how much it would cost to breed her female malamute. I quoted her a price and she indicated that she'd think about it. She also told me that she didn't want to wait too long to breed the dog as she recently learned that she had an advanced form of cancer. For some reason she wants her dog to have a litter. It wasn't very clear to me. It seemed to me that her thoughts were quite irrational."

"Yes, I'll be glad to check it out for you. Could you give me her name and where she lives?" Lynn, much more composed now, went to her index file and took out a card.

"Her name is Matilda Rose and she lives on East Road outside of Turin. Her house is white and she has a dog run attached to her garage. She takes care of her elderly father, Henry Rose. If you go by, you will see her malamute in the run."

"Lynn, I have some time to spare today. I will go over there and check it out for you. Now don't worry. If she's got Brian, I'll get him back. Is that satisfactory with you?" I could see that she was trying to maintain her composure.

"I want to pay you for this."

"No, you're not. You have taken such good care of Ruben for me in the past, that this is a freebie. Anyway," I added, "we don't even know if Matilda has Brian."

"That's true. But I have a feeling that she might have him. The reason I think this is that her cancer is progressing and she wants to have her malamute bred before she passes on. It is sad, Jason. Had I realized that it meant so much to her, I would have bred her dog at no charge."

"Well, we'll see. I'll leave Ruben with you and head over there right now. If I locate Brian, I'll have a heart-to-heart talk with Matilda Rose." I wanted to do this favor for Lynn. I took Ruben out of the Bronco, and Lynn placed Ruben in another run. I bid goodbye to Lynn, and left.

I headed south toward Old Forge. Traffic was medium. I was not in a big hurry, but this was important. I didn't enjoy seeing Lynn so down. There were a few people walking toward John's Diner. I glanced over at their parking lot. I spotted Wilt Chambers' big Dodge pickup. He must have stopped for toast and tea. I was sure that he wasn't ordering the triple cheeseburgers anymore since his weight loss.

I turned onto the Moose River Road and pointed the Bronco toward Port Leyden and Turin. It was a pleasure to drive on macadam for a change. The highway department had done a good job on this two-lane highway. The Moose River Road was curvy and you had to drive those curves with care and caution. I met only two vehicles. They were probably headed to work in Old Forge. There were a few Boonville residents who made the trip every day to work.

I spotted the two-story white home. The grounds were neat and well manicured. I looked carefully into the long dog run. There were two dogs in it. A frail woman was standing at the fence watching them. Both were malamutes. I was sure one of them was Brian of Widmere. I pulled into the driveway and got out of the Bronco. The woman came toward me, walking slowly, carrying a dog's leather leash.

I spoke first. "Good day, ma'am. My name is Jason Black from Old Forge. Are you Matilda Rose?" She appeared pale and drawn.

"Yes, I am. How can I help you, mister?" Her voice sounded so weak. I would have to be gentle in handling this situation.

"Matilda, you and I have something in common. In fact, possibly two things. One is our friendship with Lynn from the Eagle Bay kennel, and the other is that we are fond of canines. Those two malamutes you have in the dog run are something to look at." I sensed that the larger dog was Brian of Widmere.

"Matilda, is the larger malamute in the dog run Brian of Widmere?" I spoke softly to her.

"Yes...yes, it is." She lowered her head.

"Lynn asked me to locate and return the dog, Matilda. That is why I'm here."

"I was wrong to take her dog," she said, sobbing.

"Well, I'll tell you up front that Lynn doesn't want to take any criminal action against you, but it is necessary for me to take Brian of Widmere back to his owner."

Her hands trembled. She looked up at me and said, "Bless her. I knew what I did was wrong, and I am truly sorry for what I have done. Yes, please return Brian of Widmere to Lynn." She began to cry. Matilda handed me the leash with the name "Brian of Widmere" sewed into the leather. I took it and proceeded to the dog run. The malamutes did not bark, and both greeted me at the gate. One's collar plate bore the name of the missing dog.

"Matilda, Lynn will be in touch with you."

I took a short handwritten statement from Matilda, which she signed. I could understand why Lynn didn't want to pursue an action against Matilda. I proceeded to place a cooperative Brian of Widmere into the Bronco, then shut the rear gate and bid farewell to Ms. Rose. I looked toward her home and observed an elderly man peering out the front window. He didn't wave, nor did I.

Brian of Widmere had lay down in the rear of the Bronco and he was sniffing, undoubtedly sensing another dog's territory. I wondered if Ruben would detect that another dog had ridden in the back. It was mid-afternoon when I pulled the Bronco in front of the Eagle Bay Kennel. I got out and went into Lynn's office. She looked up over her glasses and asked anxiously, "Well, was I correct?"

I advised her to come outside with me. We went out together and I opened up the rear gate of the Bronco. The tail of Brian of Widmere started to wag. Lynn was so overjoyed that Brian had returned to his home.

"Jason, how much do I owe you?" she asked as she smilingly began petting and hugging Brian of Widmere.

"Lynn, you owe me nothing. You are correct; Matilda is very ill. She had to have a lot of true grit to drive over here and remove Brian from the dog run." I couldn't help but feel that Matilda had had some assistance from another person. This would be one mystery that would not be solved, as no one would pursue the matter.

Ruben jumped up on me as Lynn removed him from the dog run. I placed him in the Bronco and the big K-9 avidly sniffed and sniffed sensing that another canine had ridden in his spot: I couldn't help but chuckle, as we made our way home to the serenity of our little part of the Great Adirondacks, where the chipmunks, the bears, the deer and all those other wild animals also call home.

I let Ruben out of the Bronco near his dog run. He ran around in circles. I could tell he wanted to play. I took his leash and laid it on the hood of the Bronco. It was time that Ruben and I should wander into the woods for a little exercise.

As Ruben and I entered the forest, a medium-sized black bear sauntered across our path, about twelve feet away. Ruben's ears pointed straight to the heavens. "Stay, Ruben," I said. Ruben stood without making a move. The bear stopped and looked at us. In a couple of moments the animal continued on his way. We watched until he was out of sight and then continued our walk. A couple of frisky chippies screeched as they ran into a pile of brush. Ruben sniffed around, but didn't encounter them.

We finished our walk after about forty-five minutes, and I returned Ruben to his dog run. I then swept the run and my porch. I decided that I would broil some haddock for supper. When I finished sweeping, I placed the broom in the corner of the porch and went inside my log home.

In my office the answering machine was blinking. Four calls had come in. One was from Lieutenant Jack Doyle. It was brief: "Call me." I immediately glanced at the wall clock: 5:15 p.m. I called Troop S Headquarters.

"State Police, may I help you?" the dispatcher said.

"Yes, this is Jason Black. Is Lieutenant Doyle in?"

"Just a moment," she responded. I heard the buzzer.

"Jack Doyle speaking." I couldn't miss the Irish brogue.

"Jason Black here, returning your call."

"Jason, I just want you to know that things are moving along well on the Draper case. We'll be getting together in the near future to discuss it. I just wanted to keep you informed."

"I'll look forward to that, Jack." We said our good-byes and hung up.

I listened to the remaining calls. Two were from bad check clients and the last was from Town of Webb Chief of Police Todd

Wilson. He said, "Jason, give me a call tonight at my residence." I wondered what Todd wanted.

I cleared off my desk and straightened up a couple of my files. I then went into the bathroom and washed my hands. It was time to begin supper. I placed four potatoes in a cooking pan with water and lit the burner. I added three good-sized carrots. I then proceeded to set the table. Just before the potatoes were done, I arranged the haddock on foil and placed it in the broiler below the oven. I added breadcrumbs and Johnny-Bob's Rub for seasoning. (I had previously used it on a small pork roast and thoroughly enjoyed the results.) To add to my menu, I quickly made some coleslaw. By the time I had mashed two of the four potatoes, the carrots were done. The aroma from my broiled haddock filled the kitchen. I placed the two remaining cooked spuds in the refrigerator, ready to use for home fries in the morning. I wished that Patty could have joined me for supper, but she was working.

Everything was prepared, and my supper was steaming. Since I preferred my meals hot, I looked out to check Ruben before I sat down to enjoy the cuisine. Ruben was sitting facing the forest with his back to me. I'm certain the aroma from the kitchen had reached his sensitive nostrils. This was Ruben's way of ignoring me, especially when I hadn't asked him to join me inside.

I poured myself a glass of Chardonnay and began eating. The haddock was tender and seasoned just right. The Johnny-Bob-Rub went well with the tender white flakes of haddock. Usually I prepare my own tartar sauce for the fish, but tonight Johnny-Bob reigned on my dinner table. I had chilled the coleslaw and had added a little sugar to it. The potatoes had mashed well, and again my only wish was that Patty could have been sitting across from me. I imagined her blue eyes and blond hair before me, sparkling in the candle light. Here I was getting sentimental, or was it that glass of wine? I felt warm inside. The haddock was superb, and wouldn't you know it that Patty couldn't attest to this prize-winning entrée. The wine relaxed me. Before I cleared the table I glanced at the newspaper. The article I read brought sadness to my heart. Some paper mills were closing in the Adirondacks. I couldn't help but feel sorry for the workers and their families. It was always the almighty dollar that determined the destiny of the worker at the bottom of the ladder. So often have our working people been jerked around by the decisions made in boardrooms across the nation.

I cleared the table and placed the coleslaw, carrots, and mashed potatoes in the refrigerator after covering them. I washed the dishes and cleaned up the kitchen.

The clock showed 6:30 p.m. I decided that I would call Todd a little later, as he would probably be having his supper at this hour.

Ruben's water dish needed refreshing, so I proceeded outside. Just as I went outdoors, I heard two blasts of an air horn and the roar of Charlie Perkins' log truck returning from Vermont. I couldn't see it from my yard, but I knew it was my buddy. He had to keep moving constantly in order to feed that large family. He was a fellow that you could count on. Charlie Perkins, Wilt Chambers, Jack Falsey and Dale Rush had always been there for me. And to that list I could add many more of these Adirondackers. All of them are hardworking people.

I let Ruben out of the dog run and he made a dash for the woods. He soon returned and went to his gate. I let him into the run and went back inside.

At 7:30 p.m., I called Todd. The phone rang twice. The Chief answered.

"Chief, this is Jason returning your call."

"Hello, Jason. Just wanted you to know that the semi-trailer from Arizona passed through town today. One of my police officers made the observation. Also, Jason, the semi had a tail on it."

"Was it a car, Chief?" I was inquisitive.

"Your friend, Lieutenant Doyle is clever, Jason." I was aware that the semi was under surveillance by the undercover people. Todd didn't answer my question.

"You can say that again, Todd. He is a very dedicated guy."

"Just wanted to let you know, Jason." I appreciated Todd's call.

"Thanks, Todd. I'll be in touch." We both hung up at the same time. I would fill Todd in later, but I didn't want to say too much on the telephone. I realized he didn't want to tell me over the telephone the kind of vehicle shadowing the big semi-trailer truck.

About 9:00 p.m., I called Patty at her home. At first I thought she might still be at John's Diner, but when her answering machine didn't come on I assumed she was at home. She answered.

"Hi, honey. Did you have a busy day?"

She sounded exhausted. "Jason, I'm very tired. It was hectic all day long. I even assisted Lila with twenty pie orders for the pie-eating contest, which takes place tomorrow afternoon."

"Is it going to be in Boonville?" I asked her.

"In Boonville. Wilt is putting on the contest this year. He placed the order with Lila as well as Charlie Brown's. Charlie's baker is making twenty pies, so there will be a total of forty in the contest."

"I thought the contest was a little later in the year."

"It was supposed to be in the fall, but Wilt was contacted by several participants and urged to have the contest before summer. Apparently many of the people are going on a fall cruise," she added.

"Oh!! That explains it then."

"Honey, you know how Wilt likes to please everyone," she said with a laugh.

"Yes, sweetheart, I know how Wilt is about things, especially the pie-eating contests."

"I know you do, Jason. Now, before the contest begins, the participants are going to have a beef barbecue that John and Lila are preparing. Actually, John is making it, and he is going to serve it to the participants at the Boonville Park."

"He is!!!" I was surprised.

"It's all Wilt's idea. He wanted to try something different."

"Honey! Can you imagine that? Wilt hadn't told me the about forthcoming contest. Maybe he didn't want me to know, especially with the diet he was supposed to be on." Wait till I see Wilt, I thought.

"Oh, Jason, how's Ruben?"

"Fine, honey. He is lying in his favorite spot, and he senses we're discussing him, as his ears are straight up.

"Give him a hug for me. I'm tired, Jason. I'll say good night, as you know 6:00 a.m. comes early. Goodnight, sweetheart."

"Goodnight, Patty." I heard the click as she hung up the phone.

I let Ruben outside so he could make his fast run into the

woods. I went into my office and checked my schedule. I could see that I had nothing on for the next afternoon. I'd try to show up at Wilt's pie eating contest.

Ruben returned hurriedly and I let him in. He went directly to his bed and lay down. I went into the bathroom, brushed my teeth, and got ready for bed. I set the Big Ben alarm clock for 6:00 a.m. I thought I'd surprise Patty and go to John's Diner early for breakfast. Before I got into bed, I went back into my office and made a notation to call Lieutenant Doyle in the morning. I checked the front door and hit the sack. I was tired, too. I couldn't help but think about Patty. I wished that she was here instead of across town.

CHAPTER THIRTEEN

I heard a loud ring far away and it took me a few seconds to realize that the alarm clock had gone off. I reached out from under the covers and pushed the button on top. Ruben came bounding into the room. He began tugging on the covers.

"Ruben, stop it!!" I shouted sleepily.

The big K-9 released the covers and went back to his sleeping pad. I threw the covers back and got out of bed. It was very cool in my log home this morning, so I turned the furnace on. I could hear the roar as it ignited. The chilliness soon disappeared. I went to the bathroom and splashed some cold water into my face. I dried my face with a towel as I let Ruben out for his hasty run to the woods. While I had the door open, I heard two distinct blasts on Charlie Perkins' air horns. Charlie was headed to Vermont again with a load of logs. I hadn't seen him for awhile, and hoped that he and his family were doing well. I realized Charlie would miss the pie-eating contest in Boonville that afternoon, for there was no way he could return in time to view Wilt and the contestants pitted against each other.

I shaved, combed my hair, and got dressed. I made the bed and put Ruben into his dog run. His food and water dishes were full. I then locked my log home and climbed into the Bronco. I looked over at Ruben, and again he was sitting in the run with his back toward me. I knew that he had wanted to go with me, but John and Lila don't allow pets in their diner. I turned the ignition switch and the Bronco started up. I warmed the engine for a few minutes, then headed to John's Diner for breakfast. Just before I turned on to Route 28, a large doe lumbered into the forest. I looked for a fawn, but didn't see any. Traffic on Route 28 was light. I pulled into John's parking lot, and as soon as I did I realized why the traffic had been light. All the locals were here. I found a parking space way down at the end of the lot. I recognized about every car and truck in town and immediately spotted Dale's Chevrolet SUV and Wilt's big white Dodge pickup. I climbed the steps to the entrance. I noted that John had a couple of wet paint signs displayed along the railings. Apparently he had forgotten to remove them.

When I entered the well known eating establishment, my nostrils immediately picked up the aroma of bacon being fried on the grill. Everybody was talking and laughing. I heard a few "Hello, Jasons." I waved at the folks and walked directly to a small table in the corner. Patty was carrying a tray to a large table where a group of power company men were eagerly waiting for John's and Lila's great cooking. Wilt was sitting at the counter with Dale Rush and they both said "hello." I could tell they were in deep conversation. I could imagine that Wilt was filling Dale in on all the details surrounding the afternoon's contest. Mostly everyone had been served. When Patty finished serving the men at the large table, she went back to the counter, picked up a fresh pot of coffee and headed my way.

"Good morning, Jason." She wore a big smile. "I didn't see you come in."

"Good morning, sweetheart."

She turned over my cup and filled it with hot coffee. "What are you having this morning?" she asked, looking into my eyes.

"I'll have a short stack with an easy-over egg, a large glass of orange juice, and some extra-crisp bacon."

She wrote the order quickly. "Jason, am I going to see you this evening? I'd love to cook dinner for us." She put the order pad into her uniform pocket.

"Honey, that's a good idea. Why don't you plan being at my place about 5:30?"

"I've missed you so much, Jason." She left to place my order. I watched her as she crossed the floor. I was a lucky guy.

I glanced at the Utica paper while I waited for my food. Several men left the diner and nodded as they went by my table. Many of these fellows were craftsmen—excellent carpenters and masons. Several loggers and wood-product people had stopped in for breakfast. They all loved the woods and the area as I did. They worked hard to earn a decent living in order to raise their families in a respectable manner.

It wasn't long before Patty delivered my breakfast. It was steaming hot. There were three kinds of syrups, and I selected my favorite, maple. I thanked Patty and started one of my favorite pastimes, enjoying good food. Wilt and Dale went by on their way out of the diner and nodded as they passed me. The three of us were good friends, but Wilt and Dale knew that when I was eating, I didn't want to be disturbed. For years while I was on the job and wearing the gray uniform, wonderful people would come up to me and ask for directions or tell me their stories. I promised myself that after I retired from the state, when I was eating out in a restaurant, the requests and the stories would have to wait until I was finished. And people seemed to understand that. I made it a practice not to bother anyone while they were enjoying their meals.

I finished my breakfast. Patty brought me the check, and I paid her. I told her that I looked forward to seeing her later.

"Jason, I'm bringing supper with me, so all you have to do is set the table."

"Honey, you don't have to do that." I thought that was a nice gesture.

"Jason, I'm going to do that and I don't want to hear any argument from you." She was insistent.

I leaned over and gave her a kiss on the forehead before I left the diner. Lila and John bid me farewell as I left.

Most of the cars and pickups had left the parking area. I walked to the end of the lot and climbed into the Bronco. I spotted Jim and Judy going into their real estate office and gave them a toot as I left the parking lot. I headed to the post office.

There were a number of cars in the post office parking area. I pulled in and shut the motor off. I checked my box and found it was full of letters and publications. Several letters were from banks. There was a postcard from Jack Flynn from Newport, Oregon. I looked at it. All it indicated was that Jack was working on a missing person's case and that the weather was good. It was signed Jack F. with a P.S. "I'll call you when I return to Phoenix." I would be glad to hear from Jack and to see if he had any more information concerning Bernie Draper. I purchased two rolls of postage stamps and went home.

When I pulled into the yard I could see Ruben sitting in his dog run. His ears were at attention. He let out a bark. I got out of the Bronco and went over to him. I opened the run and let the big K-9 take a run into the woods. While Ruben was probably chasing a chippie, I checked the oil in the Bronco. It was down a quart, so I added one. Ruben returned shortly and I put him back into his run. I then went inside and proceeded to my office. The red light was flashing on the answering machine. I listened to the recording. "This is Luther, Jason. Give me a call." I hadn't heard from Luther in some time. I immediately made a telephone call to him.

The phone rang four times and Luther answered it.

"Luther, this is Jason returning your call. What's up?"

"Just wanted to fill you in. This fellow, Austin, that works for that trucking company, is really getting around town. He's in the gin mills every night. Another bit of information that you might be interested in is that the gift shop at the end of that building on Route 56 is open for business. Now, one more thing, this Austin, I learned, has purchased a couple of small cabin cruisers and they are located at a marina near Waddington." Luther spoke in a modulated tone.

"That's interesting, Luther. I appreciate the information." I could always count on Luther.

"Remember those two painters with the beards I had mentioned to you? Well, by golly, I went by that converted barn and gift shop and saw these two fellows on ladders painting the building. Must be that Austin had hired them to do the painting. I don't know who these fellows are. They're not from these parts. There has been one big semi-trailer truck backed up to the new dock in the rear of the building. It has Arizona plates on both the tractor and the trailer. That trailer is a fifty-three footer, a big one." Luther sounded a little excited.

"That's good information. Is that all you have for me?"

"Yes, that's all I have right now."

I was aware that the two bearded painters were undercover. I trusted Luther very much, but I didn't make any comment to him about my knowledge due to the confidentiality of the matter. I thanked Luther for the information and told him that I would take him out to dinner sometime when I was in the region.

"Take care, Luther."

"Be careful, Jason. I feel that outfit is up to no good."

We hung up and I immediately called Troop S Headquarters. I wanted to speak with Lieutenant Jack Doyle. The receptionist who answered the telephone was very courteous, though I didn't recognize her voice.

"Just a moment. I'll ring the lieutenant's office."

"Lieutenant Doyle speaking." His voice was authoritative and direct.

"This is Jason. I have some information for you."

"Jason, how are you? I figured I'd hear from you sooner rather than later. What's up?"

I related all the information to Jack that I had received from Luther. Jack listened intently.

"Jason, thank you for this information. We had already developed some of this; however, I wasn't aware of the two cruisers. That's interesting. These people must be thinking about smuggling their contraband into Canada by watercraft. I can't go into detail with you, Jason, but we've got a wire on that operation. I'm certain that things will unfold to our satisfaction. It is sort of a watch-and-wait situation at the moment. Any information you obtain, we'd appreciate." He sounded pleased with the developments.

"I'll keep you posted, Jack." I wanted to help all I could.

"Jason, take care. I want you to know we appreciate everything you've done on this matter. Believe me when I tell you that we are looking closely at their new operation on Route 56. They thought they were clever. This gift shop concept is just a front for bigger things to come. Stay in touch."

"Take care, Lieutenant." I hung up the phone.

I knew that Jack Doyle would handle this case with profession-alism. I only hoped that he would be careful, as this Phoenix, Arizona, group could be involved with a large cartel operation. Bernie Draper was now under a magnifying glass and Jack Doyle was hot on his tail.

CHAPTER FOURTEEN

The letters that I picked up at the mailbox concerned several bad check cases I was working on. The letters that I had sent out to the check passers had paid off. The banks informed me that their insufficient fund check cases were cleared and closed. I filed the letters with the case folders and then cleaned off my desk. Due to the fact that Patty was bringing over the supper this evening, I decided to do some cleaning—to dust and to wash a few windows. I surmised that when Patty and I were married, she'd undoubtedly share those duties around the house.

I took the dust-cloth and applied it to every piece of Colonial furniture in the log home. The Kirby cleaner I used to clean the rugs was antiquated, but ran well. The next step was to wash the kitchen floor on my hands and knees. After the floor dried, I put on a coat of liquid wax. I did live alone, but with Ruben's traveling in and out, dirt did get tracked in. I glanced at my wristwatch. Patty would be arriving in about half an hour. As soon as the wax dried, I washed my hands and set the table for dinner. I set out two candles and put a bottle of red wine on the table. I remembered she had told me not to prepare anything, as she was bringing the complete meal with dessert.

Ruben let out a series of barks announcing Patty's arrival. She drove her Jeep close to the back door. Ruben was quiet as he watched her open her rear gate. I hurriedly went out to give her some assistance.

"Hello, sweetheart," I said.

"Hi, honey! Hold the door open for me." Patty came toward me with a large tray wrapped in foil. I held open the door as she looked up at me and smiled. She put the tray on the stove.

I embraced Patty and our lips met. The kiss was warm and generous.

"Later, Jason, later. I have one more tray in the Jeep. Would you bring it in for me?" she asked with another smile.

I went outside and took the tray from the rear of vehicle. This one was also wrapped in foil.

"Looks as though you've done a lot of fussing for supper," I scolded.

"Jason, it was no bother. Lila let me prepare our dinner on one of her smaller stoves. I hope you like it."

"What wonderful dish did you prepare, honey?"

"Well, Harriet was cleaning out her freezer and she brought me over about two pounds of venison stew meat, so I prepared venison stew with all the trimmings. Are you hungry, honey?" She removed the foil from the medium-sized iron kettle.

I peered in closely and immediately observed delicious-looking dumplings. She had remembered how much I love stew with dumplings. The aroma captivated my taste buds. Patty had made a dish of cabbage salad and although we had dumplings, she surprised me with a loaf of Lila's homemade bread. While Patty was preparing to serve the meal, I went over and lit the candles. I then removed the red wine and uncorked the bottle. I had placed a couple of wine glasses on the table and they were ready to receive our wine for dinner. The candlelight flickered. I peeked outside, where Ruben was again sitting in his run with his back toward us. I surmised that the big K-9 was upset that he wasn't included in our dinner plans.

We sat down at the table. Patty had garnished our plates of steaming venison stew with parsley. I looked at the cut glass dish with cabbage salad and noticed that Patty had placed a tomato made into a flower on top of the salad.

"You are truly talented, Patty. You certainly went out of your way to make this dinner special." She blushed as I looked at her smiling lips.

I said grace and thanked God for our blessings. I poured the wine and we made a toast to each other with the promise of an everlasting love. We clinked our glasses and sipped the wine. The flicker of the candles enhanced Patty's beautiful eyes. Passion lurked in our hearts as we stared at each other across the table. The aroma of the venison stew teased my nostrils. We began our dinner. The cubes of venison were tender, and the carrots, peas, onions and potatoes complemented the rich brown gravy. The cabbage salad was cold and tasty with a bit of zest in each forkful. It was the dumplings that completed the stew's flavor. Patty had also brought a pint of Harriet's bread and butter pickles along with a jar of black olives. She poured more red wine into our glasses. The venison stew dinner was a thorough treat, and any pangs of hunger soon disappeared as we completed our main course.

"Honey, have I a special dessert for us! Can you guess what I've brought?" She smiled and waited eagerly for my response.

"Patty, I could guess, but I'd rather you tell me." I was eagerly waiting my dessert.

"Close your eyes," she said. I complied.

The refrigerator door opened and closed. I could hear Patty by the cabinet near the refrigerator, and then she returned to the dining area to place a dish on the table.

"When can I open my eyes, precious?" I tried not to peek.

"Right now, love," she whispered.

I opened my eyes, and before me was a dish holding one of my favorite desserts, cherry cobbler covered with a large swirl of whipped cream.

"Wow!! You really want to test my resistance. I love it!" I already had my spoon ready for action.

We enjoyed our cherry cobbler slowly, still gazing into each other's eyes.

"I love you, Jason," she said softly. Her blond hair flowed on her shoulders.

"I love you, too, Patty." I wanted to set a date for our wedding right now, but held off telling her. I was certain that eventually we would be joined in wedded bliss. Our passions were building. I could feel it within myself. Patty felt the same way.

"Well, Sherlock, did you enjoy the venison stew?" Her eyes were dancing.

"I loved it. You prepared it very well. Also, I thought your cherry cobbler was outstanding." I watched her beautiful face, and her eyes closed for a moment. She refilled our wine glasses and sipped at hers slowly. It had been a perfect dinner. The candlelight flickered. When we had finished, we both got up from the table and walked toward each other. I put my arms around her slender, delicate body and held her close. Our lips met, and the kiss lasted a long time. A long, long time. We finally pulled away.

I helped Patty clear the table as she scurried around the kitchen. She filled the sink with hot soapy water and started washing the dishes. I put things away in the refrigerator and cupboard. There was only a serving or two of the stew left. I covered the plastic container and put it into the refrigerator. While Patty washed our dishes, I went outside and checked Ruben's food and water dishes. I let him out of the run and he streaked off toward the woods. It wasn't long before he reappeared and came racing toward me. I wrestled with the big K-9 for a few minutes. Ruben was powerful and very playful. Our bond was strong. I put him back into the run and went back inside the log home. Patty had finished doing the dishes. I went to the broom closet, took out the broom, and swept the kitchen floor. The candles were still lit. We both went over to the table and smothered the flames. We embraced again and went into the living room.

"How would you like to hear some music, Patty?"

"I'd love to, honey." She shared my love of the oldies from many years before.

I went over to my record player and put some of the collectible 78's in a playing position. I put the arm down on the top of my favorite, the Glenn Miller Orchestra. "My Heart is a Hobo" started playing. We sat on the couch, held hands, and listened quietly. Tex Beneke's voice came through the speakers as we looked at each other with admiration.

After an hour of playing records, we talked about our future and soon came to the subject of our wedding. We decided that as we had previously discussed, an autumn wedding would be appropriate. We embraced on the couch. Our passion was building; however, we held to our decision to wait until our wedding night. Both of us agreed that this would be the proper approach. We managed to control the strong urge of desire. At about 9:00 p.m., Patty left for home. Before she left, she went over to the dog run and gave Ruben a big hug. I waited outside until she reached Route 28. I told her to call me the minute she arrived home. The memory of another night when Patty left for home was imbedded in my mind, and I was thankful that she had come out of that ordeal as well as she did. All the townspeople remembered that night when Jack Falsey located Patty's Jeep in a garage on the Rondaxe Road. Jack, our local plumber, had been making a stop at the home of one of his customers, and when he entered the garage, there was her Jeep. Dale and I had been searching by air, and we were called over the radio to meet Chief of Police Todd Wilson at the marina. It had been a tense moment for all of us.

I let Ruben out for his final nightly run, and soon we were back in the log home. The telephone rang and I answered it.

"Hi, hon. I'm home, everything is fine," she said in her perky voice.

"Swell. I loved your stew, Patty. Was everything quiet in town?"

"Very. No one was out around. Goodnight, sweetheart." She sounded sleepy.

"Goodnight, honey." I yawned.

I prepared for bed, and Ruben lay down on his air-mattress. I went into the bathroom, brushed my teeth, put my pajamas on and turned the covers back. I read for awhile, and as I was about to fall to sleep, turned the light off, reached down, and pulled the covers up. It was cool in the bedroom. An ideal night for sleeping.

CHAPTER FIFTEEN

The telephone sounded a long ways away as I came out of a deep sleep. I looked over at the Big Ben clock. It was 7:30 a.m. I wondered who could be calling at this early hour. Ruben was sitting at the foot of the bed. I picked the receiver up.

"Hello," I said.

"Jason Black, sorry to call you so early, but I have some information that may concern you."

"Who is this?" I asked. The voice sounded familiar.

"This is Sheriff Thomas Sullivan of Erie County." His voice was authoritative.

"Tom, how have you been? It has been a long time since I've heard from you. What can I do for you?"

"Our department received a teletype message to be on the lookout for an escapee from the Ohio State Prison. The escapee is a Jewell Norris."

I almost dropped the telephone when I heard the name.

"Wha...What? When did this happen?" I asked, very perturbed.

"Last night, Jason. I got your number from the State Police in Oneida. The information I received was to be on the look out for a stolen gray-colored Ford van bearing Ohio Registration 3V-262. On the end of the message it indicated that Norris may be headed to the Adirondack Region to settle an old score. Isn't he the bird you apprehended for the troopers last year?"

"He's the one, Tom. A bad news guy. I assume the authorities have been notified?" I was worried for Nate Jenkins, the store owner in St. Regis Falls.

"Everyone is on alert. You'd better arm yourself, Jason. Norris bragged to a cellmate before he broke out that you're on his list. Take this seriously, Jason."

"Tom, you know I will. I appreciate you calling me." I had known Tom for a long time and considered him a close friend even though he lived and worked on the other side of the state and we seldom saw each other.

"You take care of yourself. We have our road patrols on alert as well as the New York State Thruway. If I know his type, he'll be on the back roads."

"You're right, Tom. He'll be hard to catch. Thanks again for calling."

"No problem, Jason." Tom sounded very concerned.

I got out of bed and let Ruben outside. I turned the teakettle on to heat some water for coffee. While the water heated, I called Chief Todd Wilson.

"Town of Webb Police Department. Can I help you?" It was Todd who answered.

"Jason Black here. Good morning, Chief."

"I was just about to dial your telephone." He went on to tell me what I had already heard about the escapee from Ohio, Jewell Norris.

"Yes, Sheriff Tom Sullivan from Erie County called me just a few minutes ago."

"We're on the watch for him and the stolen gray Ford van. Jason, I called Lieutenant Jack Doyle at Raybrook. He is aware of the escape and has already assigned two men to the St. Regis Falls area."

"That's good. I'm glad you called him." I had faith that Jack Doyle would take care of the situation in his area. "What about Patty? She could be in danger." I was concerned for her safety.

"That's been taken care of. I have assigned a man to cover the diner. Try not to worry. We'll get him."

Todd and I talked for a few minutes longer. He assured me that his patrols would be on alert and that he would contact me if anything developed. We hung up. I called Patty at John's Diner and told her to be careful and to keep an eye open for a gray Ford van with Ohio registration plates. I finished getting dressed, while I hurriedly drank my coffee. My mind was spinning. Jewell Norris would, if he could, bring harm to anyone who was responsible for his apprehension and possessed the tenacity to carry out his evil mission. Last year at Santa Clara I had been in the right location when Norris came out of the woods after abandoning a stolen camper along Route 30. I understood at the time when I struck my 9mm semiautomatic pistol into his face that he wanted to do me in. He had been en route to St. Regis Falls for the purpose of harming store owner Nate Jenkins. He would have succeeded if it hadn't been for me. There was no doubt about it: Jewell Norris was heading our way. I prayed the New York State Troopers would apprehend him as he made his way toward the Adirondack Mountains.

One thing was certain: he wasn't going to accomplish his mission without a fight. I had seen this type before, and so had many law enforcers over the years. Although I was retired from the troopers, my right to defend myself was very much alive, and to defend myself—and Patty—against this criminal was going to be my mission if it became necessary. I hoped that it wouldn't come to that, but I had been forewarned; and, believe me, I'd be ready for this bastard.

I checked my Smith and Wesson 41-caliber revolver and hollow point ammunition. Carrying a gun was not easy for me. When I retired I promised myself: no more guns. But this was a special matter. The 41-caliber revolver would be my silent partner for awhile. I looked out at Ruben, who had gone into his dog run. I couldn't help but ponder what Ruben's action would be like if I were threatened by deadly physical force from Norris or anyone else with that mindset. Once again the hunted would become the hunter, and it was now a model wait-and-see or hide-and-seek unlike the hide-and-seek-games we played as children. I oiled the cylinder and loaded the revolver. I had confidence in the local police and the state troopers, but they, as good as they are, could not cover every square foot of territory. I was ready for Norris.

Less than three hundred miles away, Jewell Norris was behind the steering wheel of a stolen 1982 Ford F-250 van, gray in color. He had removed the Ohio registration plates and now had a set of stolen NY plates on the front and rear of the van. He was on Route 17 in the southern part of New York State, heading east. Norris had a look of hate embedded in every deep wrinkle on his face. On the floor behind the passenger seat of the van was a stolen 12-gauge semi-automatic shotgun fully loaded with deer slugs. Norris had committed a house burglary near Silvercreek, New York. The gun was covered with a blanket. Norris had also taken a six-inch pearl-handled hunting knife from the house and was wearing the knife in a sheath. He had placed a piece of white cardboard in the right rear window of the van with the printed words "FOR SALE," and a telephone number. He did this for added camouflage. Route 17 had very little traffic on it at 1:00 a.m. When daylight came he would pull off the road into a wooded area and wait till dark before travelling again.

Norris had two primary objectives: Nate Jenkins and Jason Black. A former U.S. Army Ranger who had been dishonorably discharged from the service, was self-motivated, shrewd, and tough. He had been trained to kill the enemy in the time of war.

CHAPTER SIXTEEN

BCI Lieutenant Jack Doyle had not moved his family up to Troop S. He had rented a small apartment for himself near Paul Smith's College. It was located in a large wooden building in a sparsely populated area. He kept his assigned car in a garage underneath his abode. It was Doyle's day off; nevertheless, Jack was up early and had just completed a two-mile jog along Route 30. He had returned to his apartment and lifted a few weights before making his breakfast of whole wheat toast and one poached egg. He had already downed a cup of decaf coffee. With breakfast and his daily exercises completed, he took a fast shower and put on a pair of dungarees and a light short-sleeved sweatshirt. Jack then decided to check his notebook on information that he had received from Jason. Jack was interested in this new unfolding case, where it was believed a Phoenix trucking firm was transporting drugs and other contraband into New York State with the speculation of smuggling the illegal drugs into Ontario and Quebec. The owner of the trucking firm, Bernie Draper from Phoenix, was a possible suspect in the murder of three Mexican Nationals.

With the information he had received, Lieutenant Doyle had already set his investigation in motion. It was now a waiting game. He had been in contact with the homicide division of the Phoenix Police Department, but he had been unable to develop any further information. Doyle's supervisor, Captain Roy Garrison, had been briefed on the alleged drug smuggling case. Garrison, a seasoned

BCI officer, had a great deal of confidence in Doyle and the four undercover people assigned. Doyle was not a behind-the-desk type of a lieutenant. He demanded that he be kept informed and was never very far away from his men, and that meant spending a great deal of time in the field.

Doyle was aware that Draper's man had purchased the two boats, and he knew the location of the marina where the boats were docked. His undercover officers had reported that a marina mechanic was presently working on the engines and tuning them up. One of the undercover operatives was able to learn that Bernie Draper's name was on the boat registrations and that the boats were purportedly going to be used for fishing in the St. Lawrence and on Lake Ontario. Lieutenant Doyle and his men were aware that this story about using the craft for fishing was just a cover story, and the boats were going to be used for other reasons that could be considered criminal in nature. The two crafts were Carver Cruisers and both were thirty-footers equipped with marine radios and other associated equipment.

Doyle read over his notes for a second time to make certain that he hadn't missed anything. Even though he had this one day off, his mind was on his work. Hopefully, Bernie Draper was unaware of Doyle's resolve.

CHAPTER SEVENTEEN

I was just finishing up washing the breakfast dishes when the telephone rang. It was Dale Rush asking me if I'd like to fly up to Lake Placid for lunch at the Breakshire Lodge. He had promised that he would return to the Breakshire Lodge to see the owner, Tom Huston. Seeing a good opportunity, I told him that I would, and he indicated he would pick me up in a half-hour.

Ruben ran out of the dog run as soon as I opened the gate. He was in hot pursuit of a small chippie. He lost the race as the chippie darted under some heavy brush down by the edge of the forest. He soon returned and I put him back into the run. He had plenty of water and dog food. I went back into the log home and closed a couple of windows. The chimes on the office clock indicated that 9:00 a.m. had arrived. I checked my wristwatch and reset it, for it was three minutes slow. I grabbed my jacket and went outside, locking the door as I exited. Dale was just driving into the driveway. He pulled up very close to my porch.

"Good morning, Dale. I haven't seen you in a few days." I was inquisitive.

"Jason, I've been working on my Lycoming engine. It needed some routine maintenance. You know how that is." He had a big grin on his face.

"Yes, indeed I do. Speaking of that, I've got to get the Bronco in some day for new plugs. When it's cool, the engine skips a little, and I know darn well those wires are breaking down."

"When are you going to trade in that old Bronco?" he asked, knowing how much I loved my car.

"Some day, Dale, some day." Dale made a left-hand turn onto Route 28. We were headed to Kirby's Boat Marina, where Dale keeps his Stinson Seaplane.

"Say, Jason, when are you and Patty going to tie the knot? Everybody in town is wondering, and a dozen folks have asked me that question in the last two weeks."

"I can't answer that question right now. I'll let you know in plenty of time though." I could tell that Dale was eager to know if we had set a date. This question was really beginning to annoy me.

Traffic was light on Route 28 this morning. We were soon at Kirby's Marina. Dale's vehicle bounced hard as he hit a large pothole in the driveway.

"Boy, Kirby better fill that hole before someone breaks a spring," Dale said.

"Yeah, you've got that right." I knew Kirby for what he was. I was still burned about the part he stole off my Glaspar boat. I kept my mouth shut though, because Dale kept his plane at the marina and there was no sense in raising an old issue. We drove down past the marina office and I could see Kirby sitting at his desk with a cigar shoved into his mouth. Dale parked in a space close to his red and white Stinson.

"Your Stinson looks sharp. Did you wax it?" I inquired, aware of the finish.

"Yeah, one of Kirby's workers did it for me for twenty dollars. He did a fine job on it." Dale raised his head high with pride.

"I agree with you. Looks great!"

Dale gave the Stinson a cursory inspection. Everything seemed to be okay, so we climbed aboard after pushing off from the dock area. The engine started on the first turn of the ignition, and we taxied out into the middle of the lake. The sun was rising to the heavens above. Dale turned the plane toward Inlet and gave it the power. The crystals of water spray were like diamonds in the blazing sunlight. As we lifted up over Inlet, we could see the Church steeple, a town landmark.

"What a beautiful sight below, Dale," I said as I looked out the window at the view.

"I agree, Jason. It is certainly eye-catching. I guess that's one reason I love this place so much." I knew that Dale had a love affair with the Adirondacks, as I did.

"Dale, that was nice of you to call me this morning. I couldn't resist your invitation. It saves me a trip to Lake Placid. I haven't seen Tom Huston in a while."

"Well, Jason, I'm not supposed to tell you, but Mr. Huston called me last night and invited us both for lunch. He asked me to pick you up. So don't give me away when we get there." I was surprised, but glad that he did call Dale. I remembered the last time Dale and I had visited the Breakshire and recalled that Tom had asked Dale to stop by any time.

"That's wonderful of Tom."

"Jason, lunch is on Mr. Huston. He told me that you did some good work for him and that this was his way to show his appreciation. By the way, have you been to Gertie's Diner lately?"

"Yes. They're doing fine, always working hard. You know as well as I do, this area is almost becoming a four-season affair in the mountains. Its good for the economy." I remembered the long, hard winters before the advent of the snowmobiles.

"That's true. It is."

It wasn't long before we were winging over Lake Placid and Dale was bringing the Stinson into a perfect landing. We taxied up to the docking area, and I climbed out as the plane approached the dock. Dale cut the engine. We secured the plane and took our jackets off, leaving them in the plane. We walked to the Breakshire, a little early for lunch, which started at 11:00 a.m. The new fresh green leaves on the trees were coming alive and the temperatures were warming.

"Wish that Wilt and Charlie were with us today, Dale. You're going to have to get a larger plane. Wilt wants to take a plane ride with you sometime."

"You tell Wilt Chambers and Charlie Perkins to look me up sometime and I will be more than happy to give them a ride." Dale sounded sincere.

"That's nice of you, Dale."

We went up the stairs to the Breakshire Lodge. We walked by the desk clerk, and Tom came across the lobby dressed in a brown suit with a bright yellow shirt and solid tan tie. He had a big smile, and with his gray hair he looked very distinguished. Once again I admired the large black bear that Wilt had carved for the lobby, with its realistic eyes and the sharp-looking claws.

"Hello, Jason! Hello, Dale! It is nice to see you both." He extended his hand to each one of us. He had a firm grip.

"Hello, Tom," we replied in unison.

"Fellas, it's a little early for lunch. So let's go to my office where we can chat for a few minutes."

We followed Tom into his office. I noticed that he had changed his furniture since my last visit. He had replaced his desk with a large solid cherry one. The pictures hanging on the walls were different, too. He had framed pictures from the 1980 Olympics, depicting many of the venues. Dale and I seated ourselves in the two comfortable stuffed chairs situated in front of his desk. I noted that the picture of his US Naval Officer son was still on the wall. I sensed how proud he was of his son.

"Would you gentlemen care for a cup of coffee?" Tom asked, wearing a smile.

"No, thank you, sir," we replied.

Tom seated himself and offered us each a cigar, which we declined as neither Dale nor I smoke. Tom went on to tell us that the Breakshire had had a good winter season with an unusual number of guests at Christmas and New Year's. We listened as he described the festive holiday celebrations. Tom had brought in a swing dance band from Cambridge, Massachusetts. The band consisted of excellent musicians, and they played everything from the 1941 era to the present.

The office telephone rang and Tom answered it. He indicated that his guests were ready for lunch. When he hung up the phone, he looked over at us.

"Lunch is ready, gentlemen," he said, pushing his chair back from the desk. Dale and I got up and followed Tom out of his office and down through the lobby to the restrooms, where we washed our hands before entering the elegant dining room. Our table was already set up with a linen tablecloth and silverware. Tall thin glasses of ice water were in place. We seated ourselves. The middle-aged waitress appeared and asked us what we would like to drink. All three of us ordered hot green tea. The Breakshire Lodge menu was new, and I noticed that several new entrees had been added. The three of us opted for the fresh broiled Alaskan salmon with baked potato and mixed vegetables. Dale and I were surprised when the waitress appeared with three shrimp cocktails. Each dish contained six shrimp. The shrimp were large and the bed of lettuce that surrounded them was crisp. The cocktail sauce had just the right amount of horseradish. I looked over at Dale and his eyes lit up. I then looked over at Tom, who was ready to bite into one.

"Tom, these are tasty shrimp." I complimented him. "Great quality."

"I thought you and Dale might like them. I had intended to serve clams on the half-shell, but they didn't come in."

"These are wonderful," Dale acknowledged in agreement.

I noted aloud that the cocktail sauce was very good and the bite of the horseradish was a great complement to the large shrimp. The waitress arrived with three garnished plates of salmon accompanied by Idaho baked potatoes with sour cream and chives. She carefully placed each plate before us, cautioning us that they were hot. The veggies consisted of a mixture of carrots, cauliflower, and broccoli. The conversation among the three of us ceased for a few moments as we began our lunch.

Tom then told us about his plans for a new addition to his stately inn, because more and more tourists visited the region each year. The plan called for a wing extending to the north from the main building with an additional sixteen rooms. Dale and I listened intently as Tom went on to tell us that many times his desk clerks had to turn potential guests away, especially during the busy seasons.

We finished our main course. The waitress brought a fresh pot of coffee to the table on a tray with three dishes of apple crisp topped with whipped cream. Before serving us, the waitress removed our plates. I looked over at Dale, who had his eye on the apple crisp, his favorite dessert. The crisp was served warm and the coffee was fresh and hot.

"How do you gentlemen like that apple crisp?" Tom asked with pride.

"Excellent," Dale replied, and I nodded in agreement.

"We have a new pastry chef, and his recipe is different from the recipe my former pastry chef used," he explained.

"Everything was splendid," I affirmed.

"I'm glad you gentlemen enjoyed it. I've been looking forward to this get-together for a long time."

"Tom, do you have an hour or so to spare? Jason and I would like to take you for a plane ride!" Dale asked.

"Yes, I have some time to spare. I'd love to." Tom gave Dale a warm smile.

Tom walked over to his desk clerk and told her that he was going for a plane ride and would return in an hour in case anything important should come up.

"Just a minute, fellas. I'll grab my jacket," Tom said excitedly.

The three of us walked out the front entrance of the Breakshire Lodge. Tom's gardeners were busy raking last autumn's leaves and were pruning some hedges. The older of the two gave us a wave, and Tom waved back. We walked briskly toward the lakefront and the red and white Stinson tied to the dock. Tom had on his leather jacket. He looked up to the sky.

"Dale, it looks like a great afternoon for flying." Tom seemed elated.

"Yep, it looks good, Tom." Dale looked at Tom and smiled.

Dale unlocked the door to the Stinson and helped Tom into the right front seat. I climbed into the rear seat. Dale untied the line and pushed us off away from the dock. There was a slight breeze and the lake was a little choppy. Dale turned the ignition, and the 245-horsepower Lycoming engine turned over with ease. The engine sounded smooth and powerful.

"Make certain your seat belts are fastened," Dale said.

Our belts were already in place as Dale taxied toward the middle of the lake. He put his sunglasses on. I looked over toward the shoreline where two fishermen were fishing off a dock. Dale put the power to the Stinson and we soon lifted off into the blue sky.

Tom appeared to be enjoying this experience (but this kind of small plane experience is so different!), although flying was not new to him, as he often took commercial flights to New York City from Albany and Syracuse, as well as Utica. While Dale and Tom were conversing in the front seats, I peered out the window and watched the land and forests below us pass by. The Adirondack Park was spacious and beautiful, no matter what season we were in. I could overhear Tom telling Dale about his son and his son's military adventures. Before Dale returned to the Breakshire, he flew over the venues of the 1980 Olympics. Tom took some pictures as we went by the ski-jumps. Dale brought the Stinson in for a smooth landing. The floats sliced the lake water as though it were icing on a cake. After we landed, Dale taxied toward the Breakshire's docking area. I looked over toward the shoreline, and the same two fishermen were casting their fish lines into the lake. Dale cut the engine about thirty feet from the dock. The Stinson continued toward the dock as Dale climbed out and secured the line. Tom climbed out and I followed him. We stood on the dock and said our good-byes to Tom Huston, owner of the famed Breakshire Lodge. Tom thanked Dale for taking him for a ride, and Dale and I thanked Tom for the excellent lunch.

Dale and I climbed back into the Stinson. Tom untied the line and pushed us off, then stayed on the dock and watched as Dale started the engine and took to the sky. Dale circled the dock as Tom waved at us. Dale dipped his wings and headed the Stinson southwest toward Tupper Lake.

"How is our fuel?" I asked.

"Fine. We've got enough to return to Old Forge," he replied as he checked the gauge.

I wanted to ask Dale to fly toward Cranberry Lake and over the Draper gift shop, but I didn't. I ascertained Lieutenant Jack Doyle was observing the goings and comings at the shop through the eyes of his undercover people. I was confident that Draper would be dealt proper justice in time. Knowing Jack Doyle as I did, I was sure he would definitely take Draper and his organization down if the evidence gathered reflected a violation of our penal laws. But I understood these cases can take time and that Doyle would be diligently building a case with no loopholes.

The flight back to the Old Forge area was smooth. The Lycoming engine purred like a kitten. It wasn't long before Dale was taxiing toward Kirby's Marina. As I peered out the window I could see the spray of small diamond droplets. I felt very secure flying with Dale Rush. He was one heck of a pilot. The docking area came up slowly. Dale had cut the engine, and I got out on the float ready to secure the red and white Stinson. I looked up and saw Kirby standing by his marina office door.

"Dale, there's old man Kirby watching us." I was surprised, as Kirby is usually out of sight, especially when I'm around.

"Yeah, I see him. He probably wants me to stop in the office and pay my rental fees."

"You're probably right," I responded. I knew that Dale was prompt when it came to paying his bills.

Dale checked the Stinson closely, and then we walked together up the knoll. Dale handed me his keys to his vehicle, and I proceeded to the far end parking area. He went to see Kirby and pay his rental fees for keeping his plane at the marina. As I walked to Dale's vehicle, I noted that some of the trees were already budding. Spring had sprung. I unlocked the passenger side door and was about to get in when I noticed a full breasted robin land near a picnic table. Kirby had set up two tables for his customers and workers. The robin's little head was looking downward, pulling on a small worm. I couldn't help but notice this small bird struggling for the sustenance of life. I wasn't a dedicated bird watcher, nor was I a member of the Audubon Society, but this lively little bird was something to observe. When I climbed into the vehicle, the robin flew away with half the worm dangling from his small beak. I wished Patty could have been there with me. She had several bird feeders outside of her house and took a great interest in our feathered friends.

About ten minutes had elapsed before Dale opened the driver's side door and climbed in. I noticed the expression on his face. It was hard to read.

"That son-of-a-gun jacked up my monthly rental fee by fifty dollars," Dale muttered angrily.

"He did?" I could see that Dale was agitated.

"He sure did," Dale repeated, and then broke out in a cynical grin.

"Well, look at it this way, despite how I personally feel about Kirby, he does have a good location. You can take off and land with plenty of room to spare." I wanted to comfort Dale.

"Yeah, you're right, Jason. Heck, it's only money, but I think he is being greedy." Dale's face was flushed.

"I know what you mean," I retorted. I had had my hard dealings with the man.

Dale started the engine and we left Kirby's marina, heading for my log home. Dale told me that he would stay in touch and thanked me for the introduction to Tom Huston. Tom had told Dale that he could steer some business his way, especially during the hunting season, when hunters or fishermen wanted to fly into remote areas for a week of either sport. There were no cars coming when Dale let me out in front of my driveway.

"See you later, Jason," Dale said.

"Take care, and stay in touch," I shot back as I exited the car.

I watched Dale pull away and drive towards Old Forge. I surmised he would be headed for John's Diner and a late afternoon snack. Dale was predictable when it came to food and his daily visit to John's. I found myself a bit wistful that he'd be seeing Patty when I wasn't.

The walk toward my log home was invigorating. The freshness of the mountain air made one appreciate God's Mother Nature. The chippies and squirrels were darting in and out of the brush piles and up the tree trunks. Some Adirondack mountain flowers were peeking from behind some downed timber. I rounded the slight bend in my driveway and saw two ears go up as Ruben stood against the fence. He didn't bark, but instead watched me intently until I was about thirty feet from the gate to his run. His tail started wagging and I heard a low growl. I noted that his water dish was low and he needed more food. I opened the gate and went inside the run. Ruben jumped up and pushed against me. I gave the big K-9 a hug and rubbed his ears and back. I let him out of the run, and Ruben ran in circles and then off toward the woods at a fast clip. I got my key out and opened the door. When I went inside I could see the flashing light on the answering machine. I heard a noise and looked toward the door. Ruben had made a hasty return. I let him in, and he went directly to his air-mattress and sprawled out on top of it. His big head was between his front paws and his eyes were darting back and forth. I had the feeling that Ruben was happy that I was home. I bent over and petted his head.

"Good boy, Ruben, good boy." I loved my dog and I was certain he cared for me. At least it appeared that way, especially when time came to feed him or toss him one of his dog biscuits.

I went into the bathroom, washed my hands and combed my hair. I had no idea what to plan for supper. I then went into my office and listened to the phone calls on the answering machine. The first was from Lieutenant Jack Doyle, number two man in charge of the Troop S BCI unit. He requested that I call him the next day. The next call was from my honey. I listened to her soft, gentle voice.

"Jason, come down to John's Diner at about 6:00 p.m. Lila prepared chicken and biscuits, and it is delicious. We'll have supper here. I love you, sweetheart."

"I love you, too, sweetheart," I whispered.

The rest of the calls were from banks and a couple of attorneys. The banks indicated they were sending me some checks for collection, and the attorneys wanted some common-sense advice about stale-dated checks. I looked at the clock on the wall: just 5:30 p.m. I had half an hour to get ready to meet my future wife. I ran into the bathroom, shaved, and took a quick shower, then dressed, applied some shaving lotion, and combed my hair. I put Ruben out into his dog run and locked the door. I went over to the Bronco and climbed in. The engine started at the touch of the ignition switch. I turned around and headed out of the driveway. A doe ran out of the woods and crossed in front of me. She was in a hurry.

There was no traffic on Route 28 as I made my way into Old Forge. I was too late to pick up my mail, so I went directly to John's Diner. The moment I pulled into the parking lot, I spotted Wilt Chambers' big Dodge truck. Charlie Perkins' big Peterbilt tractor was parked in the rear of the parking lot. Several more pickups were parked in line along the south side of the lot. I recognized a few of them, but several of them were heavy duty trucks, some with winches on the front. Patty's red Jeep was parked in the rear of the parking lot next to John's antiquated black 1928 Ford Model A. I got out of the Bronco and went into the diner.

As I entered I could see it was almost a full house. Wilt was the first to notice me.

"Hello, Jason. Where have you been?" He was wearing a big grin.

"Took a plane ride with Dale this morning and just got back about two hours ago. By the way, Wilt, those folks at the Breakshire Lodge love your black bear. Tom Huston is working up a list of folks that would like to order one."

"Are you kidding, Jason?" I could tell that Wilt was excited, and all the folks in the diner had their eyes turned to him.

"No, I'm serious. And by the way, Tom sends his regards to you." I saw Patty in the back of the dining room motioning to me.

"I'll talk with you later, Wilt. I'm having dinner with Patty and I think she just brought the food to our table." I recognized several of Wilt's logger friends, and one of them said hello to me. I nodded at the group. It appeared that Wilt and Charlie Perkins had called a dinner meeting of their logging companies. Charlie waved at me and I gave him the high sign. I'd talk with Charlie later.

I proceeded to our table, where Patty was waiting eagerly for me. I quickly excused myself and ducked into the restroom to wash my hands. I immediately returned to Patty and gave her a hug and a peck on the cheek.

"Hi, honey. Everything looks wonderful. You have even got a candle lit."

"Jason, I know how much you love chicken and biscuits and thought it was a good idea. It will save us both cooking and cleaning up the kitchen," she explained.

"Thank you, Patty. It was very thoughtful of you. I'm hungry, but most of all I'm happy to be with you. I love you, Patty."

We seated ourselves. I looked across the table at her. She had changed from her waitress uniform and was wearing a mint green sweater and dark green slacks. Her hair flowed on her shoulders and her blue eyes sparkled. She was wearing her turquoise jewelry. I looked at the plates containing the chicken and biscuits. They were steaming hot. The veggies consisted of broccoli and cauliflower covered with cheese sauce. Two glasses of ice cold water with lemon wedges were by our plates.

"Honey, this is delicious."

"The chicken is tender and the biscuits are just right. I agree, Jason, the combination is perfect. I'm so glad you could make it."

"I'm happy to be here, Patty. I can see that Wilt and Charlie must be treating their men to Lila's chicken and biscuits, as well." I was famished.

"Lila prepared extra chicken and baked twice as many biscuits this morning. Wilt called her this morning just after we opened and asked her if she could prepare the food for his people for tonight." Patty's eyes danced with excitement.

"Lila and John always go out of their way to please their customers. And, you know, even though Wilt lives in Boonville, he still spends a great amount of time in the Old Forge area."

"Yes, he does. He told me once that he has some favorite restaurants in Boonville. He mentioned Slim's, where they make special omelets. Wilt loves the western omelets with cheese."

"Patty, Wilt loves food. I must say he has really worked on his diet, and he has lost a considerable amount of weight. Have you noticed?"

"Honey, there is an underlying reason for his weight loss. He keeps hinting to me that he wants to be best man at our wedding." Patty blushed and looked down at her plate.

We finished our dinner, and Patty poured us two cups of green tea. I studied her closely as she placed the tea bag in her cup. We continued to discuss her day's happenings. I asked her if she'd like to accompany me back to my log home. We left John's after bidding farewell to Wilt Chambers and Charlie Perkins. Their twelve men smiled and waved at us. I recognized most of them. When we went outside, I opened the passenger door to the Bronco and she got in.

"I can drive up to your place, Jason." She looked at me with a smile.

"No, I'll drive you back to your Jeep later."

"Oh, you're so thoughtful. Guess that's why I love you so much, Sherlock."

I went around to the driver's side and climbed in. I started the Bronco and we pulled out of the parking lot. Route 28 through Old Forge was quiet, and only a few cars were making their way south. I looked over at Patty as she was peering out of the passenger side window. Her blond hair flowed on her shoulders. She turned and smiled. She had placed fresh lipstick on her beautiful lips. I could feel my controlled passion building, and I had to remind myself that we had agreed to wait until our wedding before we unleashed our physical feelings toward each other. We honored each other's feelings about this matter. I was just about ready to make my left turn into my driveway, when a southbound vehicle approached over the knoll. I recognized Jack Falsey's truck. He tooted the horn and waved at us. I tooted back and made the turn.

"Jack must be working late, Patty," I remarked.

"Yes, he puts in a lot of hours. He stops in the diner and is always so pleasant to wait on. He is a gentleman."

"And someone you can truly count on to do an excellent job," I added.

Patty and I could see Ruben in his dog run. He was barking and racing back and forth. I stopped the Bronco near the dog run and told Patty to jump out and go over to Ruben. I backed around and parked, then joined Patty at the dog run. It was still daylight, so we decided to take Ruben for a short walk. I opened the gate, and Ruben rushed us both, first Patty and then me. We walked toward the woods, and Ruben darted out ahead of us. A deer was grazing nearby, but did not move or run off when Ruben passed her. We ambled through the woods for about fifteen minutes before all three of us returned to the house. I let Ruben back into his dog run, and Patty and I went inside.

The night air was getting cool, so I turned up the heat. Propane was expensive, but it would take a little too long to build a wood fire. In no time the temperature rose to a comfortable level. I put on the teakettle, and soon we were comfortably snuggled up on the couch in the living room. I turned on the record player, and the room filled with country music. We both commented about Roy Clark's masterful ability at playing the guitar and banjo. When the teakettle whistled, I went into the kitchen and returned to the living room with two cups of steaming green tea and a few chocolate chip cookies on a plate. Patty enjoyed nibbling on the cookies. So did I.

We discussed everything, from politics to weather to the poverty that still exists in our country and finally to our future wedding plans. We knew the locals' opinion.

"What are you waiting for?" they were asking. Or "When's the big day?" It was getting to be an everyday question asked by many of our friends. Partly we wished they would mind their own business, but we tried to take it in the spirit of good will that was their intention. Patty and I chuckled about it to ourselves.

"Jason, look at the clock. It is 9:30 p.m. and I have to open the diner up in the morning."

"Boy, time flies by, especially when we have a moment together."

I reached out to Patty and put my arm around her, drawing her close to me. Our lips met. We pulled apart, knowing it was time for her to leave.

"Ruben, I'll be back shortly. I have to take Patty to her car." The big dog cocked his head and whined. The security lights beamed brightly on the big K-9.

It had really cooled off outside, and I got a jacket out of the closet for Patty to put on. We embraced again.

Route 28 had no traffic. The parking lot at John's Diner was almost empty. A Town of Webb patrol car was at the far end of the lot. Chief of Police Todd Wilson was talking with some youths. I did a U-turn in front of his car and let Patty out by her Jeep. The chief waved at us. We waved back. I waited until Patty started her Jeep, then left the parking lot and headed north to home and Ruben. When I arrived, Ruben was patiently waiting by his gate. I parked, turned the Bronco off, got out, and went to the dog run to let Ruben out. He raced to the woods for his nightly chore and soon returned. I checked his food and water dishes and then we went inside. Ruben went over and lay down, and I went to the bathroom, and brushed my teeth, and got ready for bed. I was just putting on my pajamas when the telephone rang. I buttoned my pajamas and hurried into my office.

"Hello," I answered, expecting Patty's call.

"Just wanted to say good night, Sherlock. I love you," she replied softly.

"Goodnight, babe. I love you, too." I wished I had her in my arms.

I heard her hang up before I placed my own phone on the hook. I had just climbed into bed between two soft sheets and three blankets plus the bedspread, intending to read for a while, when the telephone rang again. I pushed the covers back and went to the phone. I glanced at the wall clock and I noted that it was 10:35 p.m. I had been just about to doze off.

"Hello," I said.

"Jason!! Are you sitting down?" It was Lieutenant Jack Doyle. He sounded excited.

"Yes, Lieutenant, what's up?" I was curious despite my sleepiness.

"Jason, we've got Norris. Wish you could have been there."

"Great, Jack! Where did you grab him?" I was eager to hear the details.

"Two of my investigators and I were staking out Nate Jenkins' residence in St. Regis Falls. We were in the house next door. About 8:00 p.m. a gray Ford van drove by about three times and then parked a short way from Nate's. Jewell Norris got out of the van with what appeared to be a shotgun. Norris hid behind some bushes, apparently waiting for Nate to come home from the grocery store."

"Wow! What happened next?" I listened closely.

"There were some high shrubs along the front of the Jenkins' property. We quietly left the house and crept along the hedge. One of my men had a shotgun and stood to the side of us. My other investigator and me approached Norris from the rear.   What prompted Norris to turn toward us as he did I'll never know for certain. He went down on one knee and pointed the shotgun he was holding directly at us. We were between Norris and my investigator with the shotgun. Fortunately, Jason, Jewell Norris will never escape from another correctional facility. We were seven yards from him. I took a hurried shot with my Smith and Wesson semi-automatic pistol. The slug hit him between the eyes. He was able to squeeze off one shot, which went into the air. I never saw a man with such wild-looking eyes, as he fell forward on his face. End of story, Jason." Jack spoke calmly. He was hardened by experience.

"I'm glad that you and your men weren't hurt. It's too bad that Norris had to pay the fiddler, but with his deviant behavior one could assume that he was on a journey of self-destruction." I was deeply relieved he would no longer pose a threat—especially to Patty.

"Jason, I wanted to take him alive in the worst way, but it was either him or us. I had to protect my men and myself. His shotgun was loaded with four remaining deer slugs. We had some uniformed men come in to keep the crowd that gathered away from the area. Major Temple and Captain Garrison came to the scene as well as the coroner and district attorney. We were tied up for several hours. It was self-defense. I'll have to go through the drill. Thank God that none of us were hurt or killed."

"You can say that again." I could tell the shooting must be bothering Jack, despite his experience.

"Well, Jason, that's all I can tell you about it. A teletype message has been sent to APB. I assume that your friend, Chief Wilson, will get a copy of it. Oh, by the way, can you meet me tomorrow morning?" He sounded concerned.

"I sure can, Lieutenant. Where, and what time?"

"The Tupper Lake barracks at 10:00 a.m. Okay with you?"

"I'll see you there." I assumed that we'd be discussing the smuggling case.

"Just pull around in back of the barracks. You'll see a maroon-colored van. No need to go into the barracks. Meet me in the van," he said.

"Okay, will do." *Something else must be up*, I thought.

"Sorry to bother you at this late hour," he apologized. "I figured you'd want to know."

I heard the click as Jack hung the phone up. I went into the kitchen and poured myself a glass of ice water. I sipped it slowly, put the glass into the sink, and went to the bedroom. Ruben didn't move as I passed him. I climbed back into bed and put the covers over me. I drifted off to dreamland.

CHAPTER EIGHTEEN

Two giant loons were in the front yard and a red fox was about to pounce on them when I woke up from my dream. Ruben was pulling on the bed covers. For a moment I wondered what the fate of the two loons could have been. I would never know, thanks to Ruben.

I pushed the covers back and got out of bed, then unlocked the door and let Ruben outside for his morning jaunt into the woods. He hurried out, leaped off the porch, and scooted off to the woods. Before I took my shower, I waited for his return. I looked out the door as he bolted from a brush pile. I met him at the gate and let him into his run.

"Good boy, Ruben," I said, petting his big head.

I jogged back inside and closed the door. It didn't take long to shave and shower. I decided that I wouldn't eat breakfast at home, but would stop at Gertie's Diner in Long Lake. I finished dressing and picked up the house before I left. Then I called Lynn at the Eagle Bay Kennels to see if one of her people could give Ruben a bath and a grooming. She indicated that she had an opening and that I should drop Ruben off.

"Hey! Big fella! You're going to have a bath today." I rubbed his ears.

I secured the house and put Ruben into the rear of the Bronco, and headed to the kennel. I pulled up in front and turned the Bronco off. Lynn's kennel was officially called the Kliffside Kennel. She took pride in her work and was very dependable. I had known Lynn for years. She was a good friend. Her prices were fair and she always backed up her work. Ruben knew what was in store for him. Lynn met us in her waiting room and took charge of the big K-9. I patted him on the head.

"Be a good dog, Ruben." I thanked Lynn and left. I told her that it would be late afternoon before I returned to the area. She indicated that the timing was perfect.

The morning newspapers covered the Jewell Norris case. I'd read it later when I got some time.

I pushed the Bronco a little. There was no traffic. She purred along the highway at a good clip. When I pulled in front of Gertie's Diner in Long Lake, it was shortly before 9:00 a.m. I got out and hurried up the stairs. The aroma of the sizzling bacon drifted through the air. Most of the early customers had eaten and were probably at their workplace by now. I opened the door and went inside.

"Hello, Jason, what a surprise!! Good to see you." Gertie called out with a warm smile.

"Gertie, it is good to see you, too. " I always looked forward to seeing my hard-working friend.

"Would you like breakfast?" she asked.

"I'll sit at the counter," I said as I selected a stool.

Gertie handed me a menu and I scanned it. I ordered two scrambled eggs, whole wheat toast, and a cup of coffee. Gertie informed me that her husband Bob had gone to Lake Placid for supplies. I told her to give him my regards. She assured me that she would. I finished my eggs and toast, paid the check, and left Gertie her gratuity. As I exited, she bid me farewell with her usual warm smile. I climbed into the Bronco and headed towards Tupper Lake.

The traffic on Route 30 was light. I crossed the bridge in Long Lake and looked to my left a few yards north of the bridge. There was the driveway to the former Skip-Jack Campsite. The owner of the campsite had passed away, and the property had been left to his son. The son gave up the business. I could almost visualize the property still being there because of all the pleasant memories when I had camped at Skip-Jack's. I drove on.

Tupper Lake was approximately twenty miles north of Long Lake, and Route 30 was in good condition. I was keeping within the speed limit and soon arrived in front of the state police barracks. I pulled to the rear of the building and spotted the maroon van. Following Jack Doyle's instruction, I got out of my vehicle and approached the van. I couldn't see into it as the windows were tinted. It was an F-250 Ford. I approached the right side and the door slid open. I climbed in. Jack Doyle was behind the steering wheel. Two bearded individuals seated in the rear nodded as I entered. They were wearing lightweight turtleneck sweaters and jackets. Jack motioned me to take the front passenger side seat.

"Good morning, Jason. You made good time. We just arrived ourselves."

Jack was wearing a sweatshirt and blue jeans. I asked him how his family was doing. He indicated that all was well on the home front. Jack started the van and we left the Tupper Lake barracks. We drove into town, picked up Route 3, and headed west toward Cranberry Lake.

"Jason, I'd like to introduce you to Ed Isaacs and Starlin Smiley," he said as he gestured to the rear seat.

I turned slightly. "Glad to meet you, gentlemen," I replied.

"Same here," a voice answered. "We've been looking forward to meeting you."

"Jason, as you know, this is a sensitive investigation. In fact, it was your phone call that initiated the process. I asked you to join us to keep you updated on our progress as we look into this Bernard Draper operation. I will not go into the content of our intelligence that we are gathering on a day-to-day basis. However, I wanted you to meet two of our best undercover people. We have enough right now to put Draper away for years, but if we bust him at this time, we're going to miss some of the people involved with him. Right now, we know that he is running heavy drugs into Canada. He is doing this in two Carver cruisers. In addition, it is believed that he is also running guns, along with stolen construction equipment."

"Whew!! Some of this is news," I responded.

"Ed and Smiley have been all over the warehouse and gift shop that Draper is operating. Draper himself doesn't spend a great deal of time at the store or the warehouse, but he has about six people working at the shop. Ed and Smiley are posing as professional painters and have painted the whole complex. Of course, they have had to accomplish some other duties involving the buildings. By the way, Jason, in the painting world they are known as Slick and Brushy," he said with a twinkle in his eyes.

I listened closely as Jack conversed with the two undercover operatives. I learned from the conversation that Ed and Smiley had been in the U.S. Navy and both had worked in naval intelligence during their enlistment. Both were originally from upstate New York and had been with the state troopers for six years. They seemed dedicated to their specific mission. Jack took the right turn onto Route 56. I noticed that a large parking lot had been leveled off near the gift shop. There were several cars in it. Apparently the southwestern jewelry business was going well.

Jack indicated that we were heading to Waddington, New York. He informed us that the two Carver cruisers had been moved to a boathouse located south of the village. It was a sunny day and traffic was light on Route 56. I could hear Ed and Smiley in the back talking in low tones. Both of them seemed to have a good sense of humor, as several times they broke out in laughter. Jack was paying close attention to his driving. A red fox darted across Route 56 in front of us. Jack turned the wheel slightly, just missing the little fellow.

"Whew, that was close," Jack said with a sigh.

"We were lucky and so was the fox," I quipped.

Lieutenant Jack Doyle did not want to be tied to a desk and actively participated in field operations of various BCI cases under his command. I felt privileged to be invited to tag along with him. Smiley and Ed had actually been brought in from another area of the state. It was obvious to me that they must have spent the past six years working on sensitive cases such as the one they were involved in now. I could tell that they were a couple of dedicated individuals, both with plenty of wit and bushels of smarts. As I continued to look out the passenger side window of the van, I noticed that Jack was headed to Massena. I didn't ask any questions. I looked over at Jack as he wheeled the F-250 toward this northern New York village.

"Thought we'd stop for some lunch before we check out those cruisers," Jack said with a big smile. We all agreed with his decision.

On the outskirts of Massena, we passed several eateries. Jack decided to stop at Guy's Restaurant. The food was good and the prices were fair. Jack parked the van at the far end of the lot. The four of us piled out and walked to the diner. By our casual dress, anyone observing us would surmise we were fishermen stopping for a bite to eat before going out on the St. Lawrence River. Jack led the way and we entered. We took a booth at the end of the room. There were only a few people in the restaurant at this time. We all took turns going to the restroom to wash our hands. The menu contained numerous lunch selections. I settled on a corned beef sandwich on rye with Russian dressing. Jack ordered the same. Ed and Smiley ordered cheeseburgers, well done, with French fries and a side of coleslaw. The waitress quickly took our order and returned to the kitchen.

We conversed while we waited for our lunch. Smiley told us about a Glaspar tri-hull boat that he owned. It was apparent that both he and Ed were also devoted fishermen and each of them possessed a good knowledge of watercraft. They were in their early thirties, and extremely capable. Jack and I listened to the small talk. This was not the place for any serious discussion. One would never surmise that Ed and Smiley were members of an elite undercover operation.

The waitress, carrying a large tray with our orders, appeared and set it on a small table close by. Each order was gently placed before us along with large glasses of ice water with lemon wedges. The server was polite and smiled at us.

"Let me know if there is anything else you need," she said as she rushed off to answer her bell to deliver another order.

It didn't take us long to consume our lunch. The waitress soon returned and refilled our water glasses. The lunch was tasty, and all agreed that it was a fine noon meal. Jack grabbed the check and we each left a tip. He thanked the waitress and paid the check at the cashier's station. We left the diner and headed across the parking lot to the van. We were soon headed toward Waddington, via Route 37, a two-lane highway that has withstood many improvements over the years.

Several locations along the highway offer a view of the great St. Lawrence River. It was about a thirty-mile trip to Waddington. The large boathouse was between Waddington and Red Mills. From the conversation between Smiley and Jack, I learned that Jack had received a call from the boathouse owner. The owner reported that he had been approached by a man in a pickup truck with Arizona plates who had asked the owner about renting the boathouse to house two Carver cruisers. The owner of the boathouse, Miles O'Rourke, told Jack that the owner of the cruisers was a Bernard Draper from Phoenix, Arizona.

Jack turned the Ford van into a narrow winding lane. To the right of the boathouse was a two-story wooden frame house hidden behind some blue spruce trees. A narrow driveway led to the house as well as the boathouse. Jack took the driveway toward the house. A large porch was attached to the house and a man could be seen in a rocking chair. He had a straw hat on and was wearing a bright red shirt. Dark-colored horned rim glasses sat on the end of his nose. When he saw us, he slowly got up from his chair and pushed his glasses up into position. Jack turned off the van and told us to remain there. He would speak with the gentleman he believed to be Mr. O'Rourke. Jack exited the vehicle and walked toward the house.

While the lieutenant was busy with the gentleman, Ed told Smiley and me about a Crestliner boat that he used to own. He went on to tell us about the time he was on Seneca Lake when a large cruiser almost smashed into his much smaller aluminum craft. The three of us agreed that it could have been a fatal boat accident.

It seemed like an eternity before Jack returned to the van, and when he did I could see he had that twinkle in his Irish eyes.

"I just had a wonderful conversation with Mr. Miles O'Rourke. Gentlemen, he has given us permission to look into the boathouse." Jack talked rapidly.

The van had to be backed up twice before Jack could make the turn. He drove slowly on the curvy drive to the branch that led to the boathouse. We all looked closely as we approached the weather-beaten gray colored structure that housed two large Carver cruisers. Jack stopped the van and all of us exited. I looked up at the peak of the building as two sea gulls took off from the worn roof, headed toward the St. Lawrence River, where the large ocean going ships travel back and forth carrying their shipments of products from foreign lands.

We made our way down a small path to the side of the building. Jack had a key in his right hand that O'Rourke had given him. He put the key into the keyhole and turned the key to the right. Jack opened the door and we entered a small office. There was another door that opened into the area where the two cruisers were tied. I sat on a chair in the office while the three troopers checked the cruisers, taking down registration numbers and other information. Both of the cruisers were rigged for fishing, and each had sophisticated equipment attached. I made my observations through a large glass window. I looked at a fishing magazine for a while. In about a half-hour the trio came back into the office. Jack talked with Ed and Smiley in low tones. That was police business and none of my business. It did make me wonder why I retired when I did. I couldn't help but feel that I was missing all the day-to-day action of a state trooper. Jack was now standing in front of me wearing that Irish grin.

"We're ready to leave, Jason," he advised me as he took one more look around the water side of the boathouse. Only a small portion of the cruisers could be seen from the outside, because there were doors pulled down to the middle of the aft of the cruisers.

We entered the van. Jack stopped at the house and returned the key. We saw Jack shake hands with Mr. O'Rourke before he returned to the van. We left the driveway and turned right toward Red Mills. When we reached Route 345, Jack turned and headed toward Madrid and into Potsdam via Route 11 and back onto Route 56 to Route 3 and on to Tupper Lake. On the way to Tupper, Jack again thanked me for my assistance and told me to thank my buddy, Jack Flynn, for him.

"You know me, Jason. I'm the kind of guy who doesn't hand out plaudits, but in your case I thank you very much. This is an important case, and I hope we can close them down. It appears to me that Draper is evil from the get-go. I want you to know that if we are successful with this case, you'll be hearing from Major Frank Temple and Captain Roy Garrison. After all, they are my supervisors, when I give them permission to be. Only kidding, Jason," he added, patting my shoulder.

"Glad to assist anytime I can, Lieutenant."

The return trip to Tupper consisted of a four-way conversation with Jack, Ed, Smiley and myself. We exchanged stories about our own upstate New York, the area where Smiley's and Ed's roots originated. I asked both of them why they had decided to apply for the New York State Troopers. Their responses were the same: "It was my boyhood dream." I could tell that they were sincere, and I got the feeling that Lieutenant Jack Doyle was fortunate to have two undercover operatives that would go that extra mile. I asked them if they belonged to the painters' union and the response was gleeful laughter followed with the word, "Negative."

When we passed the Southwestern Gift Shop and warehouse on Route 56, a large white semi-trailer outfit was backed into their loading dock. The parking lot had several cars and pickups in it. Jack slowed the van down to a crawl, and all eyes were looking out of the passenger side, except Jack's, for his eyes were focused on the highway. Bernie Draper had no idea what he was in for. I was certain that Jack had one or two other operatives working on the case under deep cover. I was privileged to have gone along with them to Waddington, and I didn't want to probe Jack with sensitive questions. I knew Jack well, and in my knowledge of this individual, he was taking care of business, and you could bet on that. The only reason Jack included me, was in recognition of my input on this major case.

There were no troop cars parked behind the Tupper Lake barracks when we pulled in. My Bronco and two pickups were at the far end of the lot. Jack got out of the van when I did and walked with me over to my Bronco. He asked me a question: "Jason, would you consider letting your dog, Ruben, return to temporary duty? We would take good care of him, and after some added training he would be useful to us. It would be just until this investigation is completed. We are short of division dogs at the moment, as they are in use in other places in the state."

I pondered Jack's question before I replied.

"Yes, for you I would consider it, but I would ask that he be taken extra good care of. Ruben and I have a strong bond."

"I understand completely how you feel about it. If you don't mind, I will have Russ Slingerland get in touch with you in a few days and you can make your own arrangements."

"That will be fine. I know Russ very well and he is an excellent trainer."

"Yes, he is one of the best we've had. As you know, he's retired and started his own dog-training service."

I bid farewell to Lieutenant Doyle, Ed and Smiley, and told them to be careful and not to spill too much paint. They grinned. I watched them leave the barracks yard and I followed shortly after warming up the Bronco. I pulled out of the driveway and headed south toward Long Lake. The sun was settling over the mountains, and the shadows of the trees were getting long. Instead of rushing back to John's Diner in Old Forge, I decided to stop at Gertie's in Long Lake for a snack and then go home. I knew that Patty would be busy and I wouldn't be able to visit with her. I'd call her later that night.

The traffic was light as I made my way toward Long Lake. It didn't seem possible that a year had passed so quickly since Patty had been abducted from Old Forge by the two Ohio killers. I couldn't get out of my mind how the folks in my town had formed massive search parties under the direction of Chief of Police Todd Wilson. All those folks giving their time and energy under tense circumstances. I was most fortunate to live in Old Forge, where people care about their neighbors and are willing to stand up and volunteer to assist in any given emergency that might arise. Patty was lucky, and so was I, to have her back after that ordeal.

Only two trucks were parked in front of Gertie's Diner when I pulled in. I got out and looked over at the local seaplane taking off from the lake. The engine made a deep droning sound as it climbed above the tree tops and turned to the right, headed toward New-comb. I turned and went into the diner. Gertie was busy wiping a table off and filling the salt and pepper shakers.

"Good afternoon, Jason. This is a pleasant surprise." She wore a big smile as she greeted me.

"Hello, Gertie. Nice to see you. How's Bob?" I asked, glancing around.

"He's lying down for a while, Jason. We've had a busy day."

"Gertie, I don't know how you keep up the pace you do. You and Bob should take a few days to yourselves and get away from the daily grind," I added with genuine concern.

"I know we should, but with our taxes coming due, and other expenses, we just feel that we have to stay with it. Maybe someday, Jason."

"Well, I hope you two will take a break, soon."

"What would you like? I have some fresh liver that I could fry up for you."

"That's the ticket! I'll have an order of liver and onions, some mashed potatoes and any veggie you have today." Her suggestion was readily taken. "Oh, and a cup of decaf, if it's fresh, please."

"I'll braise the onions for you and I have some asparagus. Is that all right?" she asked.

"That will be fine," I replied.

I sat down at a corner table and glanced at the *New York Times.* I read a couple of editorials, then went to the restroom to wash my hands. I noticed several people come into the diner. The afternoon waitress was helping out in the kitchen and I could hear Gertie call for her.

The waitress came toward me with a tray and my order. She placed the plate in front of me. I thanked her and she scurried away, returning with a large glass of ice water and a slice of lemon wedge. I tried the liver and onions. Gertie had sautéed the onions and the combination was perfect. In addition, she had put some flour on the liver and seasoned it well with pepper and salt. This was some of the best liver that I had ever tasted. Everything was great. My plate was clean. Gertie told me that she had rice pudding. Those were the magic words. The waitress served me a large dish of it with real whipped cream. It was truly a treat. I followed that up with a refill of steaming hot decaf. After I finished, I tipped the waitress and paid my check. The diner was filling up so I wasn't able to talk with Gertie before I left. She waved at me as I went out the door. "Say hello to Bob for me, Gertie," were my parting words.

I walked over to the Bronco, and before I climbed in I looked over Long Lake. The green of the forest was eye-catching. Old Forge was my favorite, but if I ever decided to have a second choice, it would have to be Long Lake. At least I had the best of the two worlds. I resided in Old Forge and I could visit Long Lake any time

I wanted to. However, to further assess the Adirondack beauty, I could only say that every hamlet and village within the Blue Line had its own unique beauty and charm, and if I was a person of means I would have a house or cabin in each of these places. Of course that can only be a dream. God was good to me. Ruben and I had a small piece of the Adirondack Park and with that we were fortunate. We didn't have to wait in lines of heavy city traffic, and we were still able to use the super highways when we had to. Speaking of Ruben, I wondered if he would appreciate my volunteering him for police-work. I knew that Russ would be the one person whom I could trust to take good care of my pal. Troop S lost a good man when Russ retired. He, too, loves the great Adirondacks.

Before I left Long Lake, I stopped at Hoss's Country Corner. I picked up a pound of cheddar cheese. I planned to prepare macaroni and cheese for dinner the next week. Patty would be surprised. I spoke with Lori and John and waved at Ginny as I left the store. They were dedicated hard working people and I admired them very much.

The trip from Long Lake took me about one hour and a half. I was hoping to reach the Eagle Bay kennel in time to pick up Ruben. When I pulled into the parking area, I saw Lynn locking the front door. When she saw the Bronco, she knew that I had come for Ruben. She quickly unlocked the door and went inside. I got out and followed her in. She had already placed the leash on Ruben, and the big dog started wagging his tail when he spotted me.

"Lynn, Ruben looks great. You folks did a super job on the big fella."

"Jason, Ruben was a good boy and liked his bath. I haven't prepared the bill and will mail you a copy of it. Is that okay?" She smiled, handing me the leash.

"That will be fine. Thank you, Lynn. Ruben thanks you, too."

"Say hello to Patty for me, Jason."

"I will. Give your mother my regards." She nodded.

Ruben pulled hard on the leash and went directly to the rear gate of the Bronco. I opened it and he jumped in. I shut the gate and got into the vehicle. Ruben and I headed home.

CHAPTER NINETEEN

Sky Harbor airport in the Phoenix, Arizona, area was bustling with lines of customers waiting for flights, boarding flights, and meeting flights. Standing in line with a group of people booking flights was Bernard Draper, aka Bernie Draper. He had one carry-on, having previously checked two other pieces of luggage. Bernie was dressed in gray slacks, a white shirt, and a three-quarter-length brown leather jacket. He got himself booked on American Airlines Flight 222 for Pittsburgh and Syracuse. He had already made arrangements to have Scott Austin meet him at the Syracuse airport, in his black Lexus that he had shipped ahead. He was traveling alone. Jack Flynn, pretending to read the *Arizona Republic*, was standing near Bernie, watching him closely. As Bernie was at the desk, Jack slipped into a telephone booth and called his buddy, Jason Black. The answering machine came on at Jason's log home. Jack left a short message. "Jason, call me when you get in. It's important."

CHAPTER TWENTY

I pulled into my drive as the sun was fading over the mountaintops. The sky was casting a maroon glow from the setting sun. I could tell that Ruben was glad to be home. I got out and let him out of the back of the Bronco. He ran in circles and then off into the woods to smell out the chippies. In a few minutes, he returned. By then I had filled his food and water dishes. I opened the gate to the dog run and unlocked the door. Ruben came racing toward his run and immediately ran in. I went back outside to close the gate. I entered my log home, went into the bathroom, and splashed cold water on my face. It had been a long day.

As I entered my office, I saw the flashing red light on my answering machine. I listened to the various messages, some from banks, one from Wilt Chambers, and the last from my friend Jack Flynn.

I called Jack in Phoenix. Ruby answered the telephone. "Flynn Investigations. May I help you?"

"Ruby, good afternoon. This is Jason in Old Forge. Is Jack in? I'm returning his call."

"Hi, Jason. Nice to hear your voice. I've missed you. In fact, we still really wish you would come out to Phoenix and come on board at Flynn Investigations," she pleaded with me.

"Ruby, you and Jack are very dear to me. I'd do almost anything for you both, but you know l will not come to that hot part of the country. I cannot take your summer temperatures, although I really love the area," I added.

"I know, sweetie, but you can't blame a girl for trying. Take care, Jason. I'll buzz Jack and let him know you're calling."

"Jack Flynn here. Jason, how have you been?"

"Good, buddy. What's up?"

"Bernie Draper is headed your way. He took American Airlines Flight 222 out of Sky Harbor Airport earlier this afternoon for Syracuse. He must be planning on an extended stay, as he took two pieces of luggage, which he checked through, and one carry-on. He was alone when he boarded. Hilda Furman wasn't with him."

"How is the investigation by the Phoenix PD going?" I asked.

"Our buddy, Captain Jay Silverstein, tells me they have a ways to go on connecting Draper to the killing of the three Mexican Nationals, but he has three detectives assigned to the triple homicide on a full-time basis."

"That's interesting. The New York State Police are investigating Draper's operation, and they are on top of it on this end, believe me," I reassured him.

"I'm glad to hear this. Draper puts up a good front, donates funds to the politicians, organizations, and any group that would tend to benefit his position in the community out here in the mountain west. I just hope they get him."

"Lieutenant Jack Doyle is a dedicated guy, and he appreciates what you've done on the case, Jack. It isn't every day that the authorities can get the jump on the bad guys. I think the good guys might be ahead on this one. Hope so, anyway."

"Okay, Jason, I'll let you go for now. If anything else comes up, I'll give you a call."

"I appreciate it, Jack. I hope you can come east sometime and spend a week or two with me in the Adirondacks."

"Oh! I'd love to do that. By the way, Jason, have you firmed up any wedding plans? That would be an ideal time to make the trip."

"In the near future. You'll be the first to know. There are several fellows who want to be best man, but I told them that my former Marine buddy has first choice if he can make it here. At least, I'm planning on it. Is that okay with you, Jack?"

"Certainly! I'm looking forward to it. Take care, buddy."

I heard the click. I knew Jack was busy and had to get going on other matters. I called Lieutenant Doyle at his apartment and shared the information with him that I had just received from Jack Flynn. He was pleased that I called and told me that they'd known Draper was coming, but hadn't known the exact day of departure from Arizona. He did share with me the possibility of Draper staying in the Tupper Lake region.

Patty answered the phone after the second ring.

"Honey, this is Jason. Are you going to stop by, or do you want me to pick you up?"

"I'll be at your place in about thirty minutes. Okay, Sherlock?"

"Looking forward to seeing you." We hung up.

I went into the bathroom, quickly shaved, and combed my hair. The freshness of the cold water and the shaving lotion gave me a cool feeling. It brought me back to life. I then checked the refrigerator. I had some corned beef and ham in the event Patty wanted a sandwich. I went outside and let Ruben out of his run. The big K-9 ran off into the woods. He soon would be in training under the direction of Russ Slingerland. I continued to be sure that Russ would give him the best of care. Ruben dropped out of sight for a few minutes. Then I could see him approach. He lovingly jumped up on me. I rubbed his ears and patted his back. He did not want to leave my side. It was almost as if he sensed that he was being pressed into service again. I put him into his dog run.

I went inside and gave Wilt Chambers a call at his home in Boonville.

"Hello, Wilt. This is Jason returning your call."

"Jason, good to hear from you. Where in the heck have you been hiding? I even asked Chief Todd Wilson if he had seen you, and he told me that you were probably up in the Tupper Lake area. I'd like to take you and Patty on the dinner boat cruise this coming Saturday. Can you make it?" he asked, hesitantly.

"Do you mean the Old Forge Lake Cruises?" I asked, as there were two dinner cruises in the area.

"Yes, that's the one. I've heard the food is excellent."

"That's a great idea. I'd love to. Patty will be here shortly. I'll check and call you back. Okay?" I asked.

"Fine. I'll wait for your call before I make reservations."

"So long for now, good friend."

I had just hung up when Patty's Jeep came into sight. She parked near the dog run, and I could see that Ruben was at full attention. His ears were straight up and his tail was wagging. I rushed outside. Patty was already out of the Jeep and over by the dog run talking to Ruben.

"Hi, sweetheart," I said.

"Hi, darling! I've missed you so very much."

I walked toward Patty. I wrapped my arms around her and our lips met. Our love seemed to grow with every encounter. I was so very happy to see her.

"Patty, I received a call from Wilt. He would like us to join him on the Old Forge Dinner Cruise. His treat. I told him I'd check with you. How's that sound to you?" I queried.

"Great. I've been wanting to suggest that myself. Saturday's fine with me!" she answered excitedly.

Patty and I went inside. I placed a call to Wilt, telling him Saturday night would be fine.

"Have you had anything for dinner?" she asked.

"Yes, I ate at Gertie's on my way back home. I do have some corned beef or ham if you'd care for a sandwich."

"No, honey, I had a sandwich before I left work. As you know, I don't cook that often, as I take many of my meals at the diner. I've watched Lila on several occasions preparing different entrees on their menu, then I've written it down. I already have a good collection of recipes. Honey, after we get married I hope to present you with some of my favorite dishes."

"You are a sweetheart, Patty. I'm looking forward to it. By now, you know what I like." I could tell she was serious about the forthcoming commitment of marriage.

"I'll always try to please you, Sherlock. You know that."

"I know you do, Patty. I appreciate that." I gave her a quick embrace.

I told Patty that Ruben was going to a dog trainer's for a while. I didn't go into detail, and she didn't ask any questions. All she said was "You'll miss him, honey." I told her that I certainly would miss the big fellow.

Patty and I took Ruben out of his dog run and went down to the woods where we had spent many hours of hiking and watching Ruben chasing the frisky inhabitants of the trees and bushes. The chippies, I believe, enjoyed their races with Ruben to the security of the brush piles that were plentiful in this wooded paradise. The squirrels were also a challenge and at times tested Ruben's endurance.

After our walk we returned Ruben to his dog run and went inside to listen to music. I didn't have many tapes, but some of the fiddle music was from another time in American society. A friend of mine, farmer Jerome Brown, had a small radio program where he played country music of the 1920's and 1930's. I was fortunate to have some of his tapes and played this music occasionally. Tonight was one of the times. Patty and I listened to this music for a couple of hours. We sat on the couch. At about 9:30 p.m., Patty told me that she had to open the diner early in the morning. She reached over and put her arms around my shoulders. We hugged for a few seconds and then we went outside.

"Good night, Ruben," she said, rubbing his ears. "Good night, Sherlock. I probably won't see you until Saturday. Tomorrow is Friday, and you know it is a big day at work. Take care, honey. Love you."

"Good night, Patty," I said as I opened her car door.

She climbed into her Jeep. It started right up. She blew the horn lightly as she headed for home.

I let Ruben out of the dog run and he went bounding off. In a few minutes he returned and we went inside. I went into my office for a while to check my appointment schedule and wrote up a couple of bad check cases. The telephone rang. I jumped.

"Hello, Sherlock. I'm ready for bed." Patty sounded sleepy.

"Hi, honey. I should have called, but I'm in the office taking care of a few things. Guess I got tied up."

"You don't have to explain. I understand. Goodnight, dear," she said.

"Goodnight. Have a good night's sleep," I responded.

I had no sooner hung up the telephone when the bell again

pierced the quiet of my log home.

"Hello," I answered.

"Jason, hello. This is Russ Slingerland from the other side of the mountain. I'm sorry to call so late, but I just got home from a meeting. I talked with Jack Doyle at Troop S Headquarters and he went over with me about giving your retired K-9 some refresher training. I have to go to Hamilton College tomorrow morning early and wondered if I could meet you in front of the Old Forge Post Office at about 3:00 p.m. on my way north," he suggested.

"Russ, that will be fine. I'll meet you at 3:00 p.m. Thanks for calling, and—don't worry—you can feel free to call here any time. I'll see you tomorrow."

"Thanks, Jason. Good night."

I hung up the telephone. I got up from my desk and went over to Ruben. I felt that he was aware something was up. He started pacing the floor. I went to him to rub his back and run my fingers over his ears.

"Come on, big boy, you'll do fine. Just be careful, just be careful."

Ruben rubbed his big head against my arm and sat down next to me. I started to have bad feelings about volunteering him for a return-to-duty assignment. I knew that Russ would take good care of Ruben. It was the danger he might face that concerned me. Time would only tell if this unusual assignment would bring my dog back to me. Ruben finally lay down on his air mattress.

I checked the doors and prepared for bed. There were several telephone calls I had to make in the morning, and I had to clean the house. It was also laundry day. I went into the bathroom, brushed my teeth, and flossed. I put on my pajamas and went to bed.

The helicopter was falling rapidly toward a large mountain peak. Smoke was billowing from the engine. We were just about to crash into the snow-covered peak when I woke up with a start. My heart was racing. All I could remember was that the pilot had jumped out and left me alone in the falling chopper. Ruben was tugging on the bedspread, growling. He wanted me to pull on the spread.

"Settle down, Ruben," I commanded.

He went to the door and stood in front of it. I went over and unlocked the door, opened it, and let him out. I glanced at the clock. It was 7:20 a.m. I looked out the door and caught a glimpse of Ruben entering the woods. I went into the bathroom and splashed some ice cold water on my face. The dream I was having when I awoke had faded and I was now fully alert. I got out of my pajamas and into the shower, soaped myself, shampooed, and rinsed off. I finished the shower with a cold-water rinse. Brrr!! It was cold!

I looked out the window, and Ruben was sitting by the gate to his dog run. I decided to quickly shave, so went back into the bathroom and lathered my face. My straight razor needed sharpening, but I managed to complete shaving without slicing my chin or nipping an ear. I applied a hot towel and then rubbed cocoa butter on my face and applied another hot towel. I completed the process with a cold towel. The final touch was a splash of shaving lotion. I dressed and combed my hair. I went outside and put Ruben in the run.

Instead of preparing breakfast at home, I decided to run to Old Forge and do my laundry. I stripped the bed and placed all the whites in one bag and the colored in another, put them all into the Bronco, locked the door, checked Ruben's dishes, and headed for town.

When I pulled into the laundry parking lot, I spotted Charlie Perkins in his big Peterbilt and trailer. He was loaded with logs heading for Vermont. He spotted me and gave a blast on his air horns. Several people on the street, including myself, waved at Charlie, who had a good relationship with a lumber company in Vermont which was producing wooden reels for power companies. Charlie loved his lumberjack life, and raising his large family in the Adirondacks. He worked many seven-day weeks to accomplish his goals.

I placed the laundry into three machines, added soap and bleach, and put the quarters into the slots. Each machine ran for a forty-minute cycle. I rechecked the machines and headed to John's Diner and Patty.

Inside the diner, Patty was carrying a large tray of food to a table of six. She flashed me a smile as I let her pass in front of me. Some of the fellows at the table nodded. I returned the nod with a wave. I found my favorite table unoccupied and sat down. The menu was on the table. I looked it over and decided what I'd like. Patty had finished serving the large table. Retrieving her order pad from her jacket, she came over to me.

"Good morning, Sherlock." She wore her usual warm smile.

"Hi, honey. I'll have two scrambled eggs, whole wheat toast and a cup of hot tea." I wasn't too hungry this morning.

"Is that all, sweetheart?" she asked.

"That'll do. I have the washing at the laundromat, and I'm going to do some housecleaning this morning."

"I wish I was off so I could assist you, you poor dear." She smiled.

"When we're married, Patty, you can do all the housecleaning, but I will help you if I'm not out on a case," I said in jest.

"Oh! You sweetheart! I'll hold you to that promise." She rushed off toward the kitchen to answer her bell.

I had just finished my last sip of tea when Dale Rush pulled up a chair.

"Jason, would you like to do a little flying this morning? I'm heading up to the Breakshire to see your friend, Tom Huston. He called me yesterday and asked me if I could stop by. It seems that he has some fishing parties lined up for me. Apparently these people are friends of his from the New England states, and they are interested in going to some remote lakes to fish later this summer."

"Dale, I'd love to, but my schedule today is unbreakable. Any other time I'd race you to the seaplane. Hope you understand, buddy," I said with disappointment.

"I understand, but you know you're welcome to join me. After all, you're the one that introduced me to Tom."

"I know that. Please give him my regards and tell him I'll be stopping at the Breakshire Lodge to see him one of these days. I'm happy that he is sending some business your way, Dale," I added.

"He's a gentleman, and he thinks highly of you, Jason."

Dale and I talked for a few more minutes, and I promised him that I would go flying with him soon. I paid my check, and exited the diner. I had wanted to speak with John and Lila, but, as usual, they were extremely busy getting the breakfasts out to their loyal customers. I was surprised not to see Wilt, but then realized I was a little early for him. He usually stopped later in the morning, if he was in the Old Forge region.

I returned to the laundromat, put my clothing and sheets into two dryers, and placed the required coins in the slot. I checked my watch. I knew that it would take approximately 40 to 45 minutes for the drying process. I left the laundromat and walked over to the Old Forge Hardware Store. I said hello to the manager, Mike, and continued to browse around the store. To this day, I never tire of going up and down the aisles. The hardware store has everything for home and camp. It is a draw to the locals and tourists alike. I purchased a water filter and some nails. As always, the staff was friendly and helpful.

"Take care, Jason, and thanks for stopping by," Mike called over as I left.

"Best to you, Michael."

I returned to the laundromat. The time was about to run out as I approached the dryers. I took the clothes out and hung the shirts on hangers. I folded the sheets and put everything into the basket.

I placed the laundry in the rear of the Bronco and hung the hangers with the shirts and trousers on the rear window hook on the passenger side. I got in, started my trusty Bronco, and headed to the post office. I had timed it just right. There were no cars in the parking area except the employees'. I got out and went inside, peeked my head through the inner door, and said, "Hello, everyone!"

"Hello, Jason!" they shouted back. I opened my post office box and took out several letters and larger brown envelopes. I placed a rubber band around the mail and left the building. I got back into the Bronco and headed for home and the housecleaning, which I didn't really look forward to; but it was necessary and good exercise.

When I pulled into the yard I could see Ruben in his dog run. I also spotted Russ Slingerland sitting in his gray Chevrolet Blazer. He got out of the Blazer as I parked the Bronco and got out.

"Hello, Jason Black. Gosh, it has been ages since I've seen you. How are you, Jason?" he asked as he reached over and grabbed my extended hand.

"Russ, it is good to see you, too. It has been a while, and many gallons of water have flowed down the Indian River since I've seen you." I was happy to see my friend.

"You haven't forgotten the time we overturned in the canoe up on Black Lake?" he jokingly reminded me.

"Do I remember? You bet I do. We both swam to shore." I chuckled.

"We were in good shape in those days. I doubt if I could make it today," he added.

"Oh! Yeah! How well I remember, Russ."

We both had to laugh at our recollections.

"Russ, I know you're here to pick up Ruben. I know that I don't have to tell you to take good care of him, because I know you will. Ruben is my pal and I don't want anything to happen to him." I needed to let Russ know how strongly I felt about this.

"Jason, you don't have to worry. I'll be with him every day, and when we're in the field for the purpose of detecting drugs, I'll be right with him. Don't worry so much."

I believed Russ's word was golden. "I know that he'll be in good hands, with you, Russ. Say, you must have been surprised to get a call from the commander of Troop S to press you back into service."

"Yes, I was. But with this possible terrorist activity threatening, it was deemed necessary. Don't forget that Lieutenant Jack Doyle is pushy, too. He's a leader that gets things done. He not only talks the talk, but he also walks the walk," he said.

"I'm very much aware of that. He's a good man. He looks down the road and can see what has to be done. Fortunately, Ruben is in good health, and can possibly aid in Jack's investigation of Bernie Draper and his illegal activity. Draper has got to be stopped," I agreed.

"Don't worry about Ruben, Jason. I'll take good care of the big fellow. I was actively involved with him in his initial training, and I had good rapport with him during his service. Furthermore, I will be with him on any assignment that Lieutenant Doyle deems necessary on the Draper matter."

Russ opened the rear of the Blazer and I assisted him with Ruben. The big dog looked at me. When he was in the back of the vehicle, Russ closed the hatch. Ruben walked around in circles inside the Blazer and started barking loudly.

I opened the driver's side rear door. "Settle down, Ruben. Be a good dog," I admonished.

"Well, Jason, I've got to be going. I'll keep you posted on his progress. I'm certain he'll fall into his duties without any problems. By the way, why don't you come to Saranac sometime? We'll take the boat out and throw the fishing line into the water. We haven't fished together in a long time."

"I'd love to, Russ. Say hello to your family for me."

"Take care, Jason. Now quit your worrying," he chided as he left.

I watched the shiny Blazer leave the yard. My heart felt empty as Ruben peered at me from the rear window of Russ's vehicle. I reached into my right trousers pocket and removed my handkerchief. I dried my eyes as the tears began to form. I was sure going to miss my big guy, but it was for a just cause. I knew, too, that Russ would treat Ruben as though he were his own.

Russ had brought some water with him as well as dog food, and he had all the necessary supplies at his kennel for the proper care of my K-9. I emptied Ruben's feeding dish and water container. I would wash them later. I missed Ruben already!

CHAPTER TWENTY-ONE

When I went into my log home I had just reached the hallway when the telephone rang. I rushed into the office and answered it.

"Hello! Jack Doyle here." I heard Jack's familiar voice.

"Good morning, Lieutenant," I replied.

"Knock the lieutenant stuff off, Jason. Just call me Jack," he said firmly.

"What's up, Jack?"

"Did Russ pick up your dog yet?" he asked, inquisitively.

"He left my yard just a few minutes ago. Is there something wrong?"

"No, I just wondered. I knew he had to go to Hamilton College early this morning, and I surmised he'd stop and pick Ruben up." He paused. "Just for your information, Draper's in a motel in Tupper Lake and we are monitoring his activities. His foreman, or whatever position he holds in the organization, is with him as we speak. You know that the gift shop and warehouse are just a front for what actually is going on."

"I concur with your statement."

"I want you to keep me updated about anything your associate might share with you on Draper." He sounded adamant concerning this law-breaker.

"You can count on it, Jack."

"So far, Jason, we believe he is running drugs and firearms, and smuggling untaxed cigarettes and liquor across the border.

There's no doubt about it. Our intelligence reports from the OPP (Ontario Provincial Police) have been very helpful to our case. Another factor to consider is the possibility that Draper is bringing illegal aliens into our country. I've had contact with the Immigration Naturalization Service, and some of their informants have mentioned Draper's name. Well, anyway, keep me posted." Jack sounded really wound up on this case.

"You can take that to the bank, my friend. I'll let you know if I hear anything from Jack Flynn."

"Your buddy Flynn must be quite a fellow, for when I was at the FBI academy his name came up from some officers from Phoenix that were taking the academy courses. I heard he was a crackerjack of an investigator in the police arena, and a former US Marine to boot."

"You bet he was. We served together in the South Pacific."

"That's right. You did tell me that a few years ago. Anyway, take care, Jason, and we'll stay in touch. I want you there when we make the bust."

"I don't think your boss, Roy Garrison, nor Frank Temple would appreciate me being on the scene."

"I want you there, Jason. My God, man, you're the one that initiated this case for us. You'd better be there. Take care, Jason."

"Good luck, Lieutenant."

I had to get my house cleaned. I missed Ruben. I bet he missed me, too. I'd be glad when this case concerning Bernard Draper was wrapped up. To think that a man with his prominence in the State of Arizona can come into New York State with criminal intentions and set up a business for the express purpose of using it as a front to transport drugs and contraband including the smuggling of guns, untaxed cigarettes, and liquor into the country of Canada was ludicrous. This case was very involved and complex in nature. Troop S had Draper under a microscope and hopefully justice would prevail.

I called to locate a carpet cleaner and discovered that the only place that had one for rent was a hardware store in town. I went to town and picked it up, loading it into the rear of my Bronco. When I returned home and was unloading the rug cleaner, a raccoon ran across my lawn about ten feet from the rear of the vehicle. Usually the coons are nearer to the wood line, but this fellow must have been looking for food. He couldn't gain entrance to the refuse can, as I have a strong strap with hooks holding the cover down. I watched the coon wander off to the edge of the woods, where he climbed a tree. I could imagine that if Ruben were here, he would have his ears at attention. Fortunately for the coon, he wasn't here.

I was just getting ready to enter my log home when Jack Falsey pulled into the yard.

"Hi, Jack. How have you been?" I was glad to see him.

"I'm okay, Jason. I thought I'd stop and check your furnace over. I received a notice about a call-back on a part, and it will only take a couple of minutes to see if I have to replace the part."

"Sure, come on in. How'd you like a cup of coffee?"

"No, Jason. Coffee and me don't seem to get along very well. I'll have a glass of ice water, if you have one."

"You're in luck, Jack. I have plenty. While you're checking the furnace I'll break out some ice cubes. How's that?"

"That's great! I'll go downstairs and check it. For some reason I'm thirsty."

I took a tray of ice cubes out of the freezer and emptied the tray into a large pitcher. I sliced a lemon and added it to the water I poured in. Jack came back upstairs wearing a big smile.

"Well, Jason, you're all set on that. The part is not defective."

I checked the cupboard and brought out some molasses cookies. They were Jack's favorite. He seldom would take time for a cup of coffee or tea, but today he apparently had a few minutes of free time before he went on to his next stop. I poured the ice water into two large glasses and made sure a lemon wedge got into each glass.

Jack and I sat at the table for over an hour nibbling on cookies, talking about current events, and sharing information about who was sick in town and who had passed away. He inquired as to Patty and our wedding plans. I told him that we had not set the date yet. We also talked about Patty and how lucky she was to escape death while she was being held by the two killers from Ohio. We both knew that Patty was one fortunate young lady not to have been raped or murdered by those men. When Jack got up to leave, he asked me a question. "Jason, is it true that that killer Jewell Norris was intending to come after you? I've heard this from several people in the area." Jack seemed concerned.

"Yes, I'm sorry to say. He apparently had me on his hit list. He didn't appreciate looking down the muzzle of my 9-mm semi automatic last year. I'll be honest with you, Jack: Patty and Nate Jenkins don't have to worry about him anymore. Norris was bent on revenge. His problems probably started in his formative years. It's too bad that he took the wrong path of life's journey."

"Yeah, that's right, you're the one that grabbed him for the troopers. It doesn't seem possible that a year has gone by. According to what I read in the papers, that BCI Lieutenant Doyle was a lucky guy not to get shot himself." Jack sat silent for a minute. "Well, Jason, thank you for those delicious cookies. Usually at night I have a glass of milk with cookies before I retire. I've been meaning to ask you, how would you like to go fishing some afternoon?" Jack loved to fish.

"I'd like that, but let's see how this case I'm involved in works out. I promise we'll go fishing sometime soon." I love to fish, too, but it had been a long time.

I walked Jack out to his van. We bid farewell and he left the yard. I thought it strange that he didn't ask where Ruben was. I went back into the house and hooked up the carpet cleaner. I filled the container with the special solution which I had mixed according to directions. I plugged in the machine and turned it on. The brush rotated and the process began. I did all the carpets, then turned off the cleaner. Now then it would have to dry. I opened all the windows.

The floor in the kitchen was next on my list. As I mopped it, I thought of my rookie days in the Marine Corps when we had to clean the barracks. The DI's wanted it their way. Some of the rookies had to use tooth brushes in the corners where it was hard to get at with the mops. I'll never forget one DI. His name was Leland O'Herne. He was about 30, 5' 10" in height, with a black hair crew cut. He had a face like a bulldog with a thick neck. He lifted weights on his off duty times. His biceps bulged like balloons. He had piercing blue eyes that seemed to penetrate right through you, and in any confrontation with him it was always nose to nose. One day on the drill field he was addressing me in such a manner, nose to nose, when a wasp landed on his ear and stung him. I can hear him now as he ran off to the medics. I always wondered where that bee came from.

I wiped off the rug-cleaning machine and the associated equipment and put the windows down and so I could wash all of them inside and out. The log home was beginning to shape up. I took a minute and called Patty. She told me that she would stop over after work. She wanted to inspect the place to see how my housecleaning had gone. I had hoped that there was no dust hiding for her to find. After I finished our conversation, I put the cleaning machine into the rear of the Bronco and took it back to the hardware store. I thanked the clerk and told him that it had worked well.

I then drove down to the post office and rechecked my box. The only thing there was a hunting and fishing magazine and some advertisements. I nodded to some of the folks outside the building and got back into the Bronco. I stopped at the Big M and picked up a head of cabbage, rolls, milk, and bread and butter pickles. The parking lot was jammed with cars and pickup trucks. One could tell it was Friday evening.

Oncoming traffic was streaming into Old Forge from the south. I sat patiently waiting for it to pass. Finally, my left-hand turn was accomplished. I pulled up in front of the house and shut the Bronco off. It coughed and then it finally shut off. It was time for a tune up. I got out with my groceries, went inside, and put them away. I then went into my office and observed the flashing light on the answering machine. I hit the button to play the messages.

"Jason, this is Luther Johnson up Star Lake way. Call me."

I dialed Luther's telephone number.

"Hello," Luther answered on the third ring.

"Luther, this is Jason Black returning your call," I said.

"The owner of that trucking company has been around Star Lake and Cranberry Lake. He is driving a black Lexus. I believe it's a rental. I heard that he is staying at a motel in Tupper Lake. The rumor is that he has a couple of Carver cruisers in a boathouse, which is located near Waddington."

"Anything else, Luther?" I asked while quickly taking notes.

"He has been in the local bars telling people that he is going to take fishermen out in the St. Lawrence to fish. Apparently he's going to advertise this fishing trip venture to the general public. He is also buying drinks for everyone. He gives the impression that he is just an all around good guy. I was sitting in one of the bars and I got a good look at him. I don't like this fellow. He's up to something. I got a good sixth sense about people," he added.

I couldn't tell Luther everything that was going on with Bernie Draper because it was an ongoing criminal investigation by the state troopers, but Luther was on target. Draper got along well with people as a con-artist capable of deceiving the unsuspecting. I remembered what my friend, Major Frank Temple, had said to me during the abduction of Patty the previous year. He warned me not to cross the line from private investigation to police investigation. Since that time I had been careful not to disappoint my former boss.

I had made a citizen's arrest of Jewell Norris and turned him over to the troopers. I remember well how frightened he looked when I pointed my 9mm Smith and Wesson semi-automatic pistol in his face. I had wanted to confront him for what he and Ted Clovis had put Patty through. Clovis met his maker when he was catapulted through the windshield into an oak tree during a high-speed pursuit by the police. Some memories are impossible to erase.

I knew that Lieutenant Doyle's undercover people would be apprised of Bernie Draper's presence and activities. Luther had furnished me with information that was already known to the troopers. I wondered to myself how Ruben was doing in his refresher training process. I reminded myself that Russ Slingerland was one of the top shelf dog trainers in the State.

I checked the house over to make certain that everything was in place. I was satisfied that all was squared away.

When Patty pulled in, I was outside raking up some small limbs that had fallen from the trees. She blew the horn and brought the Jeep to a sliding stop right in front of me. She had one of her warm smiles on her face. I put the rake against the tree, and walked over to the driver's side of the Jeep, and opened the door. She slid out and threw her arms around my neck.

"Hey!! Wha…What are you doing?" I asked.

"I love you, you big lug. I'm just in a happy mood. After all, standing on my feet all day is not exactly my favorite activity, especially when I'm toting trays of hot steaming food and beverages, but I do it. Of course I love the people I serve, and that makes for a good day, every day."

"Guess you've got a point there, sweetheart."

We embraced and kissed each other.

"Where's Ruben?" she asked, looking around.

"I thought I had mentioned it to you. He went to a dog-training kennel in Saranac for a refresher course. I know one thing: I miss him very much," I said dejectedly.

"Oh, I'll miss him, too." She adored my canine companion.

"Are you all set for tomorrow evening? Don't forget, we have to meet Wilt at the dock of the Old Forge Lake Cruises at 4:30 p.m.," I reminded her.

"All set, Sherlock. I'm really looking forward to it."

"Hungry, honey?" I was famished.

"Yes, I am. What are we going to have?"

"Let's go inside. I've got some hot dogs and some baked beans, and I'll cut up some coleslaw."

"You're making me hungry. I'll set the table while you prepare the food."

"Okay, honey. I'll take care of that."

While Patty scurried around the kitchen I took a head of cabbage, shredded it finely and mixed it with some mayo, sugar, vinegar and my favorite other ingredients. I added some shredded carrot for color, then some salt and a little pepper. I mixed it thoroughly and placed it in the refrigerator to chill. I then took a rectangular baking dish from the cupboard, opened the can of baked beans, and spooned them into the dish. I added brown sugar and diced bacon to the beans and mixed them well, then placed three strips of lean bacon on top of the beans and sprinkled more dark brown sugar on top with Worcestershire sauce. The beans alone would be wonderful, but I always liked to doctor them up, especially for my special guest, my future wife, Patty. I placed them in the oven at 350 degrees.

I looked across the kitchen as Patty set the table. Her blond hair flowed onto her shoulders and went well with her soft blue denim shirt and jeans. She turned and looked at me. Again we approached each other and I held her close to me. Our lips met again.

"Patty, what would you like to drink?" I asked as I held her.

"Iced tea. Do you have some?" she asked.

"I certainly do, my dear."

I went to the cupboard again. On the second shelf were my tall glasses. I took two of them out of the cupboard, set them on the counter, and filled them. The ice made a crackling sound when I added the tea. My next step was to take the hot dogs with natural casings and place them on my small grill. They sizzled as they cooked, bursting in the middle. I opened the oven and checked the beans. The good smell filled the room and teased our taste buds.

"Jason, the aroma of the beans. . . . I'm getting hungry."

"Me, too, babe. It won't be long before we eat. Will you get the two candles and light them, please?"

"Jason, you're so romantic. I didn't see that in you when we first met." She blushed as she reached into the cupboard.

"I had promised myself that I'd never get serious again about anyone, but now see what you've done: you've worked your way into my heart."

"You're something, Jason." She giggled.

"Guess we're all set to chow down, as they say in the Marine Corps."

Patty lit the two beige candles and they flickered. Everything was ready to serve: hot dogs split in the center from the hot grill, steaming baked beans, and chilled coleslaw. I cut several slices of dark brown bread and poured more ice tea. For dessert, we decided on canned peaches. I seated Patty and then I sat down. I said grace to thank the Lord for our food and for Patty, too. The candles flickered and Patty's eyes sparkled like diamonds in the candlelight.

"Jason, these hot dogs are excellent. This is the first time I've had baked beans fixed this way. They are also delicious." She clearly was enjoying the meal.

"Yes, they are excellent," I said proudly. I knew that my brown sugar helped to make them super special.

"I hope you tell me what is in your secret dressing that you used in the coleslaw. It truly is a treat." She always loved to give me kudos.

"Well, maybe someday after we're married," I said jokingly. I had stumbled on the ingredients just by luck.

By the time dinner was over, our appetites were fully satisfied. I got up and cleared the dishes, then I took two biscuits, heated them, cut them in half, and put some sweet butter on each half before covering the biscuits with sliced cold peaches. I went to the refrigerator, and removed the bowl that I had previously prepared, and topped each dish off with a dollop of whipped cream. Patty poured two cups of green tea. The dessert made our meal complete and our tummies full. We sat at the table for almost a half-hour talking about Ruben, our future wedding plans, etc. We ran into a dilemma in selecting our best man. Charlie Perkins, Dale Rush, Jack Falsey, Wilt Chambers and Jack Flynn had all indicated that they were looking forward to the honor of best-man status.

Patty cleared the table and I started the dishwater.

"Jason, why don't you have an automatic dishwasher? It would be so much easier for you—and for your future wife, I might add," she said jokingly.

"Honey, private investigators in this region do not make a lot of money."

"You don't need one now, but later on you could think about it. I'll help you with the cost," she said playfully.

"I can't let you do that, sweetheart." I thought for a moment. "We'll consider it after we're married."

"I'm looking forward to tomorrow night. Old Forge Lake Cruises puts on a terrific buffet, from what I hear around town."

"I am, too. I went last year and they had a wonderful selection. I really enjoyed the experience."

After the dishes were done and the kitchen put back in order, we took a long walk into the woods adjacent to my log home. The smell of pines permeated the air and the green leaves moved on the maple trees as a breeze came in from the north. Four mallard ducks swooped over the trees, headed toward Third Lake.

We took the trail that Ruben and I traveled a great deal. The K-9 and I had been stalked in the past by a large black bear. It was hoped that he had moved to another region of the forest.

Patty and I saw the coon at the same time. I wondered if it was the same raccoon I had seen earlier near my home. We noticed that the coon was moving slowly and seemed to be sickly. Tonight the coon seemed to be moving even more slowly. There was something about this animal that didn't seem right. Patty and I stopped to watch as it moved away from us. I told Patty that I would let the local game warden know that a sick coon was in the area. There was always the scare of rabies, a virus disease of the nervous system of warm-blooded animals, which could be transmitted through the bite of a rabid animal, according to *Webster's Dictionary*. I knew that I didn't want to be bitten and I didn't want Patty or anyone else to suffer from rabies, as it can be fatal to the victim and requires a series of painful injections to combat it after the bite. Patty and I turned around and went in another direction.

We returned to my log home just as the sun was going down over the nearby mountain. I have always been in awe of the beautiful Adirondack sunsets. I asked Patty to come in and we'd pop some popcorn, but she declined.

"Honey, I have to be at the diner early in the morning. You know we'll probably be up late tomorrow night. You understand, don't you, sweetheart?" she added.

"I understand, dearest."

I took her in my arms and our lips met. I didn't want to let her go home, but I knew she needed her rest. We'd be married in the near future and then things would be different. We'd go home together all the time.

"You know, honey, if that coon had turned and attacked and if it was rabid we could be bitten. I've also heard that the rabies shots are difficult to take." She looked worried.

"Yes, as I said, they can be painful," I replied. I didn't want to frighten Patty, further. I was glad that the animal had walked on away from us.

"I know, Jason. I understand your concern."

I opened the door of the Jeep and helped her in. I leaned through the window and gave her a peck on the cheek. Patty started the vehicle, backed around, and left the driveway. I stood there until she went out of sight. I looked around at Ruben's dog run. I really missed him. I walked inside, locked the doors, and went into my office to write up a couple of bad check cases. I went to the bathroom after I finished my office work to brush my teeth, then got ready for bed with a good book. I called Patty from my bedside and we talked a few minutes. I then read until I fell off to sleep.

CHAPTER TWENTY-TWO

While Jason Black slept in his log home in the Old Forge, New York area, about seventy miles northwest, as the crow flies, just going on duty were two elite undercover officers of the state troopers. Ed and Smiley worked well together and had covered many undercover assignments during their career. It was dark inside their old pickup truck. Lieutenant Jack Doyle, under the command of Captain Roy Garrison, had been sanctioned to select the two undercover people for this sensitive assignment.

Ed was looking through a pair of infrared binoculars. He was watching the new Southwestern Jewelry Store and warehouse east of Cranberry Lake. On this night there was no moon showing, nor stars. Heavy clouds added to the black of night. The store closed at 9:00 p.m., and Ed could see the workers leave one by one. The Draper organization had hired local people. It was believed that the employees were not involved in any criminal activity themselves, but that the warehouse contained other items that didn't coincide with the store's inventory. Intelligence had been developed that drugs and other contraband were to be stored in the warehouse until they were to be smuggled into Canada by the Draper organization. The undercover personnel were gathering all the information they could. Ed and Smiley knew that it would take many hours of patience on their part to successfully complete this assignment. They were not strangers to the newly constructed warehouse attached to the store. Both had painted the exterior and interior and had made themselves more than acquainted with the layout of the building. They were familiar with the storage area for the jewelry store and the storage area in the warehouse. They had taken photographs of the interior and exterior of both areas. Sophisticated equipment was in place to record all events that would take place in both the warehouse and the store. Extra caution had to be used by both of the operatives, as their bearded faces were known to the Draper employees. Now, minus the beards, but still with glued on mustaches and wire-rimmed glasses, they carried on their monitoring.

It was approximately three a.m. when a large white semi-trailer outfit wheeled into the yard of the warehouse. Ed and Smiley heard the roar of the diesel engine and the hiss of the air-brakes as the big rig came to a stop. The driver backed the rig into the docking area and then turned the engine off. The driver and his passenger got out of the cab, and in a minute or two the large overhead doors went up, permitting their entrance into the warehouse. Ed's infrared binoculars were focused on the dock and the rear of the trailer. Smiley's binoculars were pressed against his face, also monitoring the actions of the two men.

The driver broke the seal on the trailer and the rear doors were opened. The other man started a forklift and drove into the trailer. He then backed out with several wooden and cardboard boxes, set on a pallet. He backed the forklift, turned to the right, and moved the pallet to the corner of the warehouse. Ed noted that on the wooden boxes were stamped twenty-five oil paintings. There were five cases, all with the same printing. Ed could not determine what was printed on the cardboard boxes. He noted that the trailer was refrigerated, the motor on the refrigerator unit could be heard. He also noted that the remainder of the load was frozen orange juice from a company in California. The driver closed the trailer doors and affixed another seal.

The two undercover operatives sat motionless in the old pickup. Ed looked at his partner.

"Smiley, time for some coffee."

"Yep! I could stand a cup. Hope you didn't make it too strong, partner."

"No, I cut down on the spoonful of decaf."

Ed reached behind the seat and brought up a thermos of decaf coffee and a plastic bag of apple fritters. He unscrewed the cap on the thermos and poured out two cups. He gave Smiley a fritter, keeping another out of the bag for himself, and the two of them munched them down.

"Ed, they're delicious." Smiley smiled.

"I love these fritters. They have put plenty of apples in them."

Undercover operatives have to use caution. Ed and Smiley always reside in a small rented apartment within a fifty-mile radius of the focus of their investigation. The exact location is unknown to anyone, with one exception: Lieutenant Jack Doyle. Doyle is adamant about his responsibilities as second in command of his BCI unit.

Ed and Smiley finished their coffee and fritters and continued their observation of Draper's business complex. The night was black, and the only thing that could be heard was an owl in the distance. They continued to observe the building. All of a sudden a dark-colored sedan wheeled into the yard of the warehouse.

CHAPTER TWENTY-THREE

I heard the telephone ring. Pushing the covers back, I reached over for the telephone. I lifted the receiver.

"Good morning," I said.

"Hello, Sherlock. How's my sweetheart this morning?" Patty's voice was soft and gentle.

"Patty, thank you for calling. I didn't set the alarm, and Ruben isn't here to wake me up. I should have been up an hour ago. Thanks for calling."

"You need your rest, Sherlock," she said with concern.

"I know you're right. Sleep is important."

"I'll be getting out of work at about 1:00 this afternoon and thought I'd spend an hour or two cleaning my house. What time are you picking me up?"

"Hon, I'll pick you up at about 4:00 p.m. We should have a good time on the cruise. Have you seen Wilt this morning?"

"He was waiting at the door when I opened up this morning. He asked me if you'd be in."

"Okay, Patty, I'll see you later. I love you. Bye, babe."

"Me, too! See you later. Bye, hon."

There must have been a group of customers sitting around the telephone at the diner, or Patty would have talked longer. She must have been busy.

The water was cold at first, and then it warmed up when I climbed into the shower. I lathered myself with a bar of Ivory soap and then rinsed off. I tried some new shampoo to wash my hair. I noticed when I rinsed my hair that the shower head seemed to be leaking after I shut it off. I shaved and applied some shaving lotion. It felt refreshing. After I dressed, I wandered into the kitchen and took a bagel out of the refrigerator, cut it in half and put it into the toaster. After toasting it to a golden brown I spread cream cheese on it. The teakettle started to whistle. When I poured the hot water over the tea bag, I added a little lemon juice. The bagel was chewy and delicious. My decision not to prepare a larger breakfast was based on the fact that tonight we'd be having a super buffet aboard the Old Forge Cruise boat. I had better watch my intake.

I finished my light breakfast and was just about to wash the few dishes by the sink when the telephone rang. I went into my office and sat down in my comfortable swivel chair, reaching for the telephone at the same time.

"Hello," I answered.

"Jason, Jack Flynn here." His voice sounded anxious.

"How are you, buddy?" I asked.

"Payback time, Jason. Can you do me a favor?"

"Certainly. What's up?" My curiosity was aroused.

"I would like you to try and locate a Tina Belmont. She is thirty-six years old, about five feet two inches tall. I'm working for an attorney on a civil case relative to the natural death of a Louis Peidmont. This Tina Belmont is named in the will as an heir to Peidmont's estate, which is a large sum of money and property consisting of two sizable apartment houses."

"What's the relationship of Belmont to Peidmont?"

"She's his only niece. There are no other heirs. It's important that we locate her."

"Do you have a location for her?" I inquired.

"We believe she's in the Lake George area. She moved there about five years ago and since has of dropped out of sight. The decedent had been trying to locate her for the past three years, but his efforts were in vain. He expired two weeks ago from cancer."

"I'll see what I can do. If I can locate her I'll have her call you on the telephone at your office. Is that okay with you?"

"She may be working as a maid or doing waitress work and apparently doesn't have a telephone. She does have a college degree in animal husbandry. I suppose she could be working for a veterinarian. I'll send you a check to cover your expenses. Oh! By the way, Jason, our buddy at the Phoenix PD is making progress on the Draper case. Either Bernie himself or his cohorts killed those three Mexican Nationals. I wouldn't be a bit surprised that the three Mexicans found out that Draper was dirty and he silenced them or had it done. The police lab is doing some tests on the shell casings and slugs that were found at the scene of the triple homicide. I think it would be a good idea for you to have your SP contact Captain Silverstein."

"I believe Lieutenant Jack Doyle has already made the contact with him, but if he hasn't, I'll mention it to him."

"See what you can come up with on this Tina Belmont and let me know. I'd appreciate it. Have her give me a call if you're successful in locating her."

"I'll get right on it, Jack. Take care. Talk with you later. Goodbye."

"So long, Jason."

As I finished my chores, I dropped a cup and it broke on the floor. I went to the broom closet, took out the broom and swept up the pieces, putting them in the trash. Then I returned the broom to the closet.

It was Saturday, and tonight Patty and I were to meet Wilt Chambers at the dock in Old Forge. I was looking forward to the buffet and the boat cruise on the beautiful Fulton Chain of Lakes from Old Forge to Inlet and back again.

I checked my log home over carefully, making certain that everything was picked up. I decided that I would go to the post office before the noon closure. I put on my jacket that was hanging in the closet and went outside. I locked the door, walked over to the Bronco, and got in. But when I turned the key to start it, it backfired, loud as a gunshot. "What the—" I said out loud. "I'll have to check with my mechanic soon and have him check the timing." The Bronco had high mileage, but it had been a reliable vehicle.

I slowly drove out of the yard and onto Route 28. The Bronco jerked, but finally straightened out and the motor ran smoothly.

When I went by John's Diner, one of the major meeting places in Old Forge, I noticed that Wilt's big Dodge pickup was parked in the lot. I continued on to the post office and pulled into a parking space. I got out, went into the post office, and purchased a hundred stamps and fifty stamped business envelopes. The postal clerk was pleasant. I paid her for the stamps and envelopes, and she gave me a receipt. I then went out to the lobby area and opened my box. It was full of magazines and letters. I pulled everything out, went over to the table, and placed a rubber band around the mail. I nodded to several people I recognized and left the office.

On the way back home I spotted Dale Rush, who was standing in front of the Old Forge Hardware and Furniture Store. I parked just past the entrance and got out.

"Hello, Dale. How are you? Did you fly up to Lake Placid?"

"Jason, I'm good. Yes, I flew up to see Tom Huston and we had lunch together. We missed you, Jason."

"I wish I could have flown up with you. Maybe another time."

"Tom gave me the names, addresses, and telephone numbers of several men who wanted to fly into the remote areas the next deer hunting season. He also gave me a list of a few fisherman that enjoy the remote lakes. Both lists totaled about twenty-five people. I'm going to be busy flying those fellows around to different locations. I'll have to make several trips to get the job done, but it will be worth it."

"I'm happy for you, Dale. Can you imagine all the contacts that you'll be making? You're going to do all right."

"By the way, Jason, how's Patty? I heard that your wedding date is getting closer," he asked, playfully.

"She's been busy at the diner and helping her landlady." I ignored the wedding plan inquiry.

"I'm happy for you both. She's a great gal, Jason."

"Yeah! I know. I'm fortunate, Dale."

"Listen, Jason, let's get together again soon."

"We will, Dale. I've been busy with my check cases and other matters."

"I know you private investigators have to keep on the move."

"Yes, you're right. We don't get rich, but it's a healthy environment here in the woods."

"The Adirondacks is the best kept secret in the world." He spoke with pride.

"See you later, Dale. Good-bye."

"We'll be in touch. So long, Jason."

I went into the Old Forge Hardware Store and talked with Mike and Danielle for a few minutes. Sarah was at a meeting in New York City. I asked Danielle if she had any new mysteries on the shelf in the book department. She smiled and told me some had just come in with a shipment. I thanked them both and told them I'd be in soon.

Bonnie was near the entrance talking with customers. She nodded as I left the store. I nodded back and continued on. I wanted to speak with her, but didn't want to interrupt. I'd talk with her later. Her golden-colored dog was just outside the door, and people were petting the beautiful animal. I slid by the group of people and went to my Bronco. The Old Forge Hardware was busy today. I looked across the street and the Ace Hardware's parking lot was also busy. I was reminded of how good I felt about Old Forge.

The Town of Webb was a great township with a vast land area. When I permanently moved to the area I did a great deal of research at the Old Forge Library and the Town of Webb Historical Association. It was interesting to read about the area and the people who helped to make it what it is today. My exciting historical experience of peeking into the written words of yesteryear to the present contributed to my love for this area.

I drove home and decided to take a nap. I set the alarm clock. Before I drifted off, I went into the office and wrote the name "Tina Belmont" on my pad and the words "Lake George." I would check that area for her the first of next week and notify Jack Flynn of my findings.

Just before 3:15 p.m., I woke up. I reached over and turned off the alarm clock. I rubbed my left eye, which itched. Probably my allergies were acting up. I pushed the bedspread back to the bottom of the bed and got up. I went into the bathroom, threw some cold water on my face, shaved, and took a fast shower. After the hot shower and a cold one, I dried off and proceeded to get dressed. I was ready by 4:00 p.m.

I called Patty and she answered the telephone on the third ring.

"Hi, sweetheart. Are you ready?" I knew she was always prompt.

"Sherlock, I'm ready and waiting for my chariot. Will you be here soon, honey?" She sounded happy.

"I'm on my way. I'll be there in about ten minutes."

I checked the doors and windows and made certain the gas jets on the stove were turned off. I did miss Ruben, but I knew Russ Slingerland was undoubtedly taking good care of him. I assumed that Ruben would be as good as he was when he was previously on duty in Troop S. Ruben was one of the best K-9's in the Division during his service, and now he had another chance to prove himself.

The jacket I took out of the closet was Patty's favorite, a cotton one with "Old Forge" displayed on the back. It can get cool on deck, so I decided it would be wise to take it along.

The traffic on Route 28 was light and there didn't seem to be a great deal of activity on the street as I passed through Old Forge. Some tourists walked on the sidewalks window-shopping the stores. I scooted through this popular hamlet, eager to get to Patty's house. I waved at Chief of Police Todd Wilson as I met his patrol car. The chief waved back. When I pulled up in front of Patty's house, she was standing on the porch waiting for me. I tooted the horn and pulled into the driveway, then put the window down and hollered at Harriet Stone. She was sweeping off her front porch. Patty was already walking toward the Bronco.

"Jason, sometime I want you and Patty over for dinner!" Harriet shouted back.

"We would be honored, Harriet. Just let Patty know when, and I'll be there."

"We'll do that. You two have a nice time tonight." She went back to sweeping the porch.

I opened the door for Patty. "Hello, sweetheart," I said as she entered.

"Sherlock, you're right on time. I'm famished. Wilt went by a few minutes ago and honked his horn. He must have been heading to the boat landing. He seemed in a hurry." I could tell that Patty was bubbling over with happiness.

I waited for two northbound vehicles to pass before I backed out of the driveway. There was a small knoll south of Patty's driveway that required caution when backing out.

Patty slid over and sat next to me. She put her arm around my shoulder. She looked up at me and smiled. We were both happy, looking forward to dining on the water of the Fulton Chain of Lakes. Wilt Chambers was a good friend. He enjoyed playing the part of cupid in Patty's and my relationship. He had been promoting us as a couple right from the start. Wilt knew the problems that Patty had had with her former husband, Kenneth Olson. Wilt had been in the diner one night and left for home when he spotted Kenneth near Patty's red Jeep. Kenneth was not treating Patty as a gentleman should. Wilt hadn't said anything, but he'd wandered over by Kenneth and Patty and stood there with his arms folded.

"Patty, are you okay?" Wilt had asked.

Kenneth Olson had taken a look at Wilt standing there with his huge arms folded and had immediately left the parking lot as fast as he could walk. Wilt had stood by until Patty was safely in her Jeep.

When we pulled into the parking area of the Old Forge Lake Cruises, I spotted Wilt's big white Dodge pickup. He opened the driver's door when he saw us, with a big smile on his face. He was wearing new sport clothes, a pair of beige trousers and a dark brown shirt with short sleeves. Wilt had tried to have us join him previously on the dinner cruise. Now he had finally succeeded.

We both got out of the Bronco and walked toward the big-hearted lumberjack.

"Jason, Patty, you're right on time. Hope you two have a big appetite!"

"Good to see you, Wilt. Have you been waiting for us long?"

"Nope! I just arrived a few minutes ago."

"To comment about your statement, yes, we both are famished and looking forward to this buffet. We've heard so much about it from many people. Of course, Wilt, we are glad that the three of us can spend some time together socially."

"It's about time we got together!" His deep voice boomed.

Several cars pulled into the parking area. People got out and milled around the docking area as the crew readied for our dinner cruise. I recognized some of the people in the group, and nodded at several of them. Everyone was wearing casual wear and others were carrying jackets, as the night air cools on the Fulton Chain of Lakes. The people were beginning to form a line to board, so the three of us took our places at the end of the line. While I stood there, in the line, I reflected on my days in the Marines and all the lines that we were required to stand in: the chow line, the mail line, roll call line, payday line, and the line for the base theater. I couldn't help but chuckle to myself. However, this line, boarding the dinner boat, moved right along. We handed our tickets to the crew member as we boarded. I noticed all the tables set. The buffet was covered. The three of us went to the upper deck and took seats. I felt an air of excitement as we looked out over the Old Forge Pond while the dinner cruise boat turned and headed north into the channel. We looked over both sides and observed the camps and homes built on each side of the channel. You could see people preparing their evening meals along the shorelines.

When we left the channel and proceeded into First Lake, I could see two fishing boats. The fishermen were casting. They waved at the cruise boat and we all waved back. I noticed the fishermen were wearing jackets and headgear. One of them was pulling a sizable fish into the boat. A sheriff's patrol boat passed us. While he was patrolling the area, the boats observed the well-posted speed limit signs. When he was out of sight, it became a different story. Safety on the waterways is important and the sheriffs are there for everyone's benefit and protection.

Folks began to stroll down to the lower deck to be seated for dinner. I followed Patty and Wilt down the stairs. Once on the lower deck, we were guided to our table. We passed the buffet, now uncovered. It looked wonderful, and I knew that in a few minutes the three of us would be enjoying this cuisine. I seated Patty across from Wilt and then I sat down next to her. She was wearing her favorite turquoise bracelet and matching earrings. Her blond hair was flowing on her shoulders as she talked with Wilt, discussing current events. I continued to look at the tables and the people onboard the dinner cruise boat. Everyone seemed to be having an enjoyable time. I heard a couple of outbursts of laughter a few tables away from us. After sitting at our tables for a few minutes, people started to get up and make their way to the buffet. We joined them. The buffet consisted of a garden salad, chicken, beef, pasta, and rolls and butter. I was curious to see the size portion my friend Wilt was going to take. He surprised me, he took modest portions of each entrée. As his friend, I was relieved he was still working to lose weight. On his diet he had lost fifty pounds. One of his goals was to be able to get into a tuxedo for our wedding. He was making headway, and Patty and I were proud of him. He still had a long way to go. I was a bit uneasy, because Wilt wasn't the only one vying for the best man position. So were Dale Rush, Charlie Perkins, and Jack Flynn. Their expectations could present a problem in relationships and would have to be dealt with.

On the other hand, I certainly couldn't let Patty down. I was in love with her and she with me. My love for Patty was like none other, but what if our marriage failed? I could never go through the trauma of another divorce. Our decision to remarry had been made.

We spoke very little during our meal. It merited our full attention. I had a small portion of each of the offerings from this delicious buffet. For dessert, the strawberry shortcake with whipped cream was the finale to this excellent cuisine. The strawberries were bright red and the biscuits were light and warm.

"Jason and Patty, how did you like the buffet?" Wilt asked proudly.

"Wonderful!" we replied in unison. Our tummies were full.

"I thought you'd like it," Wilt commented.

"Wilt, Patty and I want to thank you for inviting us. I wish you'd let me help with the check," I pleaded.

"Nope! It's my treat. I won't have it any other way, Jason. You know me." He set his jaw. He wasn't going to budge.

"Both of us appreciate your generosity. Next time it's our turn."

Wilt had his camera with him, a small Kodak one-time-use 35 mm with 27 exposures. He asked Patty and me to stand by the upper deck railing. He took some pictures of us and of several Adirondack camps. Wilt possessed numerous photo albums on his bookshelves in his den at home. He owned several expensive cameras, but one time he had lost a 35mm Canon camera overboard when he was fishing on Indian Lake, so from that day on Wilt has used only the one-time cameras when he's on the water.

When we docked at Old Forge, after our cruise which had lasted about two hours, the Captain and crew thanked us for our patronage. It had been a great experience and most enjoyable dining on the Fulton Chain of Lakes in the great Adirondack Mountains of New York State.

CHAPTER TWENTY-FOUR

The paint sprayer was in operation at the O'Rourke boathouse a few miles from Waddington, New York. The two painters, Ed and Smiley, had just completed the back of the wooden boathouse. Mr. O'Rourke was standing at a distance so he wouldn't get sprayed. For several days Ed and Smiley had been scraping the weather-beaten gray wood. The paint that was being sprayed was a gray water-based one that covered the old wood well. The two men were not only painting the large boathouse, but were taking special care to observe the comings and goings at O'Rourke's, which once had been a very popular marina. In recent years, Mr. O'Rourke had decided to get out of the business and had taken down two of the three buildings that sat along the water's edge. Now he rented out only three or four spaces in the remaining boathouse. The only two boats in the rental area were the two Carver Cruisers.

It was mid-afternoon, and Ed was up high on a ladder using a brush to paint some trim. Smiley was taping some doors on the river side of the boathouse. Mr. O'Rourke had returned to his residence after giving the painters some lemonade. Ed, from his ladder, looked down and saw a dark-colored sedan approaching the boathouse. He talked into a small concealed microphone.

"Smiley, a black car is approaching. Looks like a Lexus," he whispered.

"Gotcha. Keep an eye on it."

"Will do."

The Lexus pulled into a parking area about a hundred feet from the boathouse. Two men got out and approached Ed's ladder. They were wearing fishermen's garb.

"Hey, you. Painter, up on that ladder. Can we go inside? We've got to put some fishing equipment on board one of the boats in there." The well-tanned man shouted up to him, "Mr. O'Rourke knows that I was coming today. I own both of those Carvers. I'm Bernie Draper." He spoke with authority.

"Yeah, go ahead, but be careful of the wet paint," Ed said, knowing full well who he was.

The two men went to the rear of the Lexus and opened the trunk. They took out a tackle box and four fish poles. Ed's eyes were focused on the two men and what they were carrying. In addition to the tackle box, they lifted out two large duffel bags, which had straps attached. Each slung a bag over his right shoulder, one picked up the tackle box and the other the poles, and they headed to the door of the boathouse.

"Be careful—watch the wet paint," Ed reminded them.

"Yeah, we will," the tanned man sharply replied.

"Are you fellas going out fishing today?" Ed asked.

"No, not today. We're just putting our equipment on board," the tanned man continued.

"Well, good luck, anyway, " Ed said, watching the men.

Ed and Smiley knew that the tanned man was Bernard Draper, aka Bernie Draper, the owner of the trucking firm from Phoenix, Arizona. They didn't recognize the other man with him. The two men went on board one of the Carver cruisers and spent about two hours on the docked craft. Ed couldn't make any observations, as the men moved around inside the cabin. Smiley, who was doing trim work on the water side of the boat house, had a bird's-eye view and could see Draper stowing the two duffel bags into a large locker. He could see him turn the key to lock it.

When the two men came out of the boathouse, Draper stopped near Ed's ladder and looked up.

"Hey, fella. When will you be finished with the painting?" Draper was probative.

Ed stopped spraying, but did not remove his mask. He looked down at Draper.

"We hope to finish up soon, but it's a little hard to tell when we'll be done. This is an old building and it takes a long time to prepare all those hard-to-get to corners. You know what I mean. Plus we had a lot of scraping."

"Yeah, I can see you'll be a while yet," Draper said in agreement.

"Well, take it easy. I've got to get back to work," Ed quickly responded.

The two men turned and walked toward the black Lexus. They entered the car. The unidentified man got behind the wheel, and turned the big car around, and headed out of O'Rourke's driveway. Ed turned the spray gun off for a minute and looked toward the departing car. He called to Smiley.

"Yeah! What do you need?" Smiley answered.

"What do you think, Smiley? I wonder what was in the two duffel bags."

"I could guess, but I won't," Smiley replied.

Ed shut his sprayer off and came down the ladder. He went around on the water side of the large boathouse and talked with his partner. Smiley had finished the trim and had brought his paint bucket and brushes down his ladder. They talked for several minutes, and then Ed left to make a quick telephone call to their boss, Lieutenant Jack Doyle, at Troop S Headquarters.

Smiley got his lunch bucket out of the old pickup before Ed left. He went around to the water side again and sat on the dock facing the Carver cruiser. He opened his thermos of hot coffee and took out his thick ham salad sandwich, which he munched down.

Ed stopped at a public telephone on Route 37 just outside Waddington and called his boss. He brought the lieutenant up to date on the events that had taken place. The undercover operative didn't mention any surnames over the telephone. The lieutenant indicated that certain information had been developed from other sources that the two large duffel bags did not contain fishing equipment, but an illegal substance. They talked for several more minutes and then hung up. Ed returned to the boathouse and his partner.

When Ed pulled in with the beat-up old pickup truck, Smiley was waiting for him. Ed got out of the truck and went around to the front of the boathouse with his lunch bucket. Smiley had finished his sandwich and was now eating an apple. They both sat down together and finished their lunches. The pieces of the Draper puzzle were beginning to take shape.

"Smiley, I gave the boss an update of what transpired today." He shared with his partner what he had learned from the phone call.

"Did he give you any idea of what's coming down?" Smiley asked with interest.

"No, he didn't. He just told me to be patient and that intelligence was gathering useful information concerning the Draper organization that would enhance our mission," he concluded.

"You told the boss about the two duffel bags?"

"Yes, I did. The lieutenant indicated that he was already aware of the two bags and a search warrant would be obtained. He wants us to pick up the Class C camper and plan to spend a few days here at O'Rourke's as two fishermen enjoying the St. Lawrence River."

"Sounds like a good idea. Hope they put some soda pop in the refrigerator."

"He indicated that it would be stocked with everything we need." Ed smiled.

"You're making me hungry," Smiley said.

The two undercover operatives continued talking for a while and then returned to their paint brushes. Mr. O'Rourke appeared on his front porch and watched the two painters transform his old boathouse into a showcase.

CHAPTER TWENTY-FIVE

Bernie Draper was confident that his new store and warehouse would bring him big profits. The southwestern jewelry and trinkets would catch the eye of tourists passing through as well as the northern New York natives. He swaggered around the store trying to impress his employees, but he didn't reveal to anyone the extent of the Draper organization. His lucrative businesses consisted of good and evil, mostly evil, but the good was identified by the donations he made to civic organizations and even to the poor and needy. In the front door of the store the customers would enter an elaborate gift shop. The items for sale were numerous. The selection of rings, bracelets, pins, western wear, artwork, and hundreds of other items were professionally displayed for the public. Sales were already good and would get better as the tourist season blossomed.

The large white semi-trailers that visited the warehouse were owned by Draper. The majority of deliveries were usually in the nighttime, when the store and warehouse were unoccupied. The salable items for the gift shop were part of the delivery. The other part of the delivery consisted of illegal items. It was the illegal part that was the focus of Lieutenant Jack Doyle's investigation.

In the southwest, Captain Jay Silverstein had fifteen of his top detectives looking into the triple slaying of three Mexican Nationals who had been found dead of bullet wounds to their heads. So far the leads had not resulted in useful information, but the search for evidence continued. Silverstein, always relentless in his efforts to bring a case to a close by arrest, kept digging as he pushed his detectives to the limit. The Phoenix Police Department had Bernie Draper under surveillance for numerous activities that did not appear honest.

Private Investigator Jack Flynn was in constant contact with Captain Silverstein regarding the Draper matter. Any useful information developed by Flynn and his hundreds of informants in the Phoenix area would be turned over to Captain Silverstein. It was believed that the three Mexican Nationals had learned of Draper's criminal activities and had met with Draper to shake him down for a large sum of money. When Draper met with the three men for the payoff, they were murdered. This knowledge was the result of Flynn's contact with his informants on the street. It was further believed that Draper was spending time in northern New York State until the heat was off in Phoenix. The hardworking Captain Silverstein wanted Draper, and he had no intention to back off his case, no matter what happens. Draper had many friends in high places in Arizona and had donated regularly to various civic groups. Nevertheless, Captain Silverstein was relentless in his efforts to terminate his investigation with the arrest of the perpetrators.

CHAPTER TWENTY-SIX

I called Patty on Sunday afternoon. We discussed the wonder-ful time we had had with Wilt on the dinner cruise from Old Forge to Inlet and back. We were both tired and decided not to see each other that day. I told her that I was going to take a run up to the Saranac Lake region the next day to see Russ and Ruben. I missed the K-9 very much and I wanted to check on him and make a cou-ple stops. Patty would not be able to join me as she had to open up John's Diner early on Monday morning. I told her how much I loved her and advised her that I would call her Monday night on my return from Saranac.

My office work was getting behind, so I spent the rest of Sun-day at my desk writing letters to banks, lawyers, and check passers. It was important to keep all reports up to date. At 11:30 p.m. I turned the light off over my desk. I could barely keep my eyes open. My throat was dry. I decided to relax a little, so lit the burner underneath my well-used teakettle. While the water was heating, I checked the windows and doors. When I peeked outside, I saw off in the distance two pairs of eyes low to the ground. I grabbed my seven-cell flashlight and pointed it in the direction of the eyes. As I'd suspected, two raccoons, who had been annoying me, were lurking out in the yard waiting for me to go to bed so they could climb a nearby tree close to my back roof. I muttered aloud, "If Ruben were here, my friends, you'd be *chased* up a tree." I pulled the window shade down and went to the kitchen to pour the hot water into my cup and inserted a green tea bag. I let it steep and then drank it slowly. When I was finished, I placed the cup by the sink and went into the bathroom. I brushed my teeth, put on pajamas, and went to bed.

It was quiet there near Bald Mountain, especially without Ruben. The only noise was that of the refrigerator and the tick-tock, tick- tock of the Big Ben alarm clock. I wasn't a part of the backroom board meetings of the corporate world. Nor was I in the running for a political office in the township of Webb or the county of Herkimer. I was only a private investigator trying to help out my fellow man or woman. Some of my work was interesting and challenging. I didn't like to work on marital cases, but once in a while I had to, for if I didn't, the lawyers would only hire someone else. My main reason for living here in the Adirondacks was to hold onto a sense of freedom and to stay away from a pressurized society as much as possible. I wasn't the only person who adored these mountains. People from all walks of life lived here, visited here, and were buried here. And I'm not saying that everyone is a pal or friend, but for the most part it was as close as you can get to heaven.

My eyelids closed. I reached for the light switch, turned off the light, and fell asleep.

I was on a roller coaster with Patty and our knuckles were white as we hung on tight. We were traveling at a high rate of speed down a steep decline and up an ascent. We left the track and shot into the air. . . . The ring of the Big Ben alarm clock ran down and I awoke, groggily. I felt my forehead; it was perspiring. My heart was beating rapidly.

The shower felt good as I soaped my arms. There's something about a hot shower followed by a cold shower that starts the day off correctly. Brrr. . . . The air was cold, too. I shaved and applied my favorite aftershave lotion. I finished drying off and went into the bedroom to dress. I had just slipped my trousers on when I heard a roar. It was Dale, just pulling out of a power dive when I looked out the bedroom window. At 7:30 a.m. I wondered where he was going.

I wanted to give Patty a call at John's Diner, but decided

against it. She had to open up early and, considering the time, I realized the place would be busy with locals starting out their day. Some would be going to carpenter jobs, many working on lakefront properties. I knew so many of these hardworking people, especially the group that frequented John's. I could see that Jack Falsey would be checking over his big van work truck. Jack had a busy schedule. Water pumps had to be replaced or repaired, furnaces needed tending to, and camps had to be maintained. Electric pumps are important here in the Adirondacks, especially if you have your own water well. Jack took over the business from his father, and he was very fair with his customers. One thing I knew about Jack—or, rather, two things I knew: he was his own man, and you could count on him to be there if you needed him. I had added Jack Falsey to the list of potential best men for our wedding. Patty and I still hadn't figured out a way to have all of them as best men for our special day. We wanted to be fair in the selection process. Maybe we'd have the whole list placed in the best man status. Although Patty had many friends, she had decided that Lila would be her matron of honor.

I still hadn't figured out why Dale had dived over my log home. I was halfway to Long Lake when I decided that I would have breakfast at Gertie's Diner, which was on the way. When I drove through Blue Mountain and passed the Adirondack Museum, I noticed many cars and other vehicles in the vast parking area. It was always a great place to visit, to view the documented history of the region. Over the years many donations have been made to the museum, including all types of boats, canoes, and other craft. Visitors travel hundreds of miles to visit this beautiful well maintained museum.

Traffic was medium this morning, and when I pulled into the parking lot of Gertie's Diner I found it crowded. I was able to squeeze the Bronco in between two campers. As I got out I barely made it without tearing a button off my jacket. The seaplane across from the diner was about ready to take off with its passengers. The pilot revved up the powerful engine and headed into the middle of the lake. I stood there for a few minutes, as I often have in the past, watching this mechanical bird with floats climb over the surrounding mountains. "Heaven on earth." I said to myself.

When I entered Gertie's I saw her husband, Bob, behind the counter flipping some flapjacks. Gertie was making two pots of fresh coffee. The one and only waitress was carrying a large order to a table. People were chattering. The place was really alive this morning. Gertie looked up.

"Jason Black, good to see you back again. How are you?" she asked.

"Hello, Gertie! I'm feeling fine. Good to see you both," I answered. "Hello, Bob, it's been a long time since I've seen you at the grill flipping flapjacks."

"I am glad to see you, Jason. Yes, Gertie's keeping me busy this morning."

"I've missed you several times."

"Yeah, I know. Maybe we can sit down sometime and talk about old times."

"We will, Bob." I moved on to a corner table, the only empty one in the diner.

The waitress had just delivered an order of French toast to a table close by. She came to my table next.

"Jason, I can finally take your order. We have been busy this morning. What would you like?"

"Tess, I'm going to have a Western omelet with home fries and rye toast and a cup of hot tea." I was famished.

"Would you like some juice?

"I'll have a small glass of cranberry juice for a change."

"Coming right up, Jason." Tess was an excellent waitress.

I glanced at a copy of the *Albany Times Union*. I read an editorial about the proposed clean up of the Hudson River, after it had been used as a dumping ground for PCB'S. This condition was caused by a large corporate company using the river to eject their industrial waste. I could imagine that many beautiful natural places throughout the United States continued to be used for such purposes, with large civil settlements taking place behind closed doors. I put the paper on the other chair, for Tess was approaching with my breakfast.

"Here we are, Jason. I hope you're hungry."

She set the plate down before me, along with the juice and the tea. The Western omelet was hot and steamy with nicely browned home fries on the side. Butter dripped off the rye toast. Everything was served fast and hot, just the way I enjoy my food.

"Thank you, Tess. Sure looks good!" I picked up my fork.

"Enjoy, Jason."

I wished that Patty was with me this morning; however, I knew she was busy at John's taking good care of her customers. We could have shared the omelet, as it was large enough for three people. Tess stopped at my table with another pot of hot water and a tea bag. I let it steep for a few minutes and sipped it slowly. After I finished, I took the check to the cash register, leaving the gratuity on the table for the waitress. Gertie met me at the register.

"Was everything okay, Jason?" she asked with a big smile.

"Everything was delicious, Gertie. How have you been?"

"I'm keeping busy, Jason, and so is Bob." They both worked hard. "How's Patty and that Ruben?"

"They're both fine, Gertie. The next time Patty and I are in Long Lake, we'll stop in for lunch, or if it is early, for breakfast."

"Tell Patty we were asking for her. By the way, when are you two going to tie the knot?" She smiled, knowing that it was a too frequently asked question.

"We don't have a date set yet, but you're on the invitation list." There goes that question again.

"Bob and I are looking forward to it. Take care, Jason."

"See you later. Be careful."

I waved at Bob and left the diner. Across the lake I saw the seaplane just getting ready to land. I went to my Bronco and got in.

Route 30 to Tupper Lake was busy. Two log trucks were holding up traffic. I gave these fellows all the room they needed. They were independent loggers and if the truth were known, they undoubtedly didn't like the slowed traffic any more than I did. I was scheduled to meet Russ Slingerland in Saranac, but there was a possibility that he could be at the Tupper Lake trooper barracks with Ruben. If that was the case, I wouldn't have to drive on to Saranac. I was behind the loggers all the way on the drive into Tupper Lake. At the troopers' barracks I saw Russ's vehicle in the parking area. I pulled into the rear of the barracks and there he was. Ruben was standing by Russ, and upon seeing the Bronco, he started barking eagerly and pulling on the leash. Russ had a struggle to hold him. I climbed out and walked over to them. Ruben's tail was wagging back and forth. He was salivating in his excitement to see me. I hugged Ruben and could see he wanted to play.

"Later, Ruben. Settle down, boy," I said, patting him on the back. "Russ, it's good to see you. How's the big fellow performing?" I was anxious to hear.

"Jason, he's doing fine. Ruben is on the ball. I can't go into it, because, as you know, his refresher course is confidential. What I *can* share with you is the fact that Ruben has been used on several drug cases and he hit every time on locating the illegal cocaine. As a result, several arrests have been made. We'll probably use Ruben for a couple more weeks, and then I'll return him to you."

"I'm proud and happy that he has been able to assist the troopers, even though it will be a short tour of duty."

"You can be proud of this shepherd. He's one heck of a good dog. He's been missing you, Jason."

"I know he has, Russ, and I've been missing him. The house is not the same without his presence and I don't sleep as well. But I knew that you'd take good care of him."

Russ and I conversed about the training of dogs for various duties and reminisced about the past. We talked about different people in the division who had made their final patrols, many whom we had both worked with. I noticed Russ checking his watch, and realized he must have a busy schedule.

Before I departed, I took Ruben for a walk on the leash. The big K-9 pushed his big head against my trouser leg. I reached down and petted him and rubbed his back and ears.

"You'll be home soon, big fellow," I said to him as he wagged his tail.

I wanted to open the rear gate of the Bronco and let him jump in, but I couldn't do that. Ruben had his own mission, and if his being away from his home and dog run helped put Draper and his organization out of business I, for one, was all for it. I led Ruben on his leash back to Russ and he put the K-9 into his vehicle.

"Russ, thank you for meeting me here at the Tupper Lake barracks. I hope I didn't interfere with your schedule." Russ was an accommodating person. I respected this man.

"Jason, would you like to stop for lunch?" he asked.

"I'll take a rain check, if that is all right with you. I just had a large breakfast." I declined, knowing how busy Russ was.

"Catch you next time," he said, walking over to his vehicle.

I went over to say goodbye to Ruben, then climbed into the Bronco and left the parking lot. Instead of heading to Old Forge, I decided to take a ride, as I wanted to look at the jewelry store and the warehouse myself. I loved this part of the country, inside the Blue Line. I did not appreciate anyone with criminal intentions coming into this region that to me was so unspoiled. Even though I was no longer with the Bureau of Criminal Investigation, my training with the state troopers would be a part of my life until I made my final patrol.

Approaching the intersection, I negotiated my right-hand turn onto Route 56 and viewed the warehouse and jewelry store. The parking lot was full of cars, many of which were from Ontario and Quebec along with several New York State registered vehicles. I made a quick decision. There was just enough room on the far end of the parking lot for the Bronco. Getting out was again a tight squeeze. My curiosity prompted me to visit the jewelry store. I wanted to acquaint myself with the inside. I knew it would be futile to try to gain entrance to the warehouse adjacent to the shop.

I couldn't believe my eyes. The store was much larger than I had anticipated. The carpet alone must have cost a fortune. It apparently had a pad underneath, as one could feel the comfort when walking upon it, and was decorated in a southwestern motif of cacti and various desert flowers. One wall tastefully showed an early western horse-drawn chuck wagon used when the cattle drives took place after roundup. It was beautiful and really established the western theme. I almost jumped when I walked around the corner and saw a curled rattlesnake pictured halfway up another wall.

Display case after display case contained Indian necklaces, earrings, rings for the fingers, and assorted jewelry pieces not common to the northeastern part of the United States. The store was crowded. Many French-speaking persons were apparently awe-struck with the elaborate display before them. Some could be seen pointing with excitement at specific pieces of the jewelry in the ostentatious displays.

The far end of the L-shaped store featured southwestern clothes and boots. There was a section for western belts and all styles of buckles. A big French Canadian man was trying on a belt about the time I passed, and he accidentally sharply elbowed me. He apologized in French. Stunned for a moment, I recovered and continued my vigilant tour of the Southwestern Jewelry Store. Oh, how I wanted to look in the warehouse, but it was impossible at this time. I did catch a glimpse of Draper talking with an Indian. I recognized him from the photo Flynn had sent me. I had noticed several Native Americans walking through the store. He was undoubtedly exchanging ideas about the jewelry business with them. Knowing that the St. Regis had gift shops, it would only be natural to talk about suppliers and compare prices on specific items. As I observed them talking, I couldn't help but wonder if he were making contacts to benefit his jewelry business. I continued on to another section, realizing that this Draper must possess some real savvy to have been able to create this store in such a short period of time. The interior decorative work was magnificent. But, I knew Bernie Draper had a dark side that his customers were undoubtedly unaware of.

I was shocked when I went down the hall to the men's restroom. Ed and Smiley were painting the trim around the door. I met them head-on, face to face. They didn't utter a word, nor did I. I used the men's room, and when I was washing my hands I couldn't believe the scent of the liquid soap. It was the same pine scent that I had noticed one time in Flagstaff, Arizona, when Jack Flynn and I had stopped at a restaurant after returning from a trip to the Grand Canyon. I dried my hands and left. When I went out into the hallway, Ed and Smiley, wearing their paint-stained coveralls, were walking out a side door with their ladder. I turned around to see where they had finished working. A small sign was attached to the wall that read "wet paint."

I just assumed that the Southwestern Jewelry Store and warehouse was bugged for sound. I longed to be back on the job, but I knew that the BCI had a good handle on the events that were taking place.

The cash registers were busy. I spotted Draper in another part of the store conversing with several of his customers. The jewelry store operation was a good "front" for his activities that were less than honorable. I was tempted to buy Patty a turquoise necklace, but not from this store. I pretended to view the display cases of jewelry. The aisles were crowded with people. One counter displayed a sign: "20% discount." I looked into the glass covered counter and noticed several watches with bands decorated with Indian symbols. The watches were catching several pairs of eyes. I hesitated momentarily, then moved on. I really *wished* that I could view the interior of the warehouse.

My sixth sense told me that Draper was shrewd. In order to enhance his smuggling operation, he had checked available properties and found a location suitable for his operation in an area that wasn't too inhabited. He had sent some of his people to our great state of New York. These people had mixed in with some of the locals in Tupper Lake, Cranberry Lake, Newton Falls, Star Lake, and other places. An uninformed observer would see a small business being formed in the area. I knew that Draper owned two Carver Cruisers housed in a large boat house near Waddington. What did Bernie Draper have in mind for our North Country? I wished that I had all the answers, but I had seen enough which certainly enlightened me as far as the "bits" and "pieces" from the dark side of this Arizona resident. I visited the restroom and then I left the store.

Walking slowly to the Bronco brought me close to the warehouse. The door was open. I longed to walk in and look around, but noticed a large sign with red letters: "Employees Only." I hesitated by the door, just standing there. Was it possible that Draper had a stash of weapons, drugs, or untaxed cigarettes and other contraband presently in the warehouse? I was tempted to take the chance, but I cherished my private investigator's license. The words of Captain-now-Major Frank Temple continued to resound in my ear: "Remember you're not on the job anymore. Your investigator's license could be in jeopardy." That had been last year in Temple's office. Reluctantly I continued my walk to the Bronco. I climbed in and drove around to the other side of the warehouse, where one of Draper's big rigs from Arizona was unloading large containers of freight. I sat there and watched the entrance for a few minutes. I was just getting ready to pull out on Route 56 when I chuckled to myself. I couldn't believe my eyes. Here were Ed and Smiley walking out of the warehouse, carrying two cans of paint in each hand. They passed right in front of the Bronco and didn't look right or left. I knew down deep that they had seen me there and probably wondered why I was parked near the entrance to the warehouse. They realized that in no way I would interfere with their ongoing detail.

I smiled as I pulled onto the highway and headed toward Tupper Lake. Today hadn't been wasted. I'd seen Ruben and knew that Russ was taking great care of the big K-9.

I'd had an opportunity to observe one part of the Draper organization, the jewelry store in operation, which added to my knowledge that Draper was in the process of readying a smuggling system into Canada. I felt good about what I had learned and what I already knew. I would contact Lieutenant Doyle in the morning to see if I could glean from him any additional facts concerning Draper. I could see that this case was complex in nature. The drug culture in the United States was obviously running rampant and the evil-doers were making millions of dollars. Draper's operation was only small potatoes compared to the whole picture, but it was significant enough to stir the emotions of the police in New York and Arizona and anywhere that the tentacles of the Draper organization reached.

When I came to the village limits of Tupper Lake, I encountered a load of logs. The big rig was doing the speed limit. I followed him to Route 30 where he headed south toward Long Lake. I didn't recognize the trailer, but when I reached a spot to pass the rig, I recognized Charlie Perkins from the Boonville area. I pulled along the side of the tractor. Charlie must have looked down and seen the Bronco, for he laid on his air horns. I beeped him back with the squawk of the Bronco horn, then continued on by him until I pulled off the highway about a mile ahead of him onto a wide shoulder. I stopped the Bronco and got out of the vehicle. Charlie hit the air brakes, turned onto the wide shoulder, and stopped. He put his flashers on. There was plenty of room.

Charlie opened the cab door and climbed down from his air-cushioned seat. He loved his Peterbilt rig. He was a ruggedly built man with broad shoulders, about five foot eight inches in height with dark brown hair. He walked toward me with a big smile on his forty-five-year-old face.

"Jason Black, how are you?" he asked, extending his hand.

"Charlie, how have you and your great family been doing?"

"We're all good. We had our share of colds over the winter, and my wife went into the hospital to have a toenail removed. But all in all, Jason, we're fine, and I'm paying the bills on time. Can't ask for more than that, can we?"

"How's the rig been running, good?"

"Sure has. I have to change the oil and a few filters. She's got plenty of power. And as you know I try to keep rolling along just about every day. I had to go downstate last week and pick up a load of apple bolts. I hauled them up to Vermont, where they'll be made into saw handles and croquet mallets. Once in a while I'm able to get a cord or two of apple-wood. I put it into the fireplace on Sundays and it certainly makes a nice fire. The embers glow brightly and the wood has a pleasant odor. We love it." Charlie cared deeply for his family and their time together.

"Oh! Charlie, you're so right. Apple-wood is great for the fire-place."

"Well, Jason, I'd better be getting down the highway. Hey! When you were on the troopers in your early days, did you come across many log book violations?"

"Yes, I did, but most of the truckers kept them right up to the minute. Why do you ask?" I was curious at his question.

"The other day I was pulled over up north on I-87 near Plattsburgh. The lady trooper was very polite. She checked my CDL and registrations and wanted to check my log book. I took it out of the case I keep it in and handed it to her. She opened it up and checked it over closely. Thank God I had it up to date. She asked me several questions about the logging business and then smiled and handed me back my log book. She thanked me and told me everything seemed in order. I thanked her for her courtesy and she was on her way."

"I'm glad to hear that the troopers are doing their duty."

"She also asked me if I was over the height limit. That's the first time a lady trooper ever stopped me. Let's face it, Jason, those folks are out there for a purpose and can you imagine what it would be like in this society if we didn't have our police forces?"

"It wouldn't be safe for any of us, Charlie."

"Well, Jason, one more question. When are you and Patty getting married? We're all waiting for the wedding." I had heard of course, that Charlie wanted to be my best man.

"Hopefully, later this year. You're on the invitation list. We'll let you know, Charlie." The question was beginning to grate on my nerves, but I tried not to show my annoyance.

"I'll see you later, Jason." He smiled.

I shook Charlie's hand and then we turned and went to our vehicles. I pulled out first. I looked back and saw him checking his tires. He was a fine gentleman. I knew I had a good friend in Charlie Perkins, and I also couldn't leave Wilt Chambers out. They were both good friends of mine and their friendship meant a great deal to me. I could imagine that Charlie wondered why I was in Tupper Lake today, but he's always been careful not to ask questions about my private investigation work.

When I passed Gertie's Diner in Long Lake, I didn't see Bob's truck. I assumed that he was in either Utica or Tupper Lake for supplies. I made a quick stop at Hoss's Country Corner. I checked the new books on the shelves and purchased a pound of their cheese. I chatted with Hoss and Lori for a while. I always enjoy stopping at their store. I have known them for years and visited the store on a daily basis when I vacationed there. Every time I'm in the region I attempt to contact them.

I stopped across the street at their custard stand and purchased a small vanilla cone. By the time I rounded the bend and headed up the hill toward Blue Mountain, I had finished the cone. My only wish was that Patty could have been with me. I thought of her all the time and hoped that she was having a good day.

Blue Mountain Museum had a full parking lot. I hadn't visited the museum this year and would tell Patty to add that to our list of things to do. When I got to the bottom of the hill I bore to the right onto Route 28 and headed toward Old Forge. I looked at the fuel gauge and saw the needle bounce between empty and a quarter tank. I figured I'd have enough until the next morning. When I passed Raquette Lake a number of boaters were coming in off the water. Traffic was light going through Inlet. Several cars and Class C campers were parked in the community parking area. I was tired as I drove into my driveway. I missed Ruben. I hoped that he would be completed with his trooper duties in a couple of weeks. I didn't worry about him, for I knew that Russ was watching over him closely.

I shut the Bronco off, and when I did, it sputtered to a stop with a "clink." I realized the timing must be off a little. I'd run it down to the garage shortly and have my mechanic check it over.

The first thing I did when I went inside my log home was to have a large glass of ice water. I squeezed some lemon into the glass and drank the water slowly. It quenched my thirst. Usually I take a bottle or two of water with me, but today I'd left in such a hurry that it had slipped my mind. I then opened the refrigerator and checked the contents. I could readily see that I had been neglecting my grocery shopping. I looked into the freezer. It was half-full of frozen meats. I saw a small package which was marked "three hot dogs."

I looked into the cupboard and located a can of baked beans. I removed them from the shelf along with the vinegar. I turned the burner on under my heavy cast iron skillet and added some butter. I put the hot dogs in the skillet and the beans in another pan. While the hot dogs sizzled, I diced some sweet onions. The aroma of the beans and hot dogs filled the kitchen. I quickly set the table for myself. When the beans and dogs were ready, I placed them on the plate with rolls and returned to the table. The diced Vidalia sweet onion mixed with the mustard on the bulging hot dogs, and sunk into the hot dog rolls: a tasty treat. The baked beans perfectly complemented the hastily prepared meal. I sat at the table and enjoyed every morsel.

After clearing the table and washing the dishes, I swept the floor. The absence of Ruben was difficult for me. I missed my big K-9 and would be glad when Russ returned him, although I kept reminding myself that the reason for his return to temporary duty in the troopers was of importance. Probably Ruben would be taken to various places where it was suspected that drugs were present. He would do his duty as a K-9 once more for the State of New York.

I hadn't yet gone into my office, or I would have seen the flashing red light on the telephone. Usually that's the first place I head for, but tonight a million things were on my mind. I pushed the play button. The calls were from Chief of Police Todd Wilson; Lieutenant Jack Doyle; Mountain Bank; and Patty. Patty would just be getting home, so I decided to call her first.

"Hello, sweetheart. How was your day?" I asked. I missed her.

"Today was hectic, Jason. I'm very tired tonight." She sounded exhausted.

"Patty, I don't think I could stand on my feet all day like you do," I said.

"Honey, I'm off tomorrow. Can we go canoeing?" Her voice sounded eager.

"Want me to pick you up?" I quickly checked my calendar to make sure it was clear.

"No, I'll come over to your place about 9:00 a.m.," she responded, waiting for my reply.

"That will be great. Would you like a little breakfast when you get here?"

"Okay! I'll bring some of Lila's sweet rolls, with the vanilla frosting, the ones you like. Oh, maybe I'd better not, we're trying to be good about our calorie intake," she added.

"That's fine, sweetheart! Bring them along. We'll do a little extra paddling to make up for it. By the way, I've got another call to make. Get to bed early because you're going to do most of the paddling tomorrow." I enjoyed kidding her.

"Oh! I am, huh?" She laughed. "We'll see about that."

"Goodnight, Patty."

"Goodnight, Jason." Her voice was soft and alluring.

I'd wait and call Jack Doyle and Mountain Bank in the morning. I dialed Todd's number. It rang four times before he answered.

"Hello, Todd Wilson here." His voice sounded authoritative.

"Hello, Chief. This is Jason Black returning your call. Hope I'm not calling too late."

"Not at all, Jason. I called to let you know that I spotted a black Lexus with Arizona Plates. I ran a check on it and it came back to a Bernard Draper from Phoenix, Arizona. Thought you'd like to know."

"Todd, how interesting. Was he just passing through town?" I was curious.

"No, in fact he stopped and parked near the post office, and he and his passenger, another male, walked around town for about two hours. They did seem to peer into some of the gift shop windows. I didn't approach them, nor did any of my officers. The driver who answered the description on the data had a tanned complexion, and I believe he was Draper."

"Of course, I don't know, but I bet your assumption was correct. The other could be one of his employees," I said, making a guess.

"Well, anyway, thought you'd like to know that we had an Arizona visitor in town. When they left they were headed north on Route 28."

"Todd, thank you for letting me know this. For your information I was up north all day. I'll fill you in when I see you in person. Thanks again." I liked Todd Wilson. He was a straight shooter and trustworthy.

After I hung the telephone up, I sat at my desk for almost an hour trying to put all the pieces of the puzzle together. There was no doubt in my mind about Bernie Draper. He put up a good front in Arizona, donating thousands of dollars to civic organizations and greasing the palms of some unsavory politicians and some CEO'S who had two major aims in their life: power, and the acquisition of money in off-shore institutions. From the information provided me from Jack Flynn, I had learned Bernie Draper golfed with these people and had spent hours on the greens at some of the plush courses in Maricopa County planning their strategies while dining in the club house, where they had no fear of being overheard by sophisticated listening devices. And because of Draper's polishing of the so-called important ones, he himself was welcome to join the highest of social circles and exhibiting his charming façade.

Jack Flynn had briefed me on Draper's divorce case. It was his ongoing affair with his mistress, Hilda Furman, that sounded the alarm that initiated the action by his wife Cynthia Draper, nee Roth. The Roth family was well off, having made their fortune in the traditional sense of hard work blended with honesty and honorable work ethics. Bernie had charmingly professed his love for Cynthia in the beginning, but from the get-go he had a dark side which often found him draped across a mahogany bar in a tavern with his mistress, red-haired Hilda. It was Bernie's own conduct that had destroyed his marriage with Cynthia.

I made a few notes and slipped them into my case folder on Bernard "Bernie" Draper. The clock in my office read a minute from 11:00 p.m. I turned the news on for a few minutes, then clicked it off. Without Ruben's presence my log home felt empty. I checked the doors. When I looked out, a doe passed by near the dog run. Even the deer missed my K-9. The security lights illuminated the yard. I turned the lights out in the office, went into the bedroom, and readied for bed. I knew I had to do some shopping soon. I was looking forward to seeing Patty. I wished that she were there with me.

CHAPTER TWENTY-SEVEN

As Jason slept, two undercover operatives were sitting in the cab of an old pickup truck. Ed and Smiley had slept most of the afternoon at their apartment. They had had one visitor in the mid-afternoon. Ed had woken up first when he heard the tap on the door. He had gotten out of bed, and slipped on a robe, and gone to the door. He hadn't opened it right away, but had looked through the peephole in the center of the door. He'd immediately recognized his boss's face, so he'd unfastened the security chain and opened the door. Lieutenant Jack Doyle had entered wearing blue jeans and a sweatshirt, with a big smile on his face.

"Hello, Ed," Jack had greeted him as Smiley had come out of his room wearing a gray-colored robe.

"Hi, Jack," Ed had replied.

"I want both of you to listen to what I have to say. This investigation, as you know, is a sensitive one, like all undercover ops. This Draper may give the appearance of a public relations guru, but he has a dark side that could mean trouble if he was ever cornered, so I stress: be cautious and extremely careful. I know that you were hired as painters for his operation, but if he ever found out the truth you both would be in jeopardy."

Smiley had spoken up.

"Boss, you know Ed and I are careful. We know what goes on inside of Draper's organization. When it's time to appear in front of the grand jury, we'll be there. We keep our eyes open, our ears listening, and our paint brushes moving when we're painting. In fact you'd be surprised how many local folks want to hire us to paint their houses and barns. Why, I even had one fellow approach me and ask me if I did carpenter work. We just told them that we're busy and we've got to go and paint all over the state." He had laughed. "I just turned around and kept painting."

"Smiley, I know that you and Ed work well together. Just be careful. Oh! By the way! The private investigator you met, Jason Black, it is his dog that we're using on the search over in Waddington. We just want to give this guy a little more rope. That's all I have to say. If you have to get a hold of me, call me on that private number. In your rounds tonight check out the jewelry store and warehouse and, if there is a delivery, try to write down the plate numbers. Take care and be safe."

"We will," they had reassured him.

Now Ed and Smiley, with their special binoculars, scanned the Draper jewelry store and warehouse. The only vehicle parked by the store was the black Lexus. A light was on in the office. The shadows of two individuals could be seen through the Anderson window. The shadows bounced off the inside walls. They were ghostly in appearance.

In about an hour, the two people in the jewelry store office turned off the light and exited the building. It appeared to Ed and Smiley that the man believed to be Draper locked the front door. Draper and the other person stood there for a few minutes and carried on a conversation by the black Lexus. Draper opened the driver's side door and started to climb in, then hesitated and apparently changed his mind. The men had further conversation and then, turning around, they walked toward the warehouse. Draper got his key out and unlocked the small entrance door, and they proceeded to go inside, leaving the door ajar. The operatives got out of the pickup and, keeping low to the ground, ran over to the front of the warehouse. Ed and Smiley peered into the dimly lit, vast warehouse and saw the two men at the far side of the building. It appeared that they were opening a wooden case. Ed and Smiley continued to observe the men. Draper held up what appeared to be an Uzi automatic weapon. He showed the weapon to the other man, who took it in his hands and examined it. Draper took back the weapon from the man and placed it in the wooden case.

As soon as the men turned around to leave that area of the warehouse, the two undercover men ran back to their pickup and climbed in. They were parked on a narrow lane, covered with bushes. Smiley grabbed his binoculars and quickly brought the two men into focus. Draper was locking the warehouse door. The two men then walked to the Lexus, got in, and sat there for a few minutes. Finally Draper started the car and turned out of the parking lot, headed toward Route 3 toward Tupper Lake.

It appeared to the undercover detail that Draper and his man had entered the warehouse and opened a wooden case containing firearms. The exact kind of weapon was not known, although the one they were handling was indeed an Uzi, which was probably going to be smuggled into Canada. Lieutenant Jack Doyle of the BCI already had intelligence information that Draper was about to smuggle contraband in his two Carver Cruisers within a month.

At about 4:00 a.m., the old pickup truck pulled onto Route 56, heading toward Potsdam and the apartment where the two dedicated painters lived. On the way to Potsdam, Smiley talked into a small microphone attached to a tape recorder. Smiley and Ed had made numerous recordings that were turned over to Doyle at Troop S Headquarters. The investigation of Bernard "Bernie" Draper was ongoing, and so far the two undercover officers had gone undetected by the rest of the population in the region. It was these two officers who would help to curtail the criminal activities of the Draper organization.

On the way to Potsdam, it was Ed who spoke first; "Smiley, I'll be glad when we close this case as far as our input is concerned. It is discouraging to see these crooks springing up in our society. The greed for the almighty dollar takes many down the wrong road, when they should be involved in activities that would make for a better lifestyle."

"Yeah, I know what you mean, but don't count on it. Can you imagine what life would be like if we didn't have police departments on all levels of government? I'll tell you, it wouldn't be safe to go outside. Crime would run rampant!"

"You can say that again. God only knows what the outcome will be."

"That's for sure. However, we can't get cynical. We've got to put these people away.

"We will."

Ed and Smiley soon reached their small apartment. The ivy-covered brick apartment house was unoccupied, with the exception of the rear apartment, where on his off duty time Ed caned some chairs and played his six string banjo with Smiley often joining him on the harmonica. The two undercover men, posing as painters, lived unnoticed in this small community. Empty paint pails were lined up in front of the garage. They both missed their families. When they were at the apartment, they took turns in preparing meals. Besides their expertise in the police profession, both were gourmet chefs. A few minutes after returning to the apartment, the two undercover officers were sound asleep. The dark window shades in each of their bedrooms were drawn to prevent the sun's rays from entering the rooms.

CHAPTER TWENTY-EIGHT

The knock on the door was loud. I stirred.

"Jason, Jason, honey, wake up!"

I was vaguely aware of Patty knocking repeatedly on the side door of the log home.

I opened my eyes and glanced at the Big Ben alarm clock. It was 9:00 a.m. Pushing the covers back, I swung my legs around onto the floor and stood up. I grabbed my robe.

"Just a moment." I rushed to the door and opened it for Patty.

"What happened to you, sweetheart?" She asked nervously.

"Honey, oh honey, I'm sorry. The alarm clock didn't go off. Guess I'll have to buy a new clock. Or maybe I forgot to set it."

"I was going to call before I left, but I thought you'd be up and raring to go this morning." Now that she knew I was all right, she had a big smile on her face and her eyes sparkled.

"My fault, dear. I'm sorry."

"Jason, I'll set the table while you get dressed."

"Okay. I'll just be a minute or two."

I went over to her, and put my arms around her petite body, and drew her close to me. Our lips met. Our passions were aroused. I looked into her eyes and she looked into mine. Maybe in part because I was still in my pajamas, we almost got carried away, but we held firm to our commitment to wait until our wedding day. Our hearts were beating rapidly. I went into the bedroom and dressed while Patty set the table.

"I'll be right there, Patty. I just have to comb my hair and brush my teeth."

"The table is set. I think you're going to love Lila's sweet rolls. She put a lot of vanilla icing on yours. She told me to tell you."

"They sure look good," I said when I returned to the kitchen. I was famished.

"Jason, do you want me to scramble you some eggs?"

"No, hon. This will be plenty." The rolls were huge and would be enough to eat.

I seated Patty. "Let's get started on these sweet rolls before they cool off." They were delicious. The green tea was hot and warmed our stomachs. We enjoyed the rolls, and the vanilla icing was sweet and tasty. Patty told me that she had had a good week at work, and she shared stories about some of the funny happenings in the diner. She told me that the majority of the customers, as usual, were wonderful, but that there were several grouches that demanded that their toast be lightly toasted and their poached eggs well cooked. When the food wasn't "just right," they sent it back. Then there was the almost deaf lady, a regular customer who comes in with her cell phone. One noon hour she was in the diner when her cell phone rang. The lady kept saying, "Hello! Hello! Hello! . . . I can't hear you! I can't hear you! . . . Speak louder! Louder!" Patty and I both chuckled.

Patty wasn't noticed only by the people she waited on, but other food businesses tried to persuade Patty to join their staff. However, Patty held firm; she thanked these other owners, but she had her mind made up to remain loyal to John and Lila and to John's Diner. When Patty had been abducted by the two Ohio killers and the massive search was conducted, it was John and Lila who offered to feed the search groups and who donated their own money to aid in this huge undertaking. It was John and Lila who offered to get Patty counseling because of the trauma she had endured during her captivity. Patty was a deeply loyal employee.

"Honey, before we leave, I have to make a couple of telephone calls. I'll be in my office for a little while."

"Okay, sweetheart. I'll do up these few dishes and straighten out the kitchen. Gee, it seems funny without Ruben. I bet you miss him." She knew I did.

"You bet I do." I missed him so much.

I went into my office and called Mountain Bank. They asked me to stop by and pick up some checks for collection. I told the administrative assistant, Mary Green, that I'd stop by the next day. I thanked her and dialed Troop S Headquarters at Raybrook.

After going through the receptionist, Lieutenant Jack Doyle picked his phone up.

"Lieutenant Doyle speaking. May I help you?" He spoke with authority.

"Jason Black, returning your call, sir."

"Jason, thanks for calling. Just wanted to give you a quick update on the Draper matter. Things are progressing well, and we'll be taking this fellow and his organization down in the near future. I had a meeting with our DEA people and the RCMP, as well as the U.S. Border Patrol and some of our uniform and BCI people. We're working on a plan to curb Draper's illegal activity, but we've got to get our ducks in a row."

"Sounds as though you're making some good progress."

"You understand I can't go into every detail with you, but it is through your efforts and those of your Marine buddy in Phoenix that we were made aware of this activity in our jurisdiction. Hell, Jason, you know the drill."

"Yes, Jack, I know the drill." How well I knew the drill!

"Oh! Jason, the RCMP people that attended the meeting know you. One was Sergeant Joseph Kelly. He indicated that he had met you at the Prince Albert Detachment in Saskatchewan a few years ago. He also told me that they flew you up to Uranium City and that some of the mounties took you over to Waskesiu Lake."

"Where is Joe stationed now?" I remembered him well.

"He's assigned to Cornwall, and he would like you to contact him, Jason."

"They're a fine group of folks. Yes, I'll do that." I often thought of Joe Kelly and some of the experiences we had had together working on difficult cases.

"That's it, Jason. If anything else develops let us know." Jack was precise with his comments.

"Will do. Take care, sir."

"Goodbye, Jason."

After I bid farewell to Lieutenant Jack Doyle, I quickly filed some papers in the cabinets and returned to Patty, who was sitting at the kitchen table reading a magazine.

"Honey, let's change our plans. I have got to go to Lake George on an attempt to locate Tina Belmont for Jack Flynn. In fact, it should have been done several days ago."

"Sure, honey, as long as we are together. I'm ready, Jason." She smiled at me and kissed me on the cheek.

We secured the house and went outside. Both of us climbed into the Bronco and I started it. I backed around and headed toward Route 28. We headed north toward Blue Mountain. I had a check that I wanted to drop off at the Eagle Bay kennel. We pulled into the parking area and I told Patty I'd be right back. I got out of the Bronco and went inside

"Lynn, I just want to drop off this check. I received your bill, and since I was driving this way, I thought I would drop it off."

"Oh! Jason, there was no rush. But I'm always glad to see you," she acknowledged.

I handed her the check.

"Thank you, Jason." Lynn was always so polite to her customers.

"Please say hello to your mom for Patty and me."

"I will, Jason, when I see her this evening." Lynn loved her mom.

"Thanks. Talk with you later." Lynn was very busy with other customers.

"Take care, Jason."

I held the door open for a customer with a huge St. Bernard dog. The animal was so gigantic that I had to wait until he was all the way into the waiting room. The dog owner thanked me. I went out and down the steps.

Patty was waiting patiently with a big smile. The large sun glasses she was wearing covered most of her face. She had just put on fresh lipstick. I wanted to kiss her, but the parking lot of the kennel was not the place. It would have to wait. We continued north on Route 28 and turned onto Route 30 toward Warrensburg. When we reached I-87, we turned south to Lake George. The post office wasn't busy in Lake George. I presented my identification to the postmaster and inquired about Tina Belmont. The postmaster smiled when I mentioned her name. He informed me that Tina had married a Clifford Harris a year or so ago. The two had divorced and Tina had moved away. The husband had made out a change of address form for her, which indicated only that she was some place in Laughlin, Nevada. I inquired as to the location of Mr. Harris and was informed that he still resided in his home on the outskirts of Lake George. I thanked the postmaster and left.

"Jason, did you locate her?" asked Patty when I got into the Bronco.

"I've got to do some further checking, Patty."

Patty and I drove to the edge of the village near I-87. The postmaster had indicated that Harris lived in a one-story wooden-frame white house. When we pulled into his yard, I could see that the front of the home was covered with ivy running all the way up to the eaves. The outside chimney of the fireplace was covered with moss. The shades were pulled down. There was a vintage Ford pickup parked in a side driveway. The place looked spooky. I told Patty to stay in the Bronco. I got out and made my way to the front door along a winding stone walkway. Some of the stones had heaved and were in need of replacement. I walked up on to the porch. There was no doorbell. I knocked on the front door.

I happened to glance at a window and caught a glimpse of movement behind the shade. Obviously the person was peering out at me. I knocked on the door for the second time. This time I knocked harder. Out of the corner of my eye, I saw a large rat run across the porch. I listened for movement in the house. I finally heard the sliding of several bolts as the person inside unlocked the front door. I peered through the front screen door laden with cobwebs and saw the door open. Before me stood a white male about forty years of age. He was wearing a bathrobe, and a parrot was perched on his left shoulder. He spoke first.

"What can I do for you, mister?" He was shaking slightly.

"My name is Jason Black. I'm a private investigator attempting to locate a Tina Belmont. Could you tell me where I can locate her?" I looked him in the eye and he looked down. I showed him my identification.

"What do you want Tina for, mister?"

"I have a message and a telephone number for her to call in Phoenix, Arizona, relative to a personal matter. Are you Clifford Harris?"

"Why do you want to know my name? Yes, I'm Clifford Harris. Tina and I were once married, but she no longer resides here. She has moved to Nevada. We're divorced." He couldn't look me in the eye. I could tell from his demeanor that this fellow was not telling me the truth.

"Do you have an address or a telephone number for her?"

"No, I do not."

"Does she have any family or friends here in the area that may know of her whereabouts?"

"No, she doesn't, mister." This fellow was a nervous wreck. He was not a sociable person. I had interviewed many people over the many years, and there was no doubt in my mind that he had a story to tell. I decided that for now I was through questioning Mr. Harris.

"Mr. Harris, thank you for your cooperation." I could see that his lower lip was quivering. "Take good care of that parrot." He must love birds.

"Goodbye," he said.

I walked back down the path and entered my Bronco. Patty looked at me with a concerned expression.

"Hi, honey. Let's get out of here," I told Patty.

"Were you able to locate an address for the party?" she asked, smiling.

"We're all set. The lady is now residing in Nevada."

I turned the Bronco around and we headed toward I-87. The scenic beauty in the Lake George region was eye-catching. Like many places in the region, the aura of the area captivated one's attention. It was common to see tourists taking pictures with their camera from the side of the highway. We continued our travel to Blue Mountain and south on Route 28 to Raquette Lake.

When we arrived at Inlet, the traffic was quite heavy. I didn't hear the seaplane's engine until it came over the mountain. Dale Rush was making a landing at Kirby's Marina. I asked Patty if she would mind if we stopped to see Dale. She agreed to see him, and we drove to Kirby's. When we arrived, he was coming toward the marina. We parked and got out of the Bronco. Both of us ran down to the dock. Dale cut the engine about thirty feet from the shore line. As the seaplane neared the dock, Dale, who had climbed out on the float, threw me a line, and I secured the Stinson.

"Hi, Dale. Good to see you!"

"Hello, Jason. Hi, Patty. I'm meeting a couple of fishermen here. Since you introduced me to Tom Huston, I've been busy flying fishermen into the back country. Some of these people are from out of state. They love to fish in our region."

"I'm happy for you, Dale. How's the plane running?" Dale was proud of his vintage seaplane.

"I just went through the engine and replaced some parts. It's purring like a kitten, " he said with pride.

"Just asking, buddy. I know how you feel about the plane."

"Jason, I've been contacted by a flying club from the mid-west and offered membership. They have about twenty Stinsons in the club. I'm thinking about signing up." I could tell that Dale was happy to be approached for membership.

"What time are your fishermen going to meet you?"

"I'm a little early." Dale always shows up ahead of time for his appointments.

We had exchanged conversation with Dale for about thirty minutes, when a green-colored Tahoe drove in and parked. Two husky fellows got out and were looking toward the plane tied up at the dock. Dale thanked us again, gave Patty a brotherly hug, and winked at me. His fishermen had arrived. We told him to have a good flight. While we watched Dale and the fishermen take off, Patty suggested that we rent a canoe from Kirby's and paddle for a while. I didn't like the idea myself, because of my past relationship with him, but wanted to please her. Kirby himself was out of town, therefore we rented the canoe from the attendant on duty.

I ran over to make certain that the Bronco was locked and to pick up my camera. Hurrying back to Patty and the canoe that she had already rented, I helped us push off from the dock, and we headed for the middle of Fourth Lake.

It was now early afternoon and we still had an ample amount of time to make it over to Second Lake and paddle back to Alger Island. We put the canoe into the water of Fourth Lake and climbed in. I paddled in the front and Patty took the rear position. The paddles were brand new. Kirby had purchased them from a local company in Old Forge. They sliced through the water nicely.

Myself, I had always tried to patronize all the business places around my town of residence, and generally they all met my needs. In this complex society with mass confusion at times, it was enjoyable to be in a region where civility was exhibited the majority of the time. Although there are many favorable places in this great country, Old Forge, Eagle Bay and Inlet are the ones that appeal to me. When the going gets difficult, there are those who will extend their goodness to help others.

"Jason, did you see that trout break water?" Patty was excited.

"I just caught a glimpse of it. Was it a big one?" I wished I had seen it better.

"It was a large trout—the largest trout I ever saw," she added.

"Are you getting tired, Patty?" I knew she was, but she had plenty of true grit.

"No, I've got plenty of steam left." She giggled.

We paddled to the entrance of Third Lake and then floated into a cove to rest for a few minutes. I didn't know all the answers to every tidbit of the Adirondack experience, but little by little we had gained considerable knowledge of the things that interested us the most. Sometimes we wondered about the stories we had heard, but generally we came up with the correct answer. I had been kicking around these precious old mountains since I was a kid. They meant a great deal to me. I loved the place and I knew that Patty did, too.

We finished resting our arms and started back toward Kirby's Marina. All of a sudden a wave-runner sped by us heading toward Fourth Lake in the same direction we were headed. The waves rocked our canoe so hard that we almost tipped over. Patty's paddle fell into the water. I hollered at the individual, but there was no way he could hear me. He was out of sight. I brought the canoe close to the paddle, reached over the edge of the canoe, and retrieved it. I handed it to Patty.

"Thanks, honey," she said, wiping the water from her face.

"No problem, sweetheart. I'd like to talk with that fellow on the wave-runner. He should have slowed down when he went by us." The operator wasn't a kid.

"He was just showing off, Jason. You know, that macho image persona!"

"Yeah! You're right. Someday they'll kill or hurt someone, and then it'll be too late."

We continued north on Fourth Lake to Kirby's Marina. We were surprised and pleased to see the same wave-runner pulled over by the Herkimer County Sheriff's boat patrol. The operator of the wave-runner was not saying anything. He sheepishly looked over at Patty and me as we paddled by. The officer was writing him out a ticket. Both of us almost cracked up with laughter, but we knew it could have been us—*if* we'd been speeding.

Alger Island was quiet that day. Usually it is a busy place with the lean-to's rented. We paddled around the island and then returned to Kirby's. When we were getting out of the canoe, the sheriff's boat patrol went by, heading toward Eagle Bay. I felt sorry for the macho man who operated the wave-runner recklessly, but we all have to learn that the laws enacted are for all of us, not just a few. The man had been out of order that day, and maybe the next time he took his runner out in the lakes he'd be more careful and operate it in a safe manner.

Patty helped me drag the canoe onto shore. I paid the attendant and we left for my log home. We discussed our day and talked about Ruben. Both of us wondered what the big dog was doing at this moment. When we pulled into the yard we were surprised to see Wilt Chambers' big white Dodge pickup. Wilt was just walking out of the woods. Both of us were puzzled. We pulled up beside his vehicle and got out. He was still a few yards from us when he spoke out in his husky voice.

"Hello, you two love birds!" He had a big smile on his face.

Wilt looked good. He appeared to be keeping his weight down and seemed to walk with a spring in his step. Both of us were very fond of this big logger. He was also a smart business man.

"Hi, Wilt. Good to see you."

"Jason, I've got a couple of things on my mind. First of all, I had stopped at John's Diner and learned that you two were seen up on Fourth Lake, so I figured that you'd be coming back here, especially because Patty would have to pick her Jeep up." Wilt was in a good mood.

I looked at the expression on Patty's face and she looked at me. We both broke out into laughter.

"News travels really fast around here, Wilt."

He looked surprised. "Gee, I hope you didn't mind me stopping."

Wilt was always welcome here. "Of course not, Wilt. We're just joking, buddy."

He loved a good laugh. "Jason, you've got two big white oaks in your woods. If you ever want me to turn them into lumber or money, just let me know."

"I will. Right now the answer is no. But I'll think about it. It's so peaceful in the woods." I could use some extra money, but the trees stay as they are, standing in the woods.

"Yeah, it is. I took a little walk down there while I waited for you."

"Wilt, would you like a cup of coffee?" I asked, changing the subject.

"I'd love it." He rolled his eyes. "As long as it's black."

"Jason, stay out here and talk to Wilt. I'll run in and fix the coffee for us." Patty offered.

"Thank you, sweetheart. I appreciate it."

I excused myself for a few minutes and called Jack Flynn in Phoenix. I told him that I had located the former husband of Tina Belmont, Clifford Harris. Jack was interested to hear this. He told me that they had already checked Laughlin, Nevada, for Tina Belmont, and the inquiry there with numerous contacts revealed that she never resided there in the past or the present. I told Jack that Harris seemed very suspicious and appeared to be a nervous wreck during my questioning of him. After we were finished talking, I assured him that if I developed any useful information I would call him immediately. He suggested that I should let the police know about this matter. I told him I would call Lieutenant Jack Doyle at Raybrook. We hung up.

I made another call, this time to Jack Doyle. When he came to the telephone, I shared with him all the information that I had. He told me that he would have the BCI of Troop H look into the matter. I thanked him and wished him continued success on the active smuggling case involving Bernie Draper. I rejoined Patty and Wilt.

While Patty was still preparing the coffee, Wilt took me over to the rear of his big Dodge. He opened the back of the truck.

"Jason, I picked up two good two-man saws for you at an auction. I paid ten dollars apiece for them. Remember, I do not forget your collection."

"Gee, they're in very good condition, Wilt. Thank you so much. I'll add them to my collection. As you know, I first became acquainted with these saws when my father was logging and pulping in the region many, many years ago. He always told me that there wasn't anything like having a good sawing partner and a good work day in the woods. He always emphasized that you'd be certain to get a good appetite and a good night's sleep after you finished sawing."

"Jason, my dad told me the same thing," Wilt said proudly.

"There's a lot to be said for the old ways of yesterday and a lot of pride in those days. The dollar went a lot further, too."

"That's true, Jason. By the way, it's been about a year since Patty's abduction. Remember that breakfast I mentioned a while back. Well, a group of us have got together and we're going to put on a breakfast at John's Diner, and Patty's going to be the honored guest. We'd like you to attend. Patty doesn't know anything about this as we would like to keep it as a surprise."

"When, and what time?" I asked, remembering that previous conversation with Wilt.

"Next Tuesday morning at 9:30 a.m.," Wilt said.

"Yes, I'll be there. Wild horses couldn't keep me away." Wilt was always thinking of other people. He was certainly a gentle giant.

"We want this to be a surprise, so Lila will take care of everything. Please don't mention it to her." Wilt spoke in a low tone so Patty wouldn't hear.

"That's great, Wilt. Don't worry; I won't say a word."

Patty opened the door and told us that the coffee was ready. I followed Wilt inside and we sat down at the table. Patty poured the three cups of coffee. We chatted about local events in town and in Boonville. Wilt told us about some of the programs that were being planned by the Woodsmen's Field Days organization. Patty and I listened with interest. He indicated that he was working on four chainsaw-carved bears. Wilt had received several orders for the bears from Tom Huston. Wilt's gift of a large black bear to Tom had resulted in a great amount of interest by guests at the lodge, which resulted in the subsequent orders. Wilt told us he was more than pleased and was grateful to Tom.

"Wilt, you should quit your logging operation and carve the bears full-time. It appears your hobby is growing," I said.

"Jason, I can't do that, for I promised my late father that I would not sell the logging operation. I have two nephews that will be in line to take over when I can't work any longer, but I'm destined to work until I drop."

"I know how you feel about it, and you have too much invested to change your direction."

"Wilt, I'd miss you at the diner." Patty chuckled with a big smile.

"Patty, it means a lot to me, stopping in John's Diner to see you and visit with all the locals I know. Sort of like family."

"Well, we think a great deal of you, Wilt. You have many friends in this town."

"Thanks, Patty. By the way, Jason, where's Ruben? I was surprised not to see him when I pulled in the yard."

"He's on a mission, Wilt. That's all I can say."

Wilt didn't push the issue. He knew that I would have told him, if I could have. We finished our coffee. Wilt gave me the bill for the two two-man saws. I gave Wilt two ten dollar bills. He put them in his wallet. I thanked him, and he thanked the two of us for the coffee. Patty and I watched Wilt climb into his big white Dodge pickup truck. He backed around and tooted as he headed for Route 28.

We watched him go out of sight. I turned and looked at Patty, sweeping her up in my arms. I then carried her into the house. When we got inside, I kissed her warmly, and sat her down on the davenport. We talked and then decided to watch some television. Patty wanted to pop some popcorn. I went to the cupboard, removed the jar of popcorn, and handed it to Patty. While she prepared to pop the corn, I went into my office and checked my schedule. In a few minutes, I heard her calling me.

"Honey, it's ready. I put some melted butter on it. Are you ready?"

"I'll be right there, sweetheart." I could smell the freshly popped popcorn.

We went into the living room and sat on the davenport. I turned off the television and decided to insert an Anne Murray CD into the machine, and turned the volume down. We took turns removing the buttered popcorn from the dish. Patty had salted it just enough. Delicious! We finished the popcorn, and I took the bowl to the kitchen. I returned to the living room. Patty motioned to me to come and sit right beside her. We both enjoyed Anne Murray's melodic voice and could have listened to her all night. We held each other closely.

At about 9:00 p.m. Patty left for home. I walked her to her Jeep. Before she climbed in behind the steering wheel, she turned toward me and put her arms around my neck. She drew me close and kissed me on the nose. I looked down into her eyes.

"Jason, I'll be so happy when Ruben returns to you. I miss him, too, and those gigantic ears that stand up straight when I pull in the yard." She reached over and gave me a peck on the cheek. "Honey, I love you so very much. I'll be glad when we're married."

My mind raced. I looked down at her beautiful oval-shaped face and didn't say anything. I was looking for the right words.

"Patty, I will be, too." She smiled and I held her close.

"Good night, Jason."

"Good night, Patty." I loved her so very much.

I told Patty to call me as soon as she arrived home. I watched her as she drove her Jeep toward Route 28. I then went into the house and secured it for the evening. I had been sitting at my desk

for about ten minutes when the telephone rang. I picked up the receiver.

"Hi, honey, I'm home. I have to open the diner at 6:30 a.m.
Goodnight, sweetheart."

"Thank you for calling. I'll talk with you tomorrow."

I had no sooner hung up then the telephone rang. I was going to
let it activate my answering machine, but instead I picked up the
receiver.

"Hello."

"Jason, Jack Flynn here. Sorry to call you so late."

"No problem, buddy. How have you been? How's Ruby and
Jay?"

"Everyone's great. I have hired five more operatives."

"How many operatives do you have now?"

"I've expanded. I have ten men and five women. Most of them
are retired from the Phoenix PD and a couple are from Flagstaff.
That way I have the State of Arizona pretty well covered."

"I'm happy for you, Jack. You deserve it. You've put a great
deal of effort into Flynn Investigations."

"Jason, you have no idea how busy it is out here. Hundreds of
homes are being built. Every Tom, Dick and Harry are moving to
Phoenix, including a lot of fine people, but we also attract the un-
desirables. I wanted to let you know that the Phoenix PD is closing
in on Draper. They are working with informants who know him.
It's just a matter of time."

"That's good to hear. The troopers here in New York are working diligently on this end to bring Draper to justice."

"Oh, by the way, we have added onto the shopping center, and
we have five new tenants. We have an office equipment store, a
dress shop, and a salad deli. For your information concerning the
Tina Belmont matter, there is something strange about her disappearance. I've had some of my operatives checking airlines, trains,
and buses for any possible information that she may have traveled
with their respective organizations. All these checks have been
without results. It is as though she dropped off the end of the
earth." His voice sounded puzzled.

"I'm getting the same feeling about it, Jack. I have notified the authorities, and if I hear of any information about Tina or her ex-husband Clifford Harris, I'll let you know right away."

"I'll appreciate that, buddy. Have to hang up now; I have another call."

"Talk with you later, Jack." I knew he was busy.

I forgot to tell Jack Flynn about Ruben and his recall to duty. I'd tell him in the future.

Getting ready for bed was a ritual. I brushed my teeth, then went to the refrigerator and poured myself a cold glass of water.

I went into my bedroom and pulled the covers back. Before climbing into bed, I went into my office and removed *Brady's Book on Checks* and returned to the bedroom. I climbed into bed and turned the lamp on the end table up another notch. The printing in the book is not large, and the brighter light was needed. I read the section on stale-dated checks and endorsements. Transactional crimes are a commonality in the world of banking, and it is important to refresh one's knowledge on the subject. My eyelids became heavy. I closed the book and placed it on the bedside table, turned the light off, and drifted off to sleep.

CHAPTER TWENTY-NINE

Ruben was tugging at the bed covers. I woke up with a start and looked down at the foot of the bed. But Ruben wasn't there tugging on the bedspread as he has so many times in the past. My dream seemed so real. I lay there in bed on my back staring at the ceiling. I mused to myself about my decision to live in these beautiful mountains in a log home, when I could be in Phoenix, Arizona, working for Flynn Investigations with the plush office that Jack Flynn had promised me and an air-conditioned condo. Instead, I had opted to reside here in the North Woods where the air and temperature range were more bearable and the population less crowded. No! For me I had made the correct decision. Patty and I would be joined in marriage in the future, and we'd have a comfortable existence, along with our K-9, Ruben. I pushed the covers back and got out of bed.

I showered, shaved, and dressed. I decided I'd do my washing at the laundromat and stop at Doctor Don's Garage to have the timing checked on the Bronco. After a cup of green tea and an English muffin, I went into my office and dialed Troop S Headquarters. The receptionist was very polite. I asked to speak with Lieutenant Jack Doyle of the BCI.

"Lieutenant Jack Doyle speaking." His voice was authoritative, as usual.

"Good morning, Lieutenant. Jason Black calling."

"Sorry that I haven't gotten down your way to see you, but you can imagine how busy we are with this Draper matter. It's going to be a joint operation with the feds and the authorities in Canada and our division people. I hate to tell you this, Jason, but I was called into a meeting with Major Frank Temple and Captain Roy Garrison. I'm not going to be able to have you there when this goes down." He seemed uncomfortable sharing this information with me. "On the Tina Belmont matter, Troop H, BCI, have adopted a case, and it looks as though Clifford Harris may have committed a homicide. They have some good investigators looking at Harris. We appreciated your input on that."

Somehow, this came as no surprise. "I figured as much."

"It isn't that we wouldn't want you on board, but you're not an active duty member, and that's just the way it is. This is difficult for me to tell you; you know that." I heard the disappointment in his voice.

"You don't have to say any more. I understand." I sighed. "By the way, have you heard any word as to when Ruben will be returned?"

"I'll make it a point to get him back to you in a few days. He is a great K-9, Jason."

"Thank you, Jack. I appreciate your comments."

I reiterated the conversation that I had had with Jack Flynn. The lieutenant appreciated the information and told me not to be upset about not being able to have me on the bust. He indicated that if there should be "gun play" and I ended up with a slug, how could that be explained away? I agreed with him. He informed me that this decision was official, but added "I can't tell you what to do, either." He further advised me that I was on my own. I knew what he meant. I'd be there. I knew that I would be, despite the Ghosts of the Past.

Jack Doyle and I concluded our telephone conversation. I thanked him for the information and his assurance that Ruben would be coming home soon. I respected the lieutenant. We both had the same ingredient in our veins, dedication in our pursuits. We promised that we'd have lunch sometime soon.

I made a few notes after I hung up the telephone and cleared some of the clutter from the top of my desk.

The laundry bag was full to the top. I could barely tie the cord at the top. I took out some soap and bleach from underneath the cabinet and placed them in a large plastic bag. I put everything into the Bronco, locked the house, and headed for town. When I arrived at the laundromat, the parking lot was full. I pulled in next to a big red Ford pickup. I squeezed out of the door without hitting the side of the red truck, took my things out of the back, and went inside. Two machines weren't being used. I filled both of them. I didn't have any colored clothes that day. I put the soap and bleach in the opening on top of the washer and inserted four quarters into each machine. The time meter reflected that I had forty minutes to wait for the cycles to be completed.

I had forgotten to put the laundry basket into the Bronco. I went home, picked it up, and headed to Dr. Don's garage. When I arrived he was busy, but indicated that he would quickly help me. He raised the hood and with his strobe light checked the timing. He indicated that it was off a couple of degrees, which he corrected. I handed him a ten-dollar bill and he gave me a five-dollar return. I thanked Dr. Don and headed back to the laundromat, took the laundry basket out of the Bronco, and went inside. The machines had a few minutes to complete the cycles. I stood next to the machines and watched the timer go to two minutes and to one and to zero. The machines clicked off one minute apart. I placed the wet laundry into two dryers.

While the laundry was drying, I left the laundromat and went to the post office to pick up the mail.

I parked at the end of the parking lot, which was full, and went inside. I took the key and opened the box. It was full of letters and some publications. The majority of the mail was from banks and people answering my letters relative to their passing of insufficient fund checks. I put a rubber band around the letters to keep them from slipping behind the seat in the Bronco. There were many local people picking up their mail. Several of them nodded and said hello as I left the office. I had plenty of U.S. postage stamps, so I didn't have to stand in the long line. I mused at all the lines I had had to stand in from time to time. I couldn't help but wonder what the cost factor of lost time would add up to.

Just before I opened the Bronco driver's side door, I saw Jack Falsey pull in. I walked over to his truck. He had a big smile on his face. He got out of his truck and walked around to the front end.

"Hello, Jason. Where have you been? Haven't seen you for a couple of weeks."

"Hi, Jack. I've been thinking about you. I've got some work for you to do. Could you put my name on your list?"

"I'll do it right now." He pulled out a small note pad and wrote down my name.

"I've got leaky faucets in both the bathroom and the kitchen. I think I'll have you install new faucets and put a cold water faucet for outside use. I could water the little lawn that I do have."

"Jason, I'll take care of that for you the first of next week. I'll be working up on Fourth Lake this week, and I should have that job completed, say, on Wednesday. Then I'll shoot down and take care of it." Jack was a dependable person, and his plumbing craft was the best in the Adirondacks, in my personal opinion.

"I'll certainly appreciate it. The water is good, but a little on the hard side. Someday, I'll save enough money and have you put a water softener system in. Well, Jack, I've got the laundry drying at the laundromat, so I'd better get down there and take care of it. It was great seeing you, buddy."

"Take care, Jason. I'll talk with you later."

I reached the laundromat just in time. There were two people waiting for dryers. I emptied both units, and folded my laundry, and stacked it neatly in the basket. I placed the basket of laundry along with the soap and bleach in the rear of the Bronco and locked it up. I decided to walk over to John's Diner and have a bowl of soup before I headed home. I was halfway to the diner when Charlie Perkins passed me. He looked over for an instant and gave me a blast on his air-horn. I waved at him. When I went into the diner, Lila smiled. I saw Patty carrying a large tray laden down with assorted sandwiches. The table where she was headed was a large one with about seven people seated around it. She set the tray down on a small table and carefully served her customers. The people appeared friendly, and I could hear laughter generating from the table. John was assisting Lila at the grill. The entire place was busy.

I sought out a smaller table in the corner and sat down. Jim, from the real estate office across the street, stopped by my table and said hello. We chatted a few minutes, and then he indicated that he had an appointment with a potential buyer. There was a Utica paper on one of the chairs. I picked it up and glanced at the news.

In about five minutes, Patty came over to the table with a glass of ice water and a setting of silverware.

"Hi, honey! What would you like?"

"You are busy, precious. I'm going to have a bowl of split pea soup with crackers and a cup of green tea. That's all."

"We've been busy like this all morning. Can I get you anything else, honey?"

"I'm trying to lose a couple of pounds, so I'm planning on keeping my lunches on the light side."

"Will I see you tonight, Jason?"

"Want me to pick you up about 7:00 p.m.?"

She was waiting for that question. "I'll be ready, sweetheart." She smiled and brushed against my shoulder.

When the soup came, it was steaming in a large white bowl. Patty brought me extra crackers and a cup of green tea. The soup was delicious. I sipped the tea and refilled the tea cup when it was empty. When I was done eating, I paid my check.

"Did you enjoy the soup, Jason?" Lila asked.

"It was delicious, Lila." I nodded to John. He had a big smile. I left the diner and headed home.

When I pulled into my driveway, I was taken by surprise. There was the biggest black bear that I had ever seen. It was standing up with its right front leg reaching up into the tree. I drove slowly by. I looked at the bear and the animal looked at me. Then putting all four legs on the ground, the bear sauntered off in the direction of Bald Mountain. I wouldn't want to run into that big fella in the dark of night or any other time either. I stopped the Bronco near my entrance door. I looked around before I climbed out, just in case the big bear cut back toward my house. The coast was clear. I removed the laundry basket and put the soap and bleach under the sink.

I refolded the clothes, towels, underwear, socks, and handkerchiefs and put them in their respective places. When I finished with the laundry, I decided to run the vacuum cleaner and do some dusting. Even here in the mountains things get dusty. I finished the project and decided that while I was in an ambitious mode, I'd wash the windows. I made a solution of vinegar and water and did all the windows on the inside and outside. They sparkled like diamonds when the sunlight shone on them. I checked Ruben's dog run and swept it out. I then took some boiling hot water with bleach and scrubbed it. I had to have it ready for his return. I could see why Lieutenant Doyle had called. He had wanted to let me down easily. I might not be eyeball to eyeball with Draper when they made the bust, but this was my Adirondacks, too. I'd go where I wanted to and still comply with the whims of those Ghosts of the Past. Draper had no right to bring criminal activity to our state. I was more than happy to know that Lieutenant Jack Doyle was on his trail. It was going to be interesting to see how this played out.

I called Forest Ranger Gary Leach and told him about the gigantic bear in the area.

"Jason, we've heard about that bear. If you get a chance to take a picture, make certain you use a telescopic lens. This may be the bear that clawed a photographer up by Inlet. He could have lost an arm. You have to be careful. No one should be feeding them either." Gary was adamant about it.

"Gary, that's right. Some of our tourists should exercise good common sense around any wild animal."

"You got that right. Thanks for calling. I have another call coming in."

I hung up the phone. I knew that Gary must have been busy or he would have chatted.

I checked my Weatherby .308 rifle. I wanted to be ready in case the bear decided to take up occupancy in my log home. There certainly wasn't room for both of us, and I was darn certain I wasn't moving. Hopefully the big bear would seek food in another area. I never feed the deer or the bear, and I keep my refuse container in a secure location. People would have less difficulty if they didn't expose their refuse.

I had just finished the last bit of dusting in my office when the telephone rang. I put the dust cloth on the back of a wooden chair and answered the telephone.

"Hello," I said.

"Jason, this is Tom Huston from Lake Placid. How are you?"

"Good morning, Tom. It's good hearing from you."

"Jason, I believe I have an interesting case for you. When will you be coming up to Lake Placid?"

"Tom, I'll drive up in the morning. What time would you like me to drop by?"

"How about 10:00 a.m.? Is that okay with you?" he asked.

"That will be fine. See you then."

"See you, Jason. Goodbye."

"So long."

I wondered what type of case Tom Huston wanted to discuss with me. I remembered the case of the strange-acting guest, who turned out to be an escapee from a Washington State Correctional facility. I remembered that I had contacted Roy Garrison of the BCI, then Lieutenant now a Captain. The guest had been arrested for a homicide that had occurred in Sedona, Arizona. Tom Huston was appreciative of how the matter was handled and praised the troopers in the apprehension without disturbing the lodge's business operations. I was looking forward to seeing Tom.

The dustcloth on the chair was soiled, so I placed it in the laundry basket. I checked the entire log home for anything I had missed. I found some smudges on the bathroom mirror, which I removed with some glass cleaner. I was pleased with my inspection. All I can say is that the drill sergeant I had had in the US Marine Corps years ago had left a definite impression on my housecleaning activities. I can see him now, wearing those white gloves, checking the top of the doors in the barracks.

I made myself a cup of hot coffee and walked into my office, where I went through my mail. I put letters into their respective folders and placed them back into the file cabinet. I made telephone calls to several business places and typed letters.

Patty called at mid-afternoon and asked me if I would like her to take care of dinner. She would bring beef barbecue, homemade rolls, and coleslaw, and arrive about 6:00 p.m., as she was able to leave early. I said I had not made any plans, and her suggestion was fine.

I looked at my watch: 3:15 p.m. I placed my typed letters in their respective envelopes, sealed them, and put stamps on them. I locked the house and climbed into the Bronco. The vehicle started up immediately. Dr. Don had found the problem when he'd adjusted the timing. While pulling out of the driveway, I spotted Jack Falsey heading toward Eagle Bay at a pretty good clip. It was spring, so he would be busy opening camps, starting the water systems after the long, cold winter.

The post office parking lot was empty. I could have deposited the letters in the outside box, but since I needed stamps, I went inside and put the letters through the mail slot for out-of-town mail. I decided to purchase twenty dollars' worth of stamps and stamped business envelopes.

I was just getting ready to climb into the Bronco when Chief Todd Wilson pulled into the parking lot. He beckoned to me to come over to his car. I sauntered over and he got out from behind the wheel.

"Jason, can I bother you for a few minutes?" he asked.

"Anything new on the Draper case?"

"Todd, I don't have much information. You probably know more than I do. Lieutenant Jack Doyle at Troop S is on top of the case, and I imagine in the near future we'll be reading some interesting news in the paper."

"We've had about three sightings of Draper in our community. He has contacted a couple of gift stores with a sales pitch about his southwestern jewelry. So far there's been no takers here in town. Draper did leave a catalog at each of the stores. The store personnel I talked with tell me Draper has a sales pitch that's hard to beat."

"The personality kid, huh?" Draper was a smooth operator.

"We know different, Jason. It's an act and he's good at it. Where is he residing?"

"He's living in Tupper Lake."

"Interesting. He's driving the black Lexus, and the Arizona plates are still displayed. My people have been informed to notify me when he's in town."

"Sounds as though he is trying to branch out."

"Probably. Jason, this case is being primarily handled by the troopers, who are doing most of the work. The feds will be there when the bust goes down."

"Oh, yeah! You can count on that. It has to do with all the tentacles that exist. There are both federal and state charges involved."

"I've got to be on my way. Stay in touch, Jason. Good talking to you."

Todd excused himself and headed in to the post office. I climbed into the Bronco and stopped at the Old Forge Hardware and Furniture Store. I went into the book department to check for a road atlas. The atlas I had at home was torn and needed to be replaced. I purchased one and paid the cashier. I nodded to Mike, the manager, on the way out. He was in the process of holding a staff meeting with the store personnel. He flashed me a smile. I walked across the street to my Bronco and climbed in. I checked my watch: 4:50 p.m. Patty would be at the house in an hour and ten minutes, if she was on time. I headed home.

At five minutes to six, Patty arrived. I heard the brakes on her red Jeep squeal when she pulled up in front and stopped. I was standing just inside the doorway. She got out, opened up the rear passenger door, and took out a medium-sized cardboard box containing several dishes of food.

"Can I help you, Patty?" I asked.

"No, I've got it, hon. Just hold the door for me." She closed the door on the Jeep with her elbow.

"Something smells good, sweetheart! You're making me hungry."

Patty set the large box on the table and took out a dish of coleslaw, a dish of baked beans, a package of fresh homemade rolls, and a small iron pot containing beef barbecue. It was still steaming when she removed the cover. She told me to set the table and she would finish preparing our feast. She placed the coleslaw in the refrigerator and turned the burner on under the iron pot of beef barbecue and the baked beans. The aroma from the barbecue sauce filled the log home. I set the table and poured two large glasses of ice water. I then placed two candles on the table.

"You're going to love this barbecue, Jason. Not to boast, but I prepared it myself."

"I'm looking forward to it, honey."

"Everything will be ready in a few minutes," she assured me.

I put some music on and turned it down low. It consisted of oldies: "Ebb Tide," "Blue Moon," "My Heart is a Hobo," "Falling Leaves" and "Don't Cry Joe." I remembered my mother and father playing them when I was a small child. These songs were my parents' favorites. Patty left the stove for a minute and came toward me. We embraced and did a few dance steps in the kitchen. We stopped and held each other closely, which ended in a kiss. I could feel the warmth of her face against mine.

"Are you ready for dinner, Jason?" She looked up at me.

"I'm ready, dear."

She told me to sit down and that she would wait on me. I lit the candles, and Patty served the meal. She grilled the fresh rolls and placed them on my plate. She placed the succulent barbecue on the bottoms of the two rolls on my plate. I placed a spoonful of coleslaw on top of each one and put the tops over them. Patty did the same to one roll. Before we began our meal, I said the blessings, thanking God for our gifts.

The baked beans were sizzling. Unbeknownst to me, Patty had placed four strips of lean bacon and some brown sugar on the top of the beans. The candles flickered as we savored our food. The barbecue sauce excited my taste buds; a treat that I had never experienced before. The music was playing in the background in this perfect moment in time. I looked into Patty's eyes from across the table. She met my stare with a warm smile.

"I have never tasted barbecue beef like this before. You haven't only captured my heart, but you have taken me on a culinary adventure that is a first for me." My compliment filled Patty's eyes with tears of happiness.

"Honey, my mother taught me how to make the barbecue sauce and, believe me, she held me responsible for getting it right. So you see, I had a great tutor in the kitchen. I'm glad you like it." She beamed.

"I love it."

When we finished eating, I helped Patty with the dishes, and we had the kitchen put back in order in no time. We skipped dessert and went outside for a walk. I locked the door on the way out. With the rabies scare, I slipped my .380 caliber semi-automatic pistol into my jacket pocket. I took Patty's hand. We walked over to the edge of the forest and walked slowly, enjoying the unwavering elegance of our region. Her small hand was warm and surprisingly soft for all the hard work she had to endure.

We took the path that was so familiar to Ruben and myself. The trail was worn, and several brush piles lined the trail. The chippies considered it their playground, and several darted in and out of the piles in front of us. They probably missed seeing Ruben, but that hopefully would change soon, when he returned from his mission with New York State. Patty and I missed Ruben. I located the two large white oak trees that Wilt had seen. I pointed them out to Patty and told her that they were ours. Those two giant trees were like money in the bank.

"Jason, I love the woods and the animals that live here. I wish the tourists wouldn't feed the deer or the bear. It isn't right, honey."

"No, it isn't. I've been on the South Shore Road and have been almost hit several times because of the traffic congestion caused by the deer lovers feeding them. I would have to say that common sense should be used. Hey! We all love the animals, but we have to use our heads when it comes to viewing them. This is not a private zoo. It belongs to all of us, and people should be careful not to impede other users of the highway."

She nodded her head in agreement. "You're right, Jason."

We talked about our forthcoming wedding plans and debated the issue of who was going to be best man. It was becoming a dilemma for such a blessed event. I personally wanted all my male friends to be the best man, but that was impossible. We'd have to discuss the subject further. And, as of that moment, we still hadn't decided on a specific date for the wedding.

The sun was going down behind the mountain, and we headed back toward the house. I told Patty about the giant bear that was in the area and how this wouldn't be a good time to run into the big fellow. It was true my name was on the deed, but the bears go where they want to. Patty asked me what we would do if he happened along the trail. We looked at each other at that moment and laughed nervously. As we neared the log home, we were both relieved that our tramp through the woods was accomplished without incident. We went inside and turned on the CD player. This time we listened to some country music. We both loved it. I told Patty that I'd take her to a symphony sometime in the future. She had never attended a classical music presentation.

"Honey, it's 9:30 p.m. I've got to go home. I have to open the diner in the morning." She sounded disappointed.

I reached over and put my arm around her shoulder to draw her close to me. Our lips met and we kissed. We then rose from the davenport. I took her arm and walked her into the kitchen.

"Patty, we had a wonderful dinner and a great evening. I have to go to Lake Placid tomorrow to see Tom Huston at the Breakshire Lodge, so I won't be home until late tomorrow evening. Wish you could go with me, but maybe you can in the future. I love you, Patty." We held each other closely, so close that we could hear each other's heartbeat.

"I love you, too, sweetheart." She looked up at me smiling.

I thanked Patty for bringing the barbecue, beans, and coleslaw, and told her that next time it was my turn. I walked her to her Jeep and we again embraced. I opened the driver's door and she got in.

"Goodnight, Jason."

"Goodnight and be safe. Call me when you get home."

I watched her drive out of the driveway and then went back inside. I finished picking up the living room and kitchen and checked the doors. When I went into the bathroom, I noticed that the toothpaste was just about gone. I'd have to remember to add it to my grocery list. I undressed and slipped into my pajamas. I was drinking a glass of milk when the telephone rang.

"Hello," I said, expecting Patty's call.

"Goodnight, honey. I'm home. I love you."

"I love you, too."

I got into bed and read for a while. I reached toward the bed lamp and turned it out as my eyelids were heavy.

CHAPTER THIRTY

I woke up at about 5:30 a.m. The neighborhood raccoon had just slipped onto my rear roof from the adjacent tree. I got up and went into the kitchen. I took the broom by the handle and hit the ceiling several times. I could hear the coon moving around. I then opened up the door and looked toward the tree. The security lights illuminated his piercing eyes. He was on a lower limb. The coon came down the tree and scampered off toward the woods. When Ruben returned, we would have very few visits from the raccoons. I went back inside into the bedroom, and lay down on the bed on my back, and stared up at the ceiling. Mr. Raccoon had cheated me out of an hour of needed sleep.

I apparently had dozed off, as I was awakened by the telephone ringing. I reached over and lifted the receiver.

"Hello, hello, Jason. Dale here!"

"Dale, do you realize what time it is?" I answered, a little annoyed.

"It is 6:31 to be exact, according to my watch," he replied.

"Okay, what's up?" I said, trying to get my wits about me.

"I'm flying to Lake Placid. I have to return a couple of daring fishermen to the lodge. Tom Huston called me late last night and asked me if I could fly over to Fern Lake near Black Brook. The fishermen have been there for about a week. Would you like to fly with me this morning?"

"I can't believe it, Dale! I'm supposed to drive to Lake Placid

251

today to see Tom. Do you mind if I ride along? What a coincidence!" I added.

"That's what I'm calling for, buddy. Tom mentioned that. I'll pick you up at 7:30 a.m."

"I'll be ready. Thanks! That will save me driving alone," I said gratefully.

I hung the receiver up, and pushed the covers back, and slowly arose from one of my favorite places. I made the bed and went into the bathroom. The hot water felt good on my back. The new shower head was adjustable and the pulsating mode was my favorite. It helped to relax my muscles. I shaved next and combed my hair. I dressed, putting on a pair of Dockers and a burnt-orange long-sleeved shirt.

After dressing, I turned the burner on under the teakettle. I then toasted two slices of Lila's homemade bread. I was soon drinking my coffee and eating my toast. The grape jelly and the crunchiness of the toast blended well. I was just finishing when Dale drove into the yard. I was surprised when he told me that he had purchased a new Chevrolet SUV four-wheel drive. I opened the door for him, and he stepped inside for a minute while I got my leather flying jacket out of the closet. The air was cool, and Dale agreed it would be a good idea to bring the jacket along, so I slipped it on and picked up my sunglasses. We went outside and I locked the door. I went over to the passenger side of Dale's new Chevrolet, opened the door, and climbed in.

"Dale, I like it. Nice vehicle!" I said in admiration.

"I like it myself. I bought it in Utica. Right now I have 1700 miles on it."

Dale asked me if I'd like to drive it, and I told him I appreciated his offer, but I'd rather ride than drive. If I drove it and put a dent or scratch on it, I wouldn't be able to live with myself. When we reached Route 28, he turned left and showed me the fast pickup it had. It was a snappy vehicle.

"Nice SUV you've got here, Dale."

"I've always wanted to try one and thought it was a good time to trade."

It was 8:10 a.m. when we pulled into Kirby's Marina. Kirby

hadn't opened up yet. Dale drove down near the docks and parked. The red and white Stinson looked good as it pulled gently on the mooring lines.

Dale began his cursory examination. Everything appeared in order. He placed a jug of water aboard as well as a large thermos of black coffee. He told me to get in and he would untie the lines and push us off. I climbed in and closed the cabin door. Dale pushed us off and climbed in. He closed his door and checked the cockpit. The Stinson turned over when Dale engaged the ignition switch. The prop turned slowly at first, then gained momentum. The 245-horsepower Lycoming engine didn't miss a beat. It was known throughout the South Central Adirondack region that Dale Rush kept his prized possession in tip-top condition. He was one proud pilot with superb flying skill. Dale headed the seaplane toward the center of Fourth Lake. I looked out across the lake. There wasn't a boat on the lake in this area. Dale turned toward Inlet and put the power to the engine. Inlet was below us. We climbed to 3500 feet and leveled off.

"We're early. Shall we stop at Long Lake for coffee at Gertie's Diner?"

"Good idea, Dale. I was going to suggest it. I'm buying."

"I won't argue with you," Dale shot back.

We flew over the parking lot of the Adirondack Museum. There were only a few cars in the employees' parking section. I had visited the museum on numerous occasions and found it to be educational and informative in relation to the Adirondack region. For anyone visiting our mountains, the museum at Blue Mountain Lake and the Interpretive Center at Newcomb are a must stop in order to comprehend the Eco-System of the Adirondacks.

"Dale, Blue Mountain Lake is a unique place. The scenery is always breathtaking."

We circled Long Lake twice before Dale set the seaplane down on the blue waters of this popular region. He turned and slowly taxied toward the public docking area. I opened the door and climbed out onto the float. Dale cut the engine about thirty feet from the dock. The seaplane glided into position, and I tied the line. We had anticipated flying directly to Lake Placid, but Dale wanted to stop by the Adirondack Hotel and leave a few brochures advertising the fact that he was ready, able, and willing to fly fishermen or hunters into the back country area of the Adirondacks, of course for a fee. He had taken a few of the brochures and placed them in two brown envelopes, one for the hotel and one for Gertie's Diner.

As we climbed the stairs to the diner, Dale experienced a cramp in his left leg. He pushed hard on the step to help relieve the tension and the excruciating pain. It took a few minutes before the cramp loosened up. I waited with Dale and observed his face go into a series of contortions.

"Wow! That was a tough one, Jason. I've experienced it before, ever since the time I parachuted over Pensacola, Florida. It sure hurts."

"I've had a couple of those myself. They can cause a great deal of discomfort."

I opened the door and let Dale enter Gertie's first. We received a few glances from some of the regular customers.

"Hi, you two!" Gertie greeted us.

"Hello, Gertie," we replied.

Dale and I looked around for a table and located one by the jukebox. We sat down. The waitress came over with two glasses of ice water.

"Good morning, fellows. May I bring you some coffee while you look the menu over?"

Dale ordered decaf and I ordered a cup of regular coffee. She brought the beverages to the table. Dale ordered flap-jacks with one egg over medium on top. I opted to skip any more breakfast. While his order was being prepared, we talked about Dale's successful bush pilot life and his business venture. He hoped to expand his undertaking, especially during fishing and hunting seasons. Some of the back country trips would require another flight into those areas, as some of the hunting groups would consist of more than three hunters. It was all explained on his new brochure. He was proud of his creation.

The flap-jacks with the egg were set before Dale by the friendly waitress. Dale was surprised at the size of the pancakes.

Dale dove in to sample his breakfast. It was delicious. I could see Gertie standing next to the grill, waiting for approval. She was wearing a big smile. Dale gave her a thumb's up. We both waved at her.

"How come you're not eating, Jason?" she asked in concern.

"I had breakfast at home, Gertie," I called back to her.

"Boy, Jason. You certainly have good friends here in Bob and Gertie."

"They're wonderful folks, Dale," I said proudly.

Dale finished his breakfast. I left a tip on the table and paid the check, and Dale thanked me. He appeared a little upset that I beat him to it, but Dale had helped me over the years, both on the job and off the job. This was just a small payback. I winked at Gertie on the way out. She blushed as she always does and told us both to hurry back. I told her to say hello to Bob, for he had stepped out of the diner. We had noticed him go out the front door earlier with errands to be run.

We walked down the steps. I walked across Route 30, while Dale went over to the Adirondack Hotel and Hoss's Country Corner. He told me that he'd be a few minutes. Dale wanted to get the word out about his flying service. All the hardworking people in the Adirondacks were doing their thing and now Dale was doing his.

After forty minutes, I saw Dale walking toward me at a fast clip.

"Did you walk that cramp out of your leg? I thought you said a few minutes."

"I know that's what I said, but Hoss didn't want me to leave. He told me that he may be sending me some prospects. He knows a great many people." Dale was smiling sheepishly.

Dale and I walked toward the seaplane and, when we reached it, he gave it a cursory examination. He kept a close eye on the Stinson. It was in good shape, but he wanted to make certain that it stayed that way. I climbed in, and Dale unfastened the line and pushed us into deeper water. He got in and started us up, telling me the Lycoming is a good engine as we slowly taxied further into even deeper water. He checked the wind current and took off down the lake. He put the throttle to it and, as we climbed, I looked out my side and took in nature's picturesque view. Our Adirondack region has so much to offer.

The remainder of the flight was uneventful, except for a large herd of deer near Saranac Lake. Dale circled them once and then continued on to Lake Placid. It was his intention to drop me off and then continue to Fern Lake to pick up the fishermen. Dale made a smooth landing and took me close to the dock area. He turned the engine off and we glided to within arms' reach of the tie lines. I thanked Dale for dropping me off.

"I don't know what time I'll be back, but figure on a couple of hours. They'll want to take pictures of their catch in front of the plane, and then I'll be returning them here," he said.

"No problem. Take your time. When I'm done conducting business with Tom, I'll take a walk around the grounds and maybe downtown for a few minutes. I'll meet you in the lobby in about three hours," I remarked.

"See you later, Buddy," Dale said.

"Have a good flight—and watch the geese, Dale," I retorted.

Dale was wearing his aviator sunglasses and started to smile.

"Jason, are you referring to the flock of geese that got in my path a long time ago?" Dale chuckled.

"Just kidding! Have a good trip."

I watched my friend as he climbed in behind the controls. The Stinson started right away, and Dale taxied away from the dock. He put the power to the engine and took off, heading for Fern Lake and some tall fish stories. I waited until he was airborne before I turned and started walking toward the Breakshire Lodge. I was curious about what type of case Tom Huston had for me.

CHAPTER THIRTY-ONE

The two painters, Ed and Smiley, were at their apartment in Potsdam, when the telephone rang. Smiley answered. "Hello," he said.

"Hello, Smiley, this is Scott Austin. Could you and Ed start painting a house tomorrow in Tupper Lake? Mr. Draper, my boss, has purchased an old home which is in desperate need of a paint job."

"Ed is in the shower right now. I'll have him call you back as soon as he gets out. I'm not exactly sure what he has on our schedule."

"I'll appreciate that, Smiley."

Smiley hung up the receiver and immediately called Lieutenant Jack Doyle, advising Doyle of the Austin request. Doyle was gleeful and told Smiley to take the job immediately. They finished their conversation. Ed got out of the shower and Smiley told Ed what Doyle had said. Ed called Scott Austin back.

"Hello," Scott answered.

"This is Ed. Sorry I was in the shower when you called," he explained.

"No problem. Can you and your buddy start painting tomorrow morning? My boss, Mr. Draper, has acquired a piece of property, and the house is in need of a paint job. It is located on Route 30 on the edge of Tupper Lake on the south side of the Village. You can't miss it. The previous owner lost the property to the bank and in his state of rage splashed pink paint all over the front of it."

"I've seen that house when I was fishing over that way. What an eyesore!" he remarked. "We'll certainly work it into our schedule."

"Sure is. Okay, Ed. I'll tell my boss that you fellows will give it a coat of paint." Scott was always very decent to Ed, but there was another side to Scott Austin.

"Smiley and I will look the place over. If we have to do any scraping, we'll have to do that first. Find out the color Mr. Draper wants and let us know. We'll include it all in our bill. It will look a lot better when we get done with it."

"I've seen the work that you two fellows have done. By the way, we've got lots of gallons of beige paint, so use that. It will be on the porch by the time you arrive in Tupper Lake in the morning," he said.

"I guess we're all set then. See you tomorrow."

"Okay, I'm heading over to the jewelry store. I've got to make some shelves for the storeroom," Scott said.

"Boy, Mr. Draper's got quite a setup over there on Route 56. People seem to like that southwestern jewelry."

"Yeah, they love it. Our manager there tells me that receipts are good, especially on weekends."

"I bet they are," Ed said.

Ed and Scott completed their conversation and hung the telephone up.

The next morning Ed and Smiley arrived at Draper's newly purchased house on the outskirts of Tupper Lake. As Scott had indicated, the paint was sitting on the porch. The two undercover officers dressed in their coveralls looked the house over and began scraping off the loose paint. The old paint chipped off nicely, and after three hours of scraping, Smiley said, "Let's get this beige paint on this house. This Draper must be spending the dollars in a big way. Ed, this guy Draper is a bad dude. He just keeps spending money. He bought this house, set up the business, and look at those two expensive cruisers that he's got tied up over in Waddington. That's big bucks."

Smiley started painting the rear of the house. Draper didn't want it sprayed. He wanted it brushed on. Ed, in the meantime, checked every room in the house and went upstairs into the attic, paying close attention to the wires coming into the house. He looked up at the outside electrical service and smiled to himself.

CHAPTER THIRTY-TWO

I crossed the street and onto the red-brick walk leading to the entrance of the Breakshire Lodge. I looked at the assorted flowers that lined the walkway. The gardener was pruning the five-foot hedges that adorn the grounds of the Breakshire. I had never met the man who used his talent to maintain the grounds. He nodded as I walked past. I could hear the click of the pruning shears. You could actually compare it to the tic-tock of a grandfather's clock. I continued walking toward the entrance. Several blue jays spiraled near the hedges and then settled for the limbs of a maple tree. I climbed the slate steps into the Breakshire.

The first thing I observed was the black bear that Wilt had carved and presented to Tom Huston. To my surprise, there was a new small carved cub bear in close proximity to the larger bear. The clerk at the desk wearing a white shirt and maroon tie smiled and said, "Mr. Black, good morning. Mr. Huston is awaiting your arrival, sir. I will buzz him."

"Thank you," I said.

I walked over to the magazine rack and had started to look at a magazine when I heard, "Good morning, Jason."

Turning from the rack, I observed Mr. Huston standing by the entrance hallway to his office. He was wearing a blue suit.

"Good morning, Mr. Huston."

"Come into my office. I've ordered some coffee and pastry."

"Sounds good," I replied.

I followed Tom into his office and sat down in front of his desk. The large leather chair was comfortable. There was a slight knock at the door and Tom told the waitress to come in. She had a tray with coffee and pastry. She set the tray on the table, turned the two cups over, and poured the coffee. She put down two linen napkins, one by each cup.

"Mr. Huston, will there be anything else?" she asked.

"No, Mildred, thank you."

The waitress looked toward me and smiled, then removed the tray from the table and left the office.

"Jason, how have you been?" Tom asked.

"Good. Busy as usual," I replied.

"I assume that Dale dropped you off and continued on to Fern Lake to pick up the fishermen. Those two fishermen come up here every year to fish the Adirondack lakes, and this year they decided to try Fern Lake."

"That's certainly nice of you to contact Dale to handle their air transportation. Dale appreciates it very much, Tom," I added.

"Glad to steer some business his way. I believe everyone should have a share of the pie, so to speak." Tom was a fair man.

"You indicated that you had a matter you wanted to discuss with me," I said, curious.

"Jason, I had a visitor last week, a Bernard Draper. He called for an appointment and indicated that he owns a large trucking concern in Phoenix, Arizona, and a jewelry business between Tupper Lake and Cranberry Lake. Two days after he called, I met him here and we had lunch together. He's interested in introducing his line of southwestern jewelry to the Adirondack region and using our lodge banquet rooms for a jewelry show in the near future."

"Tom, I don't know Bernard Draper personally, but I'm familiar with him and his businesses." I felt frustrated that I couldn't reveal to Tom the ongoing investigation that was being conducted, as it was sensitive in nature.

"I see. Jason, Draper possesses an affable personality. He holds a business degree from Northern Arizona University. Apparently he is well connected in Arizona."

It was so difficult for me not to divulge the information about

Draper, but I couldn't at this time. I would, however, inform Lieu-tenant Doyle of Draper's intention. He, of course, might already be aware of Draper's desire to push his line of jewelry in the Adiron-dacks. I was placed in an awkward position. It wasn't that I didn't trust Tom, but I couldn't jeopardize an ongoing investigation. I would never forget the words of Frank Temple: "I'm going to tell you once more: you are not on the job, and I will recommend that your private investigator's license be revoked if you interfere with my investigation." That's the only reason I wouldn't share the in-formation with Tom Huston. I couldn't tell Tom that Draper's southwestern jewelry store was a front for something more sinister. Draper was on stage playing a dangerous game between good and evil. On one side, he was making donations to civic organizations and influential groups, and on the other, he was running a smug-gling organization of untaxed cigarettes, alcohol, and guns into Canada.

"Tom, from what you tell me, Draper sounds like an interesting character. If you want my advice as a former law enforcement offi-cer, all I can say is be wary of him. I can't go into detail, but I'm certain there is a lurking dark side. That's all I can say."

"I did notice that under his suit-jacket there was a slight bulge, and while at lunch he unbuttoned his jacket and I noticed a shoul-der holster containing a firearm. I didn't say anything to him about it. I just thought it was strange."

"Yes, indeed, that is strange." I knew it was predictable.

"Well, Jason, changing the subject and I may be out of order, but when are you and Patty going to get married?"

I was glad that Tom had changed the subject.

"We hope to get married sometime this year, possibly in the autumn."

"I look forward to being on the guest list," Tom said, smiling.

"You're on the list, Tom."

"I'm looking forward to it. Jason, thank you for stopping in. I'll let you know if Draper should contact me again. Oh—by the way, Draper did tell me that he invested in a piece of real estate in Tupper Lake."

"Thanks for the information, Tom."

We shook hands, and Tom followed me out of his office. Standing by the bear was Dale Rush. He apparently heard us approaching, and turned.

"Hi, Jason. Hello, Mr. Huston," Dale said, with a grin on his face.

"Dale, how was your flight to Fern Lake? I assume that everything went okay."

"Yes, it did, sir. I appreciated the lead you gave me. They were fine gentlemen, and they caught some fine looking fish. Apparently a bear gave them a little trouble, but they were able to scare the bear away from their camp."

"I imagine they were happy to see you and your seaplane," Tom said.

"They were glad to be picked up. They didn't sleep all night."

"Guess we're all set to head back to Old Forge," I said.

"You fellows have a good flight. Would you like some coffee before you take off?" Tom asked graciously.

I looked at Dale, and we decided to take a rain check on the coffee. Dale thanked Mr. Huston again for the referral, and he told Dale that he would be sending more business his way. We shook hands again with Mr. Huston and left the Breakshire Lodge.

Dale and I walked slowly down the path toward the lake. Dale chuckled about the bear story that the two fishermen had related to him. He told me that he appreciated the work Mr. Huston sent his way. We both remarked about the well-manicured grounds of the Breakshire.

We crossed the highway and walked toward the seaplane. A couple of men were looking at the plane, and when we arrived they told Dale that they, too, had once owned a gull-winged Stinson. I proceeded to climb into the seaplane, while Dale carried on a conversation with the two elderly pilots from days gone by. I heard them laugh. Dale thanked the gentlemen for their comments about his red and white Stinson. When Dale climbed in, he had a big grin on his face.

"Those fellows wanted to tell me some war stories. Both of them were B-25 pilots during WWII," Dale said.

"I bet they could tell you some good ones," I replied.

We put on our sunglasses and Dale started the Lycoming engine. He slowly taxied to the deeper part of the lake and turned the plane. We were soon skimming the treetops, heading in a southerly direction toward home. I had wanted Dale to fly over Draper's jewelry store and warehouse, but it was not on our schedule and the afternoon sun was fading fast. Dale took the plane up to an altitude of 3500 feet. The flight was smooth, and we chatted about my favorite subject, Patty. Dale, as always, wished us the best of everything. He didn't mention the time that he had asked Patty for a date, but I knew down deep that he had wanted to win her heart. Dale and I were good friends, and I knew he felt badly about the incident. Another topic that came up in our conversation was Ruben. Dale had mentioned that just about everybody in town was puzzled about the K-9's return to police duty. Like any small town in our country, people just wanted to know what was going on around them. It was human nature, although some folks didn't really care whether Ruben was in his dog run or climbing Bald Mountain or chasing chippies in the forest.

Dale brought the Stinson down on Fourth Lake smoothly. He slowly taxied toward Kirby's Boat Marina and cut the engine about twenty-five feet from the docking area. I climbed out on the float and tied the line. The marina was quiet, and Kirby had already closed his office. Out on the lake were two local fellows casting near the shoreline in a cove. Dale checked the plane over and locked the doors.

"We had a good day, Jason."

"Yes, we did," I replied.

We got into Dale's vehicle and headed toward Route 28. Dale dropped me off in front of my driveway. I thanked him for taking me on the flight with him.

"We'll fly again soon, Jason," he remarked.

"Anytime I'm free and you need a co-pilot, let me know," I said.

"See you later, Jason," he said as he drove away.

I watched Dale as he went out of sight and then started walking toward my log home. I walked slowly. There were two things on my mind. Patty and Ruben were very important to me, and I considered them my family.

I noticed that the weeds and grass were high along my driveway. I usually cut them down twice each year. As I approached my
log home I noticed a note slipped behind the screen door. I removed the piece of white paper and read it: "Don't forget tomorrow morning at John's Diner." It was signed "Wilt." I couldn't help
but smile. The big logger was precise and was most loyal to his
many friends.

I unlocked the door and entered. In my office the red light was
flashing on my answering machine. I decided that before I played
the tape I'd call Patty. I dialed her number. The telephone rang
twice before she answered.

"Hello." Her voice was hurried.

"Hi, sweetheart. I'm home. How'd your day go?"

"Busy, honey. We had two tour buses stop with senior citizens.
Lila had to close the diner about an hour early because she ran out
of food. She and John are out shopping as we speak." Patty
sounded exhausted, as she so often did.

"You must have worked hard to wait on all those folks. Are
you tired?"

"I'm bushed, Jason. I'm going to bed early. Oh! By the way,
Wilt was in three times today. What's going on with him? He's up
to something."

"I don't think so, sweetheart. Not that I know of."

I didn't tell Patty about the surprise that Wilt had planned for
her. I couldn't believe that the week had passed so quickly. I hastily checked the planner that I kept in my desk. There it was in my
handwriting: "John's Diner at 9:30 a.m. on Tuesday."

Patty and I talked for approximately a half hour. I told her that
I was also retiring early. After I hung the telephone up, I went to
the kitchen. I put the teakettle on the stove and lit the burner. I had
decided on having a cup of green tea before I listened to my calls. I
opened the freezer, took out a frozen fried cake, and placed it in the
microwave. The teakettle started whistling. I poured the water the
over the teabag, let it steep, sat down at the table, and sipped my
tea while scanning the local paper. The fried cake tasted good. The
only thing missing was my dog, Ruben.

My office was cold. I pushed the thermostat up and the furnace went on. In a matter of ten minutes, the air was comfortable and my chill disappeared. The button on the answering machine pushed hard. There were calls from Lieutenant Jack Doyle and Jack Flynn. The remainder of the calls were from banks and attorneys from the Adirondack region. I wrote down all the names and telephone numbers. I decided that I would return the calls in the morning, then prepared for bed.

CHAPTER THIRTY-THREE

A black Lexus was parked in the rear parking lot of Draper's jewelry store and warehouse. Ed and Smiley, with their infra-red binoculars pressed against their faces, were watching as a white semi-trailer outfit backed into the loading dock. The binoculars focused on the driver of the semi-trailer, who appeared to be in his thirties, with dark-wavy hair and a mustache. He was wearing a black jacket and dark trousers. He had gotten out of the tractor and gone to the rear of the long trailer and opened both rear doors. As Ed and Smiley watched, they observed the door of the warehouse open. Two men appeared on the dock. Ed made them out to be Bernie Draper and his man, Scott, believed to be a hit man for Draper. Scott disappeared for a few minutes. The two undercover operatives heard the motor of a forklift and observed it being operated by Scott. Several large wood containers were removed from the truck and placed in the warehouse. Smiley made notations on his pad.

The three men finished the unloading, and the driver closed the two rear doors on the trailer. All three huddled around each other for about fifteen minutes. The driver returned to the cab of his tractor and climbed in. Draper and Scott went back inside the warehouse and closed the door. It clanked as it hit the bottom of the steel floor. The big semi-outfit pulled away from the docking area and crossed the parking lot to the entrance. It turned left onto Route 56 headed toward Potsdam. The smoke from the diesel engine lingered in the cool night air. The side door of the warehouse opened, and Draper came out and got into his Lexus. He started the motor and screeched his tires on the pavement of Route 3 as he headed toward Tupper Lake. He was still residing at the motel, while his recently purchased house in Tupper Lake was being refurbished. In a few minutes, Scott Austin came out of the warehouse and locked the door. He climbed into his Chevrolet pickup and headed toward Cranberry Lake and his apartment.

Ed and Smiley checked their watches. It was 3:45 a.m. The black of night was silent around Draper's. Ed and Smiley were scheduled this day to finish some painting in the jewelry store adjacent to the warehouse. Two painters showing up for work, they were coming in early. Smiley inserted the key in the side door of the warehouse and the two men entered the building. They moved slowly to the area where the shipments were kept.

Ed located the cartons that had been removed from the semi-trailer; they were marked "gladiola bulbs." Smiley removed the cover on one of the cartons. It contained bulbs half-way down. The lower half of the carton contained large brown envelopes full of a white powder. It appeared that the intelligence reports were correct.

The undercover operatives tested the powdery substance, and it was pure cocaine. The carton top was replaced, and the two painters went into the jewelry and gift store to complete their painting. Ed went outside of the store and called Lieutenant Jack Doyle on his private number.

CHAPTER THIRTY-FOUR

Patty called me to inform me that she had received a call from Lila telling her not to come to work until 9:45 a.m. She wanted to let me know in the event that I stopped in for breakfast and did not want me to worry. Patty wasn't aware of the surprise breakfast party that was planned in her honor to celebrate her freedom from the ruthless Ohio killers that had taken her captive one year ago. It had been Patty's cool-headed presence and tenacity that had kept her from losing her life, although she had been injured after the killers crashed into a tree while being pursued by troopers. It had been this case that had drawn Patty and me so close together.

I arrived at John's Diner about 9:30 a.m. to discover Wilt Chambers was already there along with Charlie Perkins. The next to arrive was Chief of Police, Todd Wilson, and two men from his department. Dale Rush and Jack Falsey were next to come through the diner door. Two Econ men appeared, and ten of the search party leaders, including Fire Chief John Rush, (Dale's brother), soon arrived. John Mahaffy, an artist and designer and close friend of Patty and me, was next to make an appearance. Mr. Mahaffy was carrying a large case. Many of the local folks who were hoping to attend were unable to get the time off or the work force at their place of employment was short handed. The tables were set with John's finest silverware. Two dozen fresh red roses were placed at the head table for the guest of honor, Patty. Looking around the room and into the kitchen, I noticed that Lila and John were both

271

wearing white. John was sporting a new chef's hat. Everyone was talking and laughing. A jovial mood filled the diner. They had called in Gracie Mulligan to serve, as well as two other local women. It appeared to me that everything was ready to go, but the honored guest had not arrived yet. The five forest rangers involved in leading the search groups arrived along with two state trooper supervisors. They indicated that traffic was heavy, which made their arrival time later than anticipated.

This was Wilt Chambers' party, and he was the self-appointed chairman. He went to the middle of the floor. "May I please have your attention, folks?" The room became so silent.

"We're gathered here today to honor one of our citizens, Patty Olson, who should be coming through the front door shortly. She has no idea that this get-together is for her. We couldn't invite everyone that was involved in her search one year ago today. I appreciate you coming. It was a traumatic experience for her. Most of you folks know by now that Patty is engaged to our local private detective, Jason Black. Jason, is there anything that you'd like to offer?"

"The only thing I want to say is to thank you for arranging this for Patty. Yes, I'm the lucky fellow that Wilt is referring to." The sound of laughter could be heard.

The folks in the room applauded. I felt the blood rushing to my face. Wilt continued, "I'd appreciate it if everyone would take their seats, because our honored guest just pulled into the parking lot." The tall logger wiped his brow with a large red handkerchief. "She's coming up the steps now."

The door opened and Patty walked into the diner expecting to begin a day of work. Everyone was quiet. Patty looked around into the dining room and then she looked over at John and Lila behind the counter. She knew something was up, but wasn't certain what it was.

Wilt spoke first. "Patty, please come in here."

Patty walked toward Wilt.

The room exploded with everyone shouting, "Surprise! surprise!!!"

"Wilt, what's going on here?" Patty asked, as her face blushed.

"Patty you are at the head table with Jason, Mr. Mahaffy, Charlie, and myself."

Patty was completely surprised and taken off guard. She proceeded to the head table and sat down next to me. Wilt assisted her to her chair.

"Wilt, the flowers are beautiful. I love roses." She looked up at Wilt, confused.

Wilt's face turned crimson. He stood up again and took the floor.

"I would like to have a moment of silence in honor of Patty and for all victims of crimes in our great country."

The moment of silence lasted for almost a minute. Wilt continued.

"As you all know, Patty was abducted a year ago today by two men that she offered assistance to on Route 28 just north of our Hamlet of Old Forge. All of you know what transpired. You were all there beating the brush for her. I want to thank you all in behalf of Patty and her husband to be, Jason, for the outstanding effort you all put forth. Jack Falsey located Patty's Jeep, and Jason here ended up in the right place and kept one heck of a cool head when Jewell Norris came out of the Santa Clara woods. I've known Jason Black for a long time, and I know one thing: he is a caring man and usually a quiet man, but he's been in that situation more than once. He kept his head, and Norris was smart not to make a wrong move. As you all know by the newspapers and radio and television, Jewell Norris, one of the men who abducted Patty, escaped from the Ohio State Prison and went to St. Regis Falls to seek revenge against the store owner there. He aimed a loaded shotgun at three state troopers. Mr. Norris will not be escaping from prison again. In self-defense, one of the troopers had to take his life. Yes, it was sad, but ruled a justifiable shooting. It is believed that Norris's next stop would have been Old Forge. Jason, you're a good friend. Do me a favor: always take good care of Patty."

"You can count on that, Wilt." I stood up. "Folks, I want to thank you for appearing here this morning, and I want to thank you also for all the tireless efforts you put forth in searching for Patty. I didn't do anything that anyone of us wouldn't do if the occasion presented itself. I thank you." I sat down.

"One more thing folks," Wilt said, with a big smile. "I talked with Chef John and Lila, and we decided that our breakfast is going to be served family style, so just bear with us and you will be served shortly. After our breakfast I'll have a few more words to say about our honored guest, Patty. Then I'll open the floor to any one of you that would like to address the audience. You might say that this special breakfast is a lumberjack's special for you all and of course our very special guest, Patty."

The minute Patty had entered the diner, John and Lila had gone to work. This morning was to be special. Along with fruit juice, (orange or cranberry), the menu consisted of flapjacks, eggs, hash brown potatoes, bacon, ham and sausage, oatmeal and cream of wheat, corn flakes, bran muffins, and biscuits and white gravy or toast in place of biscuits. There were also grapefruit, bananas, and fresh oranges. The three waitresses began serving the platters of food.

Patty looked over at me in amazement. "Jason, did you know about this? I cannot believe that you didn't tell me." She was visibly shaken.

"Honey, how could I? Wilt wanted so to surprise you. It would have spoiled the surprise. Please don't be upset with me. I love you, precious. He swore me to secrecy," I pleaded, reaching over to hold her hand.

She squeezed my hand gently. "I understand, honey. I forgive you."

I looked over the crowd of people. Everyone was clearly enjoying their breakfast. I glanced at Patty, who was sampling some of everything. She looked over at me and smiled. Wilt was on the other side of her, and I noticed that he wasn't piling his plate with flapjacks as he used to. I listened to the people. The majority of them were just enjoying the wonderful breakfast before them. I was not acquainted with all the guests in the room, but had met most everyone at one time. There was no doubt about it: Wilt was like a father figure to Patty. I knew him well. He, and Charlie Perkins, Jack Falsey, and Dale Rush were special people who always were honest in their personal as well as their business lives. I was elated that my good friend, John Mahaffy, was able to attend. Patty was very, very happy. She had always gone out of her way to please her customers. She had endured difficult times with her first husband, Kenneth Olson, who had used her for a punching bag. He wouldn't anymore.

The extra waitresses came around with the coffee pots, and everyone had refills. I heard several people raving about the food. All the comments were positive. Charlie Perkins and I talked for a while. I asked him how his wonderful family was doing. He said that his children were doing well in school. He told me that he had purchased a second log truck, a Mack straight job with a loader on back. Charlie hoped that someday his oldest son would step into the business to help his dad. I was pleased to hear this, for Charlie worked hard for his family every day of the year. I asked him about his trips to Vermont. He indicated that he was still making these trips a couple of times each week.

Wilt stood up and asked the group for their attention.

"Folks, did everyone have enough to eat?" He always tried to please.

"Yes!" The response was unanimous.

"We are honored to have you all here to honor this special lady."

Patty blushed.

"Is there anyone here that would like to make a comment?" Wilt continued.

"Yes, I would. My name is Chester White. I've been a trooper for almost ten years and was involved in the search for Patty. I just want to compliment her for keeping her head. It was a tense situation for her. It could have gone the other way. It's a miracle that she survived. She handled herself well. Patty, you could apply for the troopers. I wish you well, ma'am." Trooper White looked directly at Patty as he addressed her.

"Thank you, Trooper White," Patty said, filled with emotion, fighting to hold back her tears.

The entire group agreed with Trooper White. Patty had handled the situation well by keeping her cool.

"Anyone else? . . . Well, if there are no further comments, my friend Charlie Perkins and I want to present Patty with a token of our appreciation and to honor her for her ability to survive a bad situation. You know we're sort of unique here in Old Forge, Eagle Bay, Inlet, and Boonville. Many of us know each other, and we interact in our businesses and daily activity. I love the Adirondacks and the surrounding area and the people. It's the people that make the difference. We've got good people. The world is a complex place, and we're only a little speck in the universe, but darn it, we count, too. Charlie, would you please bring it in?"

Charlie Perkins got up from the table and went outside to Wilt's big Dodge truck. He came back with a large box and set it down in front of Patty.

Patty whispered over to Jason. "I don't know how much more of this I can take. Why are they so good to me?" She fought back the tears.

I reached over and held her hand.

"Thank you, Charlie, for bringing the box in. Now, folks, there is one person that wanted to be here, but couldn't make it. Many of you know him from WWRV Boonville radio station. His name is Penny Younger and he has a country show in the afternoon. Well, Penny is a close friend of Charlie and myself. Of course, we all know him well. To make this short, the three of us put our heads together, and Penny and Charlie chipped in and I gave my time. We thought Patty would like these."

Patty was looking at the box in awe. She managed to smile as Charlie and Wilt opened the large box. "Patty, would you come around the table and finish opening this?" Wilt asked proudly.

Patty arose from the table and went to the box. She looked up at Wilt.

"Okay, Patty. Remove the cover," Wilt said in his low baritone voice.

Patty leaned over, removed the cover with trembling hands, and gasped with excitement. It was clear she couldn't believe her eyes. She reached into the box. Tears of happiness began to trickle down her cheeks. I stood up and watched as Patty brought out two small carved bear cubs standing about three feet in height and weighing approximately twenty pounds each. They appeared real in every detail. I watched as Patty went over to the table and set them down. She turned toward Wilt and went over to him. Wilt put his arms around Patty.

"They're beautiful, Wilt. Oh, thank you so very much! I'll cherish them for the rest of my life," Patty said elatedly, as tears of joy streamed down her cheeks.

"Patty, is there anything you'd like to say to the people?" Wilt asked.

Removing a tissue from her uniform pocket, she dried her cheeks. "I want to thank you, Wilt, Charlie and all for this tribute and the wonderful gifts. I also want to thank you all for coming today. You all completely surprised me. I will cherish this moment for my whole life. When I first came to this wonderful place from Kentucky, my then husband and I didn't know what to expect. Of course, many things happened and I divorced Kenneth for reasons you all know. You have all reached out to me and you have made me feel like someone special. I appreciate that, and I try each day to thank you for your generosity. I consider you all my extended family. I want you to know that my first husband, Kenneth, was a good man, until he became an alcoholic. I tried for a long time to help him, but his personality changed. He became dangerous to himself as well as others. I want to thank all that are here and I appreciate your friendship so much! I wish to thank John and Lila for giving me a place to work. I cherish their friendship, too. Thanks for everything!" Patty returned to her chair, visibly moved. I reached over and put my arm around her.

"Before I excuse you all, I want you to know that we have another special guest here today. I've know this man for many years. He is a friend of mine and a friend to many folks here in this room, including Patty and Jason. I believe he has something for Patty. Mr. Mahaffy, I'll turn this over to you," Wilt remarked.

"Thank you, Wilt Chambers. Gosh! I've known Wilt for many years, and as I look around this room, I can honestly say I know most of you. I'm honored to be here this morning for this special breakfast. When Wilt contacted me a few weeks ago, I decided to do a watercolor of a special place that we all are aware of. Instead of telling which place I mean, I'll show you." Mr. Mahaffy reached over and removed a framed picture from his large carrying case.

"Patty, I happen to know that you enjoy visiting that section of the Moose River Road where the river is closest to the highway. I've taken the liberty of painting this watercolor just for you. I've made it an autumn scene so I could use some red and yellow for the leaves on the trees."

Patty looked at Mr. Mahaffy with amazement.

"So, Patty, I'd like to present this to you. I placed it in an oak frame. I hope you'll like it." Mr. Mahaffy handed the painting to Patty.

"Mr. Mahaffy, I don't know what to say. It is beautiful and I thank you so much. I do love that section of the Moose River Road. Jason and I have spent many times there along the river. It is so peaceful and inspiring. Thank you so very much. I'm humbled." Patty held the watercolor high in the air for everyone to view. "Thank you again, Mr. Mahaffy."

"It was my pleasure, Patty. You're welcome."

Wilt again took the floor and noticed that Chief Wilson had a remark to make.

"Chief, go ahead. You have the floor."

"Before we break up, folks, I'd like to make a comment," Chief Wilson said.

"Go ahead, Chief," Wilt urged.

"Folks, I just want to add the fact that this young lady we've honored this morning is deserving of all the best. We're lucky to have Patty as a citizen in our community. My department wishes you the best, and I wish you the best, Patty"

"Thank you, Chief Wilson," Patty replied.

Wilt stood up. "Well, I guess that brings our festivities to an end. Thank you all for coming and enjoy the rest of your day." He had enjoyed his role as emcee.

The group began to mill around. Almost everyone approached Patty to thank her for her comments and to view the beautiful gifts. I stood by, but didn't join in the conversations. I was overjoyed for Patty. I could see that she had cultivated many friendships amongst the local people. I asked Wilt if I could chip in regarding the check. He looked at me with a grin.

"You haven't been thrown in the lake today, have you?" he quipped.

I didn't answer Wilt, because I knew how proud and generous he is. I thanked Wilt for the outstanding get-together. John and Lila gave Patty the rest of the day off. I talked with John Mahaffy before he left. John was a very busy man and had to get back to his office.

"John, thank you for coming and thank you for the beautiful painting you presented to Patty. The painting will look beautiful in our home."

"Jason, I wish you and Patty many years of happiness. It was my pleasure." He shook my hand and departed.

"Patty, would you like to spend the rest of the day with me?" I asked.

"I was just going to ask you the same thing, my dearest. Certainly." She was still trying to regain her composure.

"I'll check the post office, and you can get some more comfortable clothes to wear."

"I'll stop home and change into my blue jeans and meet you back at your place."

"Okay, sweetheart. See you shortly."

I talked to the forest rangers and Chief Todd Wilson in the parking lot, and we all agreed that Patty had been fortunate to survive the ordeal a year ago.

I waved at Wilt as he climbed into his truck.

I drove to the post office and picked up my mail. I talked with the postmaster for a few minutes and headed home. I had to make several telephone calls.

I drove into my driveway just in time to see the big black bear going into the woods. The big fellow must have been checking to see if I were home. He was becoming more aggressive. When I went inside the house I called Gary Leach, my forest ranger friend, and left word on his answering machine that the big bear was becoming bolder. I suspected that, as in the past, Gary would contact a biologist and they would dart the bear and move him out of the area.

I reached in the cupboard for my box of green teabags. I turned the burner on under the teakettle and took out a couple of teabags. Patty pulled into the yard and got out of her Jeep. She looked around and then came into the house.

"Hi, honey!" she said as she entered. She was wearing her blue jeans and a denim shirt.

"That didn't take you long, Patty. Say, guess what, Patty?" She turned around and looked directly at me with an inquisitive look on her face.

"What, hon?"

"I was pulling in the driveway when I spotted that big black bear skipping off into the woods. I checked the flowers next to house, and sure enough, there was his footprint. A fresh one, too."

"He's not afraid. That's not good, Jason," she said, alarmed.

"I know. That's why I called Gary Leach. He wasn't home, but I left a message on his answering machine. He'll contact the biologist."

"That was the smart thing to do." Patty looked concerned.

"Since the landfills have been closed, the bears are hungrier than usual."

"Maybe the big bear is looking you over, Jason." She smiled.

I looked at Patty and she laughed. I went over to her, and put my arms around her slender waist, and drew her close to me. Her lips met mine and we kissed.

"You know I'm only kidding you, Jason. I wouldn't want to see the big bear chasing you down."

"I know, I know." My thoughts drifted back to the diner. "By the way honey, have you recovered from the morning's excitement. What a party! What good friends!"

Her eyes welled up with tears. "Jason, you're all so good to me. How can I ever repay everyone for all they've done?"

I walked over and embraced her. She sobbed in my arms. I comforted her.

"Hey, babe, our tea's getting cold. We'd better go drink it."

She dried her eyes and we walked to the table, and drank our tea.

"Honey, could I ask you a favor?"

"Sure, what's up?"

"Would you mind running the vacuum cleaner, while I make a couple of phone calls?" The rug could use a cleaning.

"Certainly I will, and I'll do some dusting. I spotted a couple of cobwebs in the corner when I came in. What kind of a housekeeper are you, Jason?" she chided.

"Thanks, babe, I'll appreciate it." I didn't answer her question.

I took the vacuum out of the closet and gave it to Patty. While she was plugging it into an electrical outlet, I went into my office. I sat down at my desk and pushed the play button on my answering machine. The calls came one after the other. The first call I made was to Lieutenant Jack Doyle. The receptionist buzzed the lieutenant's office at Troop S Headquarters.

"Lieutenant Doyle speaking." His voice sounded hoarse.

"Hello, Jack. Jason Black here returning your call. You got a cold?" I asked.

"Thanks for calling back. No, just tired, Jason. I wanted to let you know that we're getting close to busting Bernie Draper and company. Jason, the major and captain do not want you to be there during the bust. I'm sorry, Jason, but that's the way it is. I hope you understand."

"Jack, I understand, but you know darn well if I hadn't developed the information, Draper would have already been set up to proceed with his criminal activities in New York State."

"Yeah, I know you're right, but that's the scoop, my friend." I heard a bit of sadness in his voice and remembered the many busts that we had made together.

"When's it coming down?" I inquired.

"I haven't been informed yet. I won't know until the bosses are ready."

"Have your undercover people testified before the grand jury yet?"

"They testified yesterday. The district attorney is going to move fast. The warrants will be forthcoming. And, the feds are going to be bringing charges as well."

"I wish you good luck with the grab. I know that you can't share the information with me. Has there been any word from the Phoenix Police Department?"

"All I know is that our bust probably will take place first, and when the Arizona authorities wrap up their case, they'll file their warrants with the institution that Draper is sent to. You know, Jason, if I had my way I'd have you right with me when we go through the door." His voice was reassuring.

"I know you would, Jack." We had knocked in a few doors and had almost got hit by gunfire when a druggie's gun had gone off accidentally.

"You can be proud for turning us onto this bum, so don't fret too much."

"I wish you the very best, Lieutenant." Jack was an asset to the officer corps at Troop S.

"Thanks, Jason, you're one of the best."

I heard the click when Jack hung up. I knew down deep in my heart that the troopers would do a good job in taking Bernie Draper down for his illegal activities. I wanted to be there, but that would be impossible; however there was no reason I couldn't be on the fringe of the activities. I had a sixth sense about Draper. He was slippery. We'd have to wait and see. I felt empty inside after Jack and I hung up.

I called my buddy, Jack Flynn. The telephone rang twice.

"Flynn Investigations." It was Ruby Wolkowski's voice.

"Ruby, Jason here. How are you?"

"Is that you, stranger? How come you haven't called lately?" She missed me. Ruby was probative.

"Busy and in love." I enjoyed answering her question.

"Would you like to talk with Jack? You're making me jealous, you big brute."

"Yes, dear, I would."

"Jason, I was just about to call you." Jack Flynn sounded rushed.

"How is the PD doing on the Draper matter?" I asked.

"They've found matching DNA on the triple homicide case and it now appears that Bernie Draper is the target. I don't know when the warrant will be issued, but you can bet it will be sooner rather than later."

"That's interesting, Jack. The New York authorities are getting ready to bust Draper in their jurisdiction. I believe there will be federal charges as well."

"Interesting, interesting. Now, hold on to your hat, Jason. I heard this morning that one of Draper's drivers was found dead in the cab of his assigned semi-trailer truck near Scranton, Pennsylvania. The name of the deceased was Cesar Guererro. He's about thirty-six years old and resides in the Phoenix area. He was an informant of Captain Jay Silverstein."

"This is the first I've heard of the murder. This case seems to be getting more involved every day," I said stroking my chin. "By the way, when did Jay get his promotion?" I hadn't heard about it, but was pleased for him. Jay was a hard worker and very deserving.

"He just made captain. You should have been here for the promotion party, Jason. What a time!!! We had a couple of belly dancers perform a sword dance that will go down in the history of promotion parties."

"It's been a long time since I attended a promotion party, Jack."

"That's what you get for living three thousand miles away," he chided.

"Jack, did they determine the cause of death on that truck driver in Pennsylvania?" These guys were really dangerous.

"They believe it was a blow to the head by a blunt instrument. He apparently put up a fight, as there was blood found at the scene and it wasn't the driver's. Jay felt terrible because this young man was going to Glendale Community College pursuing a business degree. In fact, that's where he trained for his tractor and trailer's CDL license," he added.

"Do you think Draper's involved?"

"Well, he could have ordered the hit. He has plenty of stooges on his payroll, and it could be one of many. The Pennsylvania authorities are presently carrying it as a suspicious death."

"Thank you for sharing the information, buddy."

"Glad to oblige when I can, Jason."

"We've been through a lot, Jack." I was thinking specifically of our South Pacific days.

"Yeah, you're right. By the way, how's Patty and when's the

big day?"

"In the fall, we hope. Don't worry; you're going to get an invitation."

"I'd better, Jason. I expect to be best man." He sounded serious.

"Well, I'd better get going. Nice talking with you."

"I'll stay in touch, Jason. Goodbye."

"Take care, Jack. So long for now. Tell Ruby to take care of herself and be careful on those Phoenix streets. A lot of crime there. So long." I knew that Ruby carried a .25 Caliber semi-automatic pistol. She had almost been raped one evening when she was at an ATM. A patrol car came by and the perps took off. Since that incident, Ruby was armed and ready. With Jack's help, she became quite proficient in its use with frequent visits to a shooting range.

I called a couple of banks and took down some bad check information for my letters that I send to bad check passers. I filed some reports and returned to the kitchen area. Patty had just finished dusting, and everything looked neat.

"Thank you, honey, for running the cleaner and dusting. You do good work."

"I'm practicing for the future, you big lug." Patty had a wonderful sense of humor and was always ready to display it.

She came toward me and we embraced. We could hear our hearts beating in rhythm. I told her that her comments to the group this morning were excellent. She laid her head against my chest.

"I love you, Jason, I love the watercolor of the Moose River that John Mahaffy presented me, and I love my bear cubs. " Her smile was alluring.

"I love you, too, sweetheart. By the way, John is an outstanding artist and paints at the master level. His painting is beautiful. He painted that for you from the heart. That's the way he is, precious," I said.

"I know, and I appreciate it very much. Honey, seeing that I have the day off, could we take a ride?" she asked softly.

"Okay, we'll head toward Blue Mountain Lake and Long Lake. We can be there in an hour or a little longer. That's a good idea."

I grabbed the camera and locked up the log home. When we went outside, I looked over at the dog run and immediately missed my big K-9. My hope was that Ruben wouldn't get too attached to Russ Slingerland, who was his former handler. I would call Russ in the morning.

I asked Patty to drive so I could ride shotgun with my trusty 35 mm camera. Patty had never driven the Bronco before, and it took her a while to adjust the seat and check out the dashboard. I told her to hold on a minute as I wanted to check to see if I had left my bedroom window open. I ran around the house and found the window down and locked. I climbed back into the passenger side.

"Let's go, sweetheart. Keep it down to the speed limit." As we started toward Route 28, Patty gave the Bronco very little acceleration. I told her to give it a little more gas. She stopped at the end of the driveway. She looked both ways before proceeding north toward Eagle Bay. When we reached the hamlet, I asked her to stop at the Eagle Bay kennel. She pulled up in front.

"Keep the engine running. I'll only be a moment, honey." She looked puzzled. I got out, shut the door, and ran up the steps. Lynn Sisson was busy behind her desk. She looked up with a big smile.

"Jason, where in the devil have you been?" she asked with her usual smile.

"Lynn, I've been busy. I just stopped for a minute. Do I owe you any more money? I just wanted to make sure. Ruben has been called back to active duty and that's another reason I haven't stopped by."

Lynn quickly checked the computer.

"No, Jason. In fact, you have a credit of two dollars. Would you like a refund?"

"No, just credit my next bill when I bring Ruben in for a bath."

"Okay, I will. How's Patty?" she asked as I headed for the door. "Say hi to her for me."

"Fine! We're going to head up to Blue Mountain Lake for a ride. Say hello to your mother for me."

"I will, Jason. Have a good trip."

I left the kennel office and returned to my vehicle. I climbed in. Patty looked at me lovingly.

"Lynn asked about you, honey," I said as she drove away.

Patty handled the Bronco very well. She kept it around fifty-miles-per-hour, but slowed down to a crawl when we went through Inlet. The local police patrol had a log truck pulled over. I didn't recognize the logger, but both the officer and the driver were laughing, so therefore it could not have been too serious. The ride to Blue Mountain Lake was scenic and without much traffic. We stopped at the stop sign for Route 30 and then proceeded toward Long Lake. The scenic beauty of this special place on Earth humbled me as my eyes roamed from the edge of the highway to the tops of the mountains and across the blue waters of Long Lake. To truly appreciate Mother Nature's mural of the Adirondack gift, one has to visit this place, go into the woods, climb to the highest point on the numerous mountains, and breathe in the fresh air. And view—for miles—God's creation.

When we arrived in Long Lake, I asked Patty to pull into Hoss's Country Corner. We got out of the Bronco and went up the stairs to the door. Lorrie was near the door and greeted us as we entered. She immediately approached with her friendly smile.

"Hello, Patty and Jason. How are you both?" she asked.

"Patty and I decided to take a ride this afternoon, and here we are in Long Lake," I .explained. "It's always good to see you. How's John?"

"He's fine. He had to fly to New York City for a trade show."

"Kindly give him our regards." He was a busy person.

"I will, Jason."

We talked for awhile and walked around the store. Patty went to the clothing area and I checked out the book section. After a while we both met in the clothing area of the store. Patty tried on a couple of sport jackets, and I looked at some medium-weight sweaters. They had a wonderful selection of clothing. Patty ended up buying a plaid jacket, and I purchased two much needed shirts.

After we paid for the items, we bid farewell to Lorrie and Ginny and then left the store. The sun was shining brightly, and as we made our way over to Gertie's Diner several people were watching a seaplane take off down Long Lake. We left the Bronco parked in Hoss's parking lot and decided that the walk would do us good.

I held the door open for Patty and we entered the diner. Gertie saw us coming and rushed around the counter to greet us.

"Well, it's about time you brought this young lady in to see me. What does he do, Patty, keep you under lock and key?" Gertie asked jokingly.

"No, Gertie. I'm always busy in Old Forge, and when I get out of work I'm bushed after standing on my feet all day," Patty said.

"I know the feeling, Patty. I get very tired after standing all day behind this counter."

Gertie led us to a table and I seated Patty. Gertie wiped her hands with a towel and handed us two menus. She told us that her soup for the day was navy bean, with a grilled cheese sandwich. We ordered two specials and tea. We didn't want to eat too much because we had had such a large breakfast at John's in Old Forge. I looked around for Bob, and Gertie shouted over the counter that he was in Tupper Lake picking up supplies. Patty and I talked about the jacket she had purchased at Hoss's.

"Jason, I have been looking all over for that type of a jacket. I love the two pockets and the design," she went on excitedly.

"It looks great on you, honey," I remarked, complimenting her.

"Flattery will get you anywhere, Jason." She laughed.

I didn't answer her. I considered myself so fortunate to have Patty. I felt that we'd be happy together. Even though we hadn't set the exact date, we were looking forward to the day when we would fully commit to share our lives.

The waitress was busy in the kitchen, so to be sure everything was nice and hot, Gertie served us. The soup was steaming and the grilled cheese sandwiches were served with a treat for both of us, crisp bacon. We both enjoyed the added touch, and thanked Gertie for the delightful surprise.

"Jason, I know that you both love bacon," she said.

The grilled cheese with bacon sandwiches were tasty. Gertie had made them using large slices of white bread. She had buttered both sides of the bread. We finished our mid-afternoon snack with a dish of tapioca pudding for each of us. We didn't need the real whipped cream on the top of it; however, it tasted good. Gertie took a minute and came over to our table and sat with us for a few minutes. The customers had left and the three of us were alone, while the waitress was busy in the kitchen.

"How many years have you and Bob been running the diner?" I asked.

Gertie thought for a minute.

"Jason, I don't know where the time has gone. We've been here twenty years. It seems like yesterday that we opened the front door. It has been good to us, but like anything else, it is hard work trying to keep your customers happy," Gertie said.

"Well, I want you and Bob to know that we appreciate you and your fine culinary ability."

"We'll keep doing it until we can't do it anymore," she said wearily.

We talked a few minutes longer and then thanked her for the fine hospitality. I told Gertie to say hello to Bob and that I hoped to catch him sometime. Gertie gave Patty a big hug and shook my hand.

"See you, Jason. Take good care of Patty. You've got a great gal there."

"Goodbye, Gertie," we answered.

I asked Patty, as we walked to the Bronco, if she would like to take a ride to the Tupper Lake area. She agreed, and we were soon motoring north toward the Village of Tupper Lake. I had all intentions of driving to Route 56 to take a look to see what was going on at Draper's, but before I did I wanted to see if there were any activity at Draper's newly acquired Adirondack home.

Patty didn't ask me any questions, but I assumed that she knew something was up, especially when I slowed down as I neared Draper's property. I noticed the black Lexus sedan was parked in the driveway in front of his garage. The shades were drawn. Patty looked over at the house.

"Jason! I've seen that car in Old Forge. It has Arizona plates on it. If that's the same guy, his name is Draper. He's the one that was in John's Diner trying to get Lila to put in a display counter for southwestern jewelry."

"Honey, how come you didn't mention that to me before?" Jason asked.

"I didn't think anything of it. There are always salesmen stopping in with their wares. If I had known it was important, naturally I would have told you."

"No harm done. Yes, his name is Bernie Draper from Phoenix, Arizona and he is a wheeler-dealer. Nothing for you to concern yourself with though."

"If I see him around Old Forge, I'll let you know."

"No problem, Patty, no problem."

I wondered when Lieutenant Doyle was going to bust Draper. There was no doubt about it: Draper was trying hard to make inroads with people and businesses in New York State and especially in the Adirondack Park.

Patty and I turned on Route 3 and headed toward Route 56 and the Draper establishment. The murdered driver for Draper must have come across some important information about Draper and his organization that prompted someone to kill him.

As we approached Draper's store and warehouse, I could see that the parking lot was full of cars and pickups. I noticed that there were cars from both Ontario and Quebec. I took time to jot some of the Canadian plate numbers down.

Patty and I did not enter the store because there was no telling what time Draper might stop by. I didn't want to expose Patty to any potential harm or interfere with Lieutenant Doyle's investigation. Jack Doyle was on top of this case. It would only be a matter of time before bracelets very different from the turquoise ones he was selling would be clicked around Bernie Draper's wrists. I turned around, and Patty and I headed back toward Tupper Lake and home.

The ride home was uneventful. I drove, and Patty came over next to me and snuggled close to my right shoulder. I kept both hands on the steering wheel. We drove past Draper's house on the outskirts of Tupper Lake. The Lexus was still in the driveway. The window shades were still pulled down. We drove south on Route 30. We listened to NPR radio. They were playing classical music.

"Honey, if you don't mind, I think we'll just drive to my log home. I was planning on preparing something light. Do you mind, dear?"

"Sounds interesting, darling. That'll be fine." She smiled in agreement

"I love you, Patty." My heart filled with emotion.

When we went by Gertie's, there were about a dozen cars and pickups parked in front of the diner.

"Gertie's busy, Patty."

"Boy! You can say that again. They must do well, honey."

"Both she and Bob are hard workers. They're friendly and they always go out of their way to please the customers."

"Something like John and Lila, Jason. They are always busy and very friendly to their customers."

I nodded my head in acknowledgement. "I agree with you."

Traffic was sparse on Route 28. Blue Mountain Lake didn't have much activity going on at this time. The sun had gone over the mountains, and I turned the headlights on. Patty had laid her head against my shoulder and her eyes were closed. I didn't wake her until we pulled into the hamlet of Inlet. She rubbed her eyes and looked up at me.

"Did I fall asleep, sweetheart?" She yawned.

"That's all right. You needed your rest," I told her. "You've had a big day."

Hodel's Pro Hardware was having a sale, and a number of customers were coming out of the store. I slowed down to let the people cross Route 28.

I thought about how Lieutenant Doyle and the rest of the command personnel at Troop S were in the planning stages of taking Bernie Draper down. As we drove south on Route 28 to my log home, my thoughts were at Raybrook. This was one of the times that I longed to be back on the job. In my head I knew that it was time to move on. But my heart would always miss the challenge. When the Draper case was concluded, Lieutenant Doyle would fill me in on the details.

A large buck was standing in my driveway when we pulled in. I slowed down to a crawl. I was about five feet from him before he took off for the woods.

"That was a big deer, Jason," Patty said excitedly.

"It sure was a big one." She loved to watch the animals.

"Jason, the deer herds get larger every year. This past winter was quite mild, and the deer were able to find food easier."

It wasn't easy for us to return to the log home and not see Ruben sitting in his dog run. I'd be happy when Russ returned him. When we got out of the Bronco we took a walk to the edge of the forest. The leaves were lazily moving in the slight breeze. We returned to the house in about one-half hour. I told Patty that I was going to begin working on a new project, the painting of a scene on one of my two-man saws. It was something I had been wanting to do. I took her downstairs to the cellar. The saw was lying on my wooden work table.

"Patty, this is new to me, but I've always wanted to paint one. I've seen saws with all kinds of scenes painted on them. The price tags are in excess of one hundred dollars. Some have forest scenes with running streams, mountains, and cabins."

"What are you planning to paint on your saw, honey?" she inquired.

"I'm going to paint a small log cabin on one end of the saw partially hidden in some pine trees. I thought that I'd add an old-style buzz saw and a stack of wood. At the top will be a blue sky with two or three mallards in flight."

"Fantastic! Jason, I bet it'll look great when you get it completed," she commented. "But do you have any art background?"

"I'm seriously considering taking a course at the art center this summer. I'll give it a good try. I believe if I take my time it will come out all right. I don't have any intention to sell it, but I thought it would look nice over the fireplace or in my office on the wall that is behind my swivel chair. I had another idea about having some old barn-wood put on that wall first and possibly hanging the saw there."

"That would look nice, Sherlock," she quipped.

"That's one thought, but who knows? Ideas do change."

"Yep, you're right there."

"How about a cup of tea and an English muffin? Sound like a good idea?"

We weren't terribly hungry after our large breakfast and our delectable lunch.

"Sounds good to me, darling." She was always amenable.

I went into the kitchen and put a teakettle of water on the burner. Patty took two English muffins out of the freezer and placed them in the toaster. In a few minutes we sat at the table sipping tea and enjoying our jelly-covered muffins. We talked about our wedding plans.

After we finished, we played some records and listened to some current music and oldies from the past.

Patty left for home at about 9:00 p.m. She indicated that as usual, she had to be at John's Diner at 6:30 a.m. I walked her out to the Jeep and helped her in. I told her to call me as soon as she got home. We kissed each other goodnight.

I went back inside the house. We had taken care of the dishes and cleaning the kitchen. It was spotless. I went into the bathroom, brushed my teeth, combed my hair, and slipped my pajamas on. I pulled the covers back on the bed. I went out of the bedroom and checked to make certain the door was locked. I had just peeked into the office to see if everything were squared away, when the telephone rang.

"Goodnight, my darling," she said in a soft voice.

"Goodnight, precious. Are you okay?" I asked.

"No problem. Everything was quiet when I passed through town."

"I'll call you tomorrow. Goodnight, Patty." I was tired.

"Goodnight."

I already missed her.

I went into the bedroom, set the Big Ben alarm clock and slid between the sheets. I rolled over, turned the light off, and fell asleep.

CHAPTER THIRTY-FIVE

The Big Ben was vibrating and winding down when I reached over to the night table and turned it off. I wanted to go back to sleep, but instead pushed the covers back and went to the bathroom. I shaved and climbed into the shower. The hot water felt soothing on my lower back. I would never forget the intoxicated driver going through the stop sign and striking the right rear of my troop car. I remembered how he tried to back up his Chevrolet sedan, but the damage had been so severe it wouldn't budge, although the tires burned rubber through the wet snow to the concrete. I remembered how the trunk opened and the radio equipment came out of the trunk and the seat belt cut into my side, leaving me with a hernia. I hadn't been able to return to duty until I had the hernia repaired. I remembered the pain very well. The hot water was soothing.

After showering, I got dressed. I then went into the kitchen and turned the burner on under the teakettle. Coffee and tea were going to be added to my next grocery list. There were only three teabags left in the box. The knife I used to cut the English muffin in half was dull. I used a fork instead. When it popped out of the toaster, I buttered both halves and put blackberry jam on them. I poured the hot water over the teabag and let it steep for a minute before I sat down at the table. It was lonesome here without Ruben; and hopefully he would be returning soon. I felt that Russ would watch over him closely.

I finished my tea, and cleaned the table, and washed the few dishes that had accumulated by the sink. I knew that Patty was busy at John's Diner, for all the locals rush there early in the morning to exchange happenings in their lives or other people's lives. The majority of the people were hard working and it was a relaxing half-hour before they started the work day. The same folks would be there to lend a hand to aid their fellow man or woman. I went into my office and placed a telephone call to Sergeant Joseph Kelly of the Royal Canadian Mounted Police. I had known Joe Kelly for many years, and he had been assigned to a detachment of RCMP near Cornwall, Ontario, for several years. It took a while for the call to go through. I finally made contact.

"Sergeant Kelly speaking. May I be of service?"

"Sergeant Kelly, Jason Black here. How have you been?" I asked.

"Jason, I haven't heard from you in years! Good to hear from you." I heard the surprise in his voice hearing from me.

I told Joe about the Draper matter and that the troopers had a dedicated investigation in progress. I shared with him the Ontario and Quebec registration plate numbers that appeared at Draper's store and warehouse facility. He informed me that untaxed cigarettes and alcohol and firearms had been coming into his district. They had been working with the Cornwall PD, endeavoring to find the source. At this point I suggested that he should contact Lieutenant Jack Doyle at Troop S Headquarters.

"I will contact the lieutenant today. I want to thank you, Jason, for the information. I might share this with you. The white semi-trailer outfits have been observed in our jurisdiction. We believe that aliens are being smuggled into the states. We've had contact with your federal folks relative to this. Thanks again. I'll get a hold of Lieutenant Doyle." Sergeant Kelly sounded interested in this case.

"Joe, thank you. If you and your wife ever come to our locality in Old Forge, New York, I'd love to see you."

"Maybe we can do that later in the year. Take care of yourself, Jason."

"Best to you, Joe."

I hung the telephone up after saying goodbye to Sergeant Kelly. He had been so helpful to me several years before, when I worked on a case of stolen logs that had ended up in a sawmill in Ontario.

I immediately called Lieutenant Jack Doyle at Raybrook. He answered his telephone on the second ring.

"Lieutenant Doyle speaking. Can I help you?"

"Jason Black here, Lieutenant. I just got off the telephone with Sergeant Joseph Kelly of the RCMP at Cornwall, Ontario. I think you should contact him. He indicated the authorities are investigating a smuggling case that may involve Bernie Draper."

"Thanks, Jason. I'll contact him."

"I happened to be in the vicinity of the Draper jewelry store and warehouse and picked up some plate numbers of Ontario and Quebec cars in their parking lot. When I was talking with Kelly I gave him the plate numbers. They may be associated with your investigation."

"I'll call Sergeant Kelly. We may have something there. We're going to take Draper down soon. I can't give you the date and time, but you can read it in the paper when it happens." He chuckled.

"The important thing is that Draper will be off the street. We don't want his type here in the Adirondacks or any other place," I commented angrily.

"The drug culture since the 1960's has been expensive and costly to the law enforcement community. This particular case is important, but it is only a small speck in the overall picture."

"You're right, Lieutenant. I have to go now."

"Thanks for calling, Jason. Stay in touch."

"So long, sir."

I gave Jack Doyle the Canadian registration plate numbers. He would run the data, and possibly they would be helpful in his ongoing investigation. Draper was smuggling the contraband into Canada via his two Carver cruisers and his semi-trailer outfits. There was a possibility that some of the drugs were being picked up at the jewelry store. I wasn't privy to the intelligence that the troopers had developed, but it didn't take long to figure out the workings of Draper's operation. Any investigation of this magnitude was expensive, and the taxpayer was bearing the final burden. It was an ongoing cancer, without a cure. Another example of a societal dilemma! If only there were some way to curb the demand.

I called Chief of Police Todd Wilson. He indicated that Draper had visited all our area gift shops without getting any accounts. Our business people had refused to carry his line of jewelry. The rumor was that he had come on too strong. The chief could not offer any further information, but asked me to contact him if I should spot Draper in Old Forge.

After I made my telephone calls, I decided to do the weekly laundry. I pulled the bed sheets off the bed and gathered all the soiled clothes, placing them in the laundry basket. I hoped that Patty would take over this job after we married, or better yet, we'd invest in a washer and dryer. I usually changed the towels twice each week. Apparently I hadn't this week. I put the bleach and the soap bottles on top of the basket and loaded them into the Bronco. I locked the door and had returned to the Bronco to get in, when I heard a vehicle coming into the yard. I looked up. It was a state police SUV. Russ Slingerland was bringing Ruben home. I closed the Bronco door and waited for Russ to pull up.

I could hear Ruben barking. Russ stopped the SUV by the dog run and got out, coming around to the rear. He opened the hatch.

"Hi, Jason. Ruben was a good dog. He made several hits for drugs at Chazy and Massena. We gave him a refresher course with the drug samples, and from then on his sniffer was on the money. I hate to return him to you, but the K-9s' are back from the Buffalo and Rochester areas. You can be proud of him."

When Russ released him, Ruben came rushing toward me. I gave him a big hug and rubbed his nose. "Good boy, Ruben, good boy. I'm glad you're home." I went over to the dog run, put the big K-9 in his run, and shut the gate.

"Jason, Ruben sure missed you. He'd whine at night before he went to sleep. My wife would get up and go out to him in the den and tell him 'It's okay, you'll be home soon.'"

"Russ, you know him well. You trained him when the division got him and you did a remarkable job. You certainly made a great team. Now he can rest and continue to enjoy his retirement."

"You'll be getting a letter from the Troop S Commander, I'm certain. He appreciated you making Ruben available to us. The shortage of the K-9s was only temporary, and now we have a number of them, with more being allotted to the division."

"Say, Russ, would you like a cup of coffee?" I asked.

"No thanks, Jason. I stopped at Gertie's coming through Long Lake and had breakfast. I try to stop there when I come through that way. They're always so accommodating. When I was stationed at Long Lake, I used to eat there frequently. Great folks, Gertie and Bob," he went on.

"You bet they are," I agreed. "If we had more people like them you'd have less trouble in the world. That's a fact."

"For sure, Jason. Well, I've got to head back to Troop S Headquarters. You know, Ruben and I have something in common. We were both called back temporarily for a cause. I'll be a regular civilian in about five hours. It's great seeing you, Jason. And Ruben, you be a good boy," he hollered over to the dog.

I walked Russ over to the SUV and shook his hand.

"Thanks, Russ, and say hello to the Mrs.," I said cordially.

"I will, Jason, and you say hello to Patty for me," he added as he got into the car.

"You're on the guest list for our wedding, Russ. We hope you can make it."

"Thanks again, Jason. We'll sure try. So long."

"So long. Have a safe drive home."

I watched Russ pull out of the driveway. Then I went over to join Ruben in his run and put my arms around the German shepherd. He pushed his big head against my trouser leg. I filled his food dish and water pan.

"I sure missed you, big guy."

I climbed back into the Bronco and headed for the laundromat. This time I took him along with me.

CHAPTER THIRTY-SIX

Lieutenant Jack Doyle was in his office with several members of the division discussing the strategy in the Bernie Draper case. He had attended a joint federal and state task force meeting a few days previously, where plans had been laid out to close down the Draper smuggling operation. It was a complex case, which included testimony before the grand jury. As a result of these proceedings, warrants had been issued for the arrest of Bernard Draper and his associates. The arrest warrants would be executed in New York State and at the offices of Draper's Trucking Company in the State of Arizona. Lieutenant Doyle, as well as BCI Captain Roy Garrison and Major Frank Temple, had been apprised of the suspicious death of Cesar Guerrero in the State of Pennsylvania and the triple homicide of the three Mexican Nationals in Arizona.

In addition to the criminal warrants were a number of search warrants for Draper's New York properties, which included the two Carver Cruisers located at the marina in Waddington. In addition, search warrants were issued for the vehicles, including two pickups and the black Lexus and any Draper semi-outfit in New York State. The same process was taking place in Arizona.

Lieutenant Doyle briefed his superiors on every minute detail concerning the case. Major Temple and Captain Garrison raised several important questions about the gathering of intelligence. Lieutenant Doyle responded to his two leaders with eloquence, pointing out specific important issues that had been accounted for.

The execution of the warrants would take place at 4:30 a.m. Lieutenant Doyle expressed his appreciation to all members involved in the investigation. He indicated that all personnel would be wearing their protective vests.

"Just a minute, Lieutenant Doyle. Can you tell us where the information came from that initiated this investigation?" an investigator asked.

"Yes, I can, Senior Hooper. It came from a former member of the BCI, one Jason Black, now a private investigator here in the Adirondack Mountains. Does that answer your question, Senior?"

"Yes it does, sir. Thank you."

"I want everyone to get a good night's sleep. So go to bed early. You're dismissed."

CHAPTER THIRTY-SEVEN

I pulled in front of the laundromat and shut the Bronco off. I removed the laundry and went inside. There were just two machines empty. I placed the whites in one and the colored clothes in another. I added the bleach and soap to the whites and just the soap to the colored. I plunked four quarters into each machine. When I hit the button, the machines started their washing cycles. They would run for forty minutes.

While the washing machines spun, I walked over to John's Diner. I noticed Wilt's big white Dodge parked in the lot. I went into the diner, and Patty came rushing over.

"Honey, I heard that Ruben has come home!" she said with excitement.

"How'd you hear that so fast?" I was amazed.

"Oh, you know how news travels. And besides, I saw him in the rear of the Bronco when you drove by." She laughed.

I shook my head. I should have known.

"What can I get for you, Jason?" She smiled her beautiful smile.

"I'll have a cup of hot tea. I only have about thirty minutes. I just put the wash in the machines," I explained.

"You could have waited. I would have done it for you, honey," she said, crinkling her nose.

"That's okay. There'll come a time when you'll be doing the washing all the time." I kidded her.

"Anything else besides the tea? We've got some fresh doughnuts." She was trying to tempt me.

"No, that's all I want, just the tea." I remained firm, trying not to be tempted.

Patty soon returned with the teapot and a full cup of hot steaming tea. She told me that she'd stop at the house after she got out of work. I noticed that Wilt was in a conversation with a customer of John's Diner. I didn't want to bother him, so I finished my tea and paid the bill. Lila nodded at me as I left the diner.

When I started walking back to the laundromat, Police Chief Todd Wilson pulled up to the curb. He motioned me to come over to his car. The chief reached across and opened the passenger side door.

"Could I talk with you for a minute, Jason?" he asked.

"Sure, Chief," I said as I climbed in.

"Jason, I got the word today that the troopers are going to go after this Draper organization very shortly. Now, Draper has been around attempting to push his jewelry line this past week. He's driving the black Lexus. I want you to know that none of the business folks are going to do business with him. They are very suspicious of him. He's been using high pressure tactics. You know our business people here in town are perceptive and they pass the word to each other."

"Chief, I know that. I can't say anything, but I'm glad they've taken that approach." I had confidence in all the locals. They had good instincts.

"I am too, Jason. I'll let you know if anything else comes up, and please contact me if you develop any information regarding that group. I heard that he has a foreman or a bodyguard by the name of Scott. I don't know the last name, but I was told he stopped at a local gas station a few days ago in a pickup with 'Draper' painted on the door. He was trying to get close to one of the female clerks and told her that he was headed to Pennsylvania. She indicated that the guy was packing a firearm in a shoulder holster."

"Are you kidding?" I asked, surprised.

"No, I'm serious. Do you think you can come up with the last name?"

"I've got it at home on my pad. When I finish my laundry I'll look it up and contact you," I advised him.

"I'll appreciate it. Thanks, Jason."

"I'll be in touch."

"Okay. So long for now." The chief pulled away from the curb after I got out of the patrol car.

I walked to the laundromat and put the clothes into the dryers. I sat down on the bench and read the Utica paper while the clothes were drying. All of a sudden I remembered Scott's last name. It was Austin, Scott Austin. I went over to the payphone. Chief Wilson answered the telephone.

"Town of Webb Police Department."

"Jason Black here, Chief. I just remembered the name. It is Scott Austin."

"Thanks, Jason."

"Check him out, Chief. He could have been involved in a possible homicide in Pennsylvania. Check with Lieutenant Jack Doyle at Raybrook. He might be able to shed some light on that. I had heard that one of Draper's drivers was found dead."

"That Scott Austin might well be involved." He sounded concerned.

"There's a possibility he could be."

"Thanks again, Jason." I heard the click.

I went over to the dryer and checked my laundry. I took the dry clothes out and folded them, placing them in the laundry basket. In about fifteen minutes I was headed to the post office. I pulled into the parking lot, got out of the Bronco, and went inside. The postal box was full of letters and another magazine. I nodded to the postmaster and left the office. I sat in the Bronco for a few minutes looking over the mail and then headed home. Ruben had waited patiently in the car.

I almost struck a doe when I pulled into my driveway. The deer herds were increasing every year. A number of deer-car accidents occur every month, and now I almost had another one to add to the list. It was a good thing that I take defensive driving seriously. I looked over toward the woods and the white tail disappeared in a flash. I pulled up to Ruben's dog run, shut the Bronco off, and got out. I opened the rear hatch. Ruben jumped down and ran to his run. I took the fresh laundry out and set it on the porch. I unlocked the door and put the basket inside, then hurried back outside to check on Ruben.

"Good to have you home, big fellow." I gave him a loving pat.

He jumped up on me and licked my face.

I reentered the house. Before I put the laundry away, I called Lieutenant Jack Doyle at Raybrook. I told him about my conversation with Chief Todd Wilson and about Scott Austin's stop at our local gas station, when he told the clerk that he was headed to Pennsylvania. I informed Jack that probably the chief would be calling him. Lieutenant Doyle made a note of the information. He indicated its importance, and that it might tie in with the investigation of the dead truck driver in Pennsylvania. I wished him well and said goodbye. I hung up the telephone and returned to my laundry.

With the clean clothes and articles put away, I went into the office and finished opening my mail. There were several bad checks from Adirondack business people that had to be collected or turned over to the police authorities.

I wrote several letters to the check passers and requested that they contact me relative to insufficient funds. I folded the letters and placed them in the envelopes along with a copy of the check in question. I always allowed the check passer to correct his or her error before initiating any type of criminal process. It was this approach that seemed to please the forgetful person. As for the blatant check passer, that person I liked to meet face-to-face. Usually, those face-to-face encounters never had to be repeated.

I had just finished filling out some labels for my files when the telephone rang. I answered, and recognized the voice right away.

"Hello, Jason Black. How are you? Haven't talked with you in a long time."

"Joanne Smith, it has been a long time. How are you and Ted?" I asked.

"We're both doing fine," she answered.

"What can I do for you, Attorney Smith?"

"Jason, I was wondering if you could locate a person for me."

"I'd be happy to try. What's the name?" I reached for my pad and pen.

"His name is Jerome Watson. He resided in Blue Mountain Lake ten years ago. I believe he is forty-five years of age. His grandmother passed away and he was named in her will. I contacted their post office and was told he moved away and left no forwarding address."

"Joanne, I'll certainly give it a good try. I've heard the name, and I have a contact in Blue Mountain Lake. An old-timer who knows everyone from the past and, surprisingly, he possesses a memory that is sharp as a tack."

"Jason, I'll take care of your time or any expenses that you may incur."

"We won't worry about that for now. I'll check this out and let you know."

"Okay, Jason, I'll appreciate that. You know, Ted and I were talking the other day about the deer hunt we went on with you several years ago. We didn't get any deer, but we had a good time." We both chuckled as we recalled the event.

"Joanne, I'll never forget that time. The food at your camp was delicious. You and Ted made me feel at home."

"We enjoyed having you there. Thank you, Jason. I expect that I'll hear from you."

"Yes, I'll contact you as soon as I have the information."

"Take care, Jason."

"Say hello to Ted, and thank you for calling me." It was always good hearing from Joanne.

We hung up, and I went to the kitchen and turned the burner on. I filled the teakettle and put it over the flame. I took the box of green tea from the pantry and extracted a teabag. It wasn't long before the teakettle was whistling. I poured the hot boiling water over the teabag. The last two sugar cookies in the cookie jar softened up when I dunked them in the tea. I had first started drinking green tea when I was in the US Marine Corps. Supposedly, it contains antioxidants which are good for your health.

I went back into my office and worked on my reports. I checked my casebook and added seventeen bad checks to the book, along with making out a case card and label for each file. I added another case, the attempt to locate one Jerome Watson. I spent an hour filing and cleaning up the office. I've always tried to keep the paperwork under control, but private investigators sometimes have an excess amount.

I was just about to go out and take Ruben for a walk, when the telephone rang.

"Hello, Jason, Sergeant Joe Kelly, RCMP calling. Have you got a minute?" he inquired.

"Hello, Joe. I certainly have time for a mountie, anytime."

"Jason, I have talked with your friend, Lieutenant Jack Doyle. Hey! That guy gets things done. We've been able to put some facts together to the Draper puzzle and the picture is clear. Draper and his organization are going down. The plate numbers you furnished us were very important. I won't go into detail but, believe me, some of those people have been suspects in drug cases, running guns, untaxed liquor and cigarettes and other smuggling violations. Our people are tying things together over here in Ontario. I called to thank you personally. This case is going to involve the New York Troopers, DEA, FBI, IRS, INS, ATF, OPP, QPP and the RCMP, as well as the Cornwall PD. It's going to be big. Very big."

"Joe, thank you for your comments. Yes, Jack Doyle lives and breathes the job twenty-four hours a day. We've got some great people at Troop S. They watch over the North Country of New York State."

"I bet you miss the job, Jason. You were always involved and active." I felt his comments were sincere.

"Indeed I do, Joe." I sighed as I reminisced.

"Well, I've got to go, but I'll speak with you soon."

"Take care, Sergeant Kelly. Best to you."

I hung up and went outside. I let Ruben out of the dog run and we took off for the woods. Ruben heeled all the way to the woods. He wouldn't leave my side.

We walked through the forest and over to the edge of Route 28. I spotted several large blue jays. Ruben had missed chasing the chippies, and now he had two of them cornered in a brush pile, but not for long. The chippies broke loose and went in opposite directions. Ruben pursued the nearest one. He loved to frolic with the chippies. We had just turned around and started to head for home when we saw the big bear. He was back. It looked like the bear that the state biologist had darted. I couldn't believe it. Ruben's ears went up at attention.

"Stay, Ruben, stay," I commanded.

Ruben didn't move, but was ready to spring at the other animal. The bear stopped, and stood up on its hind legs, and let out a growl that sent chills up my spine.

"Stay, Ruben." Ruben didn't budge. The bear was now on all fours. He moved off the trail, turning his head toward us, then lumbered off. My neck started aching. My old whiplash must have been acting up. I never know what will trigger it off.

The chills subsided, and Ruben and I headed back home. As we broke out of the woods, we spotted Patty's red Jeep pulling into the yard. Ruben took off, heading straight for Patty and the Jeep. I increased my pace. Patty got out of the car running toward Ruben. They met and Patty hugged the big K-9.

"Hey, Patty. Save me a hug, too, sweetheart!" I called over to her.

I ran directly to Patty and her outstretched arms, and we embraced.

"Have you eaten yet, Jason?" she asked.

"Not yet, honey."

"Well, you're in for a treat. I stopped at Slickers and picked up four dozen shrimp and cocktail sauce. They're still nice and hot."

"Ummm! That sounds great! " My taste buds awoke.

Patty went to the Jeep and took out the shrimp and cocktail sauce. I followed her inside after I put Ruben into the dog run. He looked disappointed. Patty set the table. We washed our hands, and Patty sat down at the table. I opened up two ice-cold drinks and poured each into a glass. The feast began.

"I didn't think they had shrimp to go."

"Jason, I'm not certain whether it was a favor for me, but here we are. Do you like them, honey?" she queried, eagerly waiting for my approval.

"I love them, Patty. The sauce is perfect and so are the shrimp. That was very nice of you to bring them. They're delicious."

"Honey, I'm off tomorrow. Would you like to do something special?"

"We could take a ride to Blue Mountain Lake, if that's okay." I had an ulterior motive.

"I'd love to, Jason."

"I'm attempting to locate a person in that area, and this would give us an opportunity to combine business with pleasure."

"That'll be fine. What time will you pick me up?" she asked eagerly.

"I'll pick you up at about 8:00 a.m. and we'll stop at Drew's Restaurant in Inlet for some breakfast. It will save us time in the long run. We won't have the clean-up."

"That sounds good to me." She nodded.

Patty and I cleaned up the kitchen, and then we went into the living room. I put some music on. I picked out a Patsy Cline CD and inserted it into my compact disk player. She sang "Crazy" and "I Go Out Walking After Midnight." We talked about our wedding plans while we listened to Patsy. We decided to try to have a small wedding. We debated whether we should have a church or a civil ceremony. We agreed to be married at the Big Moose Chapel, which would accommodate our many friends. We both loved the Adirondacks and the woods. The ceremony would take place shortly after Labor Day, after the majority of the tourists leave. Patty told me that she would send out the invitations and that Lila or Harriet would assist her.

I went into the office and took a new spiral notebook out of the file cabinet. We moved back into the kitchen and sat at the table making notations in the notebook. Even though our wedding would be small, it still necessitated our close attention to detail. We decided against a formal dress wedding with gowns and tuxedos. The men would wear dark-colored business suits, and the women would wear something less formal.

For music at the chapel, Carrie Neilson would sing "Ave Maria" and "Because God Made You Mine," accompanied on the piano by Eileen Baker. We decided to hold the reception at the Edge Water Conference Center overlooking the beautiful Old Forge Pond. Penny Younger and his band would play at the reception. Although I hadn't yet asked him, I was certain he would do it if he had the day open. I would contact him. Patty and I decided we would try to limit the guest list to one hundred people.

"Patty, would you like to invite your family from Kentucky to our wedding?"

"Honey, I don't think they could get time off to attend. I thought maybe someday after we're married we could drive down to Kentucky and visit my brothers." She looked over to see my reaction.

"I'd love to, sweetheart." I had never been to Kentucky.

"I think that would be the thing to do." She was happy at my response.

Patty and I went over our plans and checked everything we jotted down in the notebook.

"Jason, who shall we have marry us?"

"If it's all right with you, I thought Judge Joshua L. Daley would be the one to unite us."

"Honey, I was going to suggest that. I'm pleased that you selected him."

"Patty, he's a reverent person and a former U.S. Marine." I always gave preference to my Marine buddies.

"He's a wonderful person. He always takes time to say hello when he comes into John's."

"Patty, can you think of anything else that should be put on the list of things to do?"

"Oh! There are dozens of other things, cake, the food, what we will have to drink, and most important of all, where will we go for our honeymoon? We can always take care of the list later on." She was excited about our future plans.

I mentioned to Patty that if there were any of her friends that she'd like to invite, she should feel free to do so. I told her that I would probably add a few of my trooper associates to the list. We still hadn't picked out the specific date, but we would have it on a Saturday morning. I even planned to wax the Bronco. It hadn't had a wax job in a long, long time.

I put the teakettle on, lit the burner, and made us each a cup of hot green tea. I looked in the freezer and found two frozen brownies. I placed them in the microwave to defrost them. We sat down and sipped our tea.

"Are these the brownies I sent home with you about two months ago?"

"Yes, honey. I had put them in the freezer. They're still good, aren't they?"

"They taste fine to me," she said as she munched on hers.

"My dessert selection is limited around here."

Patty and I chatted for another forty-five minutes before she decided it was time for her to leave for her place. We cleared the table and washed the cups. She looked up at me.

"I feel very close to you, my darling." She spoke in a sweet, melodic tone.

"I love you too, sweetheart," I said as I embraced her.

Our lips met in a warm kiss. My knees felt weak.

"Thank you for those delicious shrimp. What a treat!" I said, changing the subject.

"I thought you'd like them."

Patty and I went outside. We let Ruben out of his dog run and he took off for the woods. I held Patty closely by her Jeep.

"Goodnight, honey," she said.

"I'll pick you up in the morning. Goodnight."

"Goodnight, Jason."

Ruben hurried back from the woods and reached me just as Patty pulled away. He placed his big head against my trouser leg. I petted him. I looked up into the sky and the millions of stars twinkled down on us. I saw the Big Dipper and the North Star. How could anyone not believe in the creator of Heaven and Earth and the complete universe. I was humbled by the spectacle above.

I followed Ruben to the door of my cozy log home and we went inside. Ruben went directly to his air mattress. I checked the kitchen and then went into my office. I had several letters ready to mail and would drop them off at the post office in the morning when I went to pick up Patty. Patty gave me a call to let me know she had arrived home safely. I prepared for bed and turned off the lights after I checked the doors.

The tick-tock of the Big Ben faded away as I drifted off to sleep.

CHAPTER THIRTY-EIGHT

It was late at Troop S Headquarters. The night desk man was checking over reports and answering the night calls. In the upstairs office of BCI Lieutenant Jack Doyle, the lights were burning brightly. Jack motioned to the group of people to follow him to the conference room. Three coffee pots were full of hot coffee, and a platter of donuts—sugared and plain—were placed on a nearby table.

"Gentlemen, fill your cups and take a donut of your choice and let's get down to work." Lieutenant Doyle's voice was authoritative. The men complied.

"As you know, people, this is a joint operation. It has been decided after many meetings with federal agencies, including our U.S. Coast Guard and the RCMP as well as the Cornwall Police Department, that the troopers will take the lead to apprehend Bernard Draper, Scott Austin, and all of Draper's associates. Our patrol boat has been brought to the Waddington area. The RCMP, U.S. Coast Guard, and the troopers will cover those two Carver Cruisers at O'Rourke's Marina. There is a special task force in Cornwall that will strike at the same time we do here in the states. There are several suspects in Cornwall. The Crown Attorney is on top of this. The RCMP, OPP, and the Cornwall Police Department will take care of the Canadian arrests.

"We'll have a detail covering the jewelry store and warehouse and a detail covering Draper's house in Tupper Lake. We have search warrants as well as criminal warrants for the two cruisers, buildings, and all vehicles associated with Draper. As we speak, a similar meeting is being held at the Phoenix Police Department in Arizona. Same subject. We'll take up our positions at 4:00 a.m. tomorrow morning. People are already in the general area of Waddington and in Cranberry Lake as well as Tupper Lake. It is imperative that you wear your protective vests.

"We know that Draper is armed at all times and so is his bodyguard, Scott Austin. Gentlemen, the reason for the vests is for your protection. I learned today that Phoenix has DNA that implicates Draper in the actual killing of three Mexican Nationals, who were day laborers in Phoenix. The story, as we have it from snitches in that jurisdiction, is that the three Mexicans discovered Draper's drug operation and tried to shake him down for money. This was a bad move on their part. He shot them in the head and dumped them in the desert. It is also believed that Scott Austin did a hit on one of Draper's drivers in Pennsylvania, while the driver was parked at a truck-stop. These people are dangerous. We've got to put them out of business. I want you all back here at 3:00 a.m. sharp. You've got about four hours to sleep. Keep this to yourself. Any questions? If not, you're excused."

CHAPTER THIRTY-NINE

I was standing on a dock watching Dale take off in his Stinson. Then I heard a bell. I opened my eyes and reached over, turning the alarm clock off. My dream ended. Ruben was pulling on the bed-spread at the foot of the bed.

"Settle down, Ruben. Be a good boy." I reached over to pat his back.

I pushed the covers back and went into the bathroom. I shaved and took a hot shower. When I turned on the cold water, I thought I had run into an iceberg. It was cold! Quickly I dressed. Ruben wanted to go outside. I unlocked the door, opening it. Ruben sprang out, racing toward the woods. Two mallards flew overhead, low and fast. In a few minutes Ruben was standing by the dog run. I went out and checked his water and food dishes. I filled his water dish. I heard the telephone ring and ran back inside.

"Hello," I said before it went on the answering machine.

"Jason, Todd Wilson here. Last night Lieutenant Doyle called me and told me to watch out for any of Draper's semi-trucks and to call Raybrook if any are spotted. I told him I would. My men have been alerted and Inlet is watching. I imagine he called the local barracks, too."

"Todd, I've got to go to Blue Mountain Lake this morning. I'll take my cell phone with me. I can't promise I'll be able to call out, but I'll have it with me. That's funny he called you. Maybe something is up. I'm taking Patty with me this morning. Todd, if you happen to be in the neighborhood today, just stop by and check on Ruben. He's back home, you know.

"I heard Ruben did a good job, too. Yes, I'll check on him for you."

"Thanks."

I locked up the house and petted Ruben. "Be a good boy. I'll see you later, fella."

I climbed into the Bronco and headed to Patty's house. A couple of pickups tooted as I passed through town. I spotted Jack Falsey's van starting out of town. Jack gave me a big wave. I knew that he must be on his way to help out someone. Plumbing and heating were important here in the North Country. A well pump could break down anytime. Jack took good care of his customers. I didn't have any complaints against the local service workers. They all took pride in their work. We have many good craftspeople in the region.

Patty came out her door the minute I pulled into her yard. She climbed into the Bronco and I backed out of the driveway. I leaned over and gave her a peck on the cheek.

"I love you, Jason."

"Love you, too, babe."

She smiled.

When we went by John's Diner I saw Wilt's big Dodge pickup parked in the lot. I reminded Patty that we were stopping at Drew's Restaurant, just north of Inlet for breakfast. I explained that I hadn't been there in a while and wanted to say hello to Mike Drew, the owner. Besides, it would do her good to have a change of scenery.

"I don't mind, my darling," she said agreeably.

The Inlet stores were opening when we passed through town. When I pulled into Drew's parking lot, Al, Mike's father, was just pulling out of the parking area in his new Cadillac. He smiled and waved. We waved back. I told Patty that Al must have been in a hurry or he would have stopped to chat for a while.

Patty and I got out of the Bronco and went inside. Mike's wife, Paula, greeted us with a warm smile and seated us by the window. The dining room consists of booths or tables and chairs. We opted for the booth. Paula placed two menus before us and asked if we'd like coffee. We ordered the coffee with cream. She soon returned with a tray holding two cups of steaming hot coffee with creamers and two glasses of ice water with lemon wedges. Our selection was #6 on the menu: two eggs, hashed-brown potatoes, and ham. We both opted for whole-wheat toast. Patty and I chatted in low tones about our wedding plans. I could tell that Patty was more than excited about it. So was I. I looked around at the knotty pine walls, which added to the quaintness of the interior.

Our breakfast order came. Paula set the large tray on a nearby table and served Patty first and then me. She immediately refilled our coffee cups and gave us more creamers. We began eating. I love plenty of pepper, no salt. Patty didn't use either. Everything was tasty and prepared just right. Paula came by with the coffee pot again and we had a third cup. She chatted with us for a couple of minutes. I told her to tell Mike, who was the chef for the day, that everything was wonderful. She thanked us and presented us with the check. Patty wanted to treat me. I told her that I'd take care of the bill. I had the correct amount, and I left a gratuity on the table.

We had just risen from the booth when I heard the news flash on the adjacent barroom television, which is mounted in the northwest corner. Patty and I were about to leave. We rushed back into the bar to listen. The television news announcer said, "A joint force of law enforcement officers have stopped a smuggling operation in the North Country. One of the main suspects, Bernard Draper, eludes capture." He indicated that the noon and 5:00 p.m. news would have further details. My adrenaline rose and my heartbeat increased. How I wished I could have been there. I looked at Patty.

"Patty, I'll be a son-of-a-gun." I could not hide my feelings.

"What are you saying, Jason?" Patty looked puzzled.

"Honey, I'll explain later. Let's go." I rushed us out of the restaurant.

Mike Drew looked out from the kitchen and waved goodbye. I couldn't take the time to tell Mike why we were in such a big hurry. I realized that I should have brought my firearm, but I hadn't. I helped Patty into the Bronco, and instead of turning toward Raquette Lake and Blue Mountain Lake, I turned toward Inlet. Patty was surprised. I'd explain in a few minutes. I floored the

Bronco; it sputtered and coughed, but finally responded and took off. I applied the brakes in front of the Inlet Hardware Store and skidded to a stop. Patty was hanging on tight.

"I'll be right back, honey." I left the Bronco running.

Chris Slocum was at the cashier's area. I told her I wanted to borrow a twelve-gauge shotgun and a box of deer slugs. She looked at me puzzled, but grabbed the key to unlock the display cabinet.

"Jason, it's not deer season. What's going on?" she asked as she put it on the counter.

"I can't go into detail, but believe me, Chris, it's important," I reassured her.

I knew Chris well; she surmised that if I wanted to borrow a shotgun and ammo, I must have a good reason for doing so.

"I appreciate this, Chris."

The shotgun was a twelve-gauge Remington semi-automatic with a deer barrel. It was a good used gun.

"Please let Marty know that I borrowed it." Marty was the owner.

"I will, but I'm certain it's okay."

"When I'm finished with it, I'll return it." I thanked her and told her that I'd explain later.

I raced outside and climbed into the Bronco, making a U turn on Route 28 so Patty and I were headed north. I told Patty to keep her eyes open for a black Lexus sedan. I asked myself, "Who screwed up?" Jack Flynn had told me in his letter that Bernie Draper was clever. It was going to be difficult to locate him, but hopefully he's still driving his black Lexus, which would be easy to spot. There aren't too many roads from Tupper Lake that he could take. Patty and I could continue with our plans to drive to Blue Mountain Lake. I reiterated to Patty to watch the road closely, I also eyed every southbound vehicle that we met. Patty was hanging on tightly. I wanted to call Lieutenant Jack Doyle, but I had already complied with his request of staying away from their investigation. I would love to continue to comply, but historically, while on the job, I had had more than one wanted person cross my path accidentally. My head was spinning.

I explained to Patty what was taking place. She had no knowl-

edge about the smuggling investigation in the North Country. I
hadn't related the facts to her. That wasn't my style. I could tell,
however, that Patty was getting a little nervous. I told her that the
troopers were looking for a dangerous wanted subject.

"Jason, is it the fellow that has been trying to sell his jewelry in
Old Forge? I have heard a little about him. He apparently thinks
he's a ladies' man, according to the rumor."

"Oh, yeah! He's a ladies' man all right." I didn't want to alarm
Patty any more than she already was.

"Jason, I'm glad that none of the businesspeople took on his
southwestern jewelry. You can't fool those Adirondackers."

"So am I, honey. Yes, he is the one the police are looking for.
Patty, if we see him, we'll have to be careful. It is believed that he
carries a firearm with him."

When we reached Raquette Lake I pulled off the road near the
diner. I backed the Bronco in beside a high hedge. I wanted to remain inconspicuous. We both watched the highway. I placed two
12-gauge deer slugs in my shirt pocket and lay the shotgun on the
back seat. I told Patty to remain calm. We had sat there for about
fifteen minutes when a black Lexus going southbound passed our
line of vision. I couldn't make out the rear registration plate, but I
was sure it wasn't New York. I started the Bronco, pulled onto
Route 28, and headed toward Inlet. I saw the Lexus ahead of me. A
log truck had just pulled onto the highway from a wooded road in
front of the Lexus. The truck was also heading south and moving
slowly. I saw the brake lights of the Lexus come on. I immediately
opened the glove compartment and removed my cell phone. I
called the administrative telephone number of the Town of Webb
Police Department.

"Chief Wilson speaking. May I help you?" he answered politely.

"Todd, this is urgent. Patty and I are between Raquette Lake
and Inlet, following a black Lexus sedan. I'm behind it just far
enough not to be able to read the plate number. A log truck just
pulled in front of the Lexus and is going slowly uphill. The Lexus
cannot pass. Set up a road block as soon as you can."

"I'm aware that Draper's on the run. I have two patrol cars out in the area as we speak. I'll head out to Eagle Bay right now. Consider it done," he responded without hesitation.

"I'm getting closer, Chief. I can't believe it! It looks like a woman is driving the car," I said, perplexed.

"We'll set it up in Eagle Bay." I heard the phone click as he cradled it.

We were in luck the Lexus couldn't pass the log truck.

"We'll just play it cool, Patty. You okay?" I could tell she was becoming edgy, as she unnecessarily fussed with her hair.

"I'm fine, honey, as long as I am with you," she answered nervously.

We were crawling slowly up the medium grade. The truck was loaded with big logs. The woman driving was impatient. She kept pulling out and back in, weaving in and out many times. I was getting nervous myself, yet sure that Todd Wilson was swinging into action. The Inlet officer would probably meet the chief in Eagle Bay. I was confident that they'd be able to check out the Lexus. I was curious as to who the woman was who was driving the Lexus. She appeared to be alone. Patty wasn't saying anything, but I was concerned that she was with me. In no way was it my intention to subject her to danger. I would be extremely careful not to place her in jeopardy.

The brake lights came on as the Lexus almost hit the rear of the log truck. I stayed back so I wouldn't alert the woman in the car, but I was close enough to see she was a blonde.

When we reached Drew's Restaurant, the log truck slowly drove into the parking area. I surmised the logger was going in for coffee. The Lexus increased its speed. I did, too. When we reached the downhill grade into Inlet, the Lexus slowed down to a crawl, but proceeded. Just south of Eagle Bay, near the donut shop, I saw a large truck parked across the highway with the hood up. The Lexus came to a screeching halt. On each end of the truck was a patrol car. Between the Lexus and the truck were three other vehicles. I saw Todd and another officer checking driver licenses. Todd was pointing at the truck, apparently telling the driver he'd have to wait. I could see that Todd was eyeballing the Lexus. I pulled the Bronco off the highway and watched.

The woman in the Lexus opened the door and got out.

"Patty, that's not a woman. It's a man wearing a blond wig. He's reaching inside his jacket. Oh my God, he's reaching for a gun."

I saw Todd move fast. He grabbed the man and put a headlock on him. The other officer came to his assistance. I could see that the chief was disarming Draper. Todd cuffed the man, whose arms were flailing. The blond wig went flying through the air. It was indeed Bernie Draper. Now he was trying to kick the officer. I got out of the Bronco.

"Be careful, Jason," Patty said with a worried look on her face.

"I will be honey. Lock the doors."

I ran over to assist Chief Wilson.

He appeared to be very strong. Draper bit Todd in the left arm. As I walked toward Draper, he kicked at me. I sidestepped and threw a left hook connecting with his jaw. He sank to the ground. I looked at Todd and noticed the blood trickling down his arm from Draper's bite.

"This Draper is tough, Jason," the chief said. Todd was in pain.

I asked the officer to get Todd's first-aid kit from his patrol car. I had never met the officer, as he was new. He appeared to be a fine young man. He brought me the kit, and I rendered first aid to Todd's upper left arm.

"Chief, you'd better have a doctor look at your arm," I cautioned him.

"I will, Jason. First, would you give me a sworn statement of your action?"

"I certainly will, from the beginning to the end. Chief, please call Lieutenant Jack Doyle at Raybrook. He's looking for Draper. According to the news the raid on the Draper Organization took place this morning, and apparently Draper must have slipped through the net. Todd, be careful of him. He's wanted by the Phoenix, AZ, Police Department for homicide."

"I'll call the lieutenant as soon as I get back to the office. The troopers in Old Forge are tied up on a bad accident near Woodgate. Believe me, I'll be careful of Mr. Draper. He apparently chooses to remain mute. He's not saying a word. Thanks, Jason, for your assistance."

"My pleasure, sir. I'm always happy to assist." I missed my duty days in the state trooper service.

Chief Wilson and the officer placed Bernard Draper in the rear of the chief's car. Patty was frantically watching the action from the Bronco. As I returned to her, I could tell by the worried expression on her face the deep concern she had for Todd, the young officer, and myself.

"It's all right, honey. Everything is finally under control."

She was shaking. "He was strong, Jason. I saw him bite Todd and kick at you. He had a gun, didn't he?" she asked, still trembling. I reached over and held her until she relaxed.

"Yes, it looked like a .45 caliber semi-automatic. Todd took out the clip and secured the weapon." I was impressed with his handling of the situation.

Patty seemed composed and her shaking had subsided. I kissed her on the cheek. After a brief discussion, it was decided that we would continue with our original plans for the day. We turned around and headed back toward Eagle Bay and Inlet. There were four or five vehicles that had stopped momentarily to watch the action. They continued on as the chief headed to Old Forge with his officer following him. Todd's vehicle had a wire-cage for the back seat and Draper could kick all he wanted to. He was secured.

"Honey, why would a supposedly successful businessman get involved in the smuggling of drugs and other things?" she asked, shaking her head.

"Patty, I have one word that defines your question. It is greed, my dear. Greed."

I thought about calling Lieutenant Doyle, but I had asked Todd to take care of the notification. I had a great deal of respect for Chief Wilson and his department. I wanted Todd and his officer to get the credit for the apprehension of Draper. It was a good arrest, and taking Draper and his kind off the street was important for the good of society. It might save a lot of kids from the horrors of the drug culture. I knew that Jack Doyle and his people had put a great deal of effort into this complex case. I imagined that Smiley and Ed were somewhere in the great State of New York ferreting out other violators of the law.

We drove into Inlet. I stopped the Bronco in order to take the shotgun and ammo into Chris and turn them over to her.

"Thank you, Chris. I didn't have to use it, thank God. I'll relate the story to you at another time. It is quite involved. I really don't have the time right now."

"I know just what you mean, Jason." She didn't ask any questions.

"Thank Marty for me, too. Talk with you later."

I left the store and returned to the Bronco.

I was thankful that I didn't have to use a weapon in apprehending Draper. I was pleased that Todd and the officer had responded so rapidly to my telephone call, and lucky that he was in his office when I called. All the way to Blue Mountain, Patty and I talked about the excitement that we had just experienced. I wondered what situation had transpired in the Phoenix raid that was to have occurred simultaneously. Jack Flynn would let me know.

CHAPTER FORTY

Pristine Blue Mountain Lake was brilliantly blue, and several tourists were taking pictures. I turned up the side street that connects Route 28 to Route 30. There is a big sign posted that through traffic is not permitted, although many people use it for a shortcut. I went to a small house that sits off the road surrounded by pine trees. I had not visited Jim French in a long time, but if he were at home, he'd be able to tell me if Jerome Watson were in the area. I pulled into the long driveway and headed toward the quaint home. I spotted Jim on his hands and knees weeding his flower garden. He looked up as I turned the Bronco off. I told Patty I'd be right back. I got out and walked toward Jim. He had been a large man, but he looked like a skeleton now. He had served with the First Marine Division in Korea during the Korean War and had been wounded. His right leg was four inches shorter than his left. He had a considerable limp.

"Jason Black, is that you?" He forced a smile on his slim face.

"Jim, yes it is. How have you been? Your flowers are beautiful." I complimented him on his garden.

"Thank you, Jason. Since my wife passed away I spend a lot of time with the flowers and in my little shop out in back. I make lawn ornaments, you know!"

"Jim, you probably heard that since I retired from the troopers I have become a private investigator."

"Yes, I know, Jason. Gertie and Bob from Long Lake mention you all the time. I've missed seeing you around."

"I know what you mean. I've been meaning to stop by before this, but I just seem to go through Blue Mountain Lake without using this road."

"I understand, Jason. What can I do for you?"

"Do you know a Jerome Watson?" I asked.

"I sure do, Jason, but he doesn't live in this area anymore. He's living in Gatlinburg, Tennessee. The son-of-a-gun works at Dollywood."

"He does, hmm?" This was going to be easier than I thought.

"If I remember correctly, Jerome is about forty-five years of age. I heard he married a young lady from Nashville. I believe she is a singer of some kind."

"I appreciate the information, Jim. I promise that I'll stop by and check on you once in a while. I might like to purchase a couple of lawn ornaments at a later date."

"I'll always have some crows and wooden ducks." His display was in his front yard.

"Well, I'd better get moving on." It was good to see Jim. It had been a long time since I had last talked with him.

"Take care, Jason." We shook hands. I could see that Jim was impatient to get back to his weeding.

I got back into the Bronco and backed out of the long driveway.

"Honey, that gentleman certainly has some beautiful flowers." Patty loved flowers.

"He works hard at them every day he can. I've known Jim French for several years, and after his wife passed away he retired and began to raise flowers in the summer and work in his small shop in the winter. His children—he has two sons—reside out of state. Jim visits the cemetery frequently. He loved his wife, Viola."

"How sad. He sounds like a wonderful person." Patty looked up at me with tears in her eyes. She was very sentimental.

"Honey, don't cry. I plan on looking in on him more frequently. I do know that some of the folks from his church stop by to see him. Adirondackers stick together for the most part."

"I know they do, Jason."

"Patty, seeing that we're only about ten miles from Long Lake, let's stop at Gertie's Diner for a sandwich and maybe some soup of the day."

"Oh! I'd love to." She leaned over and gave me a peck on the cheek.

The Adirondack Museum was busy as we passed by. The parking lot was full. We met only a few cars on the way to Long Lake. When we got to the outskirts of Long Lake, a group of Boy Scouts were standing by the road with their knapsacks and bed rolls. There were about a dozen of them. I slowed down and stopped, signaling them to cross the highway. There was no other traffic coming either way. It appeared that they were heading out on an overnight camping trip. They all hollered, "Thank you."

Patty and I continued on to Gertie's Diner. We parked the Bronco and got out. Several people were standing by the seaplane across the road, waiting for a flight. Patty and I went inside. The dining area was filled, with the exception of two tables. I asked Patty which one she preferred. She chose the one by the window. Gertie had a new waitress. She came over to our table with two menus and two glasses of ice water. I noticed her name tag: "Linda."

"I'll give you a couple of minutes. Would you like coffee?" she asked politely.

"We'll have two cups of coffee and two bowls of your split pea soup with some crackers." I enjoyed Patty smiling at me as I ordered.

The waitress left the table. When she came back in about five minutes, she had two cups of hot steaming coffee. After she served us, she returned to the kitchen for the soup. Bowls of split pea soup with crackers were placed before us. It was a cool day, and the hot soup would hit the spot.

"Jason, have you been listening to the radio? All morning they've been telling us about the large-scale smuggling ring that has been smashed." Gertie talked in a low tone. "Did you know about this, Jason?" I looked at her and didn't say anything, except that I hadn't had the radio on. I didn't feel like going into the story at this time.

"I thought you would like to know, Jason," she said as she rushed back to the counter.

"Well, Jason, did you know about the smuggling ring before today?" Patty asked me. "And you didn't tell me? Don't you trust me?"

"Honey, I'm a private investigator aka private detective. This is a sensitive case and I just could not talk about it. You understand, don't you, honey?" I asked, not wanting to hurt her feelings. "I was under strict confidentiality. If any word had slipped out, it could have jeopardized the whole operation. It's not that I don't trust you. Please try to put yourself in my shoes. Please try to understand," I pleaded.

She put her head down and didn't say anything for a minute.

"I understand, Jason," she said, pensively.

I wanted to tell Gertie about the case, but I didn't think it was my place to do so. I was no longer a member of the division and this case was Lieutenant Jack Doyle's responsibility, not mine.

"Patty, we'll have to read it in the newspaper." She had had a ringside seat to some of the action concerning Draper, but remained quiet.

"That's the way it should be." She nodded her head in agreement.

I could imagine that Jack Doyle had his hands full. The multiple agencies working together on major cases have a great deal of responsibility, and there is always the human factor to deal with within all organizations, no matter how smooth the playing field might be. I knew that Jack, along with Major Frank Temple and Captain Roy Garrison, would put all the pieces together.

Linda approached our table.

"Could I interest you in dessert? We have pies, cakes, and pudding," she asked.

"What kind of pudding?" There was always room for pudding.

"Tapioca," she replied.

"We'll each have one dish of tapioca with a creamer for each," Patty ordered.

The pudding was delicious. Patty handed me an extra napkin.

We finished our dessert, and Linda brought us our check. I thanked her. We chatted with Gertie for a few minutes, then paid our bill.

"Say hello to Bob for us, Gertie. Take care."

We went down the steps toward the Bronco. The lake before us was beautiful. The local seaplane had just landed and was approaching the shore. We watched it for a minute and then got into the Bronco.

"The soup was delicious," Patty remarked. "It sure hit the spot."

"Gertie is an excellent cook. Sometime you'll have to have some of her vegetable soup. That, too, will tease your taste buds." I agreed with Patty.

I spotted Zing Zing walking toward Hoss's Country Corner. I blew the horn and he waved in acknowledgement.

"Who's that, Jason?" she asked.

"Honey, Zing Zing and I go back a few years. He resides here in Long Lake and was a former resident of New York City, where he worked in real estate. I met him at the Adirondack Hotel several years ago, when I was hunting deer in the region. For years afterward, when I camped at the Skip Jack Camp Site, we would run into each other at various restaurants. He and his wife invited me to a pig roast. That's when I met Bob and Gertie. We've been friends ever since. Like Old Forge, Long Lake has many fine folks, too," I explained.

"I believe you have mentioned his name to me before," remarked Patty.

"I could have. He's a fixture here in town. A fine gentleman."

The highway toward home didn't have much traffic. We chatted all the way to my house. Our wedding plans were the topic of conversation. We continued to agree we wanted an informal wedding.

Ruben's ears shot up when he saw the Bronco approaching. I stopped the vehicle and we got out. We went over to Ruben. I opened the gate, and the big dog rushed toward us. Patty petted him and rubbed his back.

"Jason, do you mind if I take Ruben for a short walk? I can sure use one after the long ride."

"Sure, sweetheart, go right ahead. I'll unlock the house."

Patty snapped on Ruben's leash and they headed toward the woods.

"Honey, keep your eye out for the bear!" I hollered as she walked away.

"I will, Jason!" she shouted back.

While the loves of my life made their way toward the forest, I unlocked the door and went inside. As soon as I went into the office I saw the red light flashing on the answering machine. I sat down behind my desk and pressed the play button.

"Jason, this is Dale Rush. How about some golf in the morning? Call me."

"Jack Doyle calling. Call me ASAP."

"Jason, how are you? This is Ruby in Arizona. Call me, please."

The remaining calls were business-related: more bad check cases. I knew that Lieutenant Doyle would be in his office early in the morning. I'd call him at his headquarters then.

I dialed Dale's number, and he answered on the third ring.

"Dale, Jason here. What's up?"

"Jason, we need a golfer. Can you play in the morning?" Dale pleaded.

"Dale, I'd love to play, but I'll have to take a rain check. I hope you'll understand."

"Hey! Buddy, what's this I hear? I understand you're some kind of a hero." Dale chuckled.

"What are you talking about?"

"This morning didn't you call Chief Wilson about a south-bound Lexus?"

"Yeah, so what?" I asked, not surprised by the comment. News travels fast around here.

"Well, congratulations. I heard the guy was wearing a wig and you ended up dropping him with a left hook."

"Dale, I was defending myself and assisting the chief." I went on to explain.

"It's all over the television. The guy—I believe his name is Draper—was a big kingpin in a smuggling operation. I just wanted to congratulate you for your actions. Gee, don't get so touchy; I'm only telling you what I heard."

"I'm not touchy. Just surprised that you know so much about it. Remember, I didn't do anything that anyone else wouldn't do under the same circumstances. This Draper apparently was under the influence of drugs and was strong. I'm glad I was there to lend Todd a helping hand."

"I'm glad you were, too, Jason. I was only kidding you a little. I came through Eagle Bay about fifteen minutes after it was all over. I saw the Chief and his officer heading south. Later on I saw the Old Forge towing service putting the Lexus on a flatbed truck. The television and the newspapers have covered this story well."

"I realized you were kidding," I said apologetically.

We finished our conversation, and I wished him well on the golf course the next day. I heard Ruben bark. I got up from my desk and walked to the window. I looked out and Patty was brushing the dog's coat. Clearly Ruben was enjoying it. I went outside and watched Patty. When she had completed the task, she put Ruben back into the dog run. She cleaned the brush and placed it in the cabinet by the back door.

"How was your walk, honey?"

"Wonderful. Ruben was such a good dog. He must know all the chippies along the path. He barks at them and they chatter. I kept Ruben on a tight leash all during the walk. I only saw one deer and didn't see any bears."

"I was a little concerned about the large bear that has been in the area. The biologist has darted it in the past, but the big fellow keeps returning to this area."

"You didn't have to worry. I was watching very closely for any sign of him."

About seven o'clock, I made up some blueberry pancakes and fried some Canadian bacon. We loved the combination. I asked her if she'd like an egg with the pancakes. She declined. While I prepared them, Patty set the table. Tonight we'd have decaf coffee.

I seated Patty. I placed two blueberry pancakes on each plate with two slices of browned Canadian bacon. I added one egg over-medium to mine. I had heated the maple syrup. The sweet butter and the maple syrup combined for a tasty addition. Patty liked hers so much that she ordered two more pancakes. I poured three more on the small grill and we were soon enjoying our second helping. Patty got up from the table and refilled our coffee cups.

"Jason, your blueberry pancakes are wonderful. The berries are so tasty. Oh! I love you so very much, my darling," she added with glee.

"I love you, too, dearest. I'm pleased you enjoyed your pancakes. When I'm alone here, I often will make myself some. They're filling and easy. Any leftovers can be popped into the toaster and warmed up," I went on to explain.

"Jason, I always admire your ingenuity. You never cease to amaze me," she said half-jokingly.

Patty and I did the dishes and cleaned up the kitchen. We listened to music after our pancake supper. We discussed our wedding plans. We had finally decided that Jack Flynn would be the best man. We both knew deep down in our hearts that the other candidates for best man would understand. I would explain to them the reason for having Jack Flynn as best man.

"I'm happy that you made your decision." Patty yawned a couple of times. "Honey, I've got to go home. Six o'clock in the morning comes fast and I have to be at work by 6:30 a.m." We left the house and Patty went over to Ruben's dog run to pet the big K-9. As usual, Ruben's ears rose to the occasion.

I helped Patty into the Bronco. I got in and started the engine. I backed up in a reverse Y and headed toward Route 28. Patty came over close to sit next to me. The ride through town was quick. There was no traffic to contend with. I noticed that the all-night convenience store had a few cars for late night coffee. I pulled into Patty's driveway. We sat in the Bronco for a few minutes. I held her in my arms and gave her a goodnight kiss. She got out of the Bronco and ran up the steps. I waited till she was inside. She flashed the yard light to let me know everything was okay. I backed out of her driveway and headed back home for a good night's sleep.

CHAPTER FORTY-ONE

After a light breakfast of scrambled eggs and toast, and my usual cup of hot coffee, I took Ruben for a walk to the edge of the woods. There didn't seem to be any chippies out at the moment. Ruben sniffed around a couple of brush piles and, discouraged, returned to me and sat down looking up into my face. He put his left paw up for me to shake. We walked back to the house. I returned Ruben to his run and I went inside. I had missed the evening news the night before, but I realized that the smuggling case and the arrest of Draper and his associates would be a major item for weeks to come on radio and television, and in the newspapers.

I went into my office and replayed my answering machine calls. I looked at the clock: 9:10 a.m. I hoped that Lieutenant Doyle would be in his office. I'd return his call before typing up some bad check cases. I dialed Troop S Headquarters. The receptionist answered the telephone and indicated that she would buzz the lieutenant.

"Lieutenant Jack Doyle, speaking." His voice was hoarse.

"Good morning, sir. Have you got a cold?" I inquired.

"Jason! Just the man I want to talk to. I've got allergies, I guess."

"Sorry to hear that," I replied.

"First, I want to congratulate you on the Bernard Draper apprehension. What is it with you, Jason? You always seem to be in the right place."

He was referring to my left-hook, evidently.

"Jack, how did he miss your dragnet?" I quickly changed the subject to avoid further discussion as to my appearance at the scene of the Draper apprehension.

"Draper went out that night and had a few cocktails. He met a young woman from Montreal. He apparently went some place with her, possibly a motel or maybe they stayed all night in the Lexus. That was great that you called Chief Todd Wilson. By the way, he told me the whole story of how it went down in Eagle Bay. What's with the left-hook, Jason?" he firmly asked.

I had been hoping that question wouldn't come up.

"Sir, I was responding to a police officer in need of assistance. Draper was right out of it. He tried to kick me in the groin. I was just defending myself," I explained.

"I had to ask you that question, because Major Frank Temple and Captain Roy Garrison were interested. They wondered how you happened to be in the area at such a crucial time. I was under scrutiny for possibly having alerted you." He was probably being admonished for including me on only-a-need-to-know basis.

"I see. Strictly a coincidence. Patty and I were on our way to Blue Mountain Lake when the local news came over the TV about the bust and the disappearance of Draper. We just kept our eyes open for the Lexus. That's how it went down," I assured him. "I certainly was not privy to any internal information."

"There's no problem, Jason. Off the record, they were very pleased with the apprehension of Draper. If he had gotten to New York City, believe me, we'd be looking for a needle in a haystack." He continued to fill me in on the details. "It was a massive raid. A great deal of real property has been confiscated. The two Carver Cruisers are under the control of the U.S. Coast Guard. The jewelry store and warehouse are sealed tight. Scott Austin and about twenty-five of Draper's staff, including several truck drivers, have been arrested on a multitude of state and federal charges. It's going to take some time before we get it sorted out. The Arizona authorities did a splendid job on their end. We have recovered thousands of cartons of untaxed cigarettes and cases of alcohol. Numerous firearms have been seized. The cooperation of all the agencies involved went like clockwork. As we speak, our people with the feds are inventorying the currency, and the cocaine and other drugs. The INS people are looking into the smuggling of aliens. Draper has got a lot to answer to."

"I appreciate you sharing the information with me. I would have loved to have been on this case as an investigator."

"That's what happens when you retire early, Jason. Don't feel bad; it was your observations that brought down the Draper operation. Todd told me the story. He even told me how you rendered first aid to him when Draper bit him."

"I know, but I want Chief Wilson and his officer to take the credit for the apprehension. Think about it. I had Patty with me. If Todd hadn't been Johnny-on-the-spot, Draper would have gotten away. My Bronco couldn't have caught that Lexus if Draper had increased his speed. I would have smashed into him myself, if I had been alone, because he was pinned between a large log truck and me for a few minutes. I'm glad it worked out the way it did. Draper could have turned in Blue Mountain, but he would have run into your Indian Lake patrols."

"When our patrols picked Draper up, Todd had the blond wig in a plastic evidence bag with his personal effects. I chuckled when I saw the wig, Jason."

"It was the wig I spotted when he went by us in Raquette Lake. For some reason it drew my attention. But of course, it was a black Lexus."

"Well, I've held you up too long on the phone. I wanted to thank you personally for the information and the effort you put forth on the case. You stayed away like you were told, and yet, it was your action that was responsible for Draper's apprehension. Jason, I wish we had you aboard our unit here at Raybrook."

"Thanks for your comments, Lieutenant. Take care of yourself. The major and captain are fortunate to have a BCI Lieutenant that has the tenacity to get things done. Oh, by the way, sir, if you run into those painters, Ed and Smiley, tell them for me not only can they paint, but they're darn good undercover operatives."

"I will, Jason. I'll be sure to do that. So long for now."

I looked up at the clock. It was going on 11:00 a.m. I was glad

I had heard from the lieutenant. I knew that one of these days he would be promoted to captain. He was a dedicated, motivated, hard worker.

This would be a good time to call Joanne Smith before she left for lunch, I realized. I dialed her telephone number. I was happy that the line was free. She was a busy attorney with a sizable case load.

"Joanne Smith speaking. May I help you?" she answered.

"Joanne, Jason Black here. I have some information for you concerning Jerome Watson. Sorry I couldn't call you sooner."

"Jason, what are you doing getting back into the world of police work? That's all that is on the television and radio. Congratulations on grabbing that Draper fellow. I had to laugh about the blond wig that he was wearing." Joanne chuckled.

"Just happened to be in the right spot at the right time."

"That was good work, Jason. And now, what information do you have for me?"

"Regarding Jerome Watson. He is now married and residing in Gatlinburg, Tennessee. According to my sources, he is employed at Dollywood in that area. That's all the information I could develop, unless you want me to explore it further."

"Jason, that sounds good. I'll let you know if I need you to attain more information. We'll try going though the Dollywood organization. Where do I send my check for your services?" she asked.

"No charge on this one, Joanne. I was in the Blue Mountain area anyway and it worked out well," I explained.

"Well, I certainly appreciate your fast service. I'll certainly keep you in mind if I need a private investigator in the future. Take care, Jason, and be careful."

"Best to you, Joanne, and give Ted my regards."

"Goodbye, Jason. Stay in touch."

I spent the rest of the day catching up on bad check reports. Patty had called me about 2:00 in the afternoon to let me know that she was going to Syracuse with Lila in the morning. Lila had to go to a restaurant supply company and had asked Patty to accompany her. John was going to be the chef in charge and he had called in two waitresses to work for the day. I told Patty to go ahead and enjoy the day with Lila. I'd be fine, although I would miss her.

The teakettle started to whistle when the telephone rang. I turned the burner off and went into my office to answer the call.

"Hello," I answered.

"Jason, Joseph Kelly, RCMP. Can you talk for a minute?"

"Sarge, I certainly can. How have you been, Joe?" I knew he had been busy working with the smuggling case.

"Jason, I want you to know that we in the RCMP appreciated your call relative to the Draper case. We've been busy here along with the OPP and the QPP running down these smugglers. That's all I wanted to tell you."

"Joe, thank you for calling. I appreciate your comments. You know, Joe, joining the RCMP was my boyhood dream. My father took me to a movie a long time ago. It was called 'Sergeant Preston of the Yukon.'"

"Yes, Jason, I saw that film myself as a youngster. I hope we can get together one of these days. Thanks again, Jason. We'll stay in touch."

"We will, Joe. So long for now."

I hung up the telephone and went into the kitchen. I turned the burner on under the teakettle and put a green teabag into my cup. I returned to my office with my freshly brewed tea. On the way, I poked my head out the window and noticed that Ruben was lying down. A Monarch butterfly was lazily flying over his head. I watched as Ruben twitched his ear when the butterfly landed on it. The butterfly went airborne and spiraled around him, dipping down and then rising to the top of his gate post. I chuckled to myself as I went back to my desk. I changed the typewriter ribbon. My typing paper was getting low. I added that to my list of needed supplies.

My supply cabinet, because I am a self-employed private investigator, consists of the bottom two drawers of my four-drawer filing cabinet. It's much different than the supply closet I maintained as a station commander, while a member of the state troopers. What a contrast! Our supplies consisted of many report writing forms, paper clips, typewriter ribbons, envelopes, rubber bands, thumb tacks, erasers, pencils, pens, bond paper, posted property signs, dictaphone tapes, file folders, labels for the file folders, rulers, film for the station camera, light bulbs, flash bulbs, and numerous other mundane items. I was responsible not only for the supply cabinet, but for the entire station inventory, gas tank, assigned troop cars, furniture, and personnel. It was an experience that I will never forget. On top of that tremendous responsibility, I was expected to carry a normal workload.

I called Patty at John's Diner after the rush hour. She sounded bubbly on the telephone.

"Honey, do you like salmon patties?" she asked.

"I love them," I quickly responded.

"Lila prepared extra ones this morning, and I could purchase some. I thought we'd have them for dinner, if it's all right with you."

"That will be fine. What time, honey?" I asked in anticipation.

"I'll be there about 6:00 p.m., okay?"

"See you at 6:00 p.m., sweetheart!" We opted to eat at my log home because of Ruben. He was left alone too often when I had to fulfill my business responsibilities.

I could tell that she was in a hurry as we hung up the telephone. I finished my letters to Mountain Bank customers who had been issuing checks with insufficient funds. I cleared my desk of excess paperwork. I filed some reports and locked the filing cabinet. I always keep them locked. Sensitive material concerning pending divorce cases should always be kept under lock and key.

After I finished my office work I went outside to see Ruben. His water and food dishes needed to be refilled, which I immediately took care of. I then let the big fellow out of his dog run. He ran around me in a circle three times and took off for the woods. I figured out that Russ Slingerland must have changed Ruben's diet a little, as the old K-9 seemed spunkier than usual. I'd have to speak with Russ about that the next time I heard from him to find out what dog food he used. I walked toward the woods. Ruben was now out of sight.

As soon as I entered the woods, I whistled for the big guy. I heard a rushing in some brush and I peered toward the location of the commotion. A woodchuck ran out of the brushy area with

Ruben pursuing him. The woodchuck went into his hole near a downed maple tree and disappeared. Ruben eagerly sniffed the entrance to the woodchuck's refuge. Finally giving up, he came over to me and rubbed his head against my right pant leg.

The woods adjacent to my property not only contain the animal inhabitants of the park, but are blessed with numerous wildflowers: buttercups, St. Johnswort, and violets are just a few. Ruby-throated hummingbirds can be seen darting from one flower to the next and often visit my hummingbird feeder. I don't put out birdseed because of the black bears. Several of my friends learned early on that when the seed is in a feeder for the birds, it also attracts unwanted visits from the bears. In some instances, the bears have visited the residents' decks, frightening the home owners. It is a good policy to follow the "Do not feed the animals" warning.

After a while Ruben and I returned to the house. I went in, brought out a good-sized rubber ball, and threw it up into the air. Ruben got under the ball as it returned to earth and butted it with his nose. I repeated this two or three times, to his great enjoyment. Finally, I returned him to his dog run. When I closed his gate, he turned his back on me to let me know he was upset.

"Come on, Ruben, don't take it so hard. It's all right, fella. I love ya."

Just as I went inside, the telephone rang. It was Jack Flynn.

"Hello, Jason, how are you?" he asked.

"Jack, I thought I'd hear from you before this," I chided.

"I've been busy. I called to give you an update on the Draper case."

"I'm listening, buddy. Go ahead." I was anxious to hear his report.

"Well, the raid here in Phoenix went down at the same time as the one in New York. It's up in the air whether they'll return Draper to Phoenix right away. I heard he's attempting to make a deal with the feds. He apparently is telling the feds that he can turn them onto some real big dealers and drug lords."

"Do you believe that, Jack?" *What a crock of bull!*

"I'd say it's a wait-and-see situation at the moment. Captain Jay Silverstein has him cold on the triple homicide. The ballistics show that Draper's gun was used to murder the three Mexican Nationals. Apparently these three resided in a one-room efficiency apartment, and the detectives found scraps of paper with scribbling on them. The writings disclosed that one of the three who could speak and write English had written down some information about the Draper organization, and it was presumed he was getting ready to go to the cops with the information. The three of them were day laborers, and after they worked loading freight, Draper held off paying them, but promised to meet them later with the money. When they showed up at Draper's terminal office it was believed they argued and Draper went into a rage and killed the three of them. Then he dumped their bodies on the desert south of Phoenix." Jack's explanation provided good detail.

"Have they closed down his company?" I inquired with curiosity.

"Of course, like you, I wasn't on the Phoenix raid, but from what I was told it is completely shut down and the office is sealed. The semi-trailer trucks have been impounded, as well as all the files of the company. Draper is in trouble. It's going to be interesting to see if he has enough political clout to get some of the charges dismissed or reduced. His wife is going to be granted her divorce from Draper in a week. She is a fine woman and deserves a lot better than him. She's not implicated in any of her husband's evil deeds. She has her own finances and doesn't want anything from him."

"Jack, I certainly appreciate the update. About the New York raid, it went down smoothly and was a joint agency task force operation. Lieutenant Jack Doyle was in on the investigation from the start and did a fine job in putting all the pieces together. There were two special undercover operatives from the State of New York that also deserve a great deal of the credit."

"Some of my police contacts in New York State tell me that you were there when Draper himself was grabbed near a town—I believe they call it Eagle Bay. Is this true, Jason? I know how you operate, buddy," he said, laughing.

"Why, Jack, I don't know what you're talking about!" I retorted mockingly. "I'm only kidding. I did spot the Lexus driven by a blond female, but I had a hunch it was the Lexus we were looking for. I luckily had my cell phone with me and contacted the local chief of police, and that was it. Consequently, the blond wig fell off in a struggle, and it was Draper himself. He even had lipstick on and makeup. If he had got out of the Adirondacks, we'd still be looking for him. The chief was in the process of getting the ballistics report to the Phoenix PD and, as you indicated, it was a good match. It was a .45 Caliber semi-automatic," I added.

"Yeah, I know. Captain Silverstein has been checking the permits here in Phoenix. I'm glad they closed the case. I guess there are some loose ends, but they'll eventually bring it to a full conclusion. The drug money and drugs they confiscated are in the millions of dollars. Let's hope that this has saved a few lives on the streets of our country. You realize, Jason, that this is only the tip of the iceberg." There was no doubt how Jack felt about the drug culture and the organized cartels that spread their poison, hooking our people from all walks of life.

"I realize that. Let's hope that this action takes some of the drugs off the street. This situation could have been stopped or drastically reduced before it got such a foothold throughout the nation. It's now a scourge running over our land, and it has worked its tentacles into every fiber of our society, above ground and underground."

"You're on target. It's out of control. Jason, I must be running along, as I've got cases piled high on my desk. Let me know about the wedding date so I can plan."

"I will, Jack. I think tonight at supper Patty and I are going to set the date. I'll let you know right now that we'd like you to be the best man. You and I served together in the Marine Corps, and that in itself places you in that position. We go back a long way, buddy. You're the best man."

"Thanks, Jason. I'm honored," he said with sincerity.

I could tell that Jack was pleased in learning that he was going to be my best man. "So long, Jack. Say hello to Ruby and Jay for me. We'll be looking forward to seeing you."

"I'll do that. So long."

It was a pleasure to hear from Jack, and I appreciated the update on Draper. I decided to touch bases with Lieutenant Doyle, so

I called him. The receptionist politely put me on hold.

"Lieutenant Jack Doyle speaking." There was no mistaking his Irish brogue.

"Jason, here. How are you, Lieutenant?" I asked.

"Glad you called, Jason. We're having a get-together for all the folks involved with the Draper case, and Major Frank Temple would like you to attend. Your name has been mentioned numerous times. Have your ears been burning?"

"Not that I've noticed," I countered. "Why, are they upset I was at the scene?"

"Don't worry about it. The upper management was pleased that Draper was grabbed. If he had gotten out of our state, he has the resources to leave the country and possibly be on the lam for years. Hell, it doesn't matter who actually made the hands-on apprehension. The main thing is that he is out of commission now and under the control of the justice system. Let's hope he doesn't slip through a crack on a minor technicality. I feel that Arizona and New York have good cases against him." Jack was adamant in his belief.

"I agree with you wholeheartedly, Lieutenant."

"I want you there, Jason. Bring Patty, for all those involved are bringing their spouses or partners. It's going to be Saturday night at the Red Fox in Saranac. Be there by 7:30 p.m. Walt, the owner, is preparing a delicious beef barbecue. He makes the tastiest barbecue sauce and great coleslaw. A lot of effort was put forth on that investigation by many people. The feds have also been invited. I don't know if they'll show, but we hope so. Now, what's up? You called me."

"I just got off the telephone with Jack Flynn in Phoenix. He indicated that the Phoenix PD CID has the ballistic report, and it's a match on Draper's 45. caliber semi-automatic. The three Mexicans were killed because they knew about Draper's activities and were going to go to the feds."

"Yeah, that's what I heard from a report that Captain Roy Garrison received from their homicide division. Didn't you tell me that Draper's wife was in the midst of a divorce proceedings?"

"That's correct. She is a fine lady from all reports and just got hooked up with the wrong person. She's from an influential family who have holdings in ranching and oil. According to my buddy Jack, she's quite the lady."

"That's too bad that Draper decided to pursue the dark side of life's journey. Jason, greed is the word that applies to many of his kind. Not necessarily the kind that hits a parking meter for coin, which is wrong, too, but these white collar crooks that think they can beat the system and go for the gusto. Draper is going to probably end up in a federal institution—sometimes called the country club of the penal institutions," he added in disgust.

"He'll probably be planning his next career or else claim he found God. Many of them do, but still end up in stir after their next job. I'm glad I had a father and mother who ran our household. Today we have many of the kids telling the parents what to do." I remembered how strong my parents' influence was on my early childhood, emphasizing good over evil.

"True, but thank goodness we have many good kids that grow up to be decent hardworking Americans."

"You're right. All we ask of any young person is to enjoy life and become a productive citizen, with a good work effort." I agreed with his philosophy.

"Jason, we'll see you Saturday evening. Watch the deer. I almost hit one with my troop car. They dart across the highway so fast. Take care."

"See you Saturday, Lieutenant."

I hung the telephone up. I was pleasantly surprised that Frank wanted me to attend the barbecue at Saranac. I had always been under the impression the get-together after was for active personnel. That was a nice gesture on the major's part.

Since this included spouses or partners, Patty would look forward to attending the function. She had met both Frank and Roy Garrison when she was in the Saranac Lake Hospital after her abduction by the two escaped Ohio killers. She would like to thank them for their kindness.

I had just finished setting the table when Patty's red Jeep pulled into the yard. Ruben was sitting in his dog run, and the minute he saw Patty his ears went erect. I went outside to greet her.

"Honey, can you help me?" she asked.

I loved to help her. "Sure, sweetness." I wondered if she'd always be as sweet as this.

I walked over to the Jeep. Patty had three dishes covered with plastic wrap. One held the salmon patties, one contained potato salad, and the third was full of coleslaw. The potato salad and coleslaw were ice cold. I carried them into the house. Patty ran over and petted Ruben, while I carried the dishes inside. She soon entered the kitchen and washed her hands. I placed the potato salad and the coleslaw in the refrigerator and put the salmon patties into the microwave. In addition to the food that Patty brought, I warmed some dinner rolls. After placing the tartar sauce and the bread and butter pickles on the table, she mixed up some pink lemonade and filled the pitcher, adding some ice cubes. In a few minutes we were sitting at the table enjoying our cuisine.

We talked about our wedding plans and selected the Saturday in mid-September for the big day, hoping the day would be open at the church.

"Jason, I will send out the invitations in a week, and that will give our guests plenty of time to make their plans for attending our wedding. Is that okay?"

"That'll be fine, honey." My third marriage, I thought. My knees felt weak.

We finished our meal and cleared the table. Patty and I did the dishes together. After we cleaned up the kitchen, we went into the living room. Patty sat on the couch next to me. I reached over and placed a CD in the player. The music was from the old days of Glenn Miller's orchestra with Tex Beneke. Often we listened to this music from a different era of time. We embraced each other and held hands, just relaxing and letting our minds drift away from the pressures of society.

We rested for a while and then our conversation drifted to important subjects that we'd have to consider after we were married. They included our finances, medical insurance, a planned budget for our forthcoming household, and our present hobbies of photography, hiking, canoeing, painting mountain scenes in oil, dancing, and reading. We wanted to keep the hobbies separate from her waitress work and my work as a private investigator. We decided that we wanted to keep our lives less complicated so we could try to enjoy the beauty of these mountains that we revered. Our ideas bounced off each other for several hours. We did not want unnecessary dilemmas impacting our future as husband and wife. Maybe our union wouldn't be problem-free, but the only way we'd know that would be to live the experience and walk the path together. And together we would, with God's help. Fortunately, we knew our friends were supportive and looking forward to our marriage.

I removed the last CD from the machine at 11:00 p.m. Time had gone by so rapidly that the arrival of this late hour was unnoticed.

"Jason, look what time it is! I should have been home two hours ago!" Patty exclaimed.

"It's getting late, honey. I'll follow you home," I offered because of the hour.

"You don't have to do that, Jason. I'll call you the minute I get in the house."

We went outside. I thanked her for bringing the food for our dinner. I let Ruben out for his quick run to the woods. While we waited for him to return, Patty and I embraced. Our lips met under the star-filled sky above. Our hearts could be felt beating in harmony. Just then, Ruben came to us from the deep woods. His ears rose toward the heavens. We both watched as Patty drove out of the driveway and headed for home.

Ruben and I went inside. He went to his air mattress. I checked the doors and prepared for bedtime. I was just brushing my teeth when the telephone rang. I splashed some water on my face and answered it.

"Hi, honey, I'm home. I'll just say goodnight."

"Goodnight, sweetheart. Patty, I almost forgot to tell you, tomorrow night we've been invited to a barbecue at the Red Fox Restaurant in Saranac Lake. Would you like to go?"

"I'd love to go, honey. This is a surprise! What should I wear?"

"Just casual clothing. I'm going to wear slacks and a sport shirt and take a jacket, for it does get cool up there."

"Gee, I can't believe you didn't mention it, honey. I'll have to do my hair."

"Patty, you're beautiful. Don't worry so much about your hair. It had slipped my mind. I'm sorry. We were talking about other things. The barbecue is in recognition of the hard work by the members of the combined task force, " I went on to explain.

"It's all right, Jason, I still love you."

I told her to get a good night's sleep. We hung up simultaneously.

CHAPTER FORTY-TWO

The next day went by rapidly. I spent most of the time doing reports in my office. Ruben lounged in his dog run. When it came time to get ready for our trip to Saranac Lake, I locked my desk and checked Ruben's food and water dishes. He must have sensed that I was going to be away for the evening. He sat in his run with his back toward me.

I picked Patty up at her house and headed the Bronco north on Route 28. The trip to Saranac was uneventful and Patty sat close to me all the way. We arrived at the Red Fox Restaurant on time. The first person I saw was Lieutenant Jack Doyle. He had just exited his troop car. I introduced Jack to Patty. The three of us entered the restaurant. I saw the owner, Walter, near the entrance to the kitchen.

"Hello, Jason. It's good to see you." Walt smiled.

"Hi, Walt. Looks as though you've got a good crowd this evening."

"This is quite a group, Jason. I feel protected when they come to my place. The Draper case was really something. It's a good thing they put him out of business before he really got a foothold. I heard he was sniffing around Lake Placid for some plush property. The troops did an outstanding job, and so did the feds along with the Canadian law enforcement people." He spoke with pride.

"Yes, they did." I remembered that Walt was originally from Canada.

I looked around for Patty and saw her with Jack. It appeared that the lieutenant was introducing her to several of the active members and their wives. I spotted Russ Slingerland entering the dining room and went over to him.

"Jason, how are you and how's my favorite K-9? Ruben is one of the best dogs I ever trained." Russ always praised his dogs.

"You certainly did a great job with him, Russ. Where's the Mrs.?" I asked as I looked around.

"She wanted to attend the barbecue, but she had a meeting. You know how that can be." he added, apologetically.

"It's great talking with you, Russ. I'd better get back to Patty before they sign her up in the troopers."

"We'll talk a little later, Jason. I'm glad you and Patty could make it."

When I caught up with Patty she was talking with Major Temple and Captain Garrison. They were asking her how she was feeling now after her year-ago abduction by the Ohio killers. She had met them at that time.

"Major Temple and Captain Garrison, I'm feeling much better and I'm not as nervous. But that ordeal was something I never want to go through again." She shuddered as the memories returned.

"You were a brave young lady," Major Temple remarked.

"A very brave person," Captain Garrison added.

Patty and I talked with the two command officers. Both of them wished us the very best in our forthcoming marriage.

Patty and I walked around the crowd of my former associates. The other men and I kidded about the many root beers we had shared, along with the chili dogs, in my Troop S assignment. There were many good days.

We were all seated as the barbecue was about to be served. The barbecue sauce was one of Walt's guarded recipes, kept under lock and key. A gourmet magazine had tried but was unable to obtain it. Walt's recipe remained secure.

The five waitresses served each table with the barbecue on each plate. Side dishes of coleslaw, and baked beans were served family style. Beverages consisted of beer, soft drinks, iced tea, or coffee. Walter played dinner music as we dined and throughout the evening.

The attendees were mostly state police with a handful of federal people. Patty and I were introduced to several of the feds. I noticed the two undercover operatives, Ed and Smiley, sitting at a table in the far corner of the vast dining area. They had shaved their beards; however, they were now sporting mustaches. They did not mingle with the crowd, evidently still keeping their low profile.

I observed Major Frank Temple leave the head table where he had been seated. He walked over to Walter, who was still at the piano, and spoke to him quietly. Walter rose from the piano and headed over to the dais.

"May I have your attention, please. The major has requested that everyone take their seats, as he is about to make a few remarks to the group," Walter announced.

Everyone went to their chairs and sat down at the tables. The entire room became hushed as the major rose to speak.

"Ladies and gentlemen, welcome to our get-together this evening. Is everyone full enough after that tasty barbecue?" he asked.

The crowd reacted favorably with a round of applause.

"I believe we all should thank Walter for his culinary ability," the major said.

Everyone clapped their hands and some of the guests whistled. The major continued.

"Folks, seriously, this has been a lovely evening. We brought you all here tonight to thank the men and women who participated in the Draper case for their long hours of hard work and dedication as law enforcement people. It was a complex case. It took our investigators to Arizona, Pennsylvania and Cornwall, Ontario. It was a successful joint operation involving many agencies—state, federal and local law enforcement people. You all can be proud of this accomplishment and how you have handled yourselves." He was clear and sincere in his comments. He paused while the audience clapped. He continued, "Unfortunately, one of our informants, who was a driver for Draper, was detected by the Draper organization and was murdered in Pennsylvania. He was Cesar Guerrero. Some details of the operation are confidential and will be for some time. This evening I want to thank the person that brought the Draper organization to center stage. I'm pleased to announce that this person was one of our very own. He contacted our BCI Lieutenant Jack Doyle, who had been recently promoted to that rank. Seems that Jack Doyle and he are friends. Many of you know him: Jason Black, a former BCI Investigator who has worn out many soles on his shoes chasing bad guys. Jason, would you come up here for a minute?" he asked as he looked over at me.

I could not believe what I was hearing. I reluctantly got up and walked to the head table. As I made my way, I heard a lot of low-tone murmuring among the attendees. I couldn't make out what was being said. The major was standing there with his hand extended. I reached out and shook it.

"Thank you, Jason, for bringing the Draper case to our attention. Your action is appreciated. You made it possible for us to take a good look at him and his organization. We appreciate what you have accomplished. I'm speaking for Troop S and for all the citizens of our communities."

There was great emotion in his voice. I felt his comments were genuine. I was overcome.

"Thank you, Major, for your comments. It is my policy as a private investigator to contact the police if important information comes to my attention. I appreciated Lieutenant Doyle's interest in this matter and the handling of his investigation. I'm aware it involved several agencies and, of course, their cooperation. I'm pleased with the outcome. Although it is like removing a single drop of sand from a large pile, it is, however, a good start. Thank you, Major, for your comments."

I turned and walked back to my seat and Patty, while the room broke out in applause and whistles. My chest filled with pride. The mission had been accomplished. Draper was behind bars along with many of his people.

I looked at my watch and noted that it was getting late. Patty was in the process of talking with some of the troopers' wives, and I made my rounds saying hello to numerous members whom I knew, and meeting some of the new men. I wished them all well in their careers.

On the way back to Patty, I ran into Captain Roy Garrison. We shook hands and talked for a moment. I hurriedly went over to

Walter and told him that his barbecue was super, as well as his piano playing. I came across Major Temple as he was leaving. We chatted for a moment, and he sincerely wished Patty and me a wonderful marriage.

I returned to our table.

"Did you have a good time, darling?" I asked Patty, as she was radiant.

"Wonderful, Jason. I love you." She smiled alluringly.

"I love you too, precious." I reached out and patted her hand.

On the way out the door, we bid farewell to several members and their wives. It had been a delightful evening for everyone.

The ride back to Old Forge was uneventful. I dropped Patty off at her house and went directly home. We were both tired after the long trip from Saranac. I checked Ruben, and took him out for a short run. We went inside. I was so tired, I fell off to sleep immediately after hitting the pillow.

CHAPTER FORTY-THREE

The summer flew by. I went on with my normal private investigative activities. Patty continued working at the diner. The wedding day that seemed so distant was rapidly approaching. I was getting butterflies in my stomach as the days drew closer to our wedding in mid-September. Ruben seemed to know in his dog sense that I was deep in thought. Suppose it didn't work out? I was in a quandary. I never wanted to face another divorce proceeding in my life. Too many people get hurt, and the judgmental critics have a heyday working you and your reputation over the coals. It was a big step that I was about to take. I had to rid myself of these cowardly thoughts. Patty was a fine woman: sincere, passionate in her thinking, hard worker and beautiful. And, I already knew she could stand with the best in the culinary world.

Prior to our September wedding, Patty and I had driven to Lake Placid and had dinner with Tom Huston. Patty and Tom got along wonderfully. Tom talked about his son, and how much he missed his late wife. After dinner he took us on a guided tour of the stately Breakshire Lodge and showed us some of the new improvements. We listened intently as he explained the new heating plant and the installation of the new swimming pool. Of all the improvements that were made to the lodge, he considered the new beds for the rooms the top of his agenda.

When we finished the tour, we stood in the lobby. Tom raved about the big black bear and the cub that Wilt had carved for him.

351

He thanked me also, after remembering that Wilt and I had presented the bears to him personally. Patty asked Tom about the interior decorations. He explained to her that a decorator from New York City had spent a month at the lodge taking measurements and photos and attending meetings with Tom and his staff relative to the work to be done. Both of us remarked to Tom how nice the lodge appeared and thanked him for the exquisitely prepared dinner. Tom's choice of chefs was well known throughout the Adirondacks.

As we were about to leave for Old Forge, Tom surprised me.

"Jason, when you retire from the private investigation business, I'd like you to consider joining my staff here at the lodge in a security and public relations position."

I was startled, but flattered. I realized that Tom Huston was sincere.

"Tom, I'd certainly consider your offer. Thank you, sir, for your confidence in me."

Tom looked at my bride-to-be. "Patty, I'd love to have you for our hostess."

"Mr. Huston, I appreciate your offer, but that would depend on what Jason decides."

"I know it is a little premature, but I thought I'd mention it to you both," Tom said. "Think it over. Lake Placid is a great place to live."

We both thanked Tom again. After shaking hands with him, Patty and I left for Old Forge.

It was dark when we pulled into my yard. Ruben barked incessantly, happy to see us home.

"Settle down, boy!" I said, reaching over to pat him and rub his back.

I helped Patty out and walked her to the Jeep. We embraced under the stars.

"I love you, Patty. I'll be glad when we're married."

"Honey, I love you, too. Yes, then we can get down to just being husband and wife." She smiled, adding, "And live happily ever after."

We said goodnight to each other and I helped Patty into her

Jeep. Ruben and I watched her leave the driveway and head for home.

Patty mailed one hundred wedding invitations to our friends. Patty had definitely decided not to invite her brothers from Kentucky, as they were on demanding jobs and had to live on tight budgets. We held to the idea that we'd visit them in the near future sometime after our wedding day.

I spent my days working on several of my check cases and serving a few civil process papers for a couple of attorneys. By the latter part of August, the tourists were beginning to return to their homes. One evening I called Lynn at the Eagle Bay kennel and made an appointment to have Ruben bathed and groomed in the morning.

Sleep did not come easily that night as I lay in bed thinking about the fast approaching day of our wedding. I was not prepared for the Big Ben alarm as it went off at 7:00 a.m. sharp. I reached over and pushed down the alarm button, turning it off. Ruben came into the bedroom and started pulling on the bedspread. I pushed the covers back and got up making my way to the bathroom. I splashed some ice cold Adirondack water into my face. It was truly frigid. Ruben was circling around the front door and I knew he had a mission. I opened the door and let him out. He bounded off the porch and headed towards the forest.

I ran back into the bathroom and dried my face. I could feel the whiskers protruding from my chin, so decided I'd better shave. I looked into the cabinet, brought out the shaving mug with the soap and added a little hot water. I made a good amount of lather and slapped it on my face. With my straight razor I carefully shaved. Afterwards I applied some cocoa butter and placed a couple of hot towels over my face. I then applied some after-shave lotion and put a cold towel on my face. It was refreshing. After a shower and shampoo, I was ready for breakfast. I looked outside and saw that Ruben had gone into his run and was leaning over his food dish, eating.

My wardrobe was diminishing. I located a pair of Dockers and a sport shirt. I felt like a new man; nevertheless, I was approaching the half-century mark. I was just about finished when the telephone rang.

"Hello. Jason Black here," I answered.

"Jason, I'm going up this morning for a while. Do you want to ride along with me? I have to fly down to Brewerton, New York, and pick up a part for Kirby's Marina."

"I'd love to, Dale, but first I've got to drop Ruben off at the Eagle Bay kennel."

"How is the K-9?" Dale asked.

"He's fine, Dale. He's going for a grooming," I explained.

"Okay. Meet me at Kirby's after you drop the dog off, in about an hour."

I didn't want to disturb Patty at work, but I wanted to advise her of my plans. Lila answered and called her to the phone.

"Hello," Patty said in a rushed voice.

"Honey, I'll make this quick. I'm taking Ruben to the kennel and then I'm going to Kirby's to meet Dale. He asked me to fly to Brewerton with him for an engine part."

"Okay, dearest. Take care of yourself. Have to get back to work. I'll call you tonight. The invitations are all mailed," she reminded me, hurriedly.

"Great! See you. Love you."

The phone clicked and I hung up.

I quickly made myself a fried-egg sandwich on an English muffin. I added a slice of Canadian bacon to the egg. I made a hot cup of green tea. I usually took time for a leisurely breakfast, but I didn't want to keep Dale waiting. I put the dishes in the sink after I rinsed them off.

I locked the house after taking a jacket from the closet. I let Ruben take a quick run into the woods. He bounded back, sensing he was going for a ride. I opened the back gate of the Bronco and he leaped into the rear compartment.

After I left Ruben with Lynn at the kennel, I headed for Kirby's. I had mentioned to Lynn that I was going for a ride to Brewerton with Dale, and wasn't sure when I would be able to pick him up. She volunteered that her mother would gladly put him in my dog run later, as she had errands to take care of in Old Forge.

When I pulled into the driveway, I saw Dale waiting. The minute he saw me, he started the engine. The red and white gull-winged Stinson seaplane looked sharp. I parked the Bronco and hurriedly walked toward the plane.

"You didn't have to rush that fast, Jason," he admonished.

"No problem, Dale. Good to see you," I acknowledged.

I climbed in, and one of Kirby's workers pushed us off away from the dock. The 245 Horsepower Lycoming engine sounded powerful as Dale turned the plane for take-off. We took off toward Inlet and climbed to 3500 feet. Dale banked it to the right and headed southwesterly. Our destination was the Brewerton Marina. The flight to Oneida Lake was smooth. We crossed over the town of Ava and circled Camden, as Dale had a cousin residing there on a dairy farm. He pointed out the farm to me. The cars below looked small as they made their way down one highway to another. I asked Dale if he had ever met Bud Hausen, a well-known pilot who used to fly into Fourth Lake. Dale indicated that he had flown with Bud on several occasions. That's where his love of flying had first begun.

Our landing on Oneida Lake was a little rough. A wind had come up and a few white caps were noticeable. Dale asked me to stay with the plane while he went into the Marina. Kirby had called down the day before, and the part was to be ready for pick-up. Dale had shut the engine off.

He was back in about fifteen minutes with the part. He had a big smile on his face. He climbed in and, after checking the plane, started the engine. It wasn't long before we were winging our way back toward the Adirondacks. Dale was happiest when he was behind the controls of a plane. I'd known Dale for several years, and that was his forte.

On the way back, Dale mentioned that he had received our wedding invitation and told me that some of the fellows wanted to take me out to dinner on Friday night. He indicated that he was spokesman for the group and that I should be at the Edge Water by 6:30 p.m. that Friday.

"It's just a week away, Jason, so make certain that you show up," he said.

"That's very nice of you and the fellows, but it isn't necessary."

"Be there, Jason, or we'll come looking for you." He was adamant.

"Okay, okay. I'll be there. I wouldn't want those fellas after me," I agreed.

Dale took us down to 1200 feet over the Tug Hill region. Some of the trees were beginning to change colors. It was difficult to believe that the summer had passed so quickly.

"I'm going down a little closer. There's something on that hill. Yes, it is a bull moose."

I looked out the window as Dale came in for a closer look. The moose was huge. He moved into a group of trees.

"Dale, he was a big one," I said.

"Yeah, every once in a while I spot one when I'm flying around. According to my forest ranger friend, there are supposed to be around sixty in the state."

"It seems that I've heard that before," I responded.

Dale circled the moose once more and then we headed for Kirby's Marina. The flight had been a good one. Dale made a smooth landing. He taxied toward the marina and cut the engine about twenty-five feet from the docking area. I got out on the float and grabbed a line when we reached the dock area. Dale checked the plane over and then locked it up. He took the engine part to Kirby's office. I walked to my Bronco and waited for Dale to finish his business with Kirby.

He wasn't in the office very long. When he came out, he walked over to where I was standing.

"Jason, Kirby's happy to get his part. Thanks for riding along with me. We'll see you Friday night at 6:30 p.m., Jason."

"I'll be there. Thanks for the ride. I always enjoy flying with you, Dale."

We both left Kirby's. Dale indicated that he was going to go and do some work around his Victorian home. I drove down to the post office and picked up my mail, then stopped at the gas station and filled up the Bronco with gas. One of the local troopers waved at me as he went by. I waved back. I had started to get into the Bronco when Chief of Police Todd Wilson went by following the state police car. I imagined that they were going on a complaint together or to investigate a bad accident. I was headed back toward my home when I met the Old Forge Rescue, siren blaring and lights flashing. I assumed that there had been an accident some-where south of Old Forge, possibly on Route 28. We're fortunate, in our area to have a high-caliber volunteer fire department with well-equipped ambulances and rescue equipment. The men and women of the department are well trained and respond to emer-gency calls during every season of the year, displaying outstanding professionalism. The Old Forge region, as an active tourist area, many times call upon the fire department and rescue personnel, pressed into service at a moment's notice.

Ruben was patiently waiting for me in his dog run. He barked when I got out of the Bronco. "I'll be right with you, Ruben." I took the mail into the house, laid it on the desk in my office, and went back out to Ruben. When I opened the gate, the big K-9 rushed over to me. "Have you been a good boy, Ruben?" I asked. "That was sure nice of Lynn to have you dropped off for me."

He ran off toward the woods. I waited for him to return and then put him back in the dog run. I went inside and checked my mail. There were a few checks from Mountain Bank and some ad-vertisements from a police equipment company. I took a minute to call Patty.

"Hi, darling. Just checking in with you. Have you had a busy morning?"

"Yes, we've been very busy. I love you, sweetheart."

"Ditto, babe. I'll talk with you later."

I went back to checking the rest of the mail.

They say that time waits for no man. The first week of Septem-ber passed so quickly. Patty and I went over the details for the wed-ding several times; the rings had been purchased, the ceremony would be held at the Big Moose Chapel, the Reverend Joshua Daley would officiate, and our reception would be held at the Edge Water overlooking Old Forge Pond. We had received RSVP's from many people who would be attending and only three couples who would not be able to make it because of prior commitments. They expressed their disappointment.

CHAPTER FORTY-FOUR

Finally the night of my bachelor party arrived. It was being held at the Edge Water at 6:30 p.m., the night before our wedding. When I drove into the parking lot, I noticed several vehicles that were familiar to me. I entered the bar area to find a big sign displayed on the wall. It read; "Private Party Downstairs." I proceeded down the steps to one of the private party rooms. When I walked in, the room was dark. Suddenly the lights came on and the cheers went up from my friends of several years. I was shocked when Jack Flynn came up and gave me a bear hug and said, "Semper fi." The conversation in the room was so loud it was difficult to understand what was being said. John Mahaffy came over and shook my hand.

Wilt and Dale, I soon learned, had been placed in charge. They were busy talking with two waitresses who were preparing to serve us haddock dinners. I went around the room and talked with Charlie Perkins; John, from the diner; John, from Hoss's Country Corner; Bob, from Gertie's; Lieutenant Jack Doyle, from Troop S Headquarters; Sergeant Joe Kelly, RCMP from Cornwall; Jack Falsey; Penny Younger; Mike, from the Old Forge Hardware; Chief of Police Todd Wilson; and Forest Ranger Gary Leach. Others were already so engrossed in conversation that I simply nodded as I walked by. Dr. Don from the garage was talking about his new pickup truck. I was happy to see Jim from the local real estate office, and two local attorneys.

Jack Flynn presented me with a glass of white wine, clinking his glass against mine. I was so pleased that my ex-Marine Corps buddy was able to attend.

Wilt took the floor and told everyone to sit down as our dinner was ready to be served. I noticed that some of the fellows were drinking beer and some had wine. Everyone took a seat. Soon we were served fresh garden salads with hot homemade bread and sweet butter. Before dinner, Charlie Perkins said grace. I sat between Jack Flynn and Wilt Chambers. It had already been circulated around the room that Jack was going to be the best man at the wedding. The fellows jested with me about losing my bachelorhood. The room was filled with laughter, and joviality abounded.

The two waitresses removed our empty salad plates and began serving us the fried haddock. Each fish was about a foot long. Some of the fellows had baked potatoes and others selected French fries. The vegetables, consisting of broccoli and cauliflower, and mounds of coleslaw, were served family style. Refills of the drinks flowed freely. I sipped my wine. The jokes kept coming, and I was getting hoarse from the laughter. I appreciated what my friends had done to celebrate the "loss" of my bachelorhood. I told Jack that I expected him to stay at my log home that night. He indicated that he already had his room at the Edge Water. He advised me that he had to leave soon after the wedding because of a trial in Phoenix.

Wilt leaned over toward me.

"Jason, I hope that everything meets with your approval." He seemed tentative.

"Wilt, everything is perfect. You and the fellows shouldn't have gone to all this bother." Actually, I was glad they had, and at this moment I was in my glory.

"Listen! We wanted to do it, and that's that, buddy." Wilt meant every word.

Wilt looked around the room to see if everyone had finished eating. Jack Falsey was just finishing his haddock. Everyone else had cleaned their plates. Wilt waited for a few minutes and then he stood up, banging his spoon on his water glass.

"How did you like the haddock dinner, fellas?" he said with pride.

"We loved it." Everybody spoke at once.

"Gentlemen, we're gathered here tonight to help Jason cele- brate the loss of his bachelorhood. I've known Jason for several years, and my first meeting with him was at a roadblock just com- ing into the Adirondacks. He was a little lighter in weight in those days. I looked down at him from my cab. He was most polite, and after I showed him my license and registrations he told me that he wanted to measure the height of my load of logs. Another trooper and Jason took, the tape and Jason climbed up that load of logs like a squirrel goes up a tree. I'll leave it to your imagination as to what happened on that day a long time ago. No, I didn't get a ticket, only because that trooper used good common sense. I was one quarter of an inch over height." He looked over at me and grinned. "Serious- ly, gentlemen, the very first time I laid my eyes on Jason was when he was stuck in a huge snow-bank and I pulled him out with a log chain. Jason, would you like to respond to that?" Wilt's face was reddening.

"Gentlemen, I want to thank Wilt and Dale for getting you folks together. Wilt, I certainly appreciated that tow. It was a good thing you came along. I could have frozen to death. I think it was about twenty degrees below zero. Fellows, thank you again. I ap- preciate your support and friendship. Tomorrow is a big day in my life. Many of you know my future wife and you know how lucky I am. Gentlemen, thank you for coming and thank you for this even- ing. I'll remember it always."

"Okay, fellows. Be careful driving home." Wilt cautioned the group.

We all stood around for a while telling some tall tales. Jack Flynn and I went to the lobby of the Edge Water and sat down. We discussed the Draper case, and he filled me in on some of the in- vestigative leads that had focused on Bernie Draper. He told me that it was Bernie's gun used in the slaying of the three Mexican Nationals without a doubt. From where we were sitting, we could see Jack Doyle and Joe Kelly engrossed in conversation. They were just getting ready to leave the Edge Water. We both got up and went over to them. Jack Flynn and I told them each to have a good trip. It was a long drive to Cornwall and Raybrook. They had wanted to come to the wedding, too, but other matters were preventing them from doing so.

Jack Flynn and I talked way past midnight. I told him that I'd see him at the wedding. I left the Edge Water and went home. I had all my clothes ready. I would be wearing a dark blue suit, a white shirt, a light blue tie, and wing-tips. I had no idea what Patty was wearing. The wedding was to take place at 11:00 a.m. at the Big Moose Chapel. The Reverend Joshua L. Daley was going to per- form the wedding ceremony. I had promised Patty that I wouldn't call or see her until the wedding.

I sat at the kitchen table and looked at Ruben. He was lying at my feet. I petted his head and his ears. He was such a good dog. I had made arrangements with Lynn at the Eagle Bay kennel that I'd drop Ruben off in the morning on the way to the chapel. I poured myself a cup of coffee and sipped it. I tried my best to relax. I told Ruben that there would soon be three of us living here from now on.

At about 2:00 a.m., I climbed into bed. I lay on my back staring at the ceiling. I had previously set the Big Ben alarm clock for 6:00 a.m. I fell off to sleep.

CHAPTER FORTY-FIVE

I heard a bell in the distance. I was walking on the sand at Hampton Beach, New Hampshire. My feet were sinking into the sand to the tops of my ankles. Then I felt a tugging on my feet. I finally came to and realized I had been dreaming. The Big Ben ran down. Ruben was tugging at the bedspread. I pushed the covers back and got out of bed. I went to the door and let Ruben out. He bounced off the porch and headed for the woods. I stripped the bed of the sheets and pillow cases and replaced them with fresh ones. I looked outside and noticed that Ruben was in his dog run leaning over his food dish. I went into the bathroom, and shaved, and took a hot shower. I had just finished when the telephone rang.

"Hello, buddy. Jack Flynn, here." He sounded sleepy.

"You're up early," I commented.

"I'm going to have a little breakfast here. I'll see you at the Big Moose Chapel. I forgot to ask you last night: who is going to give Patty away?" Jack asked.

"Wilt Chambers has the honors. He's like a father to her."

"That's great. Okay, I'll see you later. You feeling okay?"

"Yes, I am. A little nervous. See you later. *Semper fi.*"

"*Semper fi.*" Once a Marine, always a Marine.

I dropped Ruben off at the Eagle Bay kennel and headed toward the Big Moose Chapel. When I arrived, I parked on the side. There were many cars parked in the area. I went inside. The Reverend Joshua L. Daley was in the front of the chapel. Carrie Neilson was with him. She would be singing "Ave Maria" and "Because God Made You Mine." The bride had arrived with Wilt Chambers, but of course she wasn't in sight. Lila, her Matron of Honor was waiting in the wings. Charlie Perkins and Jack Falsey were the ushers. I was nervous. It wasn't long before Jack Flynn, my best man arrived. I could see that people were starting to arrive. Charlie and Jack did a good job escorting and seating the guests. Tom Huston from the Breakshire Lodge entered and was seated. I looked over the attendees and spotted many of our friends and acquaintances.

At 11:00 a.m., we were all in position. The wedding march began. Jack Flynn was close by. I looked toward the back of the chapel, and slowly Patty, escorted by Wilt, came toward me. My ears felt flushed. Wilt was smiling and looked distinguished in his gray suit. Patty was beautiful. Her blond hair was radiant, flowing onto her shoulders. She was wearing a lovely two-piece powder-blue suit. As always, she wore very little makeup. My knees felt wobbly as Wilt and Patty approached. Wilt presented a joyous Patty to me and she stood on my right. Reverend Daley was facing us. Flashes from cameras filled the chapel. The ceremony began. The Reverend spoke eloquently during the ceremony. Our responses were quiet. Our hands clasped each other's. The best man handed me the rings. We placed them on our fingers. My knees were shaking. I turned toward Patty. She turned toward me. He said, "I pronounce you husband and wife. You may kiss the bride." We kissed warmly. The beautiful voice of Carrie Neilson had just finished singing "Because God Made You Mine."

When we left the chapel we were surrounded by over a hundred friends. We formed a line and each person congratulated us and, of course, kissed the bride. I thanked the reverend and the ushers, Jack and Charlie. We gathered around outside of the chapel and numerous pictures were taken. We felt the rice being thrown at us.

I introduced Jack Flynn to Tom Huston and the two of them chatted for a while. I knew that my buddy, Jack Flynn, would have to leave for the airport to catch his flight to Phoenix. I bid my friend farewell. He embraced Patty and told her to take good care of me. I saw her blush. We walked to Jack's rental car with him.

Charlie Perkins drove my Bronco to the Edge Water, and Patty and I rode with Wilt. People were leaving the parking area, and from the shoulder of the Big Moose Road. More rice was being thrown at us.

The reception was something to remember forever. The Edge Water put on an outstanding buffet. Penny Younger and his band played some dinner music and, after the buffet and the speeches, everyone danced. Patty danced continuously. It was a joyous time for all of us, especially for Mr. and Mrs. Jason Black of Old Forge, New York, a private investigator and a popular waitress.

The wedding gifts were taken to our house by Wilt, Jack Falsey, and Dale Rush. Some of the attendees gave us cash.

Our good friends, Ted and Joanne Smith, deer hunting partners, came forward and wished Patty and me many years of happiness. County Judge Francis E. O'Connor Jr. and Assemblyman Paul Richter approached and wished us much happiness. It was good to see them both. I introduced them to some of my friends. We had known each other for years.

Patty and I thanked everyone for coming to our wedding. The Bronco had been secretly decorated by Charlie Perkins and Wilt Chambers and Jack Falsey. A sign attached to the rear of the vehicle boldly stated: "JUST MARRIED."

Our wedding day had been perfect. The morning sun had broken through the mist that hovered over the lakes. The early autumn had begun turning the leaves to wondrous reds and gold, which were brilliantly colored, heightened by the sun's rays. Surrounded by friends, the wedding followed by a flawless reception, had all culminated to the success of our day.

Tom Huston had reserved the bridal suite at the Breakshire for the first night of our honeymoon. The next morning we would be off to Vermont and the log cabin that I had rented for a week. Patty and I were looking forward to time alone, away from the hustle and bustle of the daily routine. There were rumors already circulating that we might be followed to our private spot in Vermont. When Patty and I heard that, we both chuckled.

We wished everyone our very best. Our luggage had been placed in the Bronco. Patty and I each gave a final wave, and I opened the passenger side door of the Bronco for her. Some of the fellows had waxed the Bronco for us and it shone, reflecting the bright sun above. I climbed in and started the engine. We were showered with rice as we left the parking lot of the Edge Water. Horns started tooting as we turned right onto Route 28 and headed north on the first stretch of our honeymoon.

I turned to Patty, "Are you prepared to face life as Mrs. Jason Black?" I asked.

She looked over at me with tears of happiness welling in her eyes, "I love you, Sherlock."

There was no need for her to respond. "I love you, too!"

Patty and I asked God for his blessings. Our new life was about to begin.

ℬ

(continued from back cover)

The author was born in Theresa, New York, moving to Central New York, where he graduated from Port Byron Central School.

He served three years and three months with Company I, 108th Infantry of the 27th Division until 1950 when he entered the U.S. Air Force during the Korean War, serving in Keflavik, Iceland. In 1953 he became a member of the New York State Police where he served in Troop D and Troop B until 1982, which included fourteen years in uniform and fourteen years as a member of the elite Bureau of Criminal Investigation. After retiring he served in the banking sector for seven years. As a long lime learner he received his B.S. degree from the State University of New York. He resides in the Adirondack Park of New York State. He is a published poet and writer of short stories.